continued...

Reader and Raelynx

"Exciting . . . Intrigue, love, and magic weave into Shinn's hallmark romantic, happy-ever-after ending."
—*Publishers Weekly*

"A magnificent conclusion to Sharon Shinn's Twelve Houses series! *Reader and Raelynx* weaves a rich tapestry of danger and magic, but it's even more about the power of friendship and love. Shinn is a master of world building, plotting, and characterization—I loved *Reader and Raelynx* so much that I immediately started rereading the series from the beginning! Not to be missed."
—Mary Jo Putney, *New York Times* bestselling author of *A Distant Magic*

"Shinn continues her powerful and richly detailed Twelve Houses series with a tale of dangerous love and open rebellion."
—*Library Journal*

"A vivid, spellbinding addition to the superb Twelve Houses saga . . . a beautiful adult fairy tale that readers will appreciate."
—*Alternative Worlds*

"Shinn neatly and delightfully wraps up a four-volume romantic-fantasy series . . . a chocolate truffle of a novel: richly indulgent, darkly sweet, and utterly satisfying . . . There are plenty of great twists, thrilling action sequences, and long-awaited comeuppances along the way."
—*Kirkus Reviews*

"The best since the first book . . . a very satisfying conclusion. The whole series is highly recommended for romance readers interested in dabbling in fantasy or fantasy readers who do not mind some mingling of the genre boundaries."
—*SFRevu*

"Shinn is one of the few fantasy writers who can make familiar situations and settings seem new and interesting, to a great extent because she creates so many believable characters. Fans of the series will not be disappointed by the way in which she winds things up."
—Don D'Ammassa, *Critical Mass*

Dark Moon Defender

"Once again Shinn expertly mixes romance with traditional fantasy for a satisfying read."   —*Publishers Weekly*

"Shinn continues to demonstrate her ability to write epic fantasy that leaves the reader wanting more."
                                    —*The Southern Pines (NC) Pilot*

"Combines storytelling expertise with a richly detailed fantasy world. Recommended."   —*Library Journal*

"A worthy read."   —*SFRevu*

"Intrigue filled."   —*Mania*

"The universe is fascinating; the characters are appealing."
                                    —*The Green Man Review*

"Shinn brings an array of fascinating characters to life and imbues them with purpose."   —*Romantic Times*

"[An] exciting and highly romantic series."   —*BookLoons*

The Thirteenth House

"Outstanding . . . a lyrical grace and deep appreciation of camaraderie reminiscent of Diane Duane at her best . . . [a] superior fantasy series."   —*Publishers Weekly*

"Lyrical and entertaining fantasy . . . peopled by well-drawn characters that readers can really bond with . . . abounds with subtle romance and high-spirited adventure. Ideal for readers who like a little romance with their fantasy."   —*Kirkus Reviews*

"Shinn seems to have an endless ability to create plausible worlds for her stories. With a blend of adventure and romance, they almost seem based on the history of a remote time rather than a place invented in her imagination."   —*St. Louis Post-Dispatch*

continued...

"Set in a world of noble Houses, shape-shifting mystics, and dexterous swordsmen, the sequel to *Mystic and Rider* further develops Shinn's new series characters and introduces new plot elements. Shinn provides a wealth of action and a balanced cast of genuinely heroic and admirable characters." —*Library Journal*

"Shinn is a strong literary writer [and is] especially good at writing realistic characters. Readers who enjoy romance and strong characterization will enjoy this book and the Twelve Houses series." —*SFRevu*

Mystic and Rider

"Engaging . . . an enjoyable yarn with characters who leave you wanting more." —*Locus*

"Shinn is an engaging storyteller who moves believable characters through a fascinating landscape and interesting adventures, [and] manages to do it with deep insights that make us reach into our own souls and wonder: If we were placed in the world of these characters, what would we do and what would we believe in?" —*St. Louis Post-Dispatch*

"*Mystic and Rider* . . . is that rarity, the opening book of a series that stands solidly as a read-alone novel. Well-developed and engaging characters, an intriguing plot, plenty of action, and unforeseen twists make *Mystic and Rider* a great book." —Robin Hobb, *New York Times* bestselling author of *Renegade's Magic*

"Clean, elegant prose . . . Shinn gives us an easy, absorbing, high-quality read." —*Booklist*

"Tailor-made for the growing audience of fantasy fans who like a good juicy romance . . . spellbinding characterizations . . . a rich beginning." —*Publishers Weekly*

"Shinn's most successful book." —*SFRevu*

Fortune
and
Fate

SHARON SHINN

ACE BOOKS, NEW YORK

THE BERKLEY PUBLISHING GROUP
Published by the Penguin Group
Penguin Group (USA) Inc.
375 Hudson Street, New York, New York 10014, USA
Penguin Group (Canada), 90 Eglinton Avenue East, Suite 700, Toronto, Ontario M4P 2Y3, Canada
(a division of Pearson Penguin Canada Inc.)
Penguin Books Ltd., 80 Strand, London WC2R 0RL, England
Penguin Group Ireland, 25 St. Stephen's Green, Dublin 2, Ireland (a division of Penguin Books Ltd.)
Penguin Group (Australia), 250 Camberwell Road, Camberwell, Victoria 3124, Australia
(a division of Pearson Australia Group Pty. Ltd.)
Penguin Books India Pvt. Ltd., 11 Community Centre, Panchsheel Park, New Delhi—110 017, India
Penguin Group (NZ), 67 Apollo Drive, Rosedale, North Shore 0632, New Zealand
(a division of Pearson New Zealand Ltd.)
Penguin Books (South Africa) (Pty.) Ltd., 24 Sturdee Avenue, Rosebank, Johannesburg 2196,
South Africa

Penguin Books Ltd., Registered Offices: 80 Strand, London WC2R 0RL, England

FORTUNE AND FATE

An Ace Book / published by arrangement with the author

PRINTING HISTORY
Ace hardcover edition / November 2008
Ace mass-market edition / September 2009

Copyright © 2008 by Sharon Shinn.
Map by Kathryn Tongay-Carr.
Cover art by Donato Giancola.
Cover design by Annette Fiore DeFex.
Interior text design by Kristin del Rosario.

ISBN: 978-0-441-01775-1

ACE
Ace Books are published by The Berkley Publishing Group,
a division of Penguin Group (USA) Inc.,
375 Hudson Street, New York, New York 10014.
ACE and the "A" design are trademarks of Penguin Group (USA) Inc.

PRINTED IN THE UNITED STATES OF AMERICA

10 9 8 7 6 5 4 3 2 1

To Matt,
who's read my manuscripts by flashlight
on the long drives to Chicago,
and who particularly liked this one;

And to the rest of his family,
Shari, Rich, and Jessica,
my eternal houseguests.

◼ Gillengaria ◼

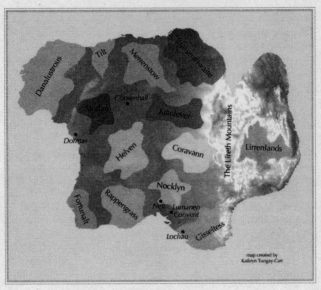

Danalustrous

Tilt

Merrenstow

Gisseltess

Storian

Chouenhall

Kianlever

Dormas

Helven

Coravann

The Lireth Mountains

Lirrenlands

Fortunalt

Rappengrass

Nocklyn

Neft Lumanen
Convent

Lochau Gisseltess

map created by
Kathryn Tongay-Carr

Chapter

1

KARRYN WAS SO GRATEFUL TO STEP OUT OF THE coach that her legs practically buckled under her as her feet touched the ground. Only Tover's hard hold on her arm kept her more or less upright. He hauled her through a muddy yard and toward the open door of a rather run-down tavern. Stumbling along behind him, Karryn glanced around, trying to get a sense of where they might be. The land was level and sparsely decorated with trees, so they might still be in northwestern Fortunalt. They had traveled fast, but she didn't think they had been on the road long enough to make it to Rappengrass.

But it was unlikely Tover planned to take her to Rappengrass anyway, she thought, as she tripped along behind him through the inn's yard. He knew a search party would have set out after them almost immediately; he would want to find the quickest and most convenient place to hole up, and that meant staying within the Fortunalt borders. She shuddered. They had been traveling since about noon yesterday, and every hour had been utterly miserable, but she had felt relatively safe as long as they were on the move. Tover had shown no disposition to ravish her in the uncomfortable confines of the coach. But once they took refuge someplace with a room and a bed . . .

Fresh panic swept through her. Did Tover plan to book accommodations here, wherever *here* was? She cast another glance behind her as Tover jerked her closer to the door. A half dozen other vehicles had come to rest inside the muddy yard. Some of the drivers were changing horses, but others appeared to merely be breaking their journey long enough to take a meal. Karryn hadn't been able to see much through the coach windows, but it had been clear that they were in a particularly desolate stretch of countryside, and this might be the only posting station for miles. A few saddled horses were also tied up outside the inn, munching on oats while their riders apparently ate breakfast inside.

Karryn's spirits rose a little. If there were many people in the taproom, she could cry out for help. Someone might recognize her or at least be willing to come to her assistance. She would have to be careful—she needed a matron traveling with her children, or sober and liveried soldiers from some nobleman's house guard. She did not want to fall into the hands of some skilled swordsman who would save her from Tover and then turn out to be *worse*. Her mother had long terrified her with stories of bandits who would kidnap little girls and torture them in ways so grotesque that Serephette had not even been able to describe them. Only now, at the age of sixteen, did Karryn understand that her mother had probably been referring to rape, not dismemberment and slow death. Though rape, should it come, would be bad enough—even if it were not at the hands of some landless mercenary.

For Tover Banlish was a serlord's son who hoped to marry his way to fortune by eloping with a serramarra. Karryn had refused his clumsy offer a little too forcefully, and he had decided to take matters into his own hands.

At the door to the tavern he suddenly yanked her around to face him, leaning forward and speaking in a menacing whisper.

"Don't try to cause trouble inside," he hissed. If he hadn't been scowling, and if she hadn't hated him, she might have thought he was attractive, for he had pleasant features framed by fine brown hair. But his blue eyes were icy and every line of his body tensed with threat. "If you so much as try to speak to anyone, I swear I'll throttle you and declare you've fainted. And if you misbehave here, I won't let you out of the coach again until we've reached our destination."

She wanted to spit in his face, but she was desperate to get inside, relieve herself, and eat something. They had only stopped four times since they started out. She was almost as mad from discomfort as she was from fear.

"You must allow me access to a chamber pot, or I'll soil the interior of your coach," she said.

He leaned even closer, sneered even more. "I'll take you myself to whatever room provides such an amenity," he said. "Just remember. Be good—or be sorry."

He waited for her affirmative. She hesitated, because she *hated* him so much; she wanted to step inside that doorway and start screaming hysterically. But fear dominated her even more than hatred did. She did not want to risk losing the opportunity to take advantage of whatever amenities this place offered.

So she nodded once, sharply. He pushed open the door and pulled her into the taproom, where again she almost fainted at the welcome warmth of the air and the delicious scents coming from the kitchen. She must have closed her eyes. When she opened them, a ragged-looking girl was approaching and waving them toward an unoccupied table.

"I suppose you want breakfast?" she was saying.

"Yes," Tover replied. "Eggs and sausage for us and our driver. Ale for my driver and me, and milk for my sister. But first—is there a place my sister can have a moment's privacy? We've been in the coach for hours."

The girl pointed down a narrow hallway. "I'll put in your order," she said, and turned away.

The "privacy" accommodations were smelly but infinitely better than a bush on the side of the road, and Karryn used the pitcher of chilly water to wash her face as well as her hands. No mirror in the small room, but she supposed that was just as well. She could only imagine how she looked, with her thick dark hair in unmanageable tangles and her green gown irretrievably wrinkled. Her face, usually rather ruddy of complexion, was no doubt pinched and a little pale. All in all, she probably *looked* as mad as Tover would claim she was if she began to throw any kind of tantrum.

She rejoined him and followed him to the table, casting surreptitious glances around the taproom as she went. Her heart sank. None of the occupants looked likely to offer her aid. At one table sat two ancient women accompanied by a granddaughter or a paid companion. At another table was a boisterous family, four shrieking children and their young and hapless parents. One solitary traveler sat up near the bar, a stocky, rather short, brown-haired man—or perhaps it was a woman—eating breakfast with a single-minded attention. A few rather villainous-looking men sat together or apart, some talking, some dicing, some looking morosely out the window.

No rescue to be hoped for from any quarter.

The unkempt barmaid approached their table bearing three large, steaming platters, and Karryn felt her stomach turn over. Food, that was what she needed. Once she ate something, she would be able to think more clearly. She would be able to figure out a plan.

She was forking up her second bite when they were joined by the driver, who pulled up a seat next to Tover. He was big, bald, and burly, with enormous hands. He had spoken very little so far on this journey, and not at all to Karryn, but she was more afraid of him than she was of Tover. There was something wicked about the way he watched her with his slitted black eyes. He wore so many weapons on his belt that he jangled every time he moved.

"Rear mare's thrown a shoe," he said to Tover as he reached for his glass of ale. "Take another thirty minutes before the smith here can get to her."

Tover looked annoyed, then he nodded. "All right. Did you have the whole team unhitched and fed?"

The driver nodded. "How much farther do you want to go today? We'll need to change the horses before long."

"We have another fifty miles to cover, mostly on back roads."

The driver nodded again. "You're going to have to take the reins, then, because I'm about dead. Unless you want to stop here for a few hours and let me sleep."

Tover glanced around the room. "Not here. Too well-traveled."

The driver looked over at Karryn and gave her a leering smile. She shrank back into her chair, trying to make herself too small to merit his attention. "Think her prissy uncle's going to be riding after her to make a daring rescue?" he said with a sneer.

Tover snorted. "Jasper Paladar couldn't rescue a cat from a garbage pail," he replied. "Still. There are guards in Forten City who were loyal to Rayson Fortunalt. Paladar could round them up to come riding after Rayson's daughter."

The guard was still smiling at Karryn. "Think your uncle Jasper's going to come after you anytime soon?" he asked in a crooning voice. "Come riding up on a big old stallion like some storybook hero?"

Without thinking, Karryn snatched up the salt cellar from the middle of the table, intending to fling it in the driver's smug face. Tover's palm slammed down over her wrist, pinning her hand to the table and nearly breaking the bones.

"I warned you to behave," he said icily into her ear. "You're a serramarra—show some decorum."

She was trying not to whimper, but his hold was so painful that it was hard to swallow the sound. She stared down at the scarred table, despising both of them.

"Look at me," Tover said in a slightly louder voice. "Serra—look at me." He pressed down on her wrist even more heavily. She smothered a yelp and looked up. He was staring at her with those cold blue eyes, and for the moment he looked even more dangerous than his companion.

"You will not throw things at Darvis," Tover said in a slow, deliberate voice. "You will not do anything to draw attention to yourself. Or I will rent a room here for the day and effectively make you my wife in this very inn. If you do not behave very, very well, that is exactly what will happen. Do you understand? Is that what you want?"

Between the pain and the fear, Karryn almost could not draw breath. She stared up at him; nothing registered but his face. Outside the outline of his cheekbones and earlobes there was only formless white space—nothing. No humanity, no hope, no rescue. She nodded.

"No," she choked out. "Please. Not here. Let us travel on."

Now Tover lifted one finger to stroke her cheek. "You hear

that, Darvis? The serramarra is not impressed by the squalid accommodations of roadside inns. She wants the luxury and comfort of Banlish Manor."

She could hear the grin still in Darvis's voice. "I think you're missing a bet if you leave here too soon."

"And I say I shall take this opportunity to prove to my lady how very gracious I can be." Tover relaxed his grip on her imprisoned hand and almost gently lifted her fingers to his mouth. He pressed a real kiss on the back of her hand. "Remember, if you will, how hard I strove to please you."

"Pardon me for interrupting," said a dry voice just a few steps away.

All three of them nearly jumped out of their seats, for not even Darvis had seen the newcomer approaching. Karryn felt a sudden wild leap of hope—*A stranger, come to rescue me?*—that instantly died away. This small, unprepossessing person was the individual she had spotted when they first walked in, the one sitting up at the bar eating a hearty breakfast. Close up, it was clear the stranger was female, though dressed in the trousers and tight-fitting jacket usually worn by men who were soldiers. Like those men, she also sported a sword and a couple of knives in her belt, though she possessed nowhere near as many weapons as Darvis.

"Ye-es?" Tover said in his haughtiest voice, drawing the word out into multiple syllables. It was his way of conveying without words the fact that he was a devvaser, the son of a serlord, and this anonymous creature was less than nobody.

The short woman completely ignored him. All her attention was on Karryn. "I just wanted to let you know something, my lady," she said in a quiet voice. "If your husband is abusing you, I can help you get free of him and take you someplace safe."

"Leave us, you insolent scum!" Tover snapped as Darvis leapt to his feet so fast his chair toppled to the floor. Karryn didn't even have to hear the whine of weapons to know the driver had drawn a blade. Tover's fingers tightened alarmingly around Karryn's wrist.

The soldier woman was completely unimpressed. She still kept her gaze locked on Karryn's, and there was a steady message in her dark brown eyes. *Trust me. I can help you.* "I have a horse out front," she said. "We can ride away from your husband right now."

Karryn made an instant, rash decision. "He's not my husband," she panted. "He's—"

Before she could complete the second sentence, Tover loosed a murderous oath and crashed to his feet, jerking her up beside him. Darvis vaulted across the table at the strange woman. Karryn screamed and tried to fling herself backward, away from Tover, away from Darvis, away from the sudden thicket of blades. But Tover held her fast and the table prevented any escape. She screamed again and cowered down, shielding her face with her free hand.

Darvis had engaged the woman in a swift and brutal knife fight. Tover was trying to haul Karryn away from the flashing blades but twice she was slammed by Darvis's weaving body, once with such force that the table screeched away from both of them when she landed heavily against it. Karryn had expected the unknown woman to be dead on the floor within thirty seconds, but no, the smaller combatant was obviously holding her own. She lunged in when Darvis expected her to feint, for he grunted in surprise and then in pain, clapping a hand to his stomach and howling in agony or rage.

Unexpectedly, Tover dropped Karryn's wrist and shook free his own sword. He fell into a stalking crouch and then flew at the woman, barely giving her time to draw her own long blade. Karryn shrieked and looked around for something heavy to fling at Tover's head, to give the woman some advantage, however slight. But it was not necessary. With three quick slices of her sword, the stranger had parried Tover's assault, knocked the blade from his hand, and run him through high on his right shoulder. Tover screamed and stumbled against the table, his hand clapped to his wound.

"I think these two are down for the moment," the woman said coolly, turning to Karryn. "Grab your things and let's run."

Karryn was already racing for the door. No one in the tavern made a move to stop her, though literally every soul in the place, even the barmaid, was staring. "All my things are in the coach, but I don't need them!" she cried. "Let's just go!"

The soldier woman was hard on her heels as they scrambled through the door. "Which coach is yours?" she inquired. "Maybe we can find a way to disable it."

Karryn came to a halt just outside the door and looked wildly around at the equipages lined up in the yard. She hadn't been on the outside of Tover's carriage often enough to know what it looked like, and he had not been stupid enough to attempt kidnapping in a carriage blazoned with his family arms. "I don't know! One of the horses needs a shoe, that's all I know."

"Good enough," the stranger said, tugging Karryn in the direction of a sturdy white gelding loosely tied to a hitching post. "That'll slow them down. We'll ride pillion till we've covered some distance and figured out what to do."

Just then the tavern door swung open and Darvis charged through, bellowing. His shirt was covered with blood, but he hefted a sword high in his left hand. But the soldier woman surprised him again, darting forward to smash her head right in the middle of his chest. He cried out and went crashing down in the doorway, just in time to trip Tover as he rushed out.

"Go, go, go!" the stranger cried, shoving Karryn toward the gelding. She had her knife out again but Karryn didn't see how she used it on either of the abductors; she was too occupied with climbing into the saddle and guiding the white horse over to the stranger's side. The woman sheathed her blade, swung into the saddle behind Karryn, and kicked the horse forward all in one seemingly effortless motion. There was a scramble and curse behind them, but they were across the muddy yard, through the gate, and racing down the road before Karryn heard any real sounds of pursuit.

She was free!

Chapter
2

WEN DIDN'T FIGURE THE TWO OF THEM COULD ride the gelding for long. He was powerful and he loved a good run, but two riders were a considerable burden, and the new passenger was taller and heavier than Wen. Also not much of a rider. She twisted and turned in the saddle, looking over her shoulder and trying to tug down the hem of her dress. Wen imagined her horse wasn't any more pleased with the fidgeting than she was.

"Sit still, if you can," she said, as civilly as possible. "We won't go far."

That, of course, made the girl crane her head around, trying to see Wen's face. "But they'll come right after us! We'll never be able to stop running!"

Wen nodded. "I know they'll pursue. We'll pull off somewhere along the road and watch them go by. Then we can proceed at a slower pace."

"What if they don't go by? What if they see us? Oh, they'll kill us both, I know they will."

Wen couldn't help grinning at that. "I don't think so. Neither of them is much of a fighter." She had to amend that after a moment's thought. "Well, the big one has strength and some training. He's probably a useful man in a brawl. But the other one, the noble—he's completely inept. I can handle both of them."

Again the girl tried to slew around in the saddle. "Who *are* you?" she demanded. "Thank you so much for coming to my rescue, but why did you? And how did you get to be good enough to fight off two grown men and win? A little thing like you?"

For a moment, Wen was tempted to push her out of the saddle. Even across the width of the posting house, it had been clear to her that this girl was the kind of person she utterly despised—wealthy, indulged, spoiled, and temperamental. Purely decorative, if she had any value at all.

But—at least back at the tavern—she was also abused and helpless, which Wen had been able to tell in an instant. Those were the traits that had sent Wen striding over to offer assistance. Wen had so much to atone for. Saving one frightened young woman might do little to assuage her guilt and grief, but abandoning the girl to certain ravishment would only have added to Wen's grim burdens.

So, making even more of an effort this time, Wen gave another civil answer. "I've been training with weapons most of my life. I might be small, but I'm very good. And I came to your aid because it was unthinkable not to."

"Tover abducted me a day and a half ago," the girl said bitterly. "I hate him! I told him I wouldn't marry him, and he said, 'We'll see about that,' and he forced me into the coach. My mother and my uncle will be so worried."

Wen hardly knew what to ask first. "Is he so in love with you, then? A fine way to show it."

The girl gave a sharp laugh. "In love with my inheritance. Not with me."

So the girl was noble-born, as Wen had guessed, and probably rich into the bargain. It wouldn't be the first time an ambitious suitor had attempted a rough wooing, but Wen had always thought the dowry would have to be awfully substantial to make up for founding your marriage on a bedrock of hatred. "I would have guessed him noble-born as well, with property of his own," Wen said.

"Indeed, he is! A devvaser—a serlord's son," the girl replied.

"But that's not good enough for him. He wants to marry a ser-ramarra and be a marlord himself one day."

That made Wen open her eyes wide and pull back a little to study what she could see of the dark-haired woman before her in the saddle. She'd saved a serramarra? From which of the Twelve Houses? They were in Fortunalt country, but not all that far from Rappengrass or Storian, and even Gisseltess was only a few days' hard riding away. Oh, gods, what irony if she had rescued Rayson Fortunalt's daughter.

"Who are you?" she asked in a quiet voice.

Her passenger spoke defiantly, as if braced for scorn. "Karryn Fortunalt."

For a moment Wen couldn't speak.

It had been almost two years ago that Rayson Fortunalt and Halchon Gisseltess had led half the Houses of Gillengaria in an uprising against the king. The resulting battle had been brief but bloody, and both of the renegade marlords had lost their lives. That was little comfort, though, for so many others had died opposing them. Coeval and Tir and Moxer. Dearest friends, truest companions. Irreplaceable and lost forever.

But no loss could be compared to the death of King Baryn, who had died in the earliest days of combat, leaving his young princess to rule after him. Wen's heart still hurt when she remembered that Baryn was gone.

When she remembered how he had died.

Wen's silence had done the trick. Karryn sat quietly before her in the saddle, huddled over the pommel. Wen no longer wanted to push her off the horse. She wanted to murder the girl with her ungloved hands.

Of course that was not an option. Neither could Wen pull up the gelding and leave the girl on the side of the road to be discovered and reclaimed by her erstwhile abductors. Karryn's story had been incomplete, but Wen felt fairly certain she'd pieced together the essential details. Serramarra Karryn would be named marlady of Fortunalt when she was old enough to hold the title. Her husband would become marlord and both of them would move in the highest circles of Gillengaria society.

This Tover fellow must be part of the new and still contro-versial second echelon of lords and landholders. Some of the

rebels who had joined the war had been the so-called lesser
lords who owed fealty to the Twelve Houses—nobles who had
always collectively, and somewhat derisively, been known as
the Thirteenth House. Those who rose up in rebellion claimed
to be tired of serving as vassals for the marlords. They wanted
to own property outright and earn titles for themselves and
their heirs.

Baryn had been cautiously in favor of prying a few minor
estates from the death grip of the marlords and bestowing them,
unencumbered, on a handful of Thirteenth House nobles. It
had fallen to his daughter, Amalie, and her various advisors to
craft a scheme to divide and apportion properties, but over the
past two years, the plan had been worked out. Now there were
Twelve Houses and Twenty-Four Manors, and any number of
confusing but jealously guarded titles. Marlords and marladies bred heirs called serramar and serramarra; the heirs to
the new serlords had been dubbed devvaser and devvaserra.
Any more subdivisions, Wen thought, and she would just
stop giving anyone an honorific. She would bow, if required
to acknowledge a noble, and maintain her silence. The gods
knew she would prefer never to speak to a single one of them
again.

Karryn whispered something in a shaky voice. Wen suspected she might be crying. Her voice chilly, Wen said, "Pardon me? I didn't hear you."

"I said, it's not my fault."

"What's not your fault?"

"My father. My father's war."

"I'm sure it's not," Wen said, her voice still icy.

Karryn lifted her head a little. "He was a horrible man,"
she said, her voice gaining strength. "You think I didn't hate
him? And yet now everyone blames me for the war. Everyone
blames me because the king is dead."

The words made Wen flinch so hard that the gelding lost
stride. Wen clucked him back in motion and responded in
an even voice. "There are many people to blame for Baryn's
death, but it's hard to imagine you are on that list."

The words were true, but that didn't make it any easier to
forgive the girl for merely existing. But, Wen reminded herself, she didn't have to forgive Karryn. She didn't have to like

the girl. She merely had to get her to a safe place and then leave her behind forever.

In fact . . . Wen glanced around at the countryside they were moving through. The road was narrow and not particularly well-traveled; the devvaser obviously had not wanted to take his captive along main routes. This region of northern Fortunalt offered fairly sparse vegetation, but they were passing through a stretch of land that provided a certain amount of cover. Some trees, some undergrowth, a little undulation in the land. They could move fifty yards off the main road and conceal themselves with relative ease.

Accordingly, Wen reined in the horse and slipped to the ground. Karryn looked down in alarm. "What are you doing? We can't stop here! There's nowhere to hide!"

Wen nodded. "They won't look for us here, I think. Come on. Off the horse. We'll hunker down." She glanced at the route behind them as if she could discern any signs of pursuit. "Quickly. I don't suppose they're more than fifteen minutes behind us."

Karryn dismounted and followed her off the road, still worried. "But if they find us—if they see us—"

"I told you. I can protect you."

Karryn took a step that was practically a flounce. "You don't even like me."

Wen held on to her temper. "I don't even know you."

"Well, it doesn't make any sense to me. Why would you help me when you hate me and everyone in my House?"

Despite the urgency, despite the fact she was listening with half an ear for sounds of oncoming horses, Wen came to a dead halt only ten yards from the road. She glared at Karryn, but the young, frightened, wild-haired, big-eyed girl glared right back.

"Well, you do," Karryn added.

Wen spoke in a tight voice. "I owe a debt. To a man I didn't save. And since I lived, and he didn't, I vowed that I would spend the rest of my life protecting others when I could. Giving them the service that I could not—did not—give to him." She twitched the reins and stalked forward, Karryn mercifully silent as she followed.

Still in silence, they found their cover in a small stand of trees blocked by a few scraggly bushes. The horse was the problem, his white coat bright enough to be seen from the road, but Wen was prepared for this contingency. She coaxed him to the ground and covered him with a saddle blanket. It was a rusty green that blended well with the vegetation, still brown on this extreme edge of spring. She and Karryn wrapped themselves in another blanket and settled to the ground right by his head.

Safe as far as it went. Wen pulled her sword and laid it across her lap. She checked the knife strapped to her wrist, and drew another one from the belt at her waist, holding it loosely in her left hand.

"What man?" Karryn asked.

Wen looked at her blankly. "What?"

"What man didn't you save?"

"Be quiet, serra. We have to listen for the sound of the dev-vaser's horse."

So Karryn whispered, "What man?"

Wen looked at her, prepared to snap a harsh reply, but the set of Karryn's face was stubborn. Wen partially revised her earlier assessment. Karryn might be rich and spoiled to some extent, but her life surely hadn't been easy. Rayson Fortunalt's daughter had probably received very little affection or attention from that driven, ambitious man. She no doubt had had to kick and scream and throw tantrums to get anything she wanted. She wasn't about to be put off by a cold answer.

"A man I worked for. I was in his guard. There were—bandits. They attacked and killed him while I was supposed to be protecting him."

Karryn's dark eyes widened. "Did you run away?"

"No, of course I didn't run away! I fought."

"Were you injured?"

Almost mortally. Better, in fact, if she *had* died. "Yes."

"Well, then it's hardly your fault. If you fought as hard as you could—"

Wen couldn't keep the utter bleakness from her voice. "I should have been dead before he was," she said. "If he had to fall, it should have been at the feet of my lifeless body."

"And you're never going to forgive yourself for being alive?"

Wen drew a sharp breath. Succinctly put. "Never."

Karryn hunched herself a little closer together. "Well, that seems pretty stupid to me."

"But then, you were stupid enough to be kidnapped by a man who wants your House, so I don't suppose your opinion has any value."

Karryn scowled at her but blessedly shut up for the moment. Wen closed her eyes and listened for pursuers. She could have killed both the devvaser and his accomplice—oh, easily—but she had chosen to wound them instead. She had seen plenty of death in that heartbreaking war. She was prepared to mete it out again if she had to, but only in direst necessity. To save the life of someone she had sworn to protect.

To save herself if, when the moment came, it seemed her life outweighed that of her attacker.

Not only had she not killed the kidnappers, she hadn't severely disabled them. She figured they could have bound their wounds and been on the road in less than twenty minutes if they had been able to rent horses or turn their carriage team into mounts.

But the sound of horses, when she heard it, came from the wrong direction. Wen cocked her head and tried to guess how many were in the traveling party. More than two; probably not more than five. And moving at a brisk but hardly breakneck pace.

Which caused her to think of a question she really should have asked before this. "Will anyone from Forten City be coming after you?" A fragment of their previous conversation surfaced in her memory. "You mentioned an uncle."

"He's not really my uncle. I just call him that."

"Whoever he is, will he be coming after you?"

"I'm sure he will." Karryn did not look sure at all. "I mean—of course he will, won't he? When he realizes I'm gone."

"Why wouldn't he know you were missing?"

Karryn glanced away. "Maybe I didn't tell him where I was going. Maybe I told him I was going someplace else."

Wen felt her breath leave her in a hiss. Oh, she would be very glad to be rid of this troublesome, disagreeable girl! "Once he realizes it," she ground out, "will he send a party after you? Will they be coming from the southwest?" She indicated the road in front of them.

Karryn looked uncertain. "I don't know. Where are we?"

Wen pointed again. "Southwest is Forten City. Is that where your uncle would be starting out from?"

Karryn nodded. "Yes. Do you think that's him coming?" Her face was suddenly hopeful.

"Maybe. Though he's brought an awfully small troop with him if it is."

"Maybe he couldn't raise too many soldiers."

An odd thing for a serramarra to say, Wen thought, but just then the first of the horses trotted into view. Wen motioned Karryn to silence, and they crouched down even farther behind the trees, though they both peered out from behind the trunks. It took another minute for the riders to pass in front of them—a party of four men, all dressed in black-and-gold livery, and mounted on exceptionally fine horses. Wen felt her heart clench in actual pain as they passed before her, elegant, alert, disciplined, deadly.

"They look like soldiers," Karryn whispered in her ear.

Wen could only nod.

"Maybe they would help us," Karryn added. "If we told them what had happened to me. Maybe they would help you fight Tover and Darvis."

Wen shook her head, still unable to speak.

"Why not?" Karryn persisted. "Do you know them? Who are they?"

The girl simply would not shut up, but it scarcely mattered now. The soldiers were out of view, not having spared one glance in the fugitives' direction.

"They're Queen's Riders," Wen managed to say. "No help to be expected from *them*."

Karryn squirmed, seeming to find it impossible either to sit still or to get comfortable. "How long will we have to sit here?"

Wen took a deep breath. Easier to do once the Riders were gone. "Until your friends ride by."

"They're not my *friends*."

Wen didn't bother answering. What were Riders doing in

this part of the world? What mission were they on for Queen Amalie? Was there some kind of trouble in Fortunalt?

Not her business. She had no connection to anyone at the royal court in Ghosenhall.

Karryn continued to fidget for the next ten minutes, but she grew quickly still when Wen sat up straighter and made a motion for silence. Yes, there was the sound she'd been waiting for—horses' hooves, probably from a pair of animals, traveling fast. In another minute, two riders galloped into view. Wen didn't need Karryn's sharp intake of breath to realize these were the devvaser and his accomplice. They appeared to be mounted on fresh horses bred for the saddle, so they'd probably rented or purchased the animals at the posting house, and they were riding hard.

Karryn only relaxed once the sound of hoofbeats had died away. "Now what do we do?" she asked.

That was, indeed, the question. "I think we find something closer to civilization," Wen said, cautiously coming to her feet. She didn't know how long the devvaser would continue onward before he began to wonder where his victim might have gone to ground—and came back to look for her. "A good-sized town, perhaps, where there might be a garrison of soldiers who would be inclined to protect you as we head back to Forten City. Wanting to earn your uncle's gratitude, you see."

Karryn nodded. "All right."

Wen surveyed her. The girl still looked defiant and sulky, but exhaustion was showing through her big eyes and rosy complexion. If she'd been abducted a day and a half ago, she'd probably been strung tight with tension ever since. "Where might the nearest sizable town be found?" she asked.

Karryn shook her head. "I don't know. I don't know where we are."

Wen's temper snapped. "By all the gods in Gillengaria, child, why *not*? You're the serramarra! When you're old enough—assuming you have the brains to survive that long, which I am starting to doubt—you will inherit every scrap of this land! Shouldn't you know where every road, every river, every town, every *house* is situated? Isn't that what it means to be marlady? That you own the land—and, in a sense, it owns you?"

"Well, I don't know!" Karryn fired back. "All my father cared about was where every gold *coin* in the land might be situated! *I* don't know how a marlady behaves! And I *don't* know where any town is! So go ahead and leave me if you want to, but stop telling me how stupid I am!"

And with that, Karryn flounced off, back toward the road, in full view of any chance passerby. Wen stood there, watching, as the girl stomped onto the road and set out in a most determined fashion in the direction they had been headed before.

The gelding gave a high whinny and clambered to his feet, tired of lying there, tired of inaction—tired, perhaps, of arguments between bad-tempered women. Wen stroked his nose, refolded the saddle blankets, and sighed heavily.

Tempting as it was, she could not abandon the girl to the many hazards of an open road in Fortunalt.

Leading the gelding by his bridle, Wen set off at a light run until she caught up with Karryn, and then she slowed to a walk. She couldn't bring herself to apologize, but it was pointless to keep quarreling. "We need a plan," she said. "I think we look for the nearest town. I didn't come this way, so I don't know what's down this road, but eventually we'll arrive at a place where we can ask directions. As soon as we can, we probably need to buy another horse." She paused a moment. "I don't suppose you have any money."

Karryn merely shook her head. She was watching her feet as if she wasn't sure she'd remember how to walk otherwise.

"And I don't suppose you have any rations."

Karryn shook her head again.

"Are you hungry? I've got some food in my bag."

"I ate at the inn," Karryn said in a subdued voice.

"Not much, I'll wager. Do you want an apple?" It was a peace offering.

Karryn accepted it. "Yes, please."

They came to a halt long enough for Wen to scoop two pieces of fruit from her bag, then they were on the move again. The exercise actually felt good, though they'd need to ride again soon. Walking would take them too long to get anywhere.

Wen remembered something that had been bothering her. After polishing off her apple, she asked, "Why did you think your uncle might have trouble rounding up soldiers to come after you?"

Karryn loosed a sigh and tossed her own core to the side of the road. "Jasper—he isn't the kind of person that soldiers listen to."

Wen digested that a moment in silence. "What kind of person is he?"

"He's a scholar. He reads books and he writes them. But he's not very physical. I can't imagine him holding a sword. Or fighting with anyone." She gave Wen a sideways glance. "He's much taller than you, but I'm sure you could knock him over without even trying."

Never having met the man, Wen was sure she could, too. "Well, even if he's not a soldier himself, he could doubtless round up the House guard to come after you. Couldn't he?"

"I suppose so," Karryn said doubtfully.

"*Is* there a House guard?"

"Sort of. Many of my father's soldiers were lost in the war."

Of course. And the queen would have had a vested interest in making sure Fortunalt didn't build up a private army again anytime soon. Still. A House had to have its own soldiers or who knew what could happen?

Well, the kidnapping of the serramarra, that's what.

"Let's go on the assumption that this uncle was able to find a dozen or so men to accompany him on a search for you," Wen said. "Would he have any reason for thinking the devvaser was the one who had run off with you?"

"I never told him about Tover asking me to marry him."

"So he probably wouldn't. And since he doesn't know where you were when you were kidnapped—gods and goddesses, you really put yourself into a bind, didn't you?"

Karryn lifted her chin. "Well, maybe he figured it out anyway. He's pretty smart."

"Who is he? How did he come to be named your guardian?"

"He's my mother's cousin. His name is Jasper Paladar. He came to stay with us after my father died."

"Did your mother invite him, or did the queen select him to look after Fortunalt until you turn twenty-one?"

Karryn shook her head. "Not my mother. Not the queen. It was the queen's consort who chose Uncle Jasper."

That made Wen widen her eyes. *Cammon* had selected Jasper Paladar to shepherd this girl through the final years of adolescence? Then the bumbling scholar that she'd been envisioning couldn't be so useless after all. Cammon never made mistakes about people. "Do you like him? Your uncle?" Wen asked abruptly.

Karryn nodded enthusiastically. "*So* much more than my own father! He's very kind. And he explains things to me. And he understands things, even when you don't tell him."

That endorsement kicked the scholar up a notch in Wen's estimation as well. Cammon trusted him, and this wretched girl admired him. Still. He hadn't provided adequate protection for someone in his charge, and Wen believed that was about the gravest error anyone could make.

"Well. We'll hope we encounter him very soon, headed our way, leading a mass of Fortunalt soldiers," Wen said. "But I think our odds will improve if we ride for a while and start looking for a settlement of any size. And this time," she added, "I'm sitting on the front of the saddle."

Karryn laughed, which made her look less like an obdurate and frightened child, and more like a privileged and carefree young lady. "If you want. I can't imagine it's too comfortable no matter how we sit."

"True enough," Wen said, tugging the horse to a halt.

She'd just put her foot in the stirrup when Karryn said, "Wait a minute. I keep forgetting to ask your name! You know mine."

Wen hesitated just a second, staring over her shoulder at the girl. Then she said, "My name is Willa."

Chapter

3

THEY RODE FOR ANOTHER TWO HOURS AT A fairly gentle pace. At first, Karryn chattered about topics that Wen found unutterably boring—her friends, her clothes, a ball she had attended last winter. But soon enough she began yawning heavily and allowing long pauses to build up between her sentences. Eventually her arms went slack around Wen's waist and her head rested against the back of Wen's. Wen waited with a sort of dour impatience for the girl to fall so deeply asleep that she loosed her hold and actually fell from the saddle.

They needed to find a place to stop, and they needed to find it soon. Fortunately, unlike Karryn, Wen actually had a moderate number of coins in her saddlebag. They'd be able to pay for food, a horse, and overnight lodgings if they needed to. If the tall, soft, wise, kind uncle didn't catch up to them first.

When they came to a crossroads that looked like a major route, Wen ruthlessly shook Karryn from her drowsy state. "Wake up. Does any of this look familiar? Where do you think this road leads?"

Karryn sighed and sat up. "I thought you said we wanted to go southwest?"

"Eventually we do. But I'm wondering if there's a bigger town closer to us if we head northeast?"

Karryn covered her mouth to hide another yawn. "I told you I don't know. I don't even know where we are."

"Just think about it," Wen said. "Marlords—and marladies—are supposed to have some mystical connection to their land. If—"

"I'm not a mystic!" Karryn exclaimed, sitting straight up. "We don't harbor mystics in Fortunalt!"

"I thought you despised your father and everything he stood for," Wen shot back. "*He's* the one who hated mystics. You should welcome them."

"I don't hate them," Karryn said stiffly. "I just don't want anyone calling me a mystic. I don't have any magic at all. I don't want any."

Wen sighed. "Well, all right. Do you think we should go left or right? Not that I'll do what you say, but I thought I'd ask your opinion."

"I think you should go straight," Karryn said crossly. "*That's* where the next town is."

There was a little silence between them for a moment. "Really?" Wen said at last.

"I don't know why I said that," Karryn replied.

Wen was grinning as she urged the gelding forward. "Well, let's just see. At any rate, I'm guessing your devvaser friend went left, chasing after us, so straight is a better choice than that."

They had only ridden another fifteen minutes when they topped a low hill and saw a market town spread out in the shallow valley below them. It was nowhere near the size of Ghosenhall or Forten City, but there were shops, there were stables, there were inns.

"You might not have magic in your veins," Wen said, a smile in her voice, "but you definitely have serramarra blood. Let's go find food and a fresh horse."

A meal revived Karryn and she claimed she didn't need to sleep. "I want to go *home*," she said. So Wen bargained with a stablemaster to buy an aging but well-behaved mare, and pretty soon they were on the road again. Not long after, they came to the crossroads and headed southwest.

"Here's where it gets tricky," Wen said. "We want to be on the road to flag down your uncle, if he's coming, but we don't want to be seen if the devvaser turns back to find you. If we hear anyone coming this way, we want to get out of sight, fast. So we need to ride slowly, and single file, listening very hard. And we need to not be very quiet."

She didn't have much real hope of Karryn falling silent, but, in fact, the girl was just tired enough to need all her energy to ride. Wen sat straight in her saddle, head bent a little, all her senses alert. She probably should have hired an escort while she was buying a horse. True, she was a much better fighter than either the devvaser or his brutish friend, but she could get unlucky; she could be hit from behind; she could take a hard blow that incapacitated her and allowed the kidnappers to snatch Karryn again. Wen didn't like the girl much, but she deserved more protection than a lone guard could provide.

They'd been on the move maybe half an hour when Wen caught the first drumming hoofbeats and muffled shouts that indicated a sizable party was headed their way. She swung the gelding off the road and Karryn hastily followed, but Wen wasn't so sure they needed to hide. This was a big group. Unless Tover had managed to recruit a whole host of equally ambitious and amoral confederates, this was probably not the devvaser.

"I think we're probably safe enough, even if this isn't your uncle," Wen said, but she made no move to steer the gelding back to the road. "We'll just stay here and let them pass, unless it's someone we're glad to see."

Two minutes later, the first riders swept into view, and even Wen knew that help had arrived. She counted ten soldiers, all dressed in gray uniforms and black sashes embroidered with white. In their midst rode a thin, bearded man wearing fine clothes and a look of worry.

Karryn kicked her mare into a run. "Uncle Jasper! Uncle Jasper!" she cried, making a headlong dash toward the oncoming riders.

Wen stayed where she was, watching with a half-smile on

her face. Naturally, Karryn's maneuver churned the whole party into chaos, as the soldiers wrenched their mounts aside to avoid riding over her. Jasper Paladar jumped from his saddle and ran over to Karryn, who was sliding off her mare as quick as could be. He *was* a tall man, Wen noted, and reedthin. Both his beard and his hair were a very dark brown streaked with gray, which gave him an air of sober distinction. He was smiling now, though, as he caught his cousin's daughter in a hard embrace. Wen was too far away to hear what he said to her, but she saw his mouth moving. A scold? A prayer of thanksgiving? A demand to know what had happened to her?

The latter, Wen decided, as Karryn pulled back a little and began an animated response. Then the formation of soldiers shifted and Wen lost sight of the glad reunion. She slowly urged her own mount back to the road. She wondered if she could ride away right now, give a friendly wave to the curious Fortunalt soldiers and disappear. Wen found expressions of gratitude and endless recountings of the adventure to be far more exhausting than the adventures themselves. She had been fortunate enough, these past two years, to aid dozens of individuals in one state of distress or another, and it was always the same. The action sustained her, the sense of purpose and even righteousness. She was at her best in those circumstances.

But she was clumsy and uncertain and even a little angry during the aftermath. *So I helped you or your husband or your daughter or your friend. It is not enough, do you understand? Your thanks only shame me. My success now only reminds me that I failed before.*

Best if she slipped down the road right now and left Karryn to look around blankly and say, "She was here just a moment ago!"

But Wen had hesitated too long. The line of soldiers parted, and Karryn came dashing through them, towing her guardian behind her. Bedraggled and exhausted as she was, Karryn finally looked pretty, Wen thought. Or maybe just happy.

"Willa! Willa! Here's my uncle Jasper. He wants to thank you."

Wen forced a smile and swung out of the saddle to make a

creditable bow in the nobleman's direction. When she straightened, he was standing right in front of her, his height making her feel so small that she started to resent it. At the same time, he had his hand outstretched to take hers, a rare mark of favor from a man of his station to a woman of hers. Reluctantly, she put her hand in his and found his grip firm, though his uncallused palm had clearly never held a weapon.

"Karryn has just told me your part in this extraordinary story," he said, and Wen marveled that such a deep and pleasant voice could come from such a slim frame. "My name is Jasper Paladar, and I'm her guardian. Thank you so much for saving her from a dreadfully grim fate."

"You're welcome," she said. "I was glad to do it."

"I would like to reward you for your efforts."

She almost smiled. It was the least original thing he could have said. "I did not befriend her hoping for a reward."

"Perhaps not, but heroism can be an expensive endeavor," he replied.

She laughed, because *that* was a phrase she hadn't heard before. "In fact, my only outlay was for the mare, which you can certainly buy from me if you like," she said. "Karryn will need to ride something, after all, as you head back to Forten City."

"She's not a very exciting horse," Karryn said. And then, when she caught Wen's look, "But of course I like her very much!"

"Karryn tells me you have exceptional skill with a sword," Jasper Paladar added. He was looking down at Wen with a mixture of curiosity and speculation, and his gray eyes were keen and considering. Even if Karryn hadn't told her so, Wen would have instantly guessed that here was a man of rare intelligence. "That's unusual for a woman, isn't it?"

"I have skill, but I don't know that it's exceptional," Wen replied coolly. "Being able to outfight a nobleman and a brigand isn't much of a challenge. Any of your guards could probably manage it."

That raised his dark eyebrows and sharpened his expression. "I would like to think that's true," he said softly. "But the caliber of soldier willing to fight for this House has deteriorated sadly since my cousin's husband went to war."

"I understand that you might face some difficulties in raising an army for your House, given its history, but even the queen would realize that you need a strong personal guard," Wen said. "If for no other reason than to prevent the sort of disaster that just happened."

Jasper Paladar's eyebrows drew together. "Karryn hasn't told me the entire story yet, but it's clear she put herself at risk, telling her mother she was heading to one destination and setting out for an entirely different destination in stealth. Even the sloppiest soldiers can be excused for not protecting her when she was not where she was supposed to be."

"Can they?" Wen said. "I don't think so."

Now his brows rose in an expression of surprise. "What do you mean?"

Wen gestured toward the soldiers. "Properly trained guards follow their master wherever the master goes. Do you think Queen Amalie ever sets foot outside the palace in Ghosenhall without at least two Riders at her back? She doesn't need to ask them to attend her. Some number of them are assigned to watch her at every hour of the day, and that is all they do."

"Still, Amalie is the queen," he replied. "There is reason to suppose she might always be in danger."

Wen shrugged. "There is reason to suppose your niece is always at risk. I don't know what kind of politics are at work here in Fortunalt, but it seems *some* of the nobles are feeling discontented. You should assume this was not a lone assault. You should plan accordingly." She looked at Karryn but she was still addressing Jasper Paladar. "You should install a well-trained and highly focused unit that follows your niece wherever she goes—whether it is to the market to buy roses or to the garden to meet a clandestine lover. And every other place in between."

"I wasn't going to meet a *lover*!" Karryn exclaimed.

Jasper Paladar's eyes had narrowed thoughtfully. "That is not an attitude that has governed Fortune since I've been there."

At first she was surprised by his use of the word, but then she remembered a stray fact she must have learned a long time ago: The principal estate owned by the marlords of Fortunalt was situated in the heart of Forten City and called by the name of Fortune. She had no idea why. Most everywhere else in Gillengaria, the marlords' estates carried names that were also used to denote the surrounding cities. It was hard to believe Rayson Fortunalt had been whimsical enough to have dreamed up this convention on his own.

She replied coolly to the lord's observation. "It's an attitude that could save her life. It's the only one, in fact, that will—if something like this happens again."

"I don't think I want a House guard that follows me everywhere I go," Karryn said with a pout. "Do you mean, everywhere? To balls? When I go to visit Lindy?"

"Everywhere," Wen said.

"How many?" Karryn's guardian asked. He gestured behind him to the Fortunalt soldiers patiently waiting in the road. "I emptied the barracks to muster this force."

Wen swept a glance over the mounted men. Hard to tell from a cursory inspection, of course, but they didn't seem like a particularly impressive group. Some too young, some too old, some too paunchy, some too slack. The best men of Fortunalt had probably been lost in the war. "The absolute minimum would be twelve," she said. "Four for each eight-hour shift around the clock. You'd be better off with sixteen or twenty. And you don't just need the soldiers. You need a captain to lead them and facilities for them to train in and equipment for them to carry. Are their swords any good? What about their horses?" Wen shook her head. "You can't just say, 'I want a strong guard.' You have to put some thought and resources into it."

Jasper Paladar let his breath out in a long sigh. "I've put most of my thought and resources into other enterprises that seemed just as important at the time," he said. "But all of that counts for nothing if the serramarra goes missing. I take your point."

Wen nodded. "Good. Then this whole misadventure had some value after all."

"Will you return to Fortune with us?" he asked abruptly. "And lead the guard?"

Wen stared at him, completely nonplussed. Karryn gave a little squeal and said, "Oh yes!" but Wen ignored her.

"No," she said shortly.

"Why not?" was the cool reply.

"You don't even know me," Wen said. "You have no reason to believe I am as good as I say—or as loyal as I would have to be."

"I think I do know both of those things," he said seriously.

"Please come back with us, Willa," Karryn begged. "I'll feel so much safer if you're there."

"No," Wen said again. "I have other—obligations."

"What obligations?" Jasper Paladar asked. "If they will not take too much of your time, we could wait for you."

She gave him a frosty look. "Obligations I am not at liberty to discuss."

Karryn spoke artlessly. "She has to make it up to somebody who died a long time ago."

That made Jasper raise his eyebrows again. Wen was furious. "My reasons are my own," she snapped. "I do not need to explain them to you. Thank you for your offer, but I am not free to accept."

"If you change your mind," he said, "do you know your way to Fortune?"

"I've never been there," she said. "But I'm sure I could find it."

Jasper gave her a small bow. "Then we shall hope you reconsider and that we see you again soon. Come, Karryn, it's time we were getting you home. Your mother is so anxious."

He put an arm around Karryn's shoulder to herd her back to her waiting horse, but Karryn broke free and flung her arms around Wen. It was wholly unexpected, and Wen froze in place, enduring the hug for the moment it lasted. "I do hope you'll come to Fortune," the girl said when she pulled back, her eyes brimming with tears. "You can't think how much we need you there."

"Karryn," Jasper called, and the girl dragged herself over to her uncle, turning back twice to give Wen a forlorn wave. Though it seemed to take forever, they were all finally mounted and on their way again. Jasper had paused long enough to count a few coins into Wen's hand—the price of the mare, and the only reward she did not decline—and then finally he was on horseback as well. Wen returned Karryn's last wave before the whole party cantered out of sight around the bend of the road.

Well. That would teach her to go rescuing serramarra. Now she felt all ruffled and peculiar, as if she'd actually seen a friend ride away.

And Karryn Fortunalt was nowhere near a friend.

Wen shook her head to clear away the confusion and swung herself onto the gelding's back. Then she just sat in the saddle a moment, not sure which direction to go.

"Well, then," she said softly. "Where was I going before I encountered the serramarra this morning?"

Ah, but that was the problem, of course. She had been headed nowhere in particular. She had no destination, no goal, no driving purpose. Nowhere to be, no one to look for. Just strangers in trouble. People who might need her for a short time, and then ride on.

Chapter
4

WEN SPENT TWO DAYS BACK AT THE LITTLE market town she and Karryn had visited, roaming the few streets and looking for work. Her funds were lower than she liked, and, as Jasper Paladar had pointed out, heroism could be expensive.

She found a job with a small freighting company that needed extra soldiers to guard a shipment to Forten City. The pay was so good for the short stretch of work that, once she made her way from the tidy business office to the chaotic loading yard to introduce herself to the captain of the guard, she couldn't resist asking what they'd be protecting.

He sized her up before answering. She guessed him to be in his late thirties, maybe eight years older than she was, and well-muscled under his worn uniform. He had short blond-brown hair, brown eyes, massive hands, and a wicked smile that he unexpectedly turned on her.

"Maybe I shouldn't discuss our cargo until I find out if you're good enough to keep it safe," he drawled.

She returned a smile that was more a smirk. She was used to proving herself to other soldiers, particularly men, and bonding over a battlefield was what she understood best about friendship. "Maybe you shouldn't," she replied. "You got any space here for a demonstration? You want to take me on or you want to turn me over to someone else?"

"Oh, I think I can handle you," he said and jerked his head to indicate the back of the yard. They made their way through a welter of carts and drivers to a relatively clear space of trampled grass and dried mud.

The captain was buttoning up his vest and pulling on his gloves. Wen settled her own clothes and slid her sword out of its sheath. She saw him give it a quick sideways appraisal, noting its superb condition. He pulled his own weapon with one fluid motion.

No one had suggested practice blades for this little encounter.

"What's your name?" the captain asked her. "I ought to know that before I slaughter you."

"Willa," she replied. "You?"

"Orson."

As if magically drawn by the promise of bloodshed, two young men drifted over, also wearing dark, serviceable clothes and sashes bearing the insignia of the freighting company. Her fellow guards, Wen presumed.

"Any particular rules?" she asked.

He grinned again. Sweet gods, he reminded her of Justin, with that lazy, cocky smile, that fair coloring, that eagerness to fight.

She would not think of Justin. She would not think of any part of that life she had so completely left behind.

"Well, neither of us will be of much use if we're disabled," he said. "Obviously, no killing blows. First blood, but I won't cut you too bad."

"Deal," she said, and lunged forward.

Her attack caught him off guard, but not for long. He was fast and aggressive, and within seconds he was on the attack and she was falling back. She let him set the pace for a while as she tried to get a sense of his reach and power. Size was in his favor, and he was strong; she felt the force of his blows against her sword all the way up to her shoulders. But he was a little too sure of himself, a little too flashy. She was careful and she

was patient, and when he feinted for her heart she skipped to
the side and raked her point down his sword arm.

He loosed a grunt of surprise and hauled back, staring
down at his arm. She heard the watching men laugh. "Fooled
you, Orson," one of them called. Orson pulled a cloth from his
pocket and swiftly bound it around the wound, tightening it
with his teeth.

Then he met her eyes, respect in his own. "Better than you
look," he said, appraising her the way he had appraised her
sword. "Where'd you learn to fight like that?"

"Fending off bandits in the northern passes of Tilt," she
said. Which was true as far as it went.

"Those must have been some bandits," he said. "You've
got the job if you want it."

She nodded and repeated her original question. "So what's
the cargo?"

"Gold doors," he replied.

"What? Gold doors? Really made of gold?"

He nodded, laughing. "Heaviest damn things you ever saw.
Looks like they're all carved with flowers and wreaths and
whatnot. Worth a fortune, apparently. They were on their way
from Storian when they got sidetracked here."

"A little skirmish on the road," one of the other men said.
"Two of the guards were wounded pretty bad."

"Which is why we need *you*," Orson added.

Wen was still astounded. "But who would want doors
made of gold?"

"Rich folk," the other guard said.

Wen instantly thought of the only rich family in Forten
City that she actually had a nodding acquaintance with. Oh,
now, that would be ironic even by the standards of her own
bitter life—to find herself delivering merchandise to Fortune.
"The serramarra?" she asked faintly.

Orson shook his head. "No—some Thirteenth House noble."

That was a relief, at any rate. Though what were the chances
Jasper Paladar would be standing on his front lawn, overseeing
the safe arrival of household decor, even if he had ordered such
items? "When do we leave?" she asked.

"Tomorrow, early," Orson said. "You have a place to sleep?
There are a few beds in the back of the barn."

She shook her head. "Got a room. I'll be back in the morning."

She was cheerful that night as she ate a solitary meal, paid for a bath, and then spent a couple hours checking all her gear. She always felt better when she had the prospect of action and companionship. Trouble was, she started to feel depressed and edgy if she stayed any one place too long—if she started to get comfortable, if she started to find comrades. *You don't deserve peace and security,* some voice in her head would nag. *You deserve hard work and a lonely path and constant penance.*

So she would move on. She hadn't spent more than a month in any one place since the war had ended. It was hard to imagine a time she would ever be able to come to rest.

ORSON expected it to take them two days to travel to Forten City, and the trip started auspiciously enough. There were six guards and a driver, decent rations, and clear skies, and by mid-afternoon of the first day, Wen was as relaxed and happy as she'd been in weeks. She and Orson were riding at the front of the small caravan, the slow wagon behind them, and they passed the time trading insults and anecdotes. He still reminded her of Justin—if Justin had aged by ten years and gained a somewhat mellow outlook—but that just helped put her at ease with him. He was the kind of man she understood instinctively, uncomplicated and forthright, ready to brawl at a moment's notice, not particularly interested in emotional displays, but thoroughly honest. She knew how hard she could push, she knew what skills he would appreciate, and she knew that, once she'd nicked him on the arm, he'd stopped thinking of her as a woman.

All of this was fine with Wen.

For the midday meal, they pulled the wagon to the side of the road, broke out the dried food, and diced for the honor of riding in the lead for the second half of the day. Wen had always had horrible luck at games of chance; she'd learned early never to bet anything she cared about.

"Willa loses again," crowed one of the other guards, a burly kid named Stef who couldn't have been more than eighteen. "You're riding in the rear."

"Glad to do it as long as *you're* up front," she replied. "Far away from me."

The driver was glancing around nervously. They were on the main road to Forten City, but this swath of Fortunalt was sparsely settled, and they hadn't passed any other traffic for an hour. "I don't like this place," he said. "Feels too lonely."

Orson was on his feet and on his horse in a few economical moves. "And we've wasted enough time already. Let's head on out."

In a few minutes, they were on their way again. Wen and a silent fellow named Carp were riding at the rear. She didn't mind the lack of conversation, since it allowed her to pay more attention to the road. Winter hadn't hit here very hard, she noted, for most of the trees and bushes were already starting to show green this early in the season. Or maybe this was just the right time for spring to make its appearance in the southern lands. She had only wandered down to Fortunalt in the past few weeks after months spent in Helven and Nocklyn. The land was unfamiliar to her, and so were its seasons. But if it was always so mild near the southern Houses, maybe she should consider spending more time here.

It would be as good a reason as any to determine where to go when.

The driver was still uneasy, she noted idly, twisting on his seat every now and then to look behind them as if expecting pursuit. She supposed he was the one who had been holding the reins when this same shipment had been attacked a few days ago, which would explain his jumpiness. *If I had a job driving pricey cargo around the country,* she thought, *I'd make sure I knew how to handle a sword.* But if he was armed, she hadn't noticed—and Wen noticed weaponry almost as a matter of course.

If you didn't know what you were guarding, she thought, the wagon would look pretty ordinary. It was just a weathered wooden cart drawn by two horses. Bits of straw stuck out through the joints; heavy canvas was spread almost flat over the bed of the wagon. But between the straw and the canvas lay the brightly polished gold doors with their intricate whorls and details. Over lunch, they'd pulled back the canvas to admire the top one until the driver got so agitated they covered it up again.

They'd been traveling maybe an hour when she heard the faintest of sounds behind them, and she wouldn't have caught even that much if she and Carp had been exchanging any conversation at all. She pulled hard on the reins and came to a halt, listening intently. Yes—riders coming at a pretty fast clip, and in a party at least as large as their own.

Her fighter's instincts prickled with warning, and she had her sword in her hand without consciously thinking about drawing it. "Orson!" she cried out. "Trouble behind us!"

The driver cursed and hauled the horses to a halt, and the other men whirled around, weapons in hand. A few seconds later, the raiding party galloped into view—seven men, all hunched over their saddles, swords at the ready.

This wasn't going to be like the scuffle at the posting house when she rescued Karryn. This was going to be a fight to the death. No point in holding back. Wen charged forward, low in her own saddle, gaining whatever advantage she could from surprise and momentum. The white gelding was a warrior's horse, fearlessly flinging himself into battle. They crashed into one of the lead bandits and Wen's thrust sent the first man to the ground, shrieking and bloody. His horse reared and snorted, trampling him where he lay.

No time to worry about him. She was already under attack from a second raider, and she swung in the saddle to parry a hard blow. Carp and Stef were finally beside her, laying about with their own swords, and then Orson, who'd had the farthest distance to cover, came pounding up. With the first man down, they were evenly matched, at least in terms of numbers. Wen had no idea how good her fellow guards were, if she could count on them to deal their share of death, or if she would have to be responsible for more than the brigand slicing away at her right now. Best to dispatch him quickly and then see which way the battle was going.

Her assailant was huge, practically twice her size, and clearly expecting to demolish her with a high, hard swing. She half parried, half twisted out of his way, and kept traveling forward, burying her sword in his throat. He choked and burbled and clawed at his neck till his eyes rolled back and his hands fell limply to his sides. She yanked her blade free and spun the gelding around, looking for the next place to strike.

She quickly saw that Orson had cut down his opponent, and Carp was holding his own, but the other guards appeared to be overmatched. "Stef!" Orson shouted at her, pointing, and she kicked her horse forward to aid the boy. With her sword added to his, they quickly routed the bandit. He suffered a hit to the shoulder, one to the knee, another to the head, and loosed a string of oaths. Then he swung his horse's head around and took off at a hard run, droplets of blood spattering the road behind him.

"Should we follow him?" Stef panted beside her.

Wen shook her head. *Protect your charge,* Tayse used to say. *Don't pay attention to any of the rest of the action.* "We help the others," she said.

But the others seemed to have matters more or less under control. Of the six guards and seven bandits who had engaged, Wen counted four still battling. There were six bodies on the ground, but only four of them appeared to be dead, and none of the corpses were defenders.

"Go see if you can help any of our people who are wounded," Wen directed Stef, and launched straight at the remaining fighters.

Just the threat of another blade against them seemed to decide the brigands. One called out to the other, and they both pulled back and turned tail. Orson chased them for twenty yards down the road, but, like Wen, he was more concerned with keeping his cargo safe. He trotted back to the scene of battle and surveyed them all from horseback.

Wen was already kneeling in the dirt and rifling through the pockets of one of the fallen men. "Not much to find here," she called up to him. "Not wearing any House colors, and they look too ragged to be paid mercenaries. Just outlaws, looking to steal our wagon."

He nodded but didn't answer her directly. "Who's wounded and how badly?" he raised his voice to ask.

"Fibbons and Jack are hurt, but Jack's not too bad off," Stef replied. His voice sounded strained. Wen wondered if this was the first time he'd seen true bloodshed. "But Fibbons has passed out."

Orson glanced down at Wen again. "You any good at fixing up folks who got hurt fighting?" he asked. "Since you're so good at fighting?"

She almost smiled. "I'm better with bones than bleeding."

Carp stirred and dropped from his horse. "I know a little about medicine," he said. "I'll see what I can do."

Orson looked over at Stef now. Wen watched him read the boy's face, try to determine how much more he could handle. "Stef, you plant yourself right in front of the wagon," Orson said, his voice matter-of-fact. "You be our lookout in case one of those fellows comes back. Willa, I guess it's up to you and me to drag these bodies out of the road."

She nodded and stood up to tug her gloves back on. She'd pulled them off to make it easier to go through the dead men's pockets. When Orson was dismounted and standing next to her, she said in a low voice, "You really think they might come back?"

He shook his head. "Only three of them left, and at least two of them were hurt pretty badly," he said. "We've got four men who are completely whole—and you and I, at least, can fight. Unless there's a lair of them not too far away, I can't think they'd come back for a third try."

"A third?" she said swiftly. "You think it's the same group that attacked the wagon before?"

"Wouldn't be surprised. Could have been following this shipment all the way from Storian. If you're going to steal something as unwieldy as a gold door, you better have an idea what you're going to do with it. I'm thinking it's a bit too much trouble for your average thief who just wants a quick bounty."

She nodded and bent over to pick up the legs of the first dead man. Orson grabbed the man's arms and they half dragged, half carried the lifeless figure off the road.

"You have a lot of trouble with bandits in these parts?" she asked him when they'd dropped the body.

He shrugged and smacked his hands together as if to rid them of the dead man's taint. "Things have been unsettled ever since the war," he said. "Lot of good men died following Rayson

Fortunalt to Ghosenhall. Lot of men refused to sign up for his war, and some of those folks found themselves stripped of their positions and their properties. Hard times came to Fortunalt and haven't really let up since."

Wen gave him a sharp look. "Are you one of those who wouldn't turn rebel against the king?"

Orson shrugged again. "Been a soldier my whole life, one way or the other. I left Forten City five years ago, when it started to look like war might come. I ended up fighting anyway, but I was in Ariane Rappengrass's army. Came back here a year or so ago, but the work hasn't been too steady. I keep thinking things will turn around for Fortunalt, so I stick." He made a small motion with his hands. "So far, not much improvement."

She turned to collect the next body, and he followed her. "What about you?" he said.

She grunted a little as she lifted the corpse's legs. This was the big man that she'd cut down; it would be a hell of a job to move *him* five inches, let alone five yards. "I told you. I come from Tilt country."

"Well, maybe originally," he said. "But you got training somewhere else when you learned to fight like that."

Like him, she shrugged, certain he wouldn't press too hard. Among people of their kind, it was just expected that there would be episodes in your past you would prefer not to discuss. Justin, for instance, had lived on the streets of Ghosenhall as a common street thief until Tayse found him. "Did some guard work here and there," she said. "I fought in the war, too, but I was on the side of the royals."

"Any sane man would have been," he said, and almost threw the big man's body down when they were off the road. Then he grinned at her again. "Or sane woman."

She crouched over the body and motioned Orson down, as if to show him something interesting on the big man's clothes. When he squatted beside her, she murmured, "I'm not so sure these were random outlaws. I'm wondering about our driver."

Orson's eyes gleamed, but he was too canny to suddenly twist his head around and stare at the wagon. "Why?" was all he said.

"Just a feeling. He seemed so edgy. He didn't like us

lingering over our meal. I think he might have made plans with this particular party to meet us at a certain point on the road."

Orson was silent a moment. "Hard to prove."

"I know. But two raids on the same wagon in three days? Only makes sense if they followed it all the way from Storian— or if the driver was giving information about his route."

"Well, let's get the rest of these fellows onto the grass, and then ask our driver a few friendly questions."

They finished clearing the road within ten minutes, then checked on the status of their hurt companions. Jack was up and walking around, cursing and flexing his sword arm, but Fibbons was still woozy.

"Is there room for him to lie down in the wagon?" Wen asked.

"Don't want to dent the doors," Orson said.

"Well, couldn't he lie *next* to them?"

It took a little effort, but they were able to reposition the cargo and make a narrow lane of space so the hurt man could lie on the straw. Orson stepped back and gave Wen a meaningful look before saying, "I'm starting to wonder how many more times this particular load might be attacked before we get to Forten City."

"Better not happen again," Carp muttered.

Orson turned deliberately to the driver. "What do you think? Hey? We likely to have to fend off thieves another time? Some more of your friends, maybe? I'm wondering just how much you know about all these attacks."

For a moment, the driver stared back at him, white-faced and slack-jawed. Then he grabbed the reins and slapped the horses into motion. The wagon lurched forward hard enough to cause Fibbons to yelp, and within seconds it was careening down the road. Orson swore and ran for his horse, for all of them had dismounted to try to make Fibbons more comfortable. Wen was the first one back in the saddle and racing after the jouncing wagon, but Orson came pounding up after her quickly enough. Orson went flying by Wen to crowd against the team, tangling their traces and forcing them to slow. Wen kept pace alongside the wagon, gauging the distance and the rate of travel. When she judged it safe enough, she swung from the gelding's back and dropped beside the driver on the bench.

He turned on her frantically, dropping the reins to try to pummel her head and shoulders. Just as she'd thought; he wasn't armed. She gave him a hard shove merely to keep his fists away from her face, then brought up her knife hand and pressed a blade to his throat. Orson had the team under control, but they were still moving at an uncomfortably fast pace, and the rocking motion threatened to drive the tip of her knife through the driver's skin.

"Don't make me kill you," she said calmly, and he sagged on the seat. Keeping the knife in one hand, she caught up the reins in the other, and slowly pulled the horses to a halt. Behind her, she was aware of Fibbons moaning and the sound of more hooves coming closer. She glanced over her shoulder to see Stef and Carp galloping alongside, Jack far behind them, leading Fibbons's horse. Her own gelding had shied away from the chaos of the runaway team and nervously paced the side of the road about ten yards back.

Orson was off his own horse and up onto the wagon on the other side of the driver. "You son of a bitch," he said roughly, and began shaking the man as if hoping to snap his head off.

"Stop it," Wen said sharply. "Either let him go or tie him up and dump him in the back so we can take him to Forten City."

Orson shook the man once more and then cuffed him hard across the face before allowing him to collapse, gasping, on the bench. "I'm not letting him go," Orson said angrily. "We could have lost two men back there because of him! I'll take him to the magistrate in Forten City, unless I decide to kill him right here."

Wen wasn't worried. Orson wasn't the type to murder a man in a fit of fury. If the driver had attacked him, well, Orson would have cut him down, but the soldier wouldn't offer any serious harm to an unarmed captive.

"Tie his hands and put him in the back of the wagon," Wen said again. "And then let's keep moving. Anyone here know how to handle a team?"

Wen was actually rather relieved when Stef answered in the affirmative. If they were going to lose another guard to driving duties, she'd rather it be the one who'd showed the least skill in fighting. It took a little more time to truss up the driver, reposition Fibbons, and tie the two extra horses to the back of the wagon, but they were finally on their way again. This time Orson rode alone in the lead, Carp and the injured Jack stayed close behind the wagon, and Wen dropped back about fifty yards to cover their trail.

She should have taken that rear position earlier today. It was something Justin always did on any expedition, riding some distance behind the main party so he could give advance warning of any hostile riders coming from that direction. She would have heard the outlaws heading their way; she could have sounded the warning sooner. Justin would never have been so lax.

Although, she had to admit, Fibbons and Jack probably would have been injured anyway. Neither of them was more than a passable swordsman, and Stef was almost hopeless. She hadn't had much chance to see Carp in action, but the fact that he had emerged unscathed made her think he could handle himself pretty well. But Orson was really good—better than he'd allowed her to see when they were fencing back in the freighting guard. Not as good as Wen, but someone she would trust to battle beside her no matter how fierce the fight.

It felt good to have a comrade in arms, however briefly.

They had traveled another couple of hours before they came to a small village huddled on one side of the road. There was no inn, but the tavernkeeper's wife agreed to let the injured Fibbons stay in their spare room for a few days in return for a little extra gold. The rest of them continued on till nightfall, when they pulled the wagon off into the underbrush and made a hasty camp. Orson even served rations to the driver, who hadn't spoken a word since the afternoon stop. They divided the watches and tried to find the least rocky patches of ground on which to spread out their blankets.

Under the stars, outside in the brisk spring air, in the company of a thief and four near-strangers, Wen slept like a lost child who had finally found her way safely back home.

THEY made Forten City a little before dusk the following day. Wen looked around her with interest. It was a busy and crowded town, one of the major seaports of the south, and within ten minutes she noticed the whole range of humanity striding by—sailors, soldiers, merchants, noblewomen, beggars, and a pickpocket or two. The smells of salt air, wet wood, fish, and horse were particularly strong, though overlaid now at dinnertime with the more appetizing scents of meat and onion.

"I hope our pay covers a real room for the night and enough money to buy a meal," Wen said as she trotted along next to Orson. No need to keep a rear guard here in the city. There was hardly enough room to maneuver the wagon down the narrow roads, let alone defend it with any kind of grace.

He nodded. "Would have covered a room last night, too, but it didn't seem worth explaining our captive," he said, indicating the driver with a jerk of his head. "And for the same reason, I'd like to get rid of him first before we deliver our shipment."

A few questions to passersby elicited the address of the magistrate, and their erstwhile driver was turned over to some rather rough-looking authorities. Wen found herself wondering if serramarra Karryn was involved in handling legal matters in Forten City. It seemed unlikely in the extreme. Perhaps that was one of the duties that Jasper Paladar was administering until Karryn attained her majority.

It was true night by the time they made their way to a large house on the western edge of town, far from the stink and bustle of the wharves. It was hard to be sure in the dark, but the house appeared to be built of glittering black stone, roofed with gleaming copper.

"Now you have to admit a pair of gold doors would be a pretty impressive sight at a place like this," Orson said to Wen, grinning.

"It would—if this was the queen's palace," she retorted. "But for a Thirteenth House lord? So grand it's foolish."

It took longer than she would have expected to unload the cargo, though there was a certain entertainment value in watching the servants struggle to lift the heavy doors and carry them into the house. Stef, in fact, couldn't restrain his laughter the second time one of the footmen stumbled and brought the whole line of bearers to their knees.

"Well, I'm glad those are off our hands and someplace they

can cause trouble for someone besides me," Orson observed. "Come on. Let's look for food and beds."

They found both in a well-appointed tavern situated comfortably close to both the harbor and the main road. Dinner was convivial, as the five of them ordered big meals and several pitchers of beer, and spent the whole meal swapping progressively less believable stories of brawls and battles they had single-handedly won. Stef did little of the talking but most of the drinking, so naturally he was sick before they'd even gotten up from the table. For some reason, that made Wen and Orson laugh even harder. They practically carried him up the stairs to the one big room they'd rented for all of them to share. Wen stripped off her outer garments and fell onto the narrow bed allotted to her, falling asleep within minutes, even happier than she'd been the night before.

But when she woke with the others and Orson suggested they get an early start on the return journey, she felt that awful clutch of panic in her stomach. This was too friendly; this was too familiar. She couldn't make these men her comrades; she couldn't train them to trust her and then fail them at some crucial juncture. She couldn't stay, and she couldn't explain.

She said nothing until she and Orson headed down the stairs together to order breakfast while the others finished shaving. "I won't be riding back with you," she told him.

He gave her a sharp look, but didn't say anything until they'd found seats in the taproom, much changed from the night before. Now the clientele was purposeful and sober, and no one lingered long at a table.

"That's some powerful demon chasing at your heels," Orson said at last. "Do you ever plan to come to rest?"

"I'd guess you knew a demon or two in your lifetime," she replied.

He nodded and forked up a bite of sausage. "I chased most of them back," he said.

"I'm working on it," she said.

He chewed and swallowed. "Well, if you change your mind, there'll always be work at the freighting office for anyone as good as you. I imagine I'll be there awhile if you were ever looking for me." He gave her a keen look. "That is, if you ever go looking for anybody."

"Not lately," she replied.

Stef, Jack, and Carp joined them then and began noisily eating breakfast. Wen excused herself from the table as if she was only going to be gone a moment, but, in fact, she stepped out of the tavern and continued on down the street, leaving Orson to make her good-byes. When she was sure they'd already left the city, she'd retrieve her gelding and ride out. She'd go straight south, following the coastline for a while. Or, if the mood took her, she might try a directly eastern route. It didn't really matter. There was nowhere she particularly wanted to go.

Chapter

5

RATHER TO HER SURPRISE, WEN SPENT THE whole day wandering Forten City. It wasn't much to look at, particularly compared to Ghosenhall, but she liked its incessant energy and its continual surprises. One street would feature a collection of respectable shops, and the next one would be nothing but taverns, brothels, and gaming establishments. More than once, Wen saw a prostitute sashaying down one side of the road while a fashionable matron strolled along the other. The divisions were more distinct in Ghosenhall, where whole districts were wealthy and well-kept, and everybody knew how to avoid the unsavory streets where the dangerous elements of society gathered.

The streets where Justin had grown up.

More than once, Wen had found herself walking through those chancy neighborhoods in Ghosenhall, her hands resting on her weapons as she wondered what it would have been like to try to survive in such surroundings. Her own childhood had been so different, tumbling through a ramshackle farmhouse with six brothers and sisters, an assortment of cousins, dogs, kittens, and the occasional duck or lizard in the mix.

She had been the middle child and easily overlooked because of her small size and her generally agreeable nature. Not until she was convinced that someone else's privilege or her own unwarranted punishment was absolutely unfair would she pitch any kind of fit, but then her temper, at least among her siblings, was legendary. Three brothers had taught her early on that she'd better learn to fight if she wanted to hold on to what was hers; three sisters had convinced her that she didn't want to expend the energy required to dress up in pretty outfits and flirt with scruffy boys. She certainly didn't want to attempt to run a household the way her mother did, or worry over finances like her father.

But she loved the camaraderie of a houseful of siblings, the rough-and-tumble affection, the bickering, the solidarity. After a while it seemed inevitable that all the forces that had shaped her would turn her into a soldier, most at home in the company of other tough, casual, physical individuals who didn't have much distinction between work and play.

And she had found her place in Ghosenhall.

And lost it.

And now she was wandering the crazy-quilt streets of Forten City and wondering what to do with herself next.

She didn't once ask for directions; she didn't even consciously begin hunting for it. But she was not surprised to find herself, early in the afternoon, staring at the compound holding the estate called Fortune. It was probably dead center in the city but cut off from the noise, the traffic, and the odors by a high, twining hedgerow of some hardy, unfamiliar evergreen. Through the snaky weave of branches, which rose higher than her head, she could see a reinforcing line of solid metal. The wrought-iron fence was hidden by the plaited green and offered what was probably the real first line of defense for the House.

Wen pushed her face deeper into the living border. Here at the very trailing edge of spring, the needles were sparse and a little yellow, allowing Wen a chance to peer past them to see a large, rambling home of graceful proportions and weathered gray stone. She grinned to see the lintels and archways constructed of the same glittering black marble used on the other lord's house. But here it looked elegant and perfectly suitable.

Wen sent her gaze around what she could see of the lawns and outbuildings. The grass was starting to preen with color, and the flower beds showed spots of yellow and lavender. A kitchen servant was hurrying up from some back path with buckets in her hands, so dairy cows were probably housed in those buildings that might be barns, and the kitchen was no doubt situated at the rear left of the house. Two soldiers slouched along the walkway that led from the main gate to the wide double doors that fronted the house.

Wen frowned. Only two guards in attendance? Hadn't Jasper Paladar learned anything from the serramarra's mishap?

She turned to the left and strolled along the perimeter, hoping to come across barracks and perhaps a training yard in the rear of the house. But the hedgerow grew thicker and more tangled the farther she progressed, and eventually the iron spikes were replaced by slats of hammered metal. She could no longer catch any glimpses of the yards surrounding Fortune.

Not that Wen cared anyway. The serramarra was no longer her concern, and the decisions of her guardian were of supreme uninterest. Wen would be on her way in the morning and have no cause to wonder about Karryn Fortunalt or Jasper Paladar again.

DAWN brought rain, gentle and steady, and Wen was tempted to stay in Forten City another day just to avoid the misery of traveling in wet weather. But choices like that would turn her soft, and she couldn't afford to be soft. She made sure her saddlebags were tightly buckled, she buttoned her coat all the way to her throat, and she gamely set out into the unpleasant weather, just to prove she would.

She picked a southeasterly direction more or less at random and plodded along without any concerns about speed or efficiency. The rain eased off to a drizzle by noon and had actually stopped when she finally broke for a meal, though the road was heavy with mud. She was far from the only one stubborn enough to travel in bad weather, for she overtook three or four wagons on the way, and pulled aside for a handful of oncoming vehicles. Not too many other solitary riders were out this day, though, at least not that she'd encountered by the time the afternoon sun began tilting over toward evening.

She was on a lonely stretch of road where all the vegetation was low but tangled; even the trees were twisted and scrubby as if too tired to stand up against the constant wind. No doubt storms blew off the ocean fiercely enough at times to keep the trees small and the shrubbery bent close to the ground.

She rounded a curve and almost rode over a small, sobbing form sprawled in the middle of the road.

Cursing, she sawed back on the reins, causing the horse to rear and whinny, but at least the figure on the ground had time to roll out of the way of the thrashing hooves. It took Wen a moment to calm the gelding, but when she was free to look around, the person who had caused all the trouble was standing at the side of the road, watching her.

He was a child, maybe ten years old, terribly thin and ragged looking, with tousled red hair and enormous dark eyes. His filthy clothes appeared to have been hacked off with a knife to suit his frame, and even in this cool weather, he was barefoot. Not even Karryn had looked so desolate or desperate.

Wen slid off her horse and approached him cautiously, not wanting to alarm him. "Hello there," she said in the voice she might have used to one of her younger sisters. "Are you lost? What are you doing out here all alone?"

He tried and failed to swallow a sob. "My sister and I were on our way to Forten City, but she got hurt," he said in a pitiful voice. "I think her leg is broken. I tried to make a camp—" He waved behind him to some vague place off the road. "But I couldn't start a fire and there's no water and I think she's passed out. I thought I could get somebody to help me, but no one will stop—" His tears welled up again, though he tried manfully to suppress them. He wiped a dirty sleeve across his eyes and whispered, "Please, could you help us? Do you know how to set a bone?"

Wen glanced around once more at the empty countryside. If ever a place was a perfect setting for a trap, this was it, and many an unwary traveler had been seduced to his doom by the appeal of a plausible waif. But the boy looked so small and frail, and there was the slim possibility he was telling the truth. "Indeed, I *can* set a bone," Wen said, "and I can make a fire, too. Show me where she is and I'll have everything sorted out in no time."

A smile broke through his grimy, tear-streaked face. "You *will*? Oh, this way, this way!" He scampered off the left edge of the road, through a maze of bushes, toward what looked like a stand of squat trees. Wen followed warily, one hand on her sword.

The boy's sister was lying on the hard ground without even a blanket to protect her from the dirt. She looked like she might be thirteen or fourteen. Her hair, a darker auburn than the boy's, spread out in a tangle all around her face, which was pinched and pale. She lay on her side, one leg curled up under her, one stretched out stiffly, as if it hurt. Wen didn't immediately see any sign of blood, which made the boy's story even more questionable.

She knelt anyway and put a hand to the girl's forehead to check for fever. At that instant, the girl's eyes flicked open, though she didn't move a muscle of her body. She looked straight at Wen and whispered a single word. "Trick."

Wen leapt to her feet, pulling blades with both hands, and whirled around seconds before she caught the crunch of feet in the undergrowth. Three bodies came barreling around the scant cover of the short trees. All men, all armed, only one of them big enough to cause her problems. Wen jumped high, kicked the closest one hard in the groin, and used the momentum of that maneuver to launch herself toward his nearest companion. The first man went down grunting, but he'd be on his feet again soon enough. She had to work fast. Midair, she raked her knife across the second man's throat, deep enough to kill him outright. Landing on her feet, she raised her sword to counter the third man's assault.

He was the biggest of the three, and he looked slow and stupid. Certainly he hadn't been prepared for his victim to turn into his attacker. "Back away," she snarled. "I'd just as soon not cut you down."

But her voice—or the realization she was a woman—was enough to spark his rage, and he bellowed and lumbered forward, swinging his own sword in a ham-handed arc. It was quickly evident that brute force, not skill, had shaped his method of fighting. All Wen had to do was keep out of his way long enough to stay alive, then dart past his flailing weapon to slice him halfway up his torso. Not a deathblow. Gods, if she could keep from killing anyone else! But enough to slow him down, to scare him, to make him lurch backward and stare down at the blooming red on his filthy shirt.

The first man was on his feet and charging toward her, more lethal than his friend, but still not much of a challenge. A few quick parries, two hard thrusts, and he was yelping with pain and cradling his useless right arm against his chest. The man on the ground never stirred.

"I'll kill you all," Wen said in a cold, calm voice, "if that's what you want."

The big man stepped forward, stepped back, looked uncertainly at his companion. But this one—a scar-faced fellow with a mean expression—grasped his sword in his left hand and dove for her again. Fury made him sloppier but more dangerous, and Wen backed up a little to keep out of his way. She heard rustling noises behind her and realized that the girl was scrambling out of her path. *No broken leg after all,* Wen thought, though she had little attention to spare for the young plotters.

The evil-looking man suddenly made a lunge for her. Wen practically rammed her sword against his in a hard parry before driving the tip of her own blade deep into his heart. Surprise loosened his sneering scowl and he made a strange whimpering sound as he collapsed to his knees. Wen wrenched her weapon free and spun around to face the last remaining attacker.

But the big man was staring at her and backing away, waving both hands in front of him as if to head her off. "No, no, no," he said. "Stay away from me." And he turned clumsily and went crashing through the bushes, making as much noise as a troop of men. She could still hear him even after she lost sight of him, and then there was the sound of hoofbeats pounding into the dusk. *They had horses, then,* she thought. *Those will come in handy.*

Best to make sure the ones she thought were taken care of were really dead. She strode between the bodies, but neither one had a pulse. Her mouth tightened as she wiped her hands clean.

Three fights in the past week. Even by her standards, that

was excessive. And this one she hadn't asked for, though she'd been careless. She'd suspected a trap, but she'd still walked right into it.

She spun around to locate the children, half-expecting them to have fled during the melee. But no, there they were, huddled together in the shadow of one of those small trees, looking worried and frightened. The girl, now standing on her obviously uninjured leg, was almost exactly Wen's height and just as dirty as her brother.

Wen strode the few steps over to them and glared, hands on her hips. "Now," she said in a stern voice. "You just tell me about your part in this little drama. Two men dead because of you. Any reason I shouldn't kill you as well?"

They had no way of knowing that was an idle threat, but the boy, at least, looked unimpressed. "It's good that they're dead—both of them!" he blazed, shaking himself free from his sister's arm. "Howard beat us and Ricky was a terrible man! I would have killed him myself, but Ginny wouldn't let me."

The chances of the little scamp killing anyone were absolutely zero, but Wen narrowed her eyes. Had they been accompanying the older men by choice or coercion? "Why were you traveling with them, then?" she asked, keeping her voice stern. "And helping them scam poor travelers? Don't you think they could have killed *me*?"

"They would have," Ginny said calmly. She pushed her auburn hair back out of her face and tried to look mature. It was the way she summoned an expression of dignity that got to Wen. Such an old look on such a young face. "We've seen them kill others. We told them we wouldn't help them, but then they—they—" She fell silent and pressed her lips together.

"They hurt Ginny," the boy said fiercely.

Wen didn't even want to know what all the "hurting" had encompassed. "How'd you end up in their care?" she said, making the last word ironic.

"Howard's our stepbrother," Ginny said. "Our mother died last year." She shrugged, letting Wen fill in what detail she wanted. "For a while, Howard took jobs as a driver or a farm worker, but he couldn't keep them. The last few weeks we've mostly been on the road. Like this."

"This is the worst," the boy said.

"Like Bryce said," Ginny added, "it's good that they're dead."

Wen drew a deep breath. "Yes. I suppose it is. Now the question is: What do we do with the two of you?"

Bryce looked up at her expectantly, his big eyes confident. *Why is he so sure I'll help them?* Wen thought irritably. But Ginny's face maintained its sober adult expression.

"We can take care of ourselves," she said. "Thank you for your assistance but we don't need you anymore."

Bryce gave his sister an indignant look. "Yes, we do! We don't have money, or water, or *food*, and we don't know where to go, and—"

"We'll find our way," Ginny said in a hard voice.

"Well, you don't have to," Wen said briskly. "I'm here, and I'm used to taking over when the situation looks dicey." Ginny opened her mouth as if to argue, and Wen grinned at her. "Don't even think about trying to get rid of me," she advised. "Didn't you see me take on your stepbrother and those men? Can't you tell I'm a fighter?"

"We don't need you," Ginny repeated.

"Don't listen to her," Bryce said. "We really do."

Wen glanced around. Nothing at the campsite except a couple of dead bodies and one threadbare duffel bag, which probably held everything the siblings owned. "I thought I heard that other fellow ride away," she said. "Are there more horses? They'd be useful."

Bryce nodded eagerly. "Two more." His face fell. "We can't ride, though."

"You'll figure it out quick enough," she said unsympathetically. "You go get the horses, bring them here. I'll check these two and see if they're carrying anything that looks interesting. Then we'll travel a little way from here and make camp." It was closing in on night; they'd be doing all this in darkness if they didn't hurry. She glanced around. "'Cause I don't think any of us wants to try to sleep tonight anywhere close to these fellows."

"Rather sleep next to them dead than alive," Bryce muttered.

Ginny hissed at him but he made a face, wholly unrepentant. Wen tried not to grin. "Go get the horses," she repeated.

As soon as they moved off, Ginny lecturing Bryce in a low voice, Wen bent over the bodies. The weapons weren't good enough to keep, but one of the men had a purse full of money. Mostly copper coins, a few silver ones. Whether this was the stepbrother or his associate, the money would still serve as something of an inheritance for the orphans, Wen thought. The other one had a few more coins in his pocket, and a belt with a fine silver buckle, worth pawning somewhere. Wen snaked it off his body and rubbed the leather in the grass to clean off the blood.

The children returned in about ten minutes with the horses. Both looked rather the worse for age and ill-treatment, and one of them kept shying at the halter, trying to bite Bryce. Wen sighed silently. She'd have to let one or both of the children ride her own well-mannered gelding while she forced one of these hardmouthed brutes to accept her commands. Tomorrow looked like an even less pleasant travel day than today.

Although today was at least proving to be more interesting than she'd anticipated. She was actually feeling pretty good, she realized. Pleased with herself for effecting another rescue. For having something worthwhile to do. Pleased at the prospect of having company over dinner. Even such miserable company as these two abandoned children.

"How far do you think we need to travel tonight?" Ginny asked in a polite voice. Whoever their mother had been—and however ill-judged her decision to marry Howard's father—she had tried to instill a sense of manners in her children. Or in her daughter, anyway.

"Not more than half a mile, I'm thinking," Wen replied. "I just want to get away from the smell of blood and the attention of the predators who will be drawn to it." She glanced at the horizon, where a thin line of white was the only evidence of differentiation between land and sky. "Better start moving."

It was a matter of moments for Ginny to retrieve their duffel bag and for Wen to round up her gelding, and then they began a slow procession away from the scene of the attack. Wen didn't even have to think about it. She headed northwest, retracing her morning's route. Back toward Forten City. She had no idea what she was going to do with these souls that had fallen under her protection, but surely they had a better

chance of survival in the city. She would figure out what to do
with them once they arrived.

THEY made camp about twenty minutes later near another
one of those stands of stumpy trees. Bryce gathered wood
for a fire while Wen unsaddled the horses and started looking through the saddlebags. Three waterskins between them,
all full. Excellent. Some packets of rations, though the apples
looked wormy and the bread was green. The dried meat still
looked decent, though. A few pairs of shirts and trousers that
she didn't even bother to repack. Nobody would ever want to
wear those again.

She tossed the saddle blankets to Ginny. "Here. Spread
those out. We'll sleep on top of two and under one, and that'll
keep us warm enough tonight."

Most of the wood was damp and smoked before it would
start, but eventually she had a fire going and food parceled out.
Bryce ate so eagerly she started to wonder if his stepbrother
had starved him to make him play his part in today's charade.
Ginny, though she appeared to be equally hungry, took dain-
tier bites and had to have second helpings urged on her.

"We have plenty of food, and money to buy more when we
get to Forten City," Wen told her. "Eat as much as you like."

The girl looked up at that. "We're going to Forten City?"

Wen took a bite of meat and chewed it carefully before
answering. "Any reason we shouldn't?"

"It's a pretty big place," Bryce said. He sounded apprehen-
sive. "We could get lost."

So they were farm children, used to open spaces and, most
likely, hard work. "Well, you won't get lost while you're with
me," Wen said. "And I'll make sure you're settled somewhere
before I go."

"Go where?" Bryce asked instantly.

Wen took another bite of meat. "Wherever I feel like
going."

"You're not from Fortunalt, are you?" Ginny asked. "Your
accent is funny."

"Tilt. You ever been that far north?"

Ginny shook her head. "Until our mother died, we'd never been more than five miles from the farm."

"So I'm guessing you can milk cows, feed animals, work in the garden, all that," Wen said.

Ginny nodded and Bryce rolled his eyes. "And chop wood and push the plow and catch the pigs if they get out," he added.

"You think we can find work in Forten City?" Ginny asked. She actually looked hopeful for the first time since Wen had encountered them.

"Not looking like that, you can't," Wen said. "But get you a bath and some clean clothes, and I think we could find an establishment to take you in." She waggled her head from side to side, considering. "The trick will be finding a place that's honest, where the proprietor won't take advantage of you—in any way," she added meaningfully.

"Oh, Bryce will make sure of that," Ginny said.

That caused Wen's eyebrows to shoot up to her scalp. "What does that mean?" she asked.

Ginny looked faintly annoyed, as if she wished she hadn't said anything. "Oh—nothing. He's just a very good judge of character."

Wen cut her eyes over toward Bryce, to find him trying to maintain an innocent expression as he munched on an apple. "How good?" she said slowly. "Are you a reader?"

The word hung over the fire for a good long moment before anyone answered. Bryce and Ginny exchanged an extended look, in which he clearly communicated something to her, and reluctantly Ginny nodded. "Yes," she said.

Wen's eyebrows were back up near her hairline. A reader could discern what other people were thinking or feeling, no matter how much they tried to conceal. A reader could sort a man's lies from his true tales or spy a woman's evil heart behind her compassionate face. Cammon, considered the most gifted reader in Gillengaria, could separate the good from the bad with no effort at all.

It seemed this lost boy could also. "You're a mystic," she said slowly.

Ginny looked alarmed—it hadn't been all that long since mystics were persecuted in Gillengaria, particularly here in the south—but Bryce nodded happily. "My mother never believed me when I said I could tell what people were thinking, but Ginny always did," he said.

Ginny put her arm around him protectively. "And he's always right."

Wen thought it over. "So—when you stopped me on the road this afternoon—"

"I knew you would help us," Bryce said with energy. "I waited and waited for the right person to come by. There were lots of people who would have stopped, but none of them would have been able to fight off Howard and the others. I knew you would. I knew you wouldn't hurt *us*, either."

It had been bad enough to fall into a trap, but to find it had been baited specifically for her made Wen feel even more peculiar. And yet, somehow she had the feeling she'd been complimented.

"That's quite a skill," she said slowly. "I'd think somebody might pay you pretty well for that."

"No," Ginny said swiftly, tightening her arm around Bryce's shoulders. "We never mention he's a reader. He'll chop wood and work in the stables—and I'll cook or clean or do whatever needs to be done—but we don't want to tell anyone he's a mystic."

"You might want to reconsider that," Wen said gently. "The world has changed in the last two years. I can think of someone who might want him just *because* he has magic."

"Who?" Ginny asked sharply. "Who would need a mystic?"

The name that had instantly popped into her head was Jasper Paladar. The serramarra's guardian might find it awfully handy to employ someone who could warn him when unscrupulous characters showed up at Fortune's door pretending to be friends. It was hard to know how much power little Bryce possessed, but enough to benefit Karryn Fortunalt? Probably.

"Someone powerful who needs a reliable advisor," Wen said. "We'll think about it while we ride to Forten City."

Ginny nodded tightly, and Wen gentled her voice. "You can trust me, you know," she said. "At least—your brother knows that, and it's true. I won't let any more harm come to you."

"I know," Ginny said. She gave Wen a straight look. "But I don't even know your name."

Wen hesitated just a moment before replying. How blatant would a lie have to be before this young mystic picked up on it? She phrased her answer carefully. "Some people call me Willa," she said. And since that was the truth, Bryce didn't contradict her.

"Then, Willa, let me thank you for what you've done for us so far," Ginny said formally. "And we will trust you to see us safely to Forten City."

Chapter
6

NEITHER CHILD WAS COMFORTABLE SITTING A horse, so the trip back to Forten City took twice as long as it had taken Wen to cover the same distance. She put Ginny on the gelding and placed Bryce before her on one of the outlaw's horses, but even so, their progress was slow. By the time they took a late lunch, they were all weary, and by the time night fell, they were still a half-day's ride from Forten City. They camped out again and made an earlier start the next morning.

They could smell the sea long before they arrived at the city itself, and eventually all the other scents of civilization began to drift their way. It didn't take a reader to tell that Ginny was getting more and more tense the closer they came to their destination, but Bryce squirmed on Wen's lap, trying to catch the first glimpse of the harbor town. Once it was in view, he drew still, staring at it with mesmerized fascination.

They clattered through the gates around noon and Wen instantly started looking for accommodations. Someplace decent enough to offer food and baths, but not grand enough to sneer at her disheveled charges. She found a suitable inn on the outskirts of town, staffed by a harried woman and her incurious husband. Within an hour, the children were washed, combed, dressed, and altogether more respectable. Ginny had even put a ragged ribbon in her auburn hair, still damp from the bath.

Wen sat them down on one of the two beds and poured out the coins she'd lifted from Howard and Ricky. Bryce's eyes widened, but Ginny's narrowed; she knew the value of each denomination and recognized that there wasn't much to crow over. "I got this off your stepbrother and his friend, so you should have it," Wen said. "We can also sell the horses—though not for much—and the gear. We'll get enough to buy you each a new set of clothes and a few decent meals. Then we need to find a place both of you can settle. Where you can do a little work to earn your keep."

"I thought I'd ask the innkeeper's wife," Ginny said in a quiet voice. "She looked like she could use some help."

Wen nodded. "She did, at that. And we can stroll around Forten City, see if anyplace strikes your fancy. Bryce can—" Wen waved her fingers over her head. "See if he senses any spot that seems like a good place for you to land." Meanwhile, she would seek out Jasper Paladar and see if he was more broad-minded about magic than the erstwhile marlord.

"You want us to go to that man who needs a mystic," Bryce said.

It really *was* sort of annoying to have him pick that idea out of her head. She'd have to ask Justin how he managed to shield his thoughts from Cammon.

No. Justin was living in Ghosenhall, and Wen never expected to see him again.

She shoved the thought aside. "I think that's an option," she said evenly. "But it's not the only one. I don't want you or your sister to have to do anything that makes you uncomfortable."

Ginny came to her feet. "Let's walk around the city," she said. "I've never been here. Let's see what it's like."

AT first both children were so overwhelmed by the sights of Forten City that they crowded close to Wen, practically tripping her every time she took a step. Bryce's eyes darted around nervously, and now and then he twitched a little, as if jerking back from a danger that Wen couldn't see. She imagined that all the sounds and emotions of the city were pressing on him hard from all directions. It might be like the sense of assault she'd felt the first time she practiced in an actual training yard, with men all around her yelling and striking each other with a musical clangor.

But she'd gotten used to it quickly enough, and Bryce made a fast recovery, too. Indeed, within an hour he seemed more intrigued than overwhelmed, and his bright curiosity had resurfaced. Ginny remained subdued but determined. She looked around at every new street they crossed as if trying to absorb and understand the mix of opportunities it offered, both for good and for ill.

Somewhat deliberately, Wen led them first through the noisier parts of town, the harbor districts and the commercial streets. Both of them, she could tell, were relieved as they made their way west from the ocean, into neighborhoods that had a little less bustle and a little more grace. By contrast, when they turned onto the wide boulevard where Fortune was situated, the street seemed almost deserted.

Bryce, of course, figured out what she was doing and ran forward to press his face against the living fence. "This is it?" he asked, trying to see through the hedge. "This is the house where you want us to work?"

Ginny followed Bryce more sedately. She bent beside him to try to catch a glimpse of the mansion. "It's very grand," she said in a doubtful voice. "I don't know that anybody here would want us."

"Grand people are the ones who like to hire grand skills," Wen replied. Then she shrugged. "I don't even know if the people who live here would want to hire a reader—and his sister. I just thought I'd show you the place. If you don't want me to make inquiries, I won't. We'll head on back to the main part of town and see what kind of work we can find for you there."

Ginny hesitated, then nodded. They turned their steps back the way they'd come. Ginny just set her shoulders and kept her attention on the street ahead of her, but twice Wen saw Bryce look over his shoulder, gazing back at Fortune.

* * *

THEY took a couple of days to just play. Wen figured neither of the siblings had ever had much time to enjoy themselves and would probably be in service the rest of their lives. Why not give them a treat now? So she took them to a museum to see fancy bits of art and strange collections of weaponry. She found a park where a troupe of actors performed comedic theatre outdoors every night. She paid the captain of a trading vessel a small fee to let the children explore the length of his ship, and then she hired one of his friends to take them sailing. Neither of them had been near the ocean before, and Bryce got sick over the railing. But both of them claimed to love the experience and asked her five times if they might go again.

She sold the horses the first day, pawning the tack separately just in case anyone would recognize the animals and their gear if they showed up together. The money was good enough to cover the cost of a couple dresses for Ginny and two complete sets of clothing for Bryce, as well as shoes for each of them. After two days of good food, hot baths, new clothing, and the absence of fear, they looked like completely different creatures. They looked like the children they must have been back when their mother loved them.

"I talked to the innkeeper's wife today," Ginny said as they prepared to go to bed on that second night. Bryce was already dead asleep.

Wen nodded. "I saw you. Did she offer you a job?"

"Yes. Room and board for me and Bryce, and pay after we've proved ourselves for three months."

"Well, that's fair. Does Bryce like her?"

"I didn't ask Bryce," Ginny said with quiet dignity. "I'm not so bad at judging a person's character myself."

Now Wen grinned. "You *are* a pretty smart girl. Then are you going to take her offer?"

Ginny was silent for a long moment as she sat beside her sleeping brother, watching his face. Wen rested on her own bed across the room, waiting. "I want him to have opportunities," Ginny said at last. "You might be right that the best place for him is a nobleman's house. If he grows up as a tavern boy, he'll be a tavern boy his whole life. If he serves a marlord—well—who knows what he might be?"

"It's not just Bryce we need to think about," Wen pointed out. "You have your life to look forward to."

Ginny shook her head. "I don't care about me. Bryce is the one I worry about."

"You'd better care about yourself. No one else is going to. Figure out what you want and go after it, because it's not going to come looking for you." Wen was surprised to hear the roughness in her own voice.

Ginny just regarded her with those big dark eyes. "Then why haven't *you* gone after what you wanted?" She gestured around the room. "Because surely *this* wasn't it."

Wen closed her eyes and sank back on the bed. To be reduced to explaining herself to a homeless girl! "I did for a while," she said on a sigh. "And it was exceptional. My own fault that it turned sour."

"Well, can't you fix it?" Ginny asked.

Wen turned on her side, facing the wall. Let Ginny lock the door and blow out the candle. "No," she said. "Not ever."

There was silence for a moment, and then the rustling sound of Ginny moving around the room. Wen heard the girl settle on the bed again before she spoke once more. "So—tomorrow? Will you go ask the noble if he's interested in hiring Bryce and me?"

Wen opened her eyes and stared blankly at the darkness. Go beg a favor of Jasper Paladar. Well, he owed her one. "I will. Go to sleep, Ginny. Tomorrow will be here before you know it."

WEN waited in Jasper Paladar's study, feeling a little more nervous than she'd expected. There had only been one soldier at the high, grillwork gate set into the living fence, which she considered inexcusable, and as far as she could tell, no guards were posted near the house itself. If *she'd* been a mercenary, she could have slipped through these halls and corridors within minutes, found Karryn Fortunalt, and abducted her with a minimum of resistance. It seemed some people were slow to learn lessons.

It might have been hard to pick her way through the house, though, for her brief glimpse of it between the front door and this study had shown it to be very imposing. A broad staircase swept up from the central foyer, and halls branched off both sides. The stairwell itself spiraled overhead into a series of stories, each with its own balcony overlooking the front entry hall. The interior of the house was nearly as severe as the gray-and-black exterior, with white marble floors inlaid with black disks, heavy carved chairs and tables in the rooms Wen could see, and dark drapes outlining every window.

She pivoted on one foot. This room wasn't quite as stark, possibly because it was messy. A massive desk was littered with papers, while stacks of books and piles of old letters made precarious columns on the floor behind it. A used wine goblet sat on the desk next to a plate still containing a half-eaten piece of bread and a hard wedge of cheese that looked like it had sat out overnight. *Must not be many mice here,* Wen thought, *or that little feast would be gone by now.*

When she heard footsteps, she straightened her posture and emptied her expression, and she was ready with a little bow when Jasper Paladar stepped in. Stupidly, her first thought was that she'd forgotten how tall he was. She'd remembered the beard, the brown-and-gray hair, the intelligent gray eyes.

"Willa," he said, and she found she'd remembered his deep voice as well. "I had not expected to see you again, but I'm pleased to find you here." He put his head out the door and she heard him ask for refreshments to be sent.

"I'm not hungry," she said at once.

He came back inside, smiled, and shut the door. "Maybe not, but I am, and I can hardly eat without offering you something. Have a seat."

He gestured at the grouping of chairs closest to the window, and sat beside her instead of behind the intimidating desk. His legs were so long she thought he could stretch them out and reach the sill. Her own barely touched the floor. She felt a moment's resentment and quickly checked it.

"So have you been in Forten City all this time since we saw you last?" he asked.

She shook her head. "No. I had no plans to come here, but I took a short-term job guarding a shipment coming this way."

"And you decided to stop by and inquire whether Karryn made it safely back once she'd left your care," he said, nodding as if that was perfectly reasonable.

She couldn't help a grin. "No, I have a question to ask you. But I do hope the serramarra is home and doing well."

"Indeed she is. She'll be sorry she missed you, however, since she's out visiting a friend who lives in the city."

Wen reviewed Karryn's artless conversation. "She has a lot of friends."

"She has a lot of acquaintances," Jasper Paladar corrected. "I don't know how many of them are truly friends."

"I hope you sent a guard with her this time," Wen said before she could stop herself.

He looked amused. "Is that why you came here? To check our fortifications?"

"No," she said—and then, because his neglect really was criminal, "but they're lousy."

"Please. Feel free to give your opinion."

She gestured. "*One* guard at the gate? That wouldn't stop *anyone*! What would happen to you if I decided to run you through? Is there anyone who could stop me? How many soldiers are on the premises? Is there a training yard? Is there a *captain*? Who's responsible for this place?" She shook her head. "Karryn's not safe, but neither are you."

"You've been spying on us, I see," he said in a level voice.

"Not spying," she said shortly. "I walked by, and that's what I saw."

He tilted his head to one side. "The offer is still open," he said. "I will hire you to be my captain and give you free rein to overhaul the guard as you see fit. I'll give you enough money to do it, too."

She pressed her lips together. "I don't want a job like that. But you ought to hire *someone* to do it."

"Why are you here, then, if not to look for work?"

"*I* don't want a position. But I have someone who might. Two someones. They're young, but one of them at least has skills that might come in handy for a serramarra."

His eyebrows rose again. "I've only had about ten minutes' worth of conversation with you over two meetings," he observed, "and you have never once said what I expected you to say. Who are these young unemployed people with special talents?"

That almost made her laugh. "A young mystic boy and his sister. I found them alongside the road in a dire situation," she said. "The boy is a reader. He knew it was safe to ask me for help. I can't tell how strong his ability is—but that's an impressive skill. The queen's consort is a reader, you know."

Jasper Paladar pursed his lips. "Indeed, I do know that. I had the opportunity to meet Cammon a couple of years ago when he decided I was the one who should be installed at Karryn's side."

"Did you not want the job, then?" she asked curiously.

"Let us say, I did not expect the offer," he replied. "I was happy enough on my own estates following my own pursuits. Seeing Karryn through the tangle that is Fortunalt politics— that has been a challenge I would have been perfectly happy to miss."

"You could have refused."

"I get the feeling people do not often refuse the royal consort," Jasper said. He read her look of surprise and smiled. "Oh, no, he offered me no threat. Merely, he presented the situation to me in such a way that I could not turn him down. *I* could not—so precisely had he judged my convictions and my honor. Some other man might have told him no and felt not the slightest guilt."

"He's a good man," Wen said in a subdued voice. "And Amalie a good queen." Though both of them were too young to be ruling the country. So much better, for so many reasons, if Baryn still wore the crown.

"Yet they have inherited a mess in Gillengaria! They do their best, better than I would have expected, but—" Jasper shrugged, then he smiled again. "But that is not what you came here to discuss with me. A mystic boy. You want me to hire him to—what? Be my advisor? Sit in on my discussions with the serlords and merchants and disgruntled landowners? The idea is quaint, my dear Willa, but impractical, don't you think?"

She held on to her temper. "I hadn't really thought about how he might aid you, my lord. Just that he might be useful." She gave him a sharp look. "Or are you one of those who despises magic?"

"I wouldn't stone a mystic in the streets, if that's what you're asking."

"Well, these days, no one would, since the act has been made a criminal offense," she replied.

"And I never condoned such actions in the past. But I've never had any dealings with mystics. Frankly, I'm not sure what good it would do me to employ such a boy."

She leaned forward. "He's a weapon. You never know how you'll employ a weapon until the situation arises."

He settled back in his chair and gave her a long look. "Well, now," he said at last. "What an interesting thing to say. A soldier's perspective, I must suppose. I have done my share of research, but I always had an end point in mind. I was trying to discover a fact, or understand a culture, or prove a theory. When I came across something that did not materially affect my investigation, no matter how unexpected it might be, I put it aside. I did not want the distraction. Sometimes I went back to it, if it was unusual enough, but then it merited its own review. I did not keep it on hand just because I thought it might be valuable someday."

Wen preserved her silence, but privately she thought that was an unforgivably shortsighted way to function. Who *didn't* pick up the odd bit of leather, the random stone, the sharp scrap of metal that might one day be turned to good use? Who *didn't* always think about how something or someone might prove helpful or might turn dangerous? How could anyone survive with such narrow focus?

"So. This boy. What can he do, besides read emotions?"

"The usual chores that you might have in a kitchen or stable," she said.

"And his sister? Her skills? How old are they, by the way?"

"I haven't actually asked them, but Bryce looks to be about ten and Ginny three or four years older. She can cook and clean and garden. They're both farm children. They're used to farm chores. But they'll both work hard at any task you put before them."

"And they're important to you why, exactly?"

She took a deep breath. "Because I found them and they trust me. And because they don't have anybody else."

"And did you approach me because you truly thought I could use this boy's services, or because you thought I owed you a little charity?"

Now she was angry, and she came swiftly to her feet. "You owe me a favor, but hiring these two wouldn't be charity," she said coldly. "They've already had an offer, and anyone who hires them will have a good bargain. I thought to match a skill with a need, but I didn't expect to be mocked for it. I'll find them other positions. Thanks for your time."

During this speech, he had come rather more leisurely to his feet. "Please don't go," he said, as she turned for the door. "I'm willing to take in your charges on one condition."

She'd taken two strides toward the exit, and she wanted to keep going. But even more she wanted to find a secure place for Bryce and Ginny. So she halted and swung around to face him, making no effort to hide her scowl. "What condition?"

"You come to work at Fortune as well."

Her expression darkened. "I told you I don't need a job."

"Maybe not, but obviously I have a job that needs you," he said. "My guard is a shambles and I fired the captain as soon as I brought Karryn back. I've been making inquiries into bringing more soldiers into the House, but I haven't a clue how to choose them or train them. You're right—Karryn's in as much danger today as she was two weeks ago, and *I* clearly don't know how to protect her. You do. Take the post, hire who you like, make the House safe. I'll take in your orphans. I think it's a good deal."

Her mind was in such a whirl she was almost trembling. She hadn't stayed in one place more than a few weeks since she'd left Ghosenhall, and the very thought filled her with both longing and dread. Even if she accepted his offer, would she be able to honor it? Would her restlessness drive her out into the night before she'd fulfilled her contract?

"How long?" she asked stiffly.

"How long would it take to get my House guard in shape?"

"Six months at least."

"Then will you stay a year?"

"No!" The word jerked out of her.

He tilted his head again. "How long would you stay?"

She took a shallow breath. Her chest hurt too badly to

allow a deep one. She could not possibly put herself in a position where people were counting on her to keep them alive. "I'm not— It's best not to rely on me," she said, almost panting the words.

He had to see her agitation, but he seemed intrigued, not alarmed. "And would your young reader agree with that assessment?" he asked. "Or would he urge me to hire you at any price?"

She glared at him and did not answer.

At that moment, there was a quiet knock on the door and a servant entered bearing a tray. "Ah. Our refreshments. Thank you very much," Jasper Paladar said.

The interruption left her confused, with emotions still at a high pitch, but some of her panic lessened as the servant arranged the tray and Jasper Paladar motioned her back to her seat. Once the footman exited, Wen perched back on the edge of her chair.

"You don't know me," she began.

"I don't," he said, handing her a fragile plate filled with a large slice of buttery cake. The dainty china looked perfectly reasonable in his elegant long-fingered hands, and perfectly ridiculous in her hardened stubby ones. "But I, too, am trying to match a skill with a need. You did not go to all the trouble of saving Karryn just to see her endangered again. I do not know how to protect her. You do. You are obviously uncomfortable at the thought of committing yourself to any long-term enterprise, and clearly not about to tell me why. So I ask again, how long would you stay? Take a bite and think about it."

Not sure she'd be able to choke down a mouthful, she obeyed. Oh, now, that *was* a most excellent taste—rich and sweet, flavored with some spice that didn't seem to have made its way to Ghosenhall. She had a second bite. "I don't want to make a promise I can't keep," she said at last.

He seemed unconcerned. "I'm sure you wouldn't. How long? Three months?"

"No."

"One month?"

"Maybe," she said reluctantly.

He considered her. "Would you agree to a month and then, at the end of that time, consider extending your contract? If the work was not done? Would that make you feel less like you were choking, to leave the terms so open-ended?"

How could he know what it felt like? She would have stared openmouthed, except she was chewing another forkful of cake. "I don't know," she said at last.

"But the month you will agree to?"

It was a long time before she answered. "The month I will agree to." She gave him a sharp look. "But you have to keep Bryce and Ginny even after I go."

He was smiling broadly. "Of course. They are only hostages to your acceptance, not your continued employment." He laid aside his plate and held out his hand. "Welcome to Fortune."

Chapter
7

SENNETH DIDN'T BOTHER KNOCKING ON THE door of Cammon's study before she strolled into the room. He had requested her attendance, and of course he knew she was on the way—he knew the exact location of his closest friends at every moment of the day, so it was impossible to come upon him by surprise. That had led some of them to rather uncivil behavior, she feared. She and Kirra, at least, would just walk in on him without ceremony, and Justin would storm into the room as if planning to throw Cammon out the window. Donnal would enter silently, sometimes shaped as the smallest of insects, and wait for Cammon to address him first. Of all of them, in fact, only Tayse showed Cammon any deference, knocking on doors and waiting to be acknowledged. But a lifetime of serving royalty had made it impossible for Tayse to be rude to anyone near the throne.

Cammon had his back to her when she entered, and he was staring out the floor-to-ceiling window that was one of the many charms of this small study. It had been Baryn's favorite room, when he was alive, and its rich colors and plush decor still reflected the old king's taste. Amalie had been too comfortable in her own pink-and-gilt study to relocate once she inherited the crown, so Cammon had taken this room as his own. Not that you could find him there very often. He was a wanderer, just as likely to be on the streets of Ghosenhall or down at the training yard watching the Riders work out as he was to be inside the walls of the palace itself.

"You wanted to see me, liege?" Senneth asked, trying to make her voice obsequious.

The question made him turn around, a scowl on his face. "Don't call me that."

She was wearing trousers, of course, so she couldn't manufacture a curtsey, but she gave him a very deep bow, just to annoy him. "But you're my king."

"I am not! I'm the royal consort."

She stayed in a subservient posture. "The common people all call you King Cammon. It's very mellifluous."

"Well, the marlords and the serlords have too much respect for titles to do anything so foolish. I *order* you to stop calling me that."

At that she couldn't restrain her laughter anymore, and she straightened up and lounged against the door. "You're quick enough to claim the privileges of royalty when you want something! You *order* me!"

He gave her his familiar boyish grin. Two years of being royal consort to Queen Amalie had changed Cammon in indefinable ways, but unless he worked very, very hard at it, he still looked like a vagabond two days off a tramp ship in some backwater harbor town. Unless his valet had styled it just ten minutes previously, his nondescript brown hair still made a rather shaggy halo around his head, and his clothes tended to magically wrinkle within an hour of being donned. His eyes had an old and hard-won wisdom to them—but they always had, Senneth reflected. Cammon had probably been born knowing things none of the rest of them would ever learn.

"Yes, I order you to treat me casually. Now sit down and tell me anything interesting that's happened."

She draped herself across one of the chairs set against the wall and he collapsed in another one nearby. "You *know* everything interesting that's happened," she said. "You know it before I do. There's no point in having a conversation with you."

He gave her a reproving look. "I know what's happening with all of *you*," he said. "But I can't keep track of *everybody*."

"Well, let's see. I heard from my brother Kiernan, and all's well in Brassenthwaite. My brother Will wrote from Danalustrous—I assume you know he and Casserah are expecting a baby?"

He nodded. "Kirra told me. Well—" He shrugged and then he laughed.

"Well, Kirra was excited to learn she'd be an aunt, and you could feel that even though she's two hundred miles away, and so you knew it," Senneth filled in. "See? I don't have to tell you anything."

He tried to assume an inquiring look. "Are the Riders back? Kelti and the others?"

"You know they are! You met with them yesterday!"

"Amalie met with them. I didn't see them. What was their news?"

Senneth eyed him, leaned back in her chair, and didn't answer.

He failed to keep a smile from his face. "All right, I wanted to talk to you because of the information the Riders brought back from the southern Houses."

She sat up a little straighter. "At last. My king is honest with me."

"I'm *not* the king!"

She waved a hand, grinning. "You're too easy. What about their report intrigued you?"

"Did you talk to them?"

"Tayse did. He said they reported all was mostly well from Gisseltess to Fortunalt, except that there still seemed to be a high number of outlaws. Travelers complain that it's not safe to journey in small parties on minor roads. His guess was that a lot of these bandits are soldiers from the war who've fallen on hard times."

"That was Amalie's opinion, too."

She tilted her head to one side. "And so? What? You want to expand the amnesty programs?"

Cammon frowned and tapped his fingers against his thigh. "I wonder if there's more to it than that," he said. "More reasons for unrest in the southern Houses."

Now he really had her attention. "You think there's instability? Like there was two years ago? Mutiny?"

His face creased; he appeared to be having trouble articulating vague impressions. "I'm not sure. I don't have a sense that anyone is plotting against the throne, but—I keep thinking it would be worthwhile to make a visit. Get a closer look."

"I thought that's what you just sent the Riders to do."

"I wouldn't want to just send Riders this time."

She opened her eyes wide. "You think *you* should go?"

He nodded. "I'm the one most likely to pick up accurate impressions of what is really going on."

Neither Cammon nor Amalie had strayed far from Ghosenhall since the war ended—not that they didn't want to. Their advisors were united in thinking it was a bad idea for the queen or her husband to travel too far outside of the well-defended, walled compound that housed the palace and a few hundred acres of property. But Amalie had refused to let herself be so confined. She made a point of walking the streets of the royal city at least once a week, and subjects from throughout Gillengaria crowded along her known routes to curtsey to her and throw flowers. Ever since she had taken the throne, she had threatened to travel the circuit of all of the Twelve Houses, just to prove she was not afraid to do so. So far Senneth and Tayse and Amalie's uncle Romar had convinced her that it was wiser to stay at home where her Riders knew every alley and hazard.

Senneth hadn't expected their pleas to hold Amalie in place forever. In fact, she was surprised they had worked this long. Amalie, though the most agreeable and easygoing of monarchs, was unbelievably stubborn when she believed she was right. And she was determined to be the people's queen, accessible to all her subjects.

But with the realm still so unsettled . . .

"It's a risk," Senneth said. "Especially if there are really outlaws crowding all the thoroughfares of Gillengaria."

"I'll take a few guards with me," Cammon said.

"A *few!*" she exclaimed, before realizing he was joking.

"You and Tayse. The two of you alone could keep me safe. Queen's mystic and Queen's Rider."

Senneth pressed her lips together. "I'm not the mystic I once was," she said quietly.

He held his hand out and she slowly gave him hers. Her skin was still warmer to the touch than his—than anyone's—but it burned at nothing like the fever pitch that used to scorch others when her magic was at its hottest.

"I haven't seen you call flame for a couple months now," he said. "Are you getting stronger?"

She pulled her hand away. "A little."

"Show me."

She clenched her fingers a moment to feel the heat build in her veins, then splayed them fast. Fire danced from every fingertip and encased her arm like a writhing red glove. She touched her hand to a pile of papers on his desk, and they went up in flames. She leaned toward the window and set the curtains on fire. The temperature in the room rose appreciably, and the smell of smoke was very strong.

"These days I can't set anything on fire unless I put my hand to it," she said. "I used to be able to fling fire halfway across a city."

"Can you still put out any fire in the vicinity just by willing it?" he asked.

"Oh, yes," she said, and curled her fingers again. Every blaze in the room went out. The curtains, the papers on the desk, showed no sign of charring. "But that's not quite as satisfying as causing an inferno to begin with."

"I'm wondering," he said, "just how much additional power you might be able to summon if you were in a desperate battle."

She gave him a somewhat sour look. "I've wondered the same thing, but since I've no wish to be in a desperate battle, I hope I don't find out."

"At any rate, you have plenty of magic for what I need," he said. "Which is to accompany me on a tour of the southern Houses."

"And you want to do—what? Visit Gisseltess, Rappengrass, and Fortunalt? Go looking for malcontents? What are you going to tell the marlords and marladies as you start poking through their properties?"

"I'll say I'm trying to determine how safe it would be for the queen to make such a tour later in the year."

"Cammon!" Now she practically jumped out of the chair. "You don't mean that, do you?"

He gave her a limpid look. "Of course I do. You know Amalie wants to travel throughout Gillengaria. She won't wait much longer. But I'd like to know that the roads—and Houses—are secure before she sets out."

She took a deep breath. Tayse wasn't going to like this. Although Tayse was always practical. If the queen insisted on touring the southern Houses, Tayse, too, would want to make sure the countryside was swept clean of brigands and rebels. "Well. Naturally Tayse and I will come. Do you want to wait till Justin comes back from the Lirrens? You know he won't want to be left out."

Cammon gestured. "I'll let him know he should meet us at Gissel Plain."

"I don't know how many Riders Tayse will want you to have—and then a whole complement of royal soldiers in addition—well, we'll just let him decide the numbers," Senneth said. "Isn't there some law about how many Riders have to always remain with the king or queen?"

"That's what Amalie says," he answered. "There must always be forty Riders available to guard the monarch. So I guess I could take nine with me."

Forty-nine Riders, Senneth thought. There should have been fifty, but eight had died in the war and four had left the royal service once the fighting ended. Not unexpectedly, there had been a host of candidates who presented themselves in Ghosenhall, auditioning for this most prestigious post, but Amalie had only slowly rebuilt her elite guard. It was a tight, almost mystical bond, the connection between ruler and Rider. Riders were unswervingly loyal, more dedicated to their king—or queen—than to their own lives; in return the monarchs trusted their Riders absolutely. It was not a casual thing to accept an individual into such intense service. It was a compact that had never been betrayed, and as far as Senneth knew, a Rider never left his ruler's service unless he or his sworn liege was dead.

There had been plenty of promising young soldiers eager

to fill that fiftieth slot, but Amalie had stopped auditioning
new candidates. "I have a full complement of Riders," she
said if anyone asked. Everyone knew that there was one missing. Everyone knew that Amalie would not replace her.

"Well—nine Riders—surely you'll be safe *then*," Senneth
said. "How quickly do you want to leave?"

"How quickly do you think Tayse can put together a
detail?"

She grinned. "Within the hour, liege, if you're in a hurry."

He laughed. "I think we can take a day or two to organize
ourselves. At any rate, I can't leave for two weeks, because
there is that dinner Romar wants me to attend."

She came to her feet. "Then that gives Tayse plenty of time
to prepare. I'll tell him to plan his route and pick his men."

"And women," Cammon said.

She gave him an inquiring look.

"I think Janni should come with us," he said.

"Certainly. Any particular reason?"

He considered. "I think she'd enjoy the trip."

So there was a reason but he didn't want to tell her. For
someone who made it impossible for others to conceal their
thoughts, Cammon could be maddeningly uncommunicative
at times. But there was no hardship in including Janni on any
long excursion. The young Rider was cheerful, skilled, and
able to hold her own with anyone, verbally and physically—
even Justin. "Anyone else you'd like us to invite for crucial but
unnamed reasons?" she asked sweetly.

He just gave her that boyish smile again. "I don't
think so."

"All right. We'll be ready to leave whenever you want us."

Chapter
8

WEN STOOD OUTSIDE THE TRAINING YARD AT
Fortune and watched her new recruits with a critical
eye.

They were not, so far, much to look at. Well, neither was
the yard. She had insisted on having a couple acres of the perfectly well-tended lawn ripped up, fenced off, and turned into
a practice field where the men under her command could hone
their skills. Now the field was churned and muddy, just as a
training yard should be—more so today because of the rain
the night before.

The men gamely battling it out were already covered to
their knees in wet dirt, and more than one had slipped on
the slick surface and gone crashing down. Good. Plenty of
skirmishes were fought on unfriendly terrain. They had to be
prepared for bad weather and unforgiving ground.

Though at the moment, they didn't look prepared for anything. It had taken Wen a week to assemble this lot, presum-
ably the best Forten City had to offer. She had rather enjoyed
the recruiting process, for she had what amounted to unlim-
ited funds and a prestigious position to offer; the men she had

approached in taverns and along the docks had listened with
interest as she outlined her proposal. *I want twenty-four of the
best fighters in Fortunalt to come work for the serramarra
Karryn. You have to be prepared to work harder than you
ever have before, and you must swear absolute loyalty to the
House. But you'll be amply compensated, and you'll have
pride in your work. . . .*

She'd dismissed the sorry remnants of the guard who had
been at the House when she arrived. Although she had invited
them all to audition for the new force, none of them had—
but more than a hundred strangers had taken up the offer. A
handful of them were women, which pleased her because Wen
had specifically sought to add a female element to the guard.
She knew from her own experience that a woman's physical strength could rarely match a man's, but many times an
encounter depended on agility, guile, and speed, in addition
to training, and the women among the Riders had always been
exceptional on those counts. Besides, she thought it would be
good for Karryn to see women among her soldiers. It would
remind the serramarra that just because she was female, she
shouldn't consider herself helpless.

It had been easy to winnow out the applicants who were
completely unqualified. And it was not particularly hard to
pick out the ones she had no interest in hiring—the arrogant,
the untrainable, the evil-tempered. The real trick was finding
the raw material that she could mold into a fighting force: the
young woman who'd never held a sword but had an uncanny
aptitude, the brawny brute who had never learned to temper his strength with finesse. Most of the time she was just
guessing.

On a whim, she'd invited Bryce to attend the final auditions to see if he had any observations to offer. He seemed
gratified by her trust and planted himself on the top rail of the
raw wood fence encircling the yard, and he sat there all morning with his face screwed up in concentration. When she had
the fighters take a break around noon, Wen hopped onto the
railing next to him and mussed his red hair.

"Well? Any thoughts?"

He looked apologetic. "I can't tell who's any good," he said.

"I thought I'd just be able to *know* who ought to be a fighter, but it's all too fuzzy. There's too much spinning around."

Wen was a little disappointed, but she grinned at him. "That's all right. I can tell who the fighters are. I just thought you might know—" She shrugged. "Something about them that's important," she ended lamely.

"Well, I know who I don't like," he said.

That was more like it. "Who? And don't point. We don't want anyone to know we're talking about them."

"That big man. Who doesn't have any hair. He's mean."

Wen glanced casually at the large bald fighter who, even at the meal break, was practicing his two-handed swings. He was one of the better combatants on the field, certainly one of the more experienced, and she'd mentally put him on the list of finalists. "Everybody seems mean when they're fighting," she said.

"*You* don't. And he's just—he reminds me of Howard."

She knew it was a common thing for a private guard to include a few bullies and outright sadists—the soldier's life attracted folks who reveled in violence. But the best soldiers had no taste for cruelty. They could be ruthless; it went without saying that they were willing to kill. But they never killed lightly, or enjoyed it, or found excuses to inflict pain. Tayse had always been her idea of the perfect soldier, extraordinarily skilled, absolutely fearless, yet deeply thoughtful. Tayse would not tolerate a vicious man in his barracks.

Neither would Wen. She nodded at Bryce. "Thanks for telling me. We don't want men like Howard in our guard."

He gave her a shy smile. "Maybe I'm wrong."

She shrugged. "And maybe not. Anybody else you don't like?"

"No, not really. Oh, but I'll tell you who I *do* like. That mystic woman."

She gave him a sharp look. "What? Who's a mystic?"

"The woman over by the fence, cleaning off her shoe."

Wen let her eyes travel around the yard until they came to rest on the woman Bryce had indicated. *Huh.* She was a few years older than Wen, a few inches taller, and a few pounds heavier. She'd acquitted herself well enough, but Wen had considered her a little too slow to ever make a top-flight soldier. But if she was a mystic . . .

"What's her power?"

"I can't tell. Does it matter?"

"I guess not." Wen watched her awhile longer. The woman carefully checked her sword and carefully sheathed it before joining the others at the lunch cart. Thoughtful. Cautious. Both good traits in a guard. "Anybody else? What do you think of that boy over there? Looks like he's not much older than Ginny."

"I think he's smart," Bryce said.

"And that man? The one with the red vest?"

She led him through the fifteen or so she'd picked out as her best prospects and found that—with the notable exceptions of the bald man and the mystic woman—their impressions mostly tallied. She couldn't decide if she should be more pleased with Bryce or with herself for their ability to read other people.

After the lunch break, she slipped back into the yard, paired up combatants again, and chose the big man as her own opponent. She hadn't gotten this close to him before, and now she focused on trying to determine personality through fighting style. He was reckless, and he wasn't intimidated by the fact that, if she hired him, she'd be his captain. In fact, the sneer on his face as he bored in for a mock kill made her think he probably had no high opinion of female soldiers and probably wouldn't take orders from her all that well. It was a problem she expected to have with most of the men, at least at first. Once she'd defeated them all a few times on the practice field, she'd have earned their respect.

She knew that because that was how she'd been forcing male soldiers to respect her for pretty much her entire career.

This fellow was pigheaded, though; she could read it in his face. As she led him through gradually more brutal exercises, breaking through his defenses every time, his sneer grew more pronounced. He couldn't believe she would continue to outfight him; he was determined to smash her down. His swings became wilder and his intention more obvious. The second time Wen stepped hastily away to avoid having her skull split in two, he gave her a wolfish grin.

"Afraid?" he said, his tone taunting. "Thought a professional like you could beat back any of us."

"Careful," she warned. "You're pushing it to the point where one of us is really going to get hurt. I'd just as soon not have my shoulder broken the first week I try to get my guard in shape." What she really meant was, *I'd just as soon not have to open up your guts right here in front of everybody,* but she was trying to phrase it politely.

"Hazard of the career," he said, and swung mightily.

She didn't even try to parry. She ducked back, waited for the momentum to carry him too far, and then darted in to carve the right side of his rib cage open. He howled in fury and staggered sideways, clapping a hand to his bloody side. "You bitch!" he cried. He took a few stumbling steps toward her, but she wasn't worried. A man like him couldn't fight with a wound like that. Tayse could have—Tayse could have cut her down if his right arm had been sawed off, and Justin wouldn't have even bothered slowing down for such an injury. But this man was made of weaker material.

"I thought I made it clear that no one was going to try to kill anyone," she told him calmly, as he gasped to a halt before her. Everyone else had stopped fighting to watch the encounter. "Looked to me like you were trying to land a real blow."

"You crippled me!" he cried.

Wen motioned over the footman who had been assigned to her, to carry messages, run errands, and look after her money. "You'll be paid for your time and inconvenience," she said coolly. "But I think it's time you were gone."

He blustered, cursed, and threw down his borrowed sword before stomping out of the yard. His performance put everyone else a little on edge, but Wen allowed no trace of her own temper to show on her face. "Back to partners," she called out, and the fighting began again.

Before long, she picked her way through the grunting bodies and singled out the mystic woman. "Take a few rounds with me," she said, and the woman's opponent peeled away. "What's your name?" she asked as they fell into position.

"Moss," the woman replied.

It was a strange name and she was a strange woman. Her hair and her skin were pale, but her features were not particularly delicate. She had round cheeks and a squat nose and a full mouth hardly defined at all by her wispy shoulder-length hair and practically invisible eyebrows. There was a look of stolidity to her, as if she clumped around in heavy work boots and heaved newborn calves out of stalls.

"Take a swing," Wen invited, and they were engaged.

Moss was strong, but a little slow. Wen could have killed her three times over. Yet the woman kept hacking away, apparently not tired at all from a half day's hard exercise. Endurance was as good as skill much of the time, and Wen could probably improve Moss's ability enough to make her a decent fighter. Never a great one, though. She just didn't have the speed.

Wen signaled that the bout was over, and Moss immediately desisted. "You've done a little fighting," Wen guessed.

Moss nodded. "Not anything fancy. Just protecting myself and my people." When Wen raised her eyebrows at that, Moss continued willingly enough, "Used to run caravans across Gillengaria. Had to fend off bandits from time to time."

"Ever lose a cargo?"

Moss shook her head. "No."

"I have a delicate question," Wen said, and wasn't surprised to see Moss's face shutter up. Wen glanced over her shoulder; no one was near enough to hear. "And you don't have to answer. But someone just whispered in my ear that you might be a mystic."

Moss's face grew even harder. "Mystics aren't too welcome in Fortunalt."

"They say the queen's a mystic and so is her consort," Wen said. "A lot safer to possess magic these days than it was before the war."

Moss's pale green eyes narrowed. "Are you saying you wouldn't mind?"

Wen shrugged. "I'd like it. I got used to working with mystics, a few posts back."

Moss hesitated a moment, then nodded abruptly. "I am. I don't talk about it much. It's never been a safe topic."

"What can you do?"

"Lift things. Move them." She jerked her head toward a

pile of unused gear at the edge of the yard. "Could shift all those swords to the other side of the fence."

This was a new one on Wen, who had mostly been familiar with shape-changers and readers and fire mystics, but she could instantly see such a power had possibilities. "You don't have to demonstrate now, in front of everyone, but I'd like to see that sometime," Wen said.

For the first time, Moss offered a tentative smile. "I don't mind saying it's a skill that's come in handy more than once. Though learning to master it when I was a little girl—" She shook her head. "I was in for more than one beating."

Wen instantly made up her mind. "Would you take a job with the House guard, if I offered?"

Moss's face closed up again. "I'm not as good as most of the others. I saw that."

"You're not," Wen said honestly. "But sometimes things matter more than raw talent. I can make you good enough—and you can bring me something extra. But you'd have to be loyal. You'd have to cut your other ties and make this House and this serramarra your foremost consideration. I'd hope you'd make it a lifetime service, but at the very least, you'd have to commit to one year."

Inside her, a voice was screaming with laughter. Demanding a year of service from others when she herself could barely promise a month! Preaching loyalty, when she had spectacularly broken her own oath! The gods, as she had always suspected, had a malicious sense of humor.

But Moss was nodding, her movements jerky but her pale eyes alight. "I will," she said. "I'll practice every day. I'll fight hard. You'll see. You'll be glad you trusted me."

Wen already was.

Chapter
9

THE VERY FIRST DAY SHE'D BEGUN RECRUIT-
ing, Jasper Paladar had invited Wen back to his
untidy office to discuss what she'd found. She quickly
learned that he expected her to come by every evening and
make a report. She was surprised but, in general, approving.
If she reported daily, she would tell him small details she
might otherwise forget to mention. Those details might mean
something to him that they did not mean to her.

The evening after she hired Moss, it was clear Lord Jasper had had his fill of formality. When she stood in his office
and began recounting the events of the day, he gestured at the
chair across from his desk. "Oh, by the Pale Lady's silver eye,
take a seat," he said impatiently. "I can't be staring up at you
for half an hour, wearing a solemn expression. It's not in my
nature."

She perched on the very edge of the chair, keeping her
back straight. Tayse used to sit in the presence of King Baryn,
she knew, and she imagined Justin was very casual with Cammon, for they had been great friends before Cammon married
the queen. But it didn't seem quite right to her. She'd managed

to be relaxed around Amalie when the girl was a princess, but she'd always been stiff and formal when Baryn was in the room.

Of course, Jasper Paladar was hardly a king.

To overcome her awkwardness, she plunged right in. "I think I've narrowed it down to the fighters I want," she said. "I offered five of them contracts on the spot today, and they all accepted. I think I'll have nineteen or twenty after the next couple of rounds, but the rest don't seem good enough to even try to improve."

"And is twenty not enough?"

"To start with," she said. "I'll keep looking."

"So who did you hire today?"

"Three men who've obviously seen service, probably in the war. My age or a little older, and they look like they'll be steady and dependable. A boy who's not much older than Karryn and who'll need some seasoning, but, sweet gods, he'll be good. And a woman."

Jasper looked only mildly surprised, but he nodded encouragingly.

"She's a mystic," Wen continued. "She's able to lift things without touching them. I had her give me a demonstration after everyone else had cleared out. She could pick up a rock that weighed almost as much as I do and hold it in the air at the height of my head for five full minutes."

Now a smile played around Jasper's mouth. "Has this been your plan all along?" he asked. "To infiltrate my house with every brand of magic? What's next—a fire-breather like that woman who advises the crown?"

"Senneth doesn't *breathe* fire," Wen shot back, annoyed. "And I haven't *planned* anything. It's just that I realized she had a special skill, and I thought we might be able to turn it to good use."

"Make her into a weapon," he said, nodding. His voice was grave but she could tell he was still laughing.

That made her sit back in her chair, cross her arms, and regard him with a certain smolder. "If you knew the first thing about fighting," she said, "you would realize that sometimes the weapon is as important as the soldier."

He held his palms out in a gesture of surrender. "I defer

to your expertise," he said. "I would not have employed you otherwise. So when do you expect to make the rest of your hires?"

"Tomorrow or the day after. There are one or two I am still not sure of. And I would like—" She hesitated.

"Yes? Please speak freely at all times, Willa."

"I would like to hire a second in command," she said. "Someone who could help me with the training and who would bring a little more experience into the mix." *Someone who might be willing to stay on after I am gone.*

He might have heard the unspoken words. Jasper Paladar was no reader, but he had an air of shrewdness that led Wen to think he always had a fair idea of what other people were thinking. Or at least, what *she* was thinking. "Someone to provide a little continuity when we have personnel changes," the lord said smoothly. "Yes, I quite see that. Did you have someone in mind?"

She nodded. "Man I worked with briefly just a couple weeks back. A veteran. If he'll take the job, you'll be able to count on him to stay."

Jasper Paladar nodded and leaned back slowly in his chair. He regarded her long enough to make Wen start fidgeting. "Tell me, Willa, I'm curious. How did you come to be a soldier?"

She uncrossed her arms to make an uncertain gesture with her hands, then laid them on her thighs. "I could fight. I was good at it. I liked it."

"But what was the point?"

She looked at him, uncomprehending.

"I mean, why fight unless you have a cause to fight for? You need to defend yourself or your property or the people you love—very well, I understand that. You meet a charismatic marlord and you believe in his values and you believe in his honor, so you take up a sword to keep him safe. I understand that as well. You see a helpless girl being abused by a rapacious abductor—catch up your sword and go to it! Cut that man down! But those are causes, do you see what I mean? Those are situations that can inspire you. Why fight just to be fighting? I don't understand the allure."

She was practically gaping at him. She had never attempted to explain what drew her to the soldier's life—had never given it a moment's thought. "But—you can't serve such a cause unless you have the skills to begin with," she said, stumbling over the words as she tried to put the concept together. "You have to train yourself to be ready."

"You see, that is where you lose me. Why would it ever occur to you to make ready in the first place? If you did not know whose honor you would be defending, how could you care enough to take up arms to protect it?"

She was having a hard time following the argument. "I suppose I always believed there would be people and places worth fighting for," she said.

"And how do you discover them?" he asked. "Have you ever found someone or something that you believed in ardently enough to defend with your life?"

Wen pressed her lips together. He had been careful, till now, not to ask her for any details of her history, but she knew he must have been curious from the very start. "There have been times, of course, when I took a job merely for the money," she said quietly. "Soldiering is a profession like any other. But I never hired on for any master I despised, nor fought for any cause that was dishonest. I can respect every choice I made."

His voice was very soft. "Then why do you hate yourself so much now?"

She was so stunned that at first she just stared at him, then she jumped to her feet. He stood up just as rapidly as she did and said in an authoritative voice, "Stay a moment, Willa. We're not quite finished with the conversation."

She stayed where she was, but she was trembling. "You are finished with *me*," she said.

He shook his head, keeping his gaze fixed on her face. "You are committed to me for a month, and I hold you to your promise," he said.

"My *promise* did not include being accused and interrogated."

"Oh, come now. I think I have been the most lenient of employers. I've scarcely asked you a word about your background. For all I know, you've used your formidable skills murdering folks from Danalustrous to Coravann. I have not required references. I've given you my absolute trust. All I asked was for you to answer a simple question."

She was silent, forcing him to repeat it.

"Why do you hate yourself so much?"

"I wasn't aware that you thought I did," she ground out. "From now on, I will try to appear like my own best friend."

He smiled slightly; it was not, of course, a real answer. "And do you, in fact, have a best friend?" he asked.

Wen felt her stomach harden as the blow hit. Janni had been the one she was closest to, but they had all been comrades of the highest caliber. So many of them dead now, and all of them lost to her forever. "I did," she said. "We've been parted for a few years."

"Family? Anyone you keep in touch with?"

This question she at least could answer. "My parents and most of my brothers and sisters all live in Tilt. I try to write them every week or two."

"And have you written them since you've been in Forten City?"

"Yes, of course I have."

"No letters have come to Fortune in reply."

Wen bit her lip. "I had them sent to a posting house in the city," she admitted.

"I suppose you thought I would intercept and read your mail," he said, his voice a little stern.

She realized she could not just say *no* and have him accept the answer. "I have gotten in the habit of moving around so much," she said, and even this reply was oblique. "I always find some local establishment and ask them to accept my mail—and then forward it on once I am gone. Many freelance soldiers do the same. I hate to make you deal with letters that might come once I have moved on."

"I do not want you to think that your privacy will be compromised while you are here," he said seriously.

She bowed her head. "I didn't think it. I didn't intend an insult."

"You just intended to be able to flee in the night without leaving behind any loose ends, should such a course of action seem advisable."

That jerked her head right up—but, in fact, she couldn't deny it. "If you find me or my work unsatisfactory, tell me so," she snapped. "Otherwise, just let me do the job I was hired for and don't meddle in my life."

So much for showing proper deference to her employer. Jasper Paladar looked amused again.

"I was actually born to be a meddler as much as you were born to be a soldier," he said, his tone almost apologetic. "I don't think I can promise not to irritate you now and then as I try to pry beneath your very prickly surface. But how is this for a bargain? You may feel free at any time to refuse to answer, or speak quite rudely to me—as long as the topic is yourself. On any other subject, of course, I insist on complete openness. But in exchange for that privilege, you must promise not to threaten to break your contract whenever I annoy you with my inquisition."

She stared at him. "You are the strangest employer I've ever had. Or is it just because you're noble that you talk like this?"

"I think you would find that, even among the Thirteenth House, I am considered unusual," he said, smiling again. "Do we have a deal?"

"I suppose so," she said ungraciously. In fact, she felt a secret rush of relief. She had been prepared to stalk out the study door and stride out the front gate, pausing only to pick up her gear, but she hadn't really wanted to. She was invested, just a little, in the notion of melding her own corps of fighters from a highly eclectic group. She wanted to see what Moss was capable of; she wanted to explore more of Bryce's abilities. She was not ready yet to leave Forten City—or Fortune itself.

"Good. Then I will see you tomorrow evening for your next report," he said, seating himself behind his desk.

She made another stiff bow and left his study.

KARRYN caught her before Wen had made it three steps down the hall. "Willa! I wanted to talk to you!"

Wen paused, absolutely mystified about what to expect from Karryn—as always. Karryn had seemed delighted to learn that Wen was joining the household, though aghast at the measures Wen expected her to take to maintain her safety. Among other things, Wen had set the rule—and Jasper Paladar had agreed to enforce it—that Karryn would never accept a social engagement or invite a guest to the house without first informing Wen. Already, Wen had been treated to a range of Karryn's attempts to overturn this law—wheedling, sullenness, mockery.

"This is why everyone hates sixteen-year-old girls," Jasper Paladar had commented without any heat after observing one of these displays. "Do your best."

"Good evening, serra," Wen greeted her cautiously.

"Did my uncle tell you that I'm going to the Coverroe house tonight?" Karryn asked in a too-casual voice.

"He didn't, and you're not, unless you give me an hour to eat and change so I can accompany you," Wen said pleasantly.

Karryn frowned and her hands made fists of irritation. "It's the *Coverroes*, Willa," Karryn repeated. "I'm absolutely safe there."

"I don't know who the Coverroes are."

"Lindy Coverroe is my best friend. I've told you about her a dozen times. You *met* her last week."

Wen rapidly reviewed the visitors who had come by Fortune since she had been in residence. Lindy Coverroe must be the giggling blonde with the rosy cheeks who had seemed to find Wen's presence in the house so odd. "I'm sure she's harmless," Wen said. "But that doesn't mean everyone else at her house is friendly toward you."

"Her mother is one of the most loyal vassals to House Fortunalt!" Karryn exclaimed. "Thirteenth House nobility!"

"And the man who abducted you is a devvaser," Wen replied.

Karryn flounced where she stood. "It's not the same thing."

"It's exactly the same thing."

"Are you going to follow me *everywhere* for the rest of my life?"

"Me or one of the other guards," Wen said cheerfully. "Get used to it."

Karryn pivoted prettily on one foot. "Mother! Willa won't let us go to Lindy's!"

Wen braced herself for the marlady's arrival on the scene. She hadn't had many encounters with Serephette Fortunalt since she'd arrived, but those few had been memorable. The woman was attractive in a lean, graying way—it was easy to tell that she and Jasper Paladar shared a heritage—but Wen was convinced she was utterly mad. Her huge eyes were sunken beneath sharp, jutting brows; her chiseled cheeks showed so little color that she always appeared absolutely haggard. She had a rather regal carriage and could turn a corner with majestic grace, as if she was used to being announced at grand assemblies, but all her movements were nervous and a little haunted. Wen imagined that living for a couple of decades with Rayson Fortunalt would be enough to turn anyone into a fidgety lunatic, but it didn't make the marlady any easier to deal with.

Serephette Fortunalt came sweeping down the hallway with her usual proud step, the heavy folds of her ornate dress falling perfectly around her form. "Captain Willa?" she said. "What is this my daughter is telling me? Naturally we must go to the Coverroes'. We accepted the invitation weeks ago." The marlady's voice always had a tremolo throb to it, as if she was about to burst into tears or admit a shocking secret.

Wen spoke with polite firmness. "I never said she couldn't go. Only that she must wait for me to accompany her." She glanced at Karryn, who had hurried up beside her mother. "If I'd had some warning that there was some event you wanted to attend tonight, I could have been ready whenever you asked."

"But we must go *now*," Serephette Fortunalt said in that urgent voice. "We will be late."

"I suppose you will," Wen said unsympathetically. "I'll be back as soon as I can." She saw the look that passed between the mother and daughter and added, "Don't even think of telling the coachman to go on without me. Lord Jasper has instructed him to never leave the House without checking with me first. He won't take you."

At that, she heard Karryn's indignant wail overriding her mother's bewildered surprise, and then they both headed down the hall to berate Jasper. Wen hurried out the front door and down to the barracks, where she could wash her hands and face and slip into her new uniform.

Jasper had had a whole set of them ordered the very day
Wen had accepted the job, promising to have more made, and
made to fit, as new recruits were added to the roster. Karryn
and her mother had expressed a keen interest in working with
the tailor to design a new style altogether for the uniforms of
Fortune, and Wen was not opposed to that at all. Bitter veterans from the war might be more inclined to serve the House
if some of the trappings were not hatefully familiar. She could
wish Karryn and Serephette were more interested in the guard
for reasons other than fashion, but she would accept whatever
attention they gave her.

"Moss? Eggles?" she called as she stepped through the
door to the barracks. Until today, she'd had the building to
herself, but of the five she'd hired, these two had been happy
to move in immediately. "I hope you've eaten something,
because we've got to set out tonight as soon as we can dress."

Eggles was sitting on one of the straight-backed chairs,
polishing his sword, but he stood up as soon as she spoke. He
was one of the veterans she'd known she would hire the instant
she saw him take his first practice swing. He was scruffy
and tough, with an inborn stillness that allowed him to pay
attention to everything going on around him without giving
much away. He was taller than Wen, but whipcord thin, with
silvery-black hair cropped so short it showed the skin beneath.
His best move was a nasty underhand thrust that had probably
kept him alive more than once.

"Where to?" he asked. He was already shrugging into
the jacket coat of the Fortunalt uniform. The material was a
charcoal gray; across it lay a black sash embroidered with the
pearls of Fortunalt.

"Some noble's house where they're giving a party."

Moss came hurrying out of the kitchen, stuffing the last
of a scone in her mouth with one hand, holding out a slice of
bread and cheese with the other. "Have *you* eaten?" she asked
around her food. "If not, this will hold you for a while."

Within five minutes, they were all more or less cleaned up,
respectably dressed, and headed back toward the mansion.
"Take horses or ride on the carriage?" Eggles asked.

"It's just through town, so on the carriage," Wen said. "You
two take the back. I'll sit up front with the driver."

No surprise that Karryn and Serephette were already seated inside. More of a surprise that Jasper Paladar stood on the front steps, watching them leave. Though dark had already fallen, Wen was sure she could see a smile on his face, and she thought it was for her. It amused him that she was so serious about her task, but it pleased him, too—and pleased him that she was not about to let Karryn's tantrums turn her back from her duty.

"Travel safely. Enjoy the dinner," he called as the driver snapped the reins. He waved good-bye, though Wen didn't see either of the women return the gesture. Of course, she didn't believe he was waving at *her.*

They traveled only a few miles in the carriage before turning into a district that Wen thought she recognized. Perhaps—surely not—oh, yes, indeed! This was the very gaudy house of glittering black stone and bright copper roof tiles. Wen was grinning broadly as she saw the ornate gold doors gleaming in the light of torches set along the front walk. Such a display didn't impress Wen at all—she tended to think more highly of people who hoarded their money and didn't boast of their accomplishments. But then, clearly the house had not been constructed to impress *her.*

One of the footmen helped the women from the coach, and Wen stepped down from the high front seat. Karryn gave her a look of horror. "You're not coming *in* with me, are you?" she demanded in a low voice. "Oh no, no, no. You can't."

"Serra, I must be able to roam the house at will," Wen replied seriously. She had heard the tales about how Justin and Tayse and Hammond and Coeval had followed Amalie into all the noble Houses one summer when they escorted her to various balls, and none of the marlords had dared to complain. A serramarra might not be as valuable as a princess, but she was just as fragile. "I must accompany you inside and get a sense of who is in attendance and how the rooms are laid out. For most of the evening, my fellow guards and I will walk the grounds and make sure no danger comes in through the gates. But if there is any alarming sound from inside, at any point in the evening, we will quickly enter to make sure nothing untoward has happened."

Serephette Fortunalt strode by with her customary sweep.

"My good Captain Willa," she said as she passed. "It is a Thirteenth House ball. Of course untoward things will be happening. But we will attempt to remain civilized even so."

Karryn followed her mother after giving Willa one brief, fulminating glare. Eggles and Moss had jumped down from the coach and watched the nobles enter the house as Wen gave them hasty instructions.

"The marlady's a bit peculiar," Eggles observed.

"And yet you will guard her life with your own and love her like your own mother," Wen said, preparing to follow Karryn and Serephette inside.

He gave her a quiet smile. "Or maybe better than that."

THEY spent the next three hours roving the house and grounds, together and apart, noting where the building was vulnerable and where the likeliest exits lay in case of trouble. In truth, one quick circuit of the interior convinced Wen that the house could be breached from almost any vantage. She occupied herself, as the night went on, by imagining how she would infiltrate it from the kitchen, from the side lawn, from the front porch, if she were trying to gain access. Eggles had a mind that worked the same way. They spent ten minutes standing in the shadow of a great ornamental tree, debating whether it would be faster to break in through the roof or a second-story window if there was a reason to get to one of the back rooms. Moss passed the time by charming the cooks in the kitchen, and came to join them carrying plates of leftover meat and pastries. Wen considered that just as valuable a contribution to the conversation as the speculation.

The evening was saved from complete tedium by the fellowship of the house guards, who patrolled the property at regular intervals. Before they'd been on the estate fifteen minutes, Eggles had reported to Wen that there were fourteen men in the Coverroes' guard and all of them looked like they could hold a weapon. Wen had made the exact same assessment, but she was pleased that Eggles had gone to the trouble of counting. They were friendly, though, and offered the serramarra's contingent a few hands of cards.

"As long as we can sit somewhere close enough to watch the

gate, I'm in," Wen said, and Eggles and Moss nodded. They played for coppers and no one won or lost anything to speak of, but it made the time go faster, and Wen was grateful.

Finally there was movement at the front door as the nobles began having the footmen signal for their carriages. Karryn and Serephette were among the last to leave, and Karryn stood in the doorway another ten minutes, whispering in Lindy Coverroe's ear, before joining her mother in the carriage.

"Thank the gods," Wen muttered to the driver. "Let's get home."

Of course, she knew better than to relax her guard at that moment. Many an ambush had been carried out late at night, when soldiers were nodding off after a long day's work. She cut her gaze from side to side, watching the shadowed streets. Once a sound behind the carriage made her twist around all the way in her seat. She was pleased to find Eggles already hanging by one hand from his strap, staring behind him to try to determine what had made the sound. When he swung around again, he shook his head. No trouble.

They made it safely to Fortune without anyone being abducted, robbed, or otherwise assaulted. Wen considered it a very successful outing, and hoped the rest of them proved as tame.

Chapter

10

IN THE MORNING, WEN WROTE A NOTE TO ORSON at the northern freighting office. She thought he would be intrigued by the offer, but that didn't mean he would take the job. If she had read him correctly, he'd had no love for Rayson Fortunalt and might not be able to stomach the marlord's daughter. But she thought he would be a formidable asset to the House guard.

By day's end, she'd hired ten more recruits, all men, and told another ten to come back the next morning for her final decision. She was a little surprised to find Ginny in the barracks, moving through the wide area that constituted the kitchen and dining room together.

"Have you been assigned the miserable job of being our cook?" Wen asked her with a grin.

Ginny looked half pleased and half annoyed. "The head cook and I had words a few times this past week, so she thought I might do better where I didn't have to mind my tongue," she said. "But I think I'll like cooking for the guard. You probably don't complain much."

"And we'll eat whatever you put in front of us," Eggles said.

"Smells good, anyway," Wen said, settling into a seat beside him. "How does the cook like your little brother, then?"

Ginny rolled her eyes. "Are you joking? Bryce knows how to make everybody love him. She's already giving him special treats and telling him not to work so hard."

Eggles eyed Wen and rubbed his shoulder as if it pained him. "Now that's a trick I'd like to learn," he said, which made everyone at the table laugh. Wen had driven them hard this day, and Eggles and Moss had had the task of making the newest recruits fight fiercely for the honor of being included.

"Things are only going to get harder," she promised him. "Once we're up to full strength we'll really start working out. Better rest now while I'm being so easy on you."

After the meal, she stepped out of the barracks to join Lord Jasper for their nightly conversation. Before heading up to the house, though, she took one quick turn around the compound, making the complete circuit around the inside of the hedge. It was something she had learned from Tayse, who walked the palace grounds at Ghosenhall once every night—sometimes more, if he was restless. Often she had wondered how such a big man managed to get by on so little sleep.

Well, ordinary rules rarely applied to Tayse.

But she would not be thinking about Tayse, about Justin, about any of them. She gave her head a hard shake and pushed through the house to seek out Lord Jasper.

He wasn't in his study, but one of the servants showed her to the library, which was on the first floor toward the rear of the house. As she stepped in, she glanced around with interest at the ceiling-high bookcases that lined every wall, and with curiosity at piles of additional volumes stacked in rather disorderly fashion on the floor. She didn't care about books, of course; she was checking for places people could hide if they'd stolen into the house. She supposed someone could crouch behind one of the pieces of furniture—a grouping of chairs before the fireplace, an arrangement of chairs and an ottoman across the room—but it was easy to see through their spindly legs and realize no one was crouching in their shadows. Someone could lurk behind the long curtains of the two tall windows, but Wen gave them a hard look and didn't think that was the case tonight.

Jasper Paladar sat in one of the chairs before the fireplace, watching her. "Do you always do that?" he asked softly. "Inspect every room when you first walk in—as if memorizing its contents?"

She shrugged. "Doesn't everyone look around when they come into a new place?"

"I'm sure they do, but I don't imagine they bring such intensity all the time."

Other people might end up dead for lack of attention, but not Wen. She changed the subject. "You have a lot of books here."

His expression showed distaste. "The ones on the shelves aren't mine."

She pointed to the ones on the floor. "Does that mean these belong to you?"

He nodded. "Some I brought with me, some I've ordered since I've been here."

She glanced around again. "It wouldn't seem like you'd need to bring *more* books here."

His voice was severe. "Most of the ones that belong in this library are valueless, acquired just for show. Neither Rayson Fortunalt nor his father was much of a scholar. Most of these volumes could be burned in the grate, and I wouldn't care. And I've always considered it a sin to burn a book."

She couldn't help herself. "Guess I shouldn't tell you about the time I was traveling with a patrol and we used the pages of a book for kindling."

A pained look crossed his face and then he laughed. "I hope you read it first."

"Mmmm, don't remember that I did."

"*Can* you read?"

"Of course I can!"

"You just choose not to. You just choose not to read for pleasure," he expanded.

"Well, it wasn't much of a pleasure in the schoolroom," she said.

All this time she had been standing near the door, not sure how long the conference would last. Now he motioned her closer and waved her to a seat across from him. Between their chairs was a small table holding an elaborately carved box. The warmth of the fire felt good after the long day outside in wet spring weather.

"You never even read Mohre's *Theories of Warfare* or Nocklyn's *Twelve Battles*? Yes, Roth Nocklyn, the ancestor of the current marlady by more generations than I can count."

"No," she said.

He settled back in his chair and steepled his hands together. "You'd like them," he said. "Full of fighting."

"They sound dull," she said. "I bet they make fighting seem boring."

"You could be right. But there are all sorts of adventure books, about young men slipping off from their fathers' farms to go seek their fortunes. Didn't you ever read any of those?"

"No," she said. "But they sound a little better than that theory book."

"I'll send away for one for you," he promised.

"And then you expect me to *read* it? I don't think that's in my contract." She was laughing, but also mostly serious.

His hands now palm-to-palm, he tapped his index fingers against his chin. "So every thought you have, every idea that's formed you, has come from actual experience?" he said, as if he couldn't believe it. "How can that be possible?"

She was bewildered. "You mean you've gotten some of your ideas from *books*? Ideas that have made you think or behave a certain way?"

"I am the man I am today because of Stolker's *Meditations*," he replied so solemnly she thought he had to be joking. "Although tempered, finally, in my thirties, by Hamton's *Notes from a Country Estate*. But if you sat down and read those collected volumes I think you'd find a tolerably accurate transcription of my soul."

She just stared at him and made no attempt to answer.

His mouth quirked up in a little smile. "So. No need to be afraid of being rude. I am not, I assure you, the only man in Gillengaria who has such a love for the printed page, but you're right to think that I'm a little more obsessive than most. Hardly anyone reads as much as I do—though hardly anyone *I* know reads as little as you."

"Well, I can hold a sword and you can't," was all she could think to say, and that made him burst out laughing.

"Indeed, we all bring to the world our unique skills, and it would be a dull place indeed if all those skills were identical," he said. "But I do respect your talents, Willa."

"Oh, and of course I respect yours! Your—ability to read."

He was still amused. "I am also a writer of some repute," he said. "I have produced two biographies and an analysis of the failure of the overseas shipping contracts during the reign of King Tamor."

Once again she didn't even try to come up with a reply.

"Don't be nervous," he added. "I would never consider making it a part of your job description to read any of those works."

"Good to know," she said. "Or you may as well fire me now."

"But in case you were ever wondering how I spent my time before I became Karryn's guardian, well, that is how."

She had, in fact, been just a little curious about that—about him. And since he had opened the door to questions, she said, "Where did you live, before you came here?"

"I have a property down on the southwestern edge of Fortunalt—quite small, by the standards of Fortune, but I'm fond of it." His voice hardened a little. "Of course, it was overrun a great deal by the Arberharst soldiers Rayson imported to fight his war, and it will take some work to restore it. But I imagine it will one day be the gracious and serene place it used to be."

"Did you leave behind a family to come take care of Karryn?" A polite way of asking, *Where's your wife?* Jasper Paladar was a handsome man, and some Thirteenth House lady would have snatched him up ages ago.

"I only have one daughter, and she's married and living in Rappengrass," he replied. "My wife died five years ago."

"Oh, I'm very sorry."

"Yes, so am I. She was quite charming—brilliant and eccentric, but warmhearted. You would have liked her. She didn't have much patience for sitting still, but she couldn't hold a sword, either."

Wen flashed him a smile for that. "Did she read your books?"

"Read them? She helped me research them. In my opening notes on the financial book I explained that it would have been impossible to write it without her help."

Jasper Paladar was describing a world Wen could scarcely comprehend and certainly couldn't imagine herself comfortable in. Wouldn't want to get comfortable in. "And your daughter?" she asked gamely. "Does she write? Or at least read?"

He nodded. "Both. And she teaches literature at a small private academy not far from Rappen Manor." He sighed. "I miss her. Perhaps I'll invite her to come to Forten City for a visit. I would travel to her but I don't like to leave Karryn—and small towns in Rappengrass don't excite Karryn too much."

Wen grinned. "Who knows? Maybe Karryn would like it. If you decide to go, let me know, and I'll put together an escort for all of you."

"And have you made more progress today toward filling the ranks of the guards?"

For several minutes they discussed her new hires and what Wen expected to happen in the next few days. He listened closely, and to her surprise remembered all the names she'd mentioned to him so far. Still, the report didn't take long, and she was waiting to be dismissed when he surprised her yet again.

"Do you play cruxanno?" he asked.

Which was when she recognized the carved box sitting on the table between them. "Not very well," she said.

He looked disappointed. "I was sure it was something you'd excel at! I thought all soldiers played strategy games as they passed the time in the barracks."

She grinned. "Soldiers are more likely to play cards or throw dice. They tend to pick games they don't have to think about too hard. They don't want to be focusing too much on something else in case there's a sudden call for troops." She gestured at the box. "Anyway, no one wants to pack something like that in a saddlebag. You'd never take it on the road."

"Do you play well enough to indulge me with a round or two?"

She was surprised. "If you want. I won't be much of a challenge for you, though, if you're any good."

He opened the box and then unfolded its sides so that it

made a rather large playing board with a deeply grooved surface. The counters and game pieces lay inside a purple velvet bag that he tossed to Wen.

"You know how to parcel out the pieces, don't you? I'll deal the cards."

So she divided the swords, the shields, the castles, the horses, the crowns, and the coins. This was a particularly fine set, with some pieces made of silver, some of gold, and small jewels inset on the hilts and tiaras. Most cruxanno games she'd seen had been made of wood, though sometimes the crowns were pewter.

"You realize we could be playing straight through till dawn and not be done," she said. "I've seen cruxanno games that lasted a month."

"I thought we'd play a few hours a night and keep the game going for as long as it takes," he said. "I have a pair of friends who played a single game that endured through a solid year. They still talk about that."

Privately, Wen thought those had to be the dullest men in Gillengaria, but of course she didn't say so. But who would spend so much time on a war game when they could have been practicing with real weapons instead?

"Ours better not take that long," she said. "I won't be here a year."

He held out a hand and she poured his counters into his palm. "Indeed, no. We'll have our own game wrapped up long before you go."

They were quiet for a few moments while they deployed their troops and chose their fortifications. Wen was usually pretty haphazard at cruxanno, but she felt some pressure to defend the honor of her profession against a man whose knowledge of warfare was entirely theoretical. So she chose her bases and her targets a little more carefully than she usually might, and frowned over the disposition of her shields.

"I claim the oaks," Jasper Paladar said.

"I yield the oaks, but I claim the southern mountains," she replied, and the game was on.

They played for nearly two hours, Wen growing more absorbed than she expected. The opening stages of cruxanno were the least interesting to watch, if you were a spectator, because most of the heavy work went on inside the opponents' heads as they worked out the strategy that would guide them for the rest of the game. Wen could tell that Jasper Paladar had his first couple dozen moves pretty well thought out, with backup maneuvers in mind to counter any threat her men might offer. She rarely planned that far ahead; she was more used to reacting than plotting an attack at the beginning.

"I see your strength is defense, not offense," he said after they had passed most of that time in silence. "Which actually makes you a tricky opponent, because you don't offer many vulnerabilities. But if I can draw you out—"

"If you want to have any hope of defeating me, you can't be telling me how you have analyzed my strategy," she said in some exasperation.

He looked up in surprise and then broke into a surprisingly sweet smile. "Perhaps that's why I frequently lose at crux-anno," he said. He pushed himself away from the table and leaned back in his chair. "I think we should pause right here for the night and think over our plans for tomorrow."

She looked doubtfully at the board. "Will anyone move our pieces? I hate to lose all my work so far."

"I will inform the housekeeper that the room is not to be entered unless I'm here to guard it." He stretched his long legs out before him. "You're better than you led me to expect, by the way, and I'm relieved to see it."

She laughed. "Why? What does it matter?"

"I have a visitor arriving in two weeks, and he is an invet-erate player. I don't expect to beat him, but I do think if I can offer him a challenging game, it will impress him. And I want to introduce him to the idea that I can be dangerous."

She surveyed him in silence. Thin, a little tired, with that bemused scholar's face and those smooth hands, Jasper Pala-dar looked anything but dangerous. "It might be hard to con-vince him, even so," she answered.

He was amused again. "Actually, more accurately, I want him to be surprised at the notion that I might be more danger-ous than he thinks."

"Well, that might be easier, I suppose. Who is this fellow?"

"Zellin Banlish." When her expression merely showed polite interest, he added, "Serlord Zellin. The father of the man who abducted Karryn."

The words made Wen scramble upright in her chair. "You've invited the serlord here? To play *games*? I've been wondering why there hasn't been some kind of retribution for what that wretched devvaser did! You should be threatening to storm his house and burn it to the ground, not having him over for tea and cruxanno!"

He laid his arms along the armrests of the chair and watched her. "Violence is not always the right response to violence, no matter what you might think," he said. "Sometimes, despite the most fervent desire a person might have, the cost of meeting brutality with brutality is simply too high."

"If someone hits me, I'm going to hit him back," she said with heat. "And anyone who goes around hitting other people should expect to be punched in the face."

"I can't prove that Tover took Karryn."

"She told you he did!"

"But I didn't see him do it. In fact, there were no witnesses at all. Tover is likely to say Karryn went with him willingly. He could say he was surprised when she chose to leave his protection—and worried for her safety once he realized she was alone on a back road of Fortunalt."

"Well, *I* saw her with him and there was no question in my mind that she was there against her will."

"But serlord Zellin is not the sort of man who would believe the protestations of an unknown soldier if they contradict the testimony of his son."

Wen's hands made tight little fists. There had been a day that anything she said would have been believed by the king himself, no questions asked, so it was doubly infuriating to hear that someone could doubt her word.

"You see the problem," Lord Jasper continued. "I want to convey the story to him in such a way that he realizes I know his son is guilty of offering harm to my ward and that I will not tolerate such actions in the future. I also want the serlord to believe I am capable of ruthless justice—and to warn his son away from ever incurring my wrath."

"I don't see how a game of cruxanno is going to prove any of that to him."

He smiled. "It will be the conversation as well as the game that will convince him." He glanced around the room. "And the setting, perhaps. Something intimidating. This room seems more imposing than my little study."

"Have a couple guards standing watch," she suggested. "Not just to make sure he doesn't try to strangle you over the game, though that's a reason, too! But to show that you're well defended."

He nodded. "Yes. You and someone else you choose."

She made a gesture. "People don't always look at me and realize they should be afraid."

"Yes, but if he really does try to choke the life out of me, I want you in the room to save me."

She grinned. "Now who's relying on brute force over strategy?"

He tilted his head, as if considering. "You're the soldier," he said. "Which would you say wins the most encounters?"

"Depends on the circumstances."

"What are the factors?"

"Terrain, fortifications, the relative size of the opposing troops, the general's skill, and luck."

"So a smaller army can defeat a larger one if enough factors swing in its favor."

"Sure," Wen said. "But if I could, I'd opt for the larger force every time."

He motioned at the cruxanno board. "Here we begin with equal forces, so strategy and skill are paramount. Strength doesn't even enter into the equation."

"It *always* enters into the equation," she said. She was laughing. "With one swipe of my hand, I could send the whole board to the floor. Brute force wins again."

"But that's not part of the game!"

"It is if it keeps you from winning."

"What about honor?" he asked.

"In a cruxanno game?" Her tone was derisive.

"In general. Surely there are tactics you would not use even in war."

"War is about killing people," she said grimly. "Surely there is nothing honorable about that."

He narrowed his eyes. "I feel like you are arguing in circles."

She spread her hands in a gesture of defeat. "Would I stab a man in the back? No. Would I harm an unarmed man? Only if he was threatening me with his bare hands. Would I take desperate measures to protect someone in my charge? I would if the threat was grave enough. I believe in the kind of honor that says I don't try to start fights. But if I am under attack, I'll be ruthless in response. And sometimes that response isn't as pretty as you'd like."

"Well, now, that seems as honest as anything you've ever said to me," he replied softly.

Why was he always trying to poke beneath her hard surface? Why was he so interested in what she thought and how she felt? All he should care about was that she was good at the service he had hired her to perform. "Do you have such conversations with your butler and your valet?" she asked shortly. "Do you always try to force them to expose the darker side of their natures?"

"Not so far," he replied in a cheerful voice. "I can't imagine anything they'd have to say would be quite as colorful as your observations, however."

She had been waiting for him to dismiss her, but now she pushed herself to her feet and prepared to take her leave. "You might meet a hundred soldiers and find all of them think exactly as I do," she said. "I'm not as unusual as you think."

"Really?" he said as she walked to the door. "I must take more time to acquaint myself with the members of my guard if they are all as interesting as you. Goodnight, Willa. I will see you tomorrow."

Chapter

11

THE TRAINING OF THE NEW GUARDS BEGAN IN earnest over the next few days, while the game of cruxanno continued in the evenings. It was clear that Jasper Paladar had no chivalrous thought of allowing Wen to win, and Wen decided early on that she would not graciously give him the upper hand merely because he paid her salary. So they advanced their troops cautiously, testing each other's strengths, and the game proceeded slowly but in a manner that satisfied them both.

They did not have any more conversations about Wen's notions of warfare. Thank the miserable gods for that.

Three days after the cruxanno game had begun, she received word that Orson had arrived in Forten City and was awaiting her at a harborside bar. She left Eggles in charge of the afternoon's training session and met Orson down on the wharf. He'd picked one of the more respectable taverns, and it was relatively quiet during this hour of the day. They took a back booth and ordered a round of beer.

"You've gone up in the world since I saw you last," Orson observed.

"It's only temporary. For me, anyway."

He was sprawled on his side of the booth, looking as relaxed as could be, but she noticed how his hands never strayed too far from his weapons. Just like hers. It was a relief, after the long discussions with Jasper Paladar, to be having a conversation with a man who didn't puzzle her. "What's the job?" he asked lazily. "And why do you think I'd like it?"

She gave him a straight look. "I've got a feeling you didn't care much for the marlord who's now dead," she said.

He nodded. "That's a mild way to put it."

"His daughter's sixteen. Will be marlady when she's old enough. Karryn is—" Wen shook her head. "Well, she's a handful and a half. Sweet one minute, stubborn the next, and stupid about half the time. But I actually like her. There's no cruelty in her, anyway, like there was in her father, and she's *certainly* never going to lead any kind of rebellion against the king. Against the queen," she corrected herself.

"Still not clear to me why this matters."

"From what I can tell, the war left Fortunalt in a mess," Wen said bluntly. "Still a lot of outlaws on the road. The ser-ramarra was kidnapped a few weeks back, and only got free through a lucky chance." No need to go into the details of that luck right now. "Apparently there was only a ragtag bunch of soldiers left behind at Fortune once the marlord died in the war, and they never did a good job of protecting Karryn. Her guardian has hired me to assemble a real guard—twenty to twenty-four men who can truly protect her."

Orson looked intrigued despite himself. "They'd have to be pretty good."

Wen nodded. "Well trained, highly disciplined, *and* loyal to the House. But that's a big enough force to hold off any petty bandits and make even a rebel lord think twice about trying to overtake it."

He nodded. "Even the queen only has fifty Riders."

Forty-nine. Or so Wen had heard. "Right. I've already organized a force of about twenty. I like who I've got so far. I think they'll come together well. But I think the job will be more than I can handle by myself."

"You want me to be a training master?"

"I want you to sign on," she said. "Be my second in command until I go—and then step up as captain."

His face didn't register surprise or even much curiosity. He'd sized her up a long time ago. Neither did he make any false statements of modesty. They'd fought beside each other once, and that was enough for both of them to have taken an accurate measure of the other. "You're thinking lifelong commitment."

"It could be. Plenty of the great lords find one watch captain they trust and stick with him till the end."

He scratched his finger along the side of the glass, where it seemed someone hadn't done a good job of scrubbing off splatter from a former patron's meal. "As you said, I've no love for House Fortunalt. I'm not sure I could look at his daughter and forgive her for having such a father."

"Maybe it helps a little if you know that she hated him even more than you do."

"Maybe," he said. "But I can't suppose a sixteen-year-old girl will be ordering the guard about anytime soon. What about this guardian you mentioned? What's he like?"

How to describe Jasper Paladar . . . "He's one of the stranger sorts I've met, but in a way that makes me like him," she answered frankly. "Very smart man—always surrounded by books, always *thinking*. Never had any weapons training and doesn't pretend to know what it's like to be a soldier. But I feel respect when he talks to me. And that makes me respect him in turn."

Orson raised his eyebrows. "Liberal with his coin?"

She grinned. "The pay's fair, if that's what you're asking."

"How long do you plan to stay?"

"I promised a month. He'd like me to stay for six. Somewhere in the middle, I'm guessing."

"Aren't you worried about me trying to undermine you? If I think I'm to be named captain next, why won't I try to assert my authority now?"

She just looked at him and didn't answer. Finally his brown eyes warmed and his face split in a smile. "No, guess I wouldn't be doing that," he said. "I don't suppose you make that many mistakes when you're judging a man."

"One mistake I hope I didn't make," she said. "Thinking you could take orders from a woman."

He shrugged. "Take orders from anyone as long as they make sense."

"And fight alongside a woman. I've got two in the group already and would hire more if I could find them."

"Looking for allies?" he asked with a smirk.

If he'd been close enough, she would have swatted him. "Looking for people who bring different strengths to the mix."

"Got no problem with anyone who can hold a sword and listen to reason."

"How about mystics? Problem with those?"

He settled back and studied her more closely for a moment. "Not you," he said at last. "The serramarra?"

"No. Couple others at the House, though, including one in the guard. If it matters to you, tell me right now, and the rest of this conversation never happened."

He scratched the underside of his chin. His face was rough with about a day's worth of stubble, which just added to his generally rakish air. He still reminded her of Justin, but he was coming into sharper focus for her as his own man. "I rode for a while with a small troop out of Coravann," he said after a moment. "One of the soldiers could shape-shift a little, just enough to look like someone different. One of our men got drunk one night, locked up by the local magistrate for starting a fight and, I can't remember why, there was some fear they might hang him. So this shiftling, he changes his face so he looks like that magistrate, and he goes striding into the building where they're holding our soldier. 'There's been an order to release this man,' he says, all mad like he thinks it's the worst idea ever. So the guard at the cell lets him go. We rode out of that town as fast as our horses would take us," he concluded. "And I've had a soft spot for mystics ever since."

"Were you the drunkard who was looking at a hanging?"

He laughed. "Not that time, but it could have been. I was young and not as smart as I am now."

"Smart enough to take this job I'm offering? You might never have to go roaming again."

"That's a funny thing to say for someone who can't sit still herself."

"Right now we're talking about you."

"I'd have to see the place," he said. "Meet the serramarra and her guardian." He eyed her. "Meet the men who'd be reporting to me and make sure they're any good."

That was intended as a jab, but it was so halfhearted she didn't bother reacting. "You wouldn't be worth much if you'd take a job like this without looking it over," she said. "Come on back to the House."

ORSON spent his first hour at Fortune in the training yard, watching some of the maneuvers and introducing himself to the guards. The veterans among the group sized him up while he was assessing them, and Wen was aware that most of them drew the correct conclusion about his presence. It didn't seem to bother anyone, particularly once he slipped over the fence and took a few practice swings with Eggles.

Bryce had wandered over to watch, as he often did, and Wen asked him his opinion of Orson. "I think I'd like him," the boy said. "Is he going to stay?"

"I hope so."

More awkward, of course, to introduce him to the serramarra and her family, though Wen figured she could count on Jasper Paladar to make this seem natural. After Orson had shaved and otherwise cleaned himself up, Wen took him to the library, where Jasper Paladar was studying the cruxanno board. The lord looked up as soon as Wen and Orson entered.

"I've spent half my day wondering when you were going to move your southern troops," he greeted her, but his eyes went quickly beyond her to Orson. He came easily to his feet and held out his hand. "I see Willa has brought a friend."

She could tell Orson appreciated the gesture as the two men shook hands. Jasper was the taller of the two, but Orson was bulkier. "Yes, my lord," Orson said. "She told me of the opportunities at the House and invited me to come look things over."

"And what do you think?"

"I think she's assembled a good troop, but there are a few basic fortifications you'd need to make to really turn this into a defensible position," he said.

Jasper regarded him with a faint smile. "I meant, what did you think about taking on a job with us?"

Orson glanced at Wen. "It sounded like an excellent post and I'm honored to be considered. But I thought you'd want to get to know me first, and I'd like to meet the serramarra if I'm to serve her."

"I'm not sure that meeting Karryn will be an inducement, but certainly I can arrange it," Jasper said. Wen laughed, and only then did Orson smile. Clearly, he hadn't been too certain the lord was joking. "We'll have to wait until the morning, though. She's gone up to her room in a temper because her mother disapproved of the style of a dress she wanted to commission."

"I have sisters," Orson said. "I remember how that goes."

Jasper glanced down at the game board. "Do you play cruxanno?" he asked.

"I play," Orson said, "but I'm better at cards." Which made Wen laugh again.

"Clearly, I need to take up cards and other games of chance," Jasper said. "Maybe someday you can teach me the games you play in the barracks."

"We usually play for money," she said. "You might want to get your skills to a respectable level before you ask to be dealt in to a soldier's game."

"Nonsense," Orson said with a grin. "We'd be happy to invite him now."

"I can see that having a House guard will prove to have educational as well as security benefits," Jasper said. "Orson, I enjoyed meeting you. Come to my study tomorrow after breakfast and I'll make sure Karryn is on hand to greet you. We can get to know each other over the next few days and you can let me know if you're interested in the position. Willa wants you to be second in command." He left unsaid the part all three of them mentally filled in: *and captain once she departs.*

"You need to decide, too," Orson said. "If you want me for the position."

Jasper glanced at Wen. "If Willa trusts you, so do I," he said. "We'd be happy to have you serve House Fortunalt."

KARRYN chose to be mature and earnest when Jasper introduced her to Orson the next morning. Wen could only imagine she was trying to impress her mother, who hovered nearby, watching them with her huge, haunted eyes.

"Have you been a soldier long?" Karryn asked him in a polite voice.

Orson kept his face serious. "All my life, except for a time I was a sailor, and even then we fought at sea more than once."

"Have you ever served in a civil guard like the one Willa wants to put together for me?"

"Once or twice I took a job with some minor lord or a wealthy merchant who liked to have a troop around him when he traveled. It was much the same."

"Willa thinks I need guards with me practically every minute of the day," Karryn said, flicking Wen a slightly accusatory look.

Orson nodded. "I'd tell you exactly the same thing."

"My father had soldiers around him, and I didn't like them," she burst out.

"I think Willa has assembled a better caliber of fighters," Orson replied quietly. "People who will neither desert you nor hurt you."

Something about that answer seemed to please Karryn. "Maybe I should meet all the new guards she's hired."

"An excellent idea," Wen answered. "Anytime you like."

Serephette chose that moment to enter the conversation. "Not today, however. The dressmaker is on her way."

Karryn assumed an expression of long-suffering. "Not today," she repeated. "But very soon. Orson, thank you so much for taking the time to meet me."

So Orson's first experience of Karryn was highly favorable and Wen was feeling pretty good about the whole situation. Two days later, though, he had a chance to see the serramarra practically at her worst.

* * *

NOW that she was close to a full complement of guards, Wen had instituted true security measures, leaving two soldiers at the gate and having another two patrol the grounds at all hours of the night and day. Whenever there was company—which was often, for Jasper frequently had appointments with merchants and vassal lords who had some grievance to air—she insisted that one guard be inside the house itself, instantly on call. Those who were off duty spent their days training, practicing both on foot and on horseback, constantly striving to improve their skills.

On this particular morning, Wen was dueling with Moss when Davey, her youngest recruit, came leaping over the fence rail. "Captain!" he called. "The serramarra's got visitors. A big fancy coach."

Cursing, Wen signaled Moss to pull back, and then handed over her weapon. When would the stubborn girl learn that she *had* to let Wen know any time guests were due at the House? A footman was all well and good for announcing who was at the door, but only a soldier could fend off a visitor who had violence on his mind.

"Orson!" Wen called, hopping the fence and detouring toward the barracks, where she'd left her uniform jacket. "Let's go make a show of force up at the House!"

Such was the speed at which the soldiers reacted that they were striding through the main doors just as Karryn came flying down the great stairway. Wen had a moment to assess the situation. That looked like Lindy Coverroe standing in the formal parlor just to the left of the foyer, and the short, fair-haired woman beside her must be her mother. They were dressed for traveling and showed no disposition to be seated, so Wen thought perhaps they had just paused here on their way somewhere else.

Nonetheless, she gave Karryn a minatory glare and the serramarra mouthed, *"I didn't know they were coming,"* as she hurried past the guards. Wen and Orson assumed impassive expressions and stationed themselves just outside the parlor, visible if anyone was looking but not, Wen hoped, obtrusive.

"Karryn, Karryn, can you come with us?" Lindy squealed in her high-pitched voice. Wen couldn't help it; she found Lindy vapid and tedious. Karryn had her faults, but Lindy didn't have any virtues that Wen could see.

"Go where?" Karryn asked.

"Coren is taking his boat out for the afternoon, and he's invited a dozen of us to come. It's all very last minute," Lindy said. "Edwin and Katlin will be there, and Helena and—oh, everybody! He told me to stop and pick you up, since he didn't have time to send out invitations to everyone."

Karryn clapped her hands together. "Let me go tell Jasper and my mother! I'll be back as soon as I can!"

She scurried from the room, and Wen and Orson fell in step right behind her. Karryn waited till they were out of earshot of the visitors and then she hissed, "And don't even *think* that you're going to come with me! On a boat! With all my friends! I will look too ridiculous."

"And don't even think that you have a chance of going on this expedition without four of us at your back," Wen said calmly.

Karryn stopped dead and spun around. "*Willa!* Who could possibly hurt me on Coren Bauler's boat? We'll be miles from anyone who means me harm! On the *ocean*!"

"I don't know Coren Bauler. Maybe he wants to throw you overboard," Wen said. "I don't know Edwin and Katlin. Maybe they don't like you."

"Maybe an Arberharst ship is lurking a few miles out of the harbor, looking to board unwary pleasure cruisers setting out from Forten City," Orson put in. "Twenty sailors could come pouring over the rail to slaughter the whole party."

"In which case, I hardly think four guards could keep me safe!" Karryn snapped.

Orson grinned. "Ah, Willa and I can account for ten sailors each."

Karryn stamped her foot. "You can't come! Everyone will say I am silly—or they'll say I'm so arrogant I have to bring guards with me everywhere I go just to prove how important I am."

"I don't care what they say," Wen said. "We go, or you don't."

"If you don't do what I say, I'll have both of you fired," Karryn fumed.

"I believe your uncle hired us, and he's the one who'll have to fire us," Wen replied.

Karryn stamped her foot again, then whirled around and

stormed down the hall toward Jasper's study. Heart sinking, Wen stole a look at Orson. This sort of behavior could not possibly endear the serramarra to the potential second in command. But he was grinning and shaking his head.

"I think she has to be saved from herself as much as she might have to be saved from anyone else," he whispered.

Jasper, when appealed to, categorically sided with Wen. "I thought I made it very clear, Karryn," he said calmly. "Willa is responsible for your safety, and her instructions are law. I happen to agree with her that I don't want you on Coren Bauler's boat without supervision. Coren Bauler! If Demaray Coverroe wasn't accompanying you, there is no way I would allow you to go anywhere near him. In fact, I'm tempted to join the party, just to prove that you are, in fact, under my watchful eye."

"Are you trying to destroy my life?" Karryn wailed. Wen saw that she was actually starting to cry. "Everyone already thinks I'm the oddest girl, with the strangest family, and now I'm to have soldiers trailing me everywhere I go? Who will ever want to marry me? Who will ever be my friend? I'm so *bizarre*!"

She started to weep in earnest, not even seeming to care that her face was blotching. Orson stood by the door expressionlessly, but Wen said, "Should I send for her mother?"

Jasper shook his head. "Serephette would hardly be of assistance." He came close enough to take Karryn in a gentle embrace. Instead of pushing him away, as Wen half expected, Karryn turned her face into his shoulder and continued to cry unabated. He stroked her thick brown hair and spoke with more patience than Wen would have been able to muster. She suddenly remembered that he had a grown daughter. Surely he had seen displays like this before.

"No one wants you to seem eccentric," he said kindly. "What you don't understand is how precious you are. Don't you know how terrified your mother and I were when you disappeared with Tover Banlish? I think I have been a very poor guardian up till now, not realizing how easily you could be snatched from my protection. I won't make that mistake a second time. You must be guarded, Karryn, and I am sorry if that makes you feel odd and alone. But I will do anything to keep you safe."

The tone of the words, or perhaps their genuine affection,

had the effect of causing Karryn to sniff and lift her head. "But what will I tell Lindy?" she whispered.

Jasper put his hands on either side of her face and kissed her forehead. "I shall tell Demaray that I am being an over-protective uncle and that I insist on burdening you with a guard. She may mock *me* all she likes. I don't care at all. Now. Would you rather I came or stayed behind? You must put up with Willa no matter what your preference, but I will not force you to endure my presence as well."

"No—you ought to come—I think you will enjoy it," Karryn said, beginning to smile through her tears. "Oh—gods and goddesses! I must look a total fright. Tell the Coverroes I will be with them as soon as I can." And without a word to Wen or Orson, she picked up her skirts and raced out the door.

Jasper stared after her and sighed. "I suppose I'd better go change as well," he said. "How quickly can you gather reinforcements and meet us at the gate?"

"Ten minutes, my lord," Wen said, and she and Orson were on their way.

They were just shy of the barracks when she demanded, "Well? Does such a tantrum make you reconsider?"

"She's a girl," he said, as if that excused ill behavior. "She cares what people think about her and, as you said before, she hasn't had an easy time of it. But she didn't lash out at anyone when she was disappointed, and she listened to reason. If anything, I like her more."

Wen couldn't hold back her sigh of relief.

They rounded up Eggles and a young woman named Amie, made sure everyone was suitably dressed in jackets and sashes, and jogged up to the gate just as the Fortunalt carriage was pulling around from the stables. Obviously, Jasper had decided there were now too many of them to fit in the Coverroe conveyance, and for the short ride to the sea, it was hardly worth bringing out horses for the guards.

"Three on back, one with the driver," Wen directed. "Let's go."

WEN almost enjoyed the outing; she had always liked being on the water. Northern Tilt spilled out onto the ocean, and although

her family had lived sixty miles inland, everyone in Tilt made
it to the seashore as often as possible. But she didn't think much
of Coren Bauler, a dissolute-looking man probably a year or
two shy of forty, who seemed to have no good reason to want to
befriend a score of people in their teens and twenties.

She also didn't think much of the way Jasper Paladar
passed virtually the entire length of the cruise chatting with
Demaray Coverroe as they strolled up and down the boat's
polished decks. The lady was animated but relaxed, gesturing
often and frequently breaking into laughter. She was enough
shorter than the tall lord that she had to tilt her head up to talk
to him; something about the posture seemed coquettish, Wen
thought. Demaray Coverroe was not precisely pretty, but her
fair hair was well-styled and her face was made up, and she
carried herself with an assurance that was attractive.

Jasper Paladar seemed to find it attractive, at any rate. He
smiled more often than he did when he was playing cruxanno
with Wen, and his replies to her sallies were spirited and made
with the aid of several forceful gestures. Wen found herself
wondering if Demaray Coverroe was as brilliant, warm, and
well-read as Jasper's own wife had been.

Or perhaps *all* the noble ladies of his acquaintance were
more likely to meet those standards than Wen could be
expected to.

Despite her distaste for the company, Wen was pleased
when everyone in the assembled group survived the outing
and made it back to shore. Even more pleased when the Fortunalt contingent was safely behind the hedge and the guards
left behind assured her that all was well. She washed her face
to rinse off the residue of sea air and ate a healthy dinner.

She hesitated before making her customary trip up to the
house—she had been with Jasper Paladar the whole day, after
all, so she had nothing to report—but she decided to check in
with him just in case he was expecting her. And indeed, she
found him in the library, brooding over the cruxanno board,
and ready with a smile when she entered the room.

"I wondered if you might be too weary to play for an hour,"
he said.

"You think I'm tired? After sitting on a ship's deck for
hours doing nothing? *Tired* is after I've spent all day trying to

prove I'm stronger than Orson even though he outweighs me by nearly a hundred pounds."

He looked interested. "And are you?"

She settled herself in the seat across from him. "Of course not. But I'm faster. And so far, I've killed him four times and he's only killed me once. So I'm better."

"Strategy over strength," he said.

"Training over natural advantage," she retorted.

He didn't bother to answer, and they were both silent awhile as they studied the board. Finally, after she made her first careful move, she said, "I didn't care much for that Bauler fellow."

"No, nor do I," Jasper answered, his eyes still on the board. "He's Thirteenth House, but he's never struck me as quite decent. The sort of man who would get his housemaid pregnant and then send her off without a copper."

She muffled a laugh at the perfect description. She repositioned a line of her soldiers and had the satisfaction of hearing Jasper suck in his breath in irritation. "He's Thirteenth House," she repeated. "Was he ever considered to be one of the new serlords?"

"Coren?" Jasper said in accents of revulsion. "Hardly."

"How were they chosen?"

He sat back in his chair and steepled his hands, as he often did when about to embark on a long explanation. "The marlords designated the properties they were willing to cede, and all their vassal lords convened and voted on who among them deserved to be elevated—a process that involved no end of brangling and bribery, as you can imagine! In Kianlever and Tilt, so I heard, it took months before a consensus could be reached, though in Brassenthwaite and Rappengrass, the voting was over in a day. But then, Kiernan Brassenthwaite and Ariane Rappengrass run exceedingly well-regulated Houses. In every case, the elected lords had to present themselves to Ghosenhall to be approved by the queen."

"Who picked the properties to give up in Fortunalt?" she asked.

"I did, but Serephette was instrumental in my decisions."

"It's hard to imagine anyone voting for Tover Banlish's father, if he's anything like his son," Wen commented.

Jasper grinned. "He's even less polished—but more honest,

I would say. Not much of a politician. Neil Holden is much the same. I confess I often think my own job would be easier if Demaray had won a title instead."

Wen gave him an inquiring look. "She wanted to be serlady?"

He made an equivocal motion with his hands. "Half the men and women of the Thirteenth House desired the new title and said so outright. Demaray was more restrained than most about showing how much she wanted it, but it was clear she liked the idea of being elected to a higher station."

Wen thought about the extravagant town house with the expensive marble facing and ostentatious gold doors. Had Demaray Coverroe built that house hoping the other lords would consider her grand enough to be voted in as serlady? If so, Wen didn't think much of Jasper's notions of restraint.

"I suppose she was very unhappy when she didn't win the votes," Wen said.

"She didn't appear to be," Jasper said. "Of course, nothing was settled for certain until the queen ratified the elections. Amalie had already rejected two other serlords—one from Tilt and one from Gisseltess, I believe. I thought Demaray might have another chance at a title if Amalie turned down Banlish or Holden. But, in fact, the queen approved them both without the slightest hesitation."

"Did *you* want to be serlord?" Wen asked curiously.

"Not even for an instant," he said. "What an impossible task! To serve as the first generation of a new stratum of society! Nothing could be so hard."

"You took on a chore that was almost as hard," Wen said. "Watching over Karryn."

"Well, but this is only a few years of turbulence and trouble," he said, smiling. "I'll be able to wash my hands of her once she's twenty-one. Not at all the same thing."

Privately, Wen thought he had accepted the more difficult assignment, but she let it go. "It's your move," she said. "Unless you're tired of the game."

He leaned forward again, eyes once more intent on the board. "Not at all," he said. "I've figured out exactly what I want to do."

Chapter
12

THE JOURNEY FROM GHOSENHALL TO GISSEL Plain required more effort than Senneth had spent on any trip, *ever*, and she had been traveling half her life. She had been certain Cammon wouldn't be able to leave the palace guarded by only nine Riders, but she hadn't expected them to bring nearly seventy additional soldiers with them, as well as various heralds, cooks, valets, and couriers.

"I thought we were a country in peacetime," she said to Tayse as she surveyed the small army of soldiers bivouacked outside the city, awaiting the signal to move out in the morning.

A brief smile lit his dark face and made his otherwise forbidding presence seem a little less intimidating. Of course, *she* was not intimidated. She had been married to the Rider for more than two years and fear had never been her predominant emotion when she was with him. "Even in peace, royalty cannot be lax," he said.

"We only brought twenty royal soldiers when we squired Amalie around three years ago!"

"And almost turned back a dozen times when danger

presented itself," he reminded her. "I'm not sure that Gisseltess is entirely tame. So we will go in well defended."

She sighed theatrically. "I used to dread going home to
Brassenthwaite because I didn't want to see my brothers,"
she said. "Now I have to dread Gisseltess for the same reason.
Because of a brother! Who would ever have expected such a
thing?"

His smile returned. "You, I believe, when you did everything in your power to make it possible for Nate to marry the
marlady Sabina."

"Well, you're the one who put her husband to death, so
you're really the one who enabled the wedding," she replied.

He bowed his head as if rebuked, but answered, "That was
not the reason I killed him."

No. Tayse had killed Halchon Gisseltess to save Senneth's
life. Everything else was just a side benefit. "And, anyway, I
don't hate Nate as much as I used to," Senneth said. "But I
can't think he'll be delighted to have to put up such a big reti-
nuc when we descend on him."

"He will have the privilege of welcoming the royal consort
to his House," Tayse said. "He should feel honored."

Senneth grinned. "I think Nate disapproves of Cammon.
He remembers him as the vagabond who dined at Brassen
Court and really didn't deserve to be sitting at the table."

"He didn't think a Rider should be sitting at the table,
either," Tayse said. "*Or* marrying his sister. If we spent too
much of our time worrying about what Nate likes, there would
be no progress at all in the world."

That made Senneth laugh, and she was still smiling when
she entered the palace to look for Cammon and tell him everything was ready for tomorrow's trip. She found him standing in his study, Amalie beside him.

"Majesties," Senneth said, bowing low.

Amalie offered her usual welcoming smile. The young
queen was barely twenty-one and absolutely radiant, with
strawberry-blond hair, fine white skin, and all the natural
glow of youth. Being queen agreed with her, Senneth thought.
Or maybe, after a reclusive adolescence spent hidden away
from the world, Amalie simply thrived on the constant bustle
and interaction that made up a queen's ordinary life.

"Is everything ready for tomorrow morning?" Amalie asked.

Senneth nodded. "We look like we're ready to invade the southern Houses but, yes, at last Tayse is satisfied that Cammon will be safe enough to travel. I was supposed to ask you if you have any lingering concerns about letting him leave the palace—"

Amalie waved her hands. "No, none at all. Go, go. Leave right now if you like."

Cammon was laughing. "She thinks once this trip is successful, Tayse and Romar will finally agree that it's safe for her to travel outside the city again," he explained. "It's not that she's so eager to get rid of *me*. She's really only interested in her own future amusement."

Senneth regarded them with a frown. "I have to say, I expected the two of you to be a little more weepy at the idea of being separated," she said. "Won't this be the first time you've been apart since you were married?"

"Since before that," Amalie said tranquilly. "We haven't been separated since he first came to the palace to guard me."

"Well, I would think you would be a little more upset."

"We'll be able to stay in touch," Cammon said. "I don't even know why Tayse is so insistent on bringing couriers."

Senneth nodded. Cammon had frequently and dramatically illustrated his ability to communicate with loved ones over impressive distances, and he and Amalie had been speaking to each other silently long before anyone else had been aware they were falling in love. For a reader, she supposed, that mental connection might be almost as sensuous and satisfying as the physical one.

"Perhaps Tayse will want to send news to other people besides the queen," she said. "Or perhaps he is merely planning how he will get news out if something happens to *you*. You know Tayse—he is always thinking of the worst thing that could possibly occur and then trying to figure out how to work around it."

"And that is why he is first among Riders," Amalie said. "I trust him to keep everyone I love absolutely safe."

DESPITE the size of the entourage, Senneth at first had been optimistic about how quickly they might be able to move. After all, she had seen Tayse hustle large groups of soldiers into battle and she knew he could run an efficient company. But she had, as was so often the case, reckoned without Cammon.

They were scarcely a half day's ride out of Ghosenhall before it became apparent that Cammon considered himself an ambassador of the crown and that his goal was to win the loyalty of every subject in Gillengaria. They stopped for a noon meal at a large inn in a prosperous town, and Cammon smiled warmly at the serving girls, the patrons, the young boys brave enough to creep close to his chair. When a little blond girl not more than five years old was permitted past the Riders and put her sticky fingers on his knee, Cammon bent down to look in her wide eyes.

"Are you the king?" she asked.

"Yes, I am," he replied, not bothering with his usual equivocation. "Would you like some of my apple pie?"

"Do you have any bread left?" she said.

"Here's a piece, but it's got gravy on it."

"I don't mind."

So he fed her his leftover food and kissed her on the cheek and sent the whole taproom into raptures. Senneth was just staring at him with her mouth open because she knew how quickly reports of this behavior would fly down the road ahead of them and what it meant for the rest of the journey.

Indeed, when they left the inn, the road was already lined with townsfolk wanting a glimpse of Cammon. He made the rest of the day's journey on horseback so he could wave and nod and otherwise acknowledge all the attention from the growing crowds. No matter how far they were from the nearest town, there were people sporadically camped along the side of the road, waiting to get a look at him. Young girls blew kisses; fathers hoisted their sons onto their shoulders and said, "That's the king," as Cammon rode by. Cammon didn't bother to try to correct any of them.

They had dinner quite late that first night since they arrived at their designated inn a good couple of hours later than expected. "Tell me," Senneth demanded. "Was this your real agenda? To go jogging through the countryside spreading goodwill? You didn't have to be so devious. You could have told us what you had planned."

"I did tell you," he said, cramming a piece of buttered

bread in his mouth. "I said I wanted to see if the southern regions would be safe for Amalie to visit."

"But I thought you meant—oh, never mind. You realize that it will take us twice as long to get to Gissel Plain if you stop to kiss every baby born since the new year."

"Well, we're not really in a hurry, are we?" he said.

"Apparently not."

She had thought the dilatory pace would irk Tayse, but, in fact, he seemed indifferent. He was the king's man, or the queen's; if they demanded of him that he crawl from one end of Gillengaria to the other, he would do so without complaint. "And I'm not exactly worried that someone will get too close to him and then try to rip his throat open," Tayse told her that night as they prepared to sleep. "If anyone can sense trouble coming, it's Cammon. So let him wave and smile and shake a few hands. If it serves Amalie, it serves us all."

In the following days, as they continued to inch their way through Gillengaria, Tayse did make use of those couriers, sending notices to innkeepers that their arrival plans might be altered by a day or two—or three or four. Cammon continued to ride, as the weather continued fairly agreeable. Senneth either rode beside him to keep him company, or slumbered in his unoccupied coach. She had learned to drowse in the saddle, but inside the coach was much more agreeable.

Since Cammon had expressed a preference for taking meals in the common dining areas—to give more people the chance to approach him—she and Tayse had determined that their only hope of private conversation lay in joining him in his room every morning before they set out. Two weeks into the trip, she and Tayse entered Cammon's room just as the valet was leaving.

"We're ready to move out when you are," Tayse said. "Have you had breakfast?"

Cammon waved toward an untouched tray sitting on a small table. "They brought food up, but I thought I'd eat downstairs before we go."

"The weather's threatening, so it would be best to start as quickly as possible," the Rider replied. "I would like to make our next stop before nightfall, which means we shouldn't dawdle too long on the road."

Cammon sighed and sat at the table, motioning for Senneth and Tayse to join him. "Everyone always tells me I *dawdle*," he said, transferring meat and eggs from a serving dish to a plate. "Lynnette must have complained about it every day when I lived with her."

"I wouldn't complain about it if I was really worried," Tayse said with a hint of a smile. "I'd just pack you up and move you out so fast your head would still be bobbing."

Senneth took the rest of the eggs and most of the bread. Tayse, she knew, had already eaten. He liked to get necessary tasks out of the way as soon as possible so he could concentrate on matters of real importance. "If it's going to rain, you should ride in the carriage," she said. "That'll speed up the trip some, too."

"Then you have to ride with me so I'm not bored," Cammon said.

"You mean, so I can use magic to keep the coach warm," she retorted.

"That, too." He chewed and swallowed and then said, as an absolute non sequitur, "I don't know, but I'll tell Sabina he asked."

Tayse and Senneth both stared at him. *"What?"* she demanded. "Are you talking to ghosts now? Or are you going mad?"

Wholly unembarrassed, he gestured toward the empty fourth chair at the table. "Amalie," he said. "She said her uncle Romar wanted to know if Nate and Sabina would be coming to Ghosenhall anytime soon. So I said I'd ask." He seemed to listen a moment and added, "Not that we're commanding them to visit. Amalie thinks Romar would just like to strengthen Gisseltess's relationship with the crown."

Senneth's eyes traveled from the unoccupied chair to Cammon to Tayse. Tayse was trying hard not to laugh, so instead he was scowling. "Amalie is here? In the room?" she said in a strangled voice.

Cammon nodded and said, "Well, sort of. I don't know if she can see and hear *you*. Oh. Yes, she can. She says, good morning, Senneth."

"Good morning, Majesty," Senneth replied a little helplessly.

Tayse was interested. "Coralinda Gisseltess could do the

same thing, couldn't she?" he asked. "Seem to project her soul across a little distance while her body was in another place?"

"Yes, but Coralinda was evil, and she's dead, and she couldn't send herself more than a mile—at least as far as we know!" Senneth exploded. She was still staring at Cammon. "How long has the queen had *this* particular trick?"

Amalie possessed a peculiar kind of magic, and they were still sorting out its ramifications. Amalie herself called it "thief magic," for she seemed to be able to steal or mimic the abilities of mystics around her. But Senneth had never heard of anyone except Coralinda Gisseltess being able to send a ghost of herself outside of her physical body to wander around investigating.

Cammon looked surprised. "Oh, ever since the war, I suppose. She's never been able to travel this far before, but we thought she might be able to track *me* down, and so far we've been right." He shrugged.

"Bright Mother burn me," Senneth muttered and shook her head. Well, Cammon's magic was peculiar as well. He could not only read emotions, he could amplify them; he could collect and magnify another mystic's power. It was not surprising that he could communicate with Amalie over great distances—Senneth would not have been astonished to learn they were conducting entire conversations as effortlessly as if they were standing together in the same room—but she hadn't expected Amalie to come strolling over the bridge of Cammon's power and settle down next to them at breakfast.

Tayse, as always, was already considering the practical applications. "This would be useful if, for instance, we need to strike some kind of deal with Sabina Gisseltess and want Amalie's approval before finalizing terms," he said. "She could actually be present in the room and listening to the discussion—even if no one else realizes she is there."

"Or believes it when we later claim she audited the whole conversation!" Senneth exclaimed.

Tayse was still working it out. "Still, it'd be unlikely that Cammon would be sent out to make treaties for the crown. Do you think, over time, Amalie could develop the same sense of communion with someone other than yourself? Another reader, perhaps? It might take experiment and practice, but perhaps she could learn to accompany an ambassador across Gillengaria when there is need for her presence at delicate negotiations."

"Probably," Cammon said. "So far I can't think of anything Amalie hasn't been able to do if she tries hard enough."

"Tell me again," Senneth said. "*Why* are people afraid of mystics?"

Tayse ignored her. "It would be even more beneficial if she could find a way to accompany an ambassador overseas. To Sovenfeld or Karyndein."

Cammon shook his head regretfully. "I don't think even Amalie's that strong," he said. "I've never heard of a mystic having any power outside of Gillengaria."

"Someone from Sovenfeld with his own kind of magic," Tayse suggested.

Cammon looked intrigued. "Now, that would be interesting—though I never heard of anyone in Sovenfeld having any magic, either," he said.

"Maybe we'll have to start paying attention to what kind of magic exists outside our borders," Tayse said.

Cammon seemed to listen a moment and then smiled. "Amalie says she'll ask pointed questions next time anyone from overseas comes calling," he reported. "She likes the idea of a magical ambassador. Maybe we'll find one soon."

AFTER that, Senneth thought she might be excused if she looked a little warily around the inside of the coach before she climbed in beside Cammon. "Is she here, too?" she asked.

"Who? Amalie? Don't be ridiculous," he replied as the driver sent the vehicle smoothly into motion.

"How is that a ridiculous question? The whole situation is preposterous."

"When she's talking to me, she can't pay attention to what's happening back in Ghosenhall," he explained. "She says it's like being in a trance. So we don't do it very long any one day."

Now Senneth was alarmed. "I hope no one walks in on her while she's staring sightlessly at the wall. They'll think she's having a lunatic fit."

"She keeps her maid in the room to watch over her and a Rider at the door," Cammon reassured her. "We're really not as careless as you think."

"Well, you've always seemed careless to *me*," she said, her voice very grouchy.

He laughed. "Oh, and you're so cautious?"

"I'm less valuable."

"I doubt that anyone who knows you would agree."

As Tayse had predicted, the weather turned nasty about an hour after they set out, and the coach was pelted with freezing rain for most of the rest of the day. Senneth had regained enough of her own magic to keep the carriage comfortably warm, though she felt sorry for the horsemen enduring the full brunt of the ice. There had been a day she would have had enough fire in her veins to move from soldier to soldier, laying her hands upon theirs and infusing them with the heat from her own body. Even now, if they had to pull off the road and make a hasty camp, she would be able to start a fire in this dismal weather, beat back the cold in a radius large enough to circle the entire troop. But it would take most of her strength and leave her with a bruising headache. She would do it if the situation were dire—but Tayse, she knew, would tell her that soldiers trained for bad weather, and she should not concern herself at all for their comfort.

"It'll be good to be inside tonight," she observed after a long silence.

Cammon yawned and seemed to shake himself awake. "It will," he agreed. "And good to see Justin again."

"Justin's meeting us today?" she said with a great deal of pleasure. "Does Tayse know?"

"I suppose so, since I had to ask him the name of the inn we're staying at. In fact, I think Justin's there already."

Indeed, when the royal procession pulled up at a modest establishment in a fairly small town, Justin was waiting for them in the doorway. Senneth supposed that if it hadn't been sleeting, he would have cantered on up the road to meet them, since Justin didn't have much patience for sitting still. She didn't even wait for Cammon to climb down from the coach first, but jumped out and rushed forward to throw her arms around the burly Rider. His answering hug almost broke her ribs.

"Justin! It's so good to see you!" she cried. He'd been gone about six weeks, and she had missed him dreadfully. "How was your visit to the Lirrens?"

He laughed and shook back his sandy hair, then clapped Cammon hard on the shoulder. Justin was always properly respectful to Amalie, but he couldn't stop treating Cammon like a little brother. "Full of lots of challenges and mock battles, as always," he said. "I swear, if I didn't lock and barricade the door, Torrin would creep in at night and see if he could take me by surprise when I was sleeping."

Torrin was Justin's brother-in-law, a wily and aggressive fighter whose greatest ambition was to defeat Justin at swordplay. "Did you duel with him?" Cammon asked, ducking inside out of the rain.

"I did."

"And did he ever beat you?"

"He did not."

"In other words, a successful visit for you," Senneth said.

Justin laughed. "Torrin will *never* beat me. Sometimes I let him get close enough to keep him from getting discouraged."

Senneth gestured vaguely toward the door. "It'll take Tayse a few minutes to get everyone settled. Have you asked for a private dining room? Cammon has been winning the hearts of the fawning multitudes by sitting in the taprooms and eating with the masses, but for tonight, at least, it would be nice to talk in privacy and hear your travel stories. If that suits you, Your Majesty," she added.

Cammon grinned. "Just for tonight, I suppose."

Justin was leading the way down a rather narrow hallway to a small room with heavy timbers and brightly painted whitewash. "I've already ordered the pitchers," he said. "Figured we'd want to talk."

By the time a very wet Tayse maneuvered his big body into the room, they were on their second set of pitchers and had started in on the food besides. Tayse and Justin, of course, did not exchange any effusive greetings, just nodded at each other and looked pleased. "Good trip?" Tayse asked, dropping to a chair.

"No troubles," Justin said.

Senneth scooted her own chair closer to Tayse's. She could

feel the cold emanating from his clothes and skin. "Give me your hand," she said, and folded both of her warm ones over his broad, icy fingers. "*You*, at least, don't have to be chilly as long as I am nearby."

Normally Tayse would shrug off any suggestion that he needed to look to his own comfort, but all this time later he still considered it a privilege to touch the hand of this particular serramarra. He laid his palm against hers and accepted the grace of her magic with a private smile. They held hands under the table and turned their attention back to their friends.

"You don't seem to have made much progress," Justin said. "I thought you'd be a hundred miles farther along by now."

"Cammon's taking the opportunity to spread goodwill, so our journey has been very slow," Senneth replied. "So tell us about your trip! Was everyone excited to see Ceribel?"

Ceribel was Justin's daughter, a little more than a year old. Her eyes and hair were as dark as her mother's, but she didn't display much of Ellynor's sweet tranquillity. No, she had Justin's energy, curiosity, will, and temper. Senneth was absolutely positive the girl would grow up to be a Rider.

Justin laughed and helped himself to more food. "Well, yes, of course they were, but I'm not sure they got what they expected," he said. "Last time we visited, Ceribel was only two months old, and she wasn't walking around smacking people and trying to grab everything for herself. The Lirren girls are all very meek, you know. But Ceribel . . ." He shook his head. "She's a handful. Ellynor can handle her, but I could tell before I left she was starting to resent her mother's comments about how we were raising her."

Senneth started to say something, glanced around the room, and then laughed. "I thought I would murmur, 'I believe all young couples find that their parents disapprove of their child-rearing methods,' or something like that, but then I realized not one of us knows a damn thing about what a normal family is like. So I'm afraid none of us can give you any advice."

Justin grinned. "Don't need any advice. Ceribel is perfect."

Tayse also looked amused. "Have you shared with Ellynor's parents the fact that you're teaching her how to hold a dagger?"

"Justin!" Senneth exclaimed.

"It's wooden. It's fine," Justin reassured her. "I wasn't going to tell them, but then she was sitting on Torrin's lap and she tried to pull his knife from his belt, so—I had to explain a little. I thought he'd pitch a fit, because Torrin is so fierce about Lirren rules, but I think the idea tickled him. I figure by the time I go back to get Ellynor, he'll have taught Ceribel how to play hoop toss—and probably win it, too."

As hoop toss involved catching metal rings on the tip of a sword, Senneth rather doubted this, but she was glad to hear the warlike Torrin seemed to be so fond of his niece. "Has her family accepted the idea that Ceribel will be raised outside of the Lirrenlands?" she asked.

Justin drained his glass and poured another one. "I don't think so, no. I could see Ellynor's mother and sisters sort of crowding her sometimes, talking very seriously. I'm sure they were trying to make the point that no Lirren girl should be raised across the Lireth Mountains. And no doubt Torrin and Hayden will add their voices as well. But I'm not too worried. Ellynor is pretty stubborn."

"Did you see Valri while you were there?" Cammon asked. He had been very close to Amalie's stepmother, who had returned to the Lirrens shortly after the war. She had not been back across the mountains to visit, but Senneth was fairly sure both Amalie and Cammon kept in touch with her regularly— Amalie by letter, and Cammon by more mystical means.

"She was there for a few days when we first arrived," Justin said. "And Arrol with her. I swear I almost didn't recognize her at first. Her hair was long—all the way down her back and covered with those strange designs—and you wouldn't believe how it changes her face. Also, she just looked different. Happy. Relaxed, maybe. She never looked that way when she was living at the palace."

Senneth sighed. "Well, I don't think any of us were looking too relaxed those last few months in Ghosenhall before the war," she said. "Valri might not recognize *us*, either."

"I don't think *I* look any different," Cammon said.

Justin laughed and scrubbed his hand through Cammon's hair, which hardly had the effect of making it look any worse than it had a moment before. "You're all cleaned up," Justin said. "Dressed in fine clothes. She'd never know who you were."

"At least I *own* decent clothes these days," Cammon said. "Unlike some people."

Justin glanced down at his muddy trousers. "I've been traveling."

"So have we," Cammon replied.

"When did you tell Ellynor you'd be back?" Senneth asked.

"Thought it would be a couple of months, but I wasn't sure how long this mission would take," Justin said, a note of inquiry in his voice. "In fact, I'm not really clear on what we're doing or where we're going, just that Cammon indicated I should join you."

"We're making a circuit of the southern Houses," Senneth said. "Gisseltess then Rappengrass then Fortunalt. I would have thought we could complete that in way under two months, but given Cammon's insistence on personally speaking to every single human being who resides within a twenty-mile radius of our route, I am beginning to think a year won't be long enough."

"And we will need to spend some time at each House, so that adds to our days," Tayse put in. "But if you feel a pressing need to return to the Lirrens, we are defended well enough. Seventy soldiers in our train, and seven other Riders."

"Who else?" Justin asked, sounding pleased. After Tayse listed the names, he said, "I'll go out and see them when we're done here. But I'm still not sure I understand the basic purpose of the trip."

At times, Senneth wasn't sure she understood it, either. She could not rid herself of a feeling that Cammon had motives that he had not shared. What kept her from being truly uneasy was the knowledge that Cammon's entire bent was for harmony and unity. If he had an unstated goal, it would be a peaceful one.

"Amalie wants to travel throughout the realm," Cammon said. "I know there's been some restlessness in the southern regions. I thought if I made the journey first I would be able to sense how safe she would be."

Justin grinned at Tayse. "Guess we couldn't keep Amalie penned up in Ghosenhall forever," he said. "*That'll* be an interesting trip."

"This one might be interesting, too," Senneth said, watching Cammon's innocent face. "You just never know."

Chapter
13

WEN HAD A LITTLE EXPERIENCE WITH MYSTICS, since she had fought alongside a handful of them during the war and even trained with one or two. Senneth Brassenthwaite had been a decent fighter intent on honing her swordsmanship without resorting to magic to win an encounter, but Cammon had been utterly incapable of going into battle without drawing upon his ability to read his opponent. That mental sensitivity had given him insurmountable defensive skills—it was literally impossible to land a blow on him. It had scarcely mattered that he had no offensive skills to speak of.

Even so, Cammon had killed three men who had tried to assassinate Amalie, or so Wen had heard. That had been the very day Baryn himself had died.

Wen shook her head and again concentrated on the task at hand—which, this morning, was figuring out how to incorporate a mystic's skills into the strategy of the battlefield. She had paired Moss with Orson, because if Moss could disrupt Orson's attack, she could outfight anybody. Well, except a Rider.

So far, it hadn't helped much to have Moss try to jerk Orson's sword from his grasp. It startled him, but he just leapt over it and assaulted Moss with his bare hands. And while she was having the life choked out of her, she couldn't focus on pelting him with small stones and other pieces of debris.

"I think you have to be more aggressive in your own attack," Wen said thoughtfully once the combatants broke apart. Moss was panting, but Orson seemed completely unaffected by the recent struggle. "Don't let him get close enough to do any damage."

"That'll be hard to manage in the heat of battle," Orson observed. "She needs to learn tricks that will help her after she's already engaged."

"We'll get to those, too," Wen said. "I want to see what advantages she can summon up most easily."

"I can drop a rock on his head," Moss said between gasps. "Minute I see him coming toward me."

"How much mass can you move all at once?" Wen asked. "How much weight?"

Moss shrugged. "I don't know. I've been practicing with different sizes of boulders. Some seem pretty heavy. But I have to concentrate to lift them and move them where I want them to go."

"What if you didn't have to *lift* it?" Wen said. "What if you just had to push it?"

Orson saw where she was going and gave her his wicked grin. "Well, let's try that," he said, dropping into a runner's crouch. "You try to shove me back."

Without any more warning than that, he sprang for Moss across five feet of trampled earth. She gave a little shriek and flung her hands up—and Orson actually seemed to *thump* against blank air before he skidded backward and landed on his rear. He was just stunned enough to sit there silently for a moment, and then he started laughing.

"*That's* the idea," he said, picking himself up. "That's exactly what you want to do."

Moss looked at her hands, a little bemused. "I never tried that before. I didn't know I could do that."

"That's what fighting for your life will teach you," Orson said. "The limits of your physical strength."

Wen was pleased. "Yes, Moss, that was very good. We'll need to keep practicing that so it becomes automatic every time you're threatened."

"Ought to see how many people she can shove aside at once," Orson suggested. "A whole line of fighters? A man on horseback? Now, that would be worth something."

"First let's see if I can knock *you* over again," Moss said. She had pushed her pale hair behind her ears and her strange eyes were bright in her broad, plain face. Wen thought she had never seen Moss look so triumphant—even though this was a relatively minor victory. Or maybe not, in Moss's life, which remained largely unknown to Wen. Such a small success might be the first one the other woman had ever had.

The three of them worked on Moss's skills for the rest of the afternoon, Wen taking her turn running at Moss in case the act of repulsion was affected by an opponent with a different center of gravity. Moss could knock Wen over with more ease, but Wen was faster to recover and managed to skid forward on her knees and bring Moss down with her.

"You're completely dead," Wen said, miming a slash to Moss's throat.

"I love to see women fight," Orson said.

Wen met Moss's eyes and shared a thought. Wen stood up and brushed herself off as Orson strolled forward to offer Moss a hand up. Instead, he got knocked flat on his back, and Wen pounced on him, pummeling his chest and shoulders. He yelped and bucked her off, but by this time Moss had used her magic to snatch up a rock about the size of her own head, and she dropped this with a satisfying *splat* right in the middle of his stomach. He groaned and rolled to his side, not making any attempt to rise.

"I love to see women fight, too," Wen said. "They're so much smarter than men."

Then she heard a sound that she had come to think did not exist. Moss's laughter.

IT turned out that Jasper Paladar had been thinking about the uses of magic, too, which Wen discovered that night as she joined him in the library. They were almost two weeks

into the cruxanno game, and she was tired of it; she had every
hope it would be finished soon.

On the other hand, the long, slow game had practically
invited the two of them to make idle conversation during the
hours they played, and Wen had come to really look forward to
the discussions. It was hard to predict what topic would catch
Lord Jasper's fancy from day to day. Sometimes he might ask
her prosaic questions about the guards and their progress;
other times he might want her opinion on a piece of news he
had learned from Ghosenhall. Just as often, he would launch
into a tale about some marlord dead these hundred years—
stories that Wen would have expected to find excruciatingly
dull, but which, in fact, could hold her interest long after they
had given up on cruxanno for the night.

She liked Jasper Paladar. She didn't understand why,
precisely. He was not like anyone she had ever met and he
didn't have any of the qualities she was used to requiring
in her friends. Merely, he was interesting to her. She found
him baffling half of the time and intriguing all of the time.
She couldn't imagine what he found in her own personality
to appeal to him, but he never seemed bored in her presence,
never seemed disappointed by her replies. Perhaps he merely
possessed the grace of his elevated social station and knew
how to put any other individual at ease, but she thought it was
more than that. He liked her, too.

At times, the knowledge filled her with a low-grade level
of warm satisfaction.

At other times, it made her want to abandon her few possessions and disappear without notice in the middle of the
night.

Her month of contracted service was due to be up in seven
days. She had wondered if he would remember, but it had
been the very first thing he said when she had joined him in
the library the night before.

"I'm not much of a training master, but even I can tell that
the guard you've assembled isn't in fighting shape," he had
greeted her. "One more week won't be nearly enough time to
train them. Will you stay another month?"

"I think that would be best," she'd said.

They had not referred to the contract again. Wen had lain

awake in a panic half the night, hearing the breathing of her fellow guards all around her in the dark barracks. Surrounded again by friends; if she lingered long enough, they would begin to feel like family. She could not afford that; she could not surrender herself to the twin embraces of trust and affection.

But it was just for another five weeks. She could stay that long, then cut herself free.

She tried to forget that every night before she entered the library to see Jasper Paladar she first had to tame both her wisp of excitement and her jangle of fear.

Tonight, fresh from trying out Moss's magic on the battlefield, she stepped into the room to find the other House mystic displaying his abilities for Lord Jasper. Bryce was perched in a chair before the fire, facing away from Jasper, who sat in his customary spot beside the cruxanno table.

"It's in your left hand," Bryce said.

"Correct again," Jasper replied. He sounded delighted.

Wen closed the door and regarded them with a smile. "What are you two up to?"

Bryce pushed his red hair away from his face. "I'm telling Lord Jasper where he's hiding a gold coin. He said he'll give it to me if I can guess right more times than not. But it's not *guessing*," he added. "So it doesn't seem fair."

"In fact, he hasn't been wrong once," Jasper said. "It's really quite remarkable."

Wen held her hand out. "Let me try," she said, and Jasper tossed her the coin. "Turn around and look at Lord Jasper," she told Bryce. When he obediently redirected his gaze, she tossed the heavy piece of gold from palm to palm a few times before closing the fingers of her right hand over it. "Now. Which hand?"

"Right one," Bryce said without hesitation.

"Correct." She repeated the process. "Now?"

"Right hand."

"Now?"

"Left hand."

She popped the coin in her mouth and looked at Jasper, who obligingly said, "Now where is it?"

"In her mouth," Bryce exclaimed. "Don't swallow my gold! If she does, you have to give me another piece."

Wen spit out the coin as Jasper laughed. "I don't think Willa is careless enough to swallow money, but if she is, I'm good for it," Jasper said. "That was a very impressive demonstration, Bryce! Do you think you can do so well tomorrow night?"

"I don't see why not."

"What's happening tomorrow night?" Wen asked.

"Zellin Banlish is paying us a visit. Don't you remember?"

"About time," she muttered.

Jasper smiled. "Give Bryce his money and let him get back to the kitchen. I understand there's a piece of berry pie awaiting him."

Once the boy was gone, Wen settled at the cruxanno table and studied Lord Jasper. "Why do you want Bryce to show off parlor tricks to the serlord?"

"I think such a demonstration will—" Jasper searched for a phrase. "Act as a metaphor."

Wen wasn't entirely sure what a metaphor was, but she said, "I think a better one would be if I held a sword to his throat."

He laughed. "Strategy, remember? Not strength."

She shrugged. "When does he arrive?"

"In time for dinner. Karryn has expressed a desire to be excused from his presence—quite understandably. She will spend the evening with Lindy Coverroe, but Demaray will join us for dinner, as will Serephette, of course. Afterward, the serlord and I will engage in our game of cruxanno, which he tells me he is quite looking forward to."

Wen was thinking rapidly. Four guards to accompany Karryn to the Coverroe house, two to watch over the dinner and then oversee the game, while two more were inside the house within easy call. Four or six more to roam the House grounds while company was present . . . The day shift would have to be light, then, so that the majority of personnel could be on hand for the evening's responsibilities.

"And you would rather have me here with you than at the Coverroes' house with Karryn?" she asked.

"Yes," he said. "I don't think any of us are in danger from Zellin, but I would like your opinion on how matters unfold here with the serlord. Which means you must be here to observe that unfolding."

That was high praise from an employer to his captain. She kept her face grave and nodded. "I'll send Orson and Moss with Karryn. And a couple of others."

"Moss—she's the mystic, right?" At her nod, he said, "Perhaps you should keep her here to join the watch with you."

Wen nodded again, a little baffled. That meant she would need two particularly seasoned warriors to be stationed inside the house—Eggles certainly should be one of them—since Moss's fighting skills still were scarcely average. "Why?" she asked.

"In case it seems expedient to offer another metaphor."

She regarded him. "For someone who was not very impressed at the idea of hiring mystics—"

"Indeed. I've changed my mind. I am learning how to brandish a weapon."

Which was so funny she couldn't help bursting into laughter. He beamed right back at her and then gestured at the game board. "Come, now. Can we finish tonight? Or I'll have to hunt up a fresh set for my encounter tomorrow."

Wen sobered and bent over the board. "Certainly we can. I think it's my turn." She shoved all her remaining armies into the northeastern quadrant, leaving the crown piece quite solitary on the southern border. "Your move."

He stared down in dismay. "But—I can't counter that."

"I know."

"That's not how you play cruxanno! You *never* leave your own territories unprotected! What if I could march my army there and slaughter your king before you could breach my defenses?"

"I don't think you can, but go ahead and try. One way or the other, we'll be done tonight."

He raised his eyes to study her. "I would never have imagined you could be so reckless."

She met his gaze steadily. "It's only a game."

"If the stakes were real, would you make such a gamble?"

"It would depend on what would be lost if I failed."

He took a deep breath. "I don't know that I've ever risked everything, leaving nothing behind as a safeguard."

She stopped the words that rose to her lips; she would not ask them of anyone, certainly not a nobleman, and her employer. *Even when you married? Even when you risked your heart?* She had no experience to compare to that. She had taken her own lovers carelessly, knowing each affair would last a short time. She had yearned after Justin with a hopeless hunger, but even that relationship hadn't demanded any commitment from her since Justin had been oblivious to her emotions. Except for its ongoing misery, it had been very easy, in fact, requiring no time, no sacrifice, no hard choices.

The one thing she would have thrown away everything else to protect was the life of the king. She would have given her own life for his. And still, he was dead and she was not, so who was she to question the stakes another man might find too high?

"I suppose most of us haven't had to make such a decision," she said at last. "But I don't care about cruxanno, so I don't care if I win or lose."

"Well, I'm not giving up without a fight," he said, regaining some of his focus. "Let's see, I shall—hmm." He fell silent, studying the board.

He made a few excellent moves as the night wore on, but it was no use. Wen's forces had overwhelmed his and he was forced to surrender. "We should have made a bet," Wen said.

"Next time, maybe."

"Aren't you tired of cruxanno? You will be after tomorrow night, won't you? I hope so."

He was amused. "Very well, we'll set the board aside. You can teach me a card game or we'll find another diversion."

I don't have to come by every night if you're growing tired of me, she thought. But she didn't say it. She didn't want him to revoke the privilege. She didn't want to give up their quiet exchanges and laughing exclamations of surprise.

It was only for another five weeks. It would not hurt anybody if she enjoyed his company that much longer.

SERLORD Zellin Banlish arrived with a flourish, in a fancy carriage drawn by six horses, and accompanied by four guards of his own. The trip between his Manor and Fortune was long enough that he would be spending the night, and so would his guards. Wen courteously offered them sleeping space in the barracks, which they instantly accepted.

So they did not plan to loom beside their master inside the House while he visited, dedicating themselves to his protection. That simplified her own task, though it made her think less of Zellin Banlish.

Though she had not thought well of him before.

During dinner, she and Moss stood at opposite ends of the dining room, wearing their sashes splashed with Fortunalt pearls and keeping their faces absolutely impassive. Serephette, who apparently had not been informed that they would be present, gave them each one long, expressive look and then ignored them for the entire evening. Zellin Banlish didn't even seem to notice that they were in the room. He was a middle-aged but relatively trim man of medium build, thinning brown hair, and eyes as blue as his son's. His face was round and might have seemed pleasant if he ever smiled, Wen thought, but on the whole he had a dour aspect that gave him an unfriendly cast. If asked to make a quick judgment of him, Wen would have written him off as neither observant nor particularly keen-witted.

Demaray Coverroe was both, however, and throughout the meal, her gaze occasionally flickered between the two guards until she returned her attention to her tablemates. It would have been a much quieter meal had she not been present, Wen thought, for Serephette never bothered to make much effort and the men were more interested in their food. Demaray's lively conversation kept the whole table talking during the first three courses, as she drew out everyone in turn. The serlord talked with some enthusiasm about his latest racehorse, while Serephette was induced to discuss a new fashion that she particularly admired. Demaray even asked Jasper about the reprinting of one of his books, something that would never have occurred to Wen to inquire after. She had to admit the lady was a polished hostess, even while in someone else's house.

When the meal was half over, Demaray sent a glance once again between Wen and Moss. "What is this new affectation, Jasper?" she asked in a teasing voice. "I *almost* understand when you insist on guards accompanying Karryn outside the walls, but here inside the house? Following *you*? Or are they guarding Serephette? Naturally I consider you both precious, but surely this is taking caution too far."

Jasper touched his napkin to his lips. "We have not told this story publicly, because Karryn begged us not to, but five weeks ago an attempt was made to abduct her," he said.

Wen was curious to see Demaray's reaction, for she had assumed Karryn had shared the story with her best friend, and Lindy with her mother. But the serlady looked sincerely horrified. "No! Abduct Karryn? Who? How did you get her back?"

"A good-hearted stranger assisted Karryn in her escape," Jasper said. "As for the man who took her— Let us say I think he believes he is safe from justice, but I am determined to let him know that is not true."

Zellin Banlish looked up from his food for almost the first time since he'd stopped talking horseflesh. "She would recognize this man if she saw him again?"

Jasper laid his napkin down. "Recognize him? She is acquainted with him," he said softly. "She has danced with him in his own home."

Demaray laid her hands flat on the table and made as if to rise. She was pale. "Jasper! But who could have been so villainous! And so bold?"

"I prefer not to name him at the moment," Jasper said. "But I will, when I have the proper evidence."

"What kind of proof could you gather now?" Banlish asked skeptically. "More than a month past the event?"

Demaray gave him a smoldering look. "I would think Karryn's word would be proof enough."

Banlish shrugged. "A girl that age might say anything. Maybe she thought to run away from home with a handsome young lord—I assume this man was noble?"

"Indeed."

"And when the affair didn't go as she expected, and her guardian came looking for her— Well, she wouldn't be the only young woman to make up a story about force when she had been intending seduction all along."

Demaray turned her back on him as if unwilling to consider such a possibility with her own daughter. "But, Jasper, was she harmed—in any way at all?" she asked.

Her delicate emphasis on these last words made it clear what she meant. Serephette spoke up for the first time. "No," she said coldly. "Her virtue is still intact, though a marlady can marry where she likes even if she is not virginal. You need have no worries on that score, Demaray."

Now Demaray was all fluttery apology, with a touch of reproof. "Serephette! That's not what I meant! I was worried about her well-being, not her marriage prospects."

"As it happens, her abductor had marriage on his mind, too," Jasper said. "It seems he had a hankering for a marlord's title and thought that a—forceful—proposal might win him his desired bride."

"That's outrageous!" Demaray exclaimed.

But Banlish was nodding. "It wouldn't be the first time a marlady had found her husband that way."

Demaray glared at him. "Which certainly does not make it acceptable now!"

"I suppose you would have to ask Jasper for a more exact date, but I don't think marrying into the Twelve Houses by force has been a common practice for at least a hundred years," Serephette said in a chilly voice. "And that it was tried on my daughter is abominable. As you might guess, I disagree strongly with Jasper on the notion of keeping Karryn's abductor a secret. If it were up to me, I would publish his name to every House and Manor across Gillengaria so that he would find it impossible to find *any* bride, let alone a serramarra."

"Then tell us," Demaray urged. "Who took Karryn against her will?"

Serephette's face took on that brooding, haunted look that was her most common expression—as if she was reviewing matters too dreadful to speak of, too powerful to forget. "She won't tell me. She does whatever Jasper says."

Zellin Banlish appeared to be slightly amused. "Seems like Jasper Paladar wields a lot of power here," he said. "Thirteenth House lord making the rules for the marlady-to-be? That seems backward."

"Zellin!" Demaray exclaimed, and Serephette gave the serlord a frosty look. But Jasper just brushed his napkin to his lips again and smiled.

"Romar Brendyn was regent to Queen Amalie before she

took her crown," he said. "He's Twelfth House, of course, but no marlord himself. I cannot think the disparity between his rank and Amalie's was any greater than mine and Karryn's—and I would happily take him for my model."

Zellin shrugged and seemed to lose interest in anything except his food. Serephette came unceremoniously to her feet.

"If you'll excuse me, I've developed a severe headache," she said. "Please enjoy the rest of your dinner."

And without another word, she strode out the door. Demaray stared after her in dismay. "Jasper—should I leave as well?" she said. "How awkward!"

"Don't go on my account," Zellin said, around his food. "I couldn't care one way or the other if Serephette is in the room."

"Oh, finish the meal, at least," Jasper replied. "The dessert is especially good. I'm sure you'll like it."

Wen was not surprised when Demaray settled back into her chair. Her impression was that the lively little noblewoman was more entertained than embarrassed by the situation, for she seemed like the kind of person who delighted in a scandal, as long as it didn't reflect on her. She also, Wen thought, was the sort of woman who craved male attention and bloomed into true prettiness when she was the center of it. There wasn't much attention to hope for from Zellin Banlish, but Jasper directed all his conversation at her for the rest of the meal. Wen had to think that Demaray Coverroe didn't truly mind that Serephette had stalked from the table in such a fury.

Still, she could make no excuse to linger once the meal was properly over. "Do let Serephette know how much I enjoyed the evening," she said, as Jasper saw her to the door. "And tell her how sorry I am for her—headache."

"We'll expect Karryn back sometime in the morning," Jasper said. "And we'll expect to see you again soon."

The instant the door was shut behind her, he winked at Wen, hovering with Moss in the shadows near the stairwell. "And now for the only truly interesting part of the entire evening," he said. "Cruxanno."

Chapter
14

ONE OF THE FOOTMEN HAD ESCORTED THE SER-lord to the library, and Banlish was already sitting in what Wen thought of as *her* chair, doling out the crux-anno pieces. He didn't even seem to notice that Wen and Moss followed Jasper into the library and took up stations on either side of the door.

"This is a fine set," he said as Jasper took his usual seat. "Was it Rayson's?"

"My own," Jasper said. "I brought it with me when I arrived. I like familiar things around me, and beautiful things, and things with value. I haven't had much opportunity to play, however, so you are doing me a great kindness tonight."

Zellin gave a noncommittal grunt. "Do you play for stakes?" he asked.

"Always," Jasper replied.

Wen couldn't help glaring at the back of his head. He hadn't played for stakes with *her*, or she'd be a few coins richer by now.

Then Jasper added, "Though the stakes aren't always money."

Banlish grunted again. "What else can you bet?"

"It's not what you bet," Jasper said, "it's what you hazard."

Banlish looked up from the board to give Jasper one hard, irritable look. "You're as odd as Serephette Fortunalt when you talk like that."

"Serephette was formed by a torturous life," Jasper replied. "All of us are shaped to some extent by forces outside our control. And to some extent by our passions—the ones we govern and the ones we allow to run unchecked."

Zellin looked even more irritated. "Do you always talk this much nonsense?" he demanded.

Jasper gave a light laugh. "Pretty much."

The serlord made his first move, a fairly standard one, from what Wen could determine. "Well, I don't mind the talking, because it won't distract me from the play, but choose a subject that's a little more coherent."

"I defer to you. Name a topic."

Zellin laughed shortly. "Demaray Coverroe."

"A most agreeable lady."

"Pretty enough," Zellin agreed, "but flighty. How long has her husband been dead now? She needs a man to settle her down."

"Do you think so? I've always thought she handled her affairs with a great deal of aplomb," Jasper replied. He was studying the board, taking time to consider his own move.

Zellin snorted. "Beggared herself to build that house, or very nearly. Though it's a magnificent place, I'll give her that. I borrowed her architect when I wanted to make improvements to Banlish Manor."

Jasper Paladar did not answer until he had shifted a few of his swords and soldiers into position. "Did you make those improvements before or after you had been elected to the serlordship?" he asked.

"After," Zellen said with a snort. "I did not consider my title secure till I had gone to the royal city and presented myself to the queen." He shrugged. "Though it wasn't Amalie who actually passed judgment on any of the new serlords. It was Cammon."

Jasper looked up, surprise on his face. The expression was perfectly presented, but Wen had the feeling that he was pretending—that this was something he had known all along.

She grew even more interested in the conversation. "The royal consort?" he repeated. "What do you mean?"

Zellin made a rude noise. "You know what they say about him. He's a mystic."

"A reader. Yes."

"Well, every serlord or serlady chosen by their fellows had to make their way to Ghosenhall to be approved by royalty. Everyone thought it was a formality, of course. But in we went, one by one, and made our bows. Amalie just sat there, looking like a child—I swear she could pass for fifteen. Cammon asked a few questions, but Amalie didn't say a word."

"What did he ask?"

Zellin gestured impatiently with the hand hovering over the cruxanno board. "Did you fight in the war, did you support Rayson Fortunalt, are your estates in good order, are you loyal to the queen? What a waste of time. I kept wishing they would just approve me and let me leave. There was so much to do back in Fortunalt. Gods and goddesses, the whole region was in disarray! Households bankrupted, hundreds of lives lost, brigands loose on the roadways. I was impatient to be home and beginning the real work of restoration, not answering the aimless questions of upstart royalty. But there were Riders in the room, ready to pounce at the smallest insult, and so I showed nothing but respect."

This extraordinary speech left Wen first angry, and then fighting hard to hold back mirth. Clearly Zellin Banlish had never been witness to Cammon's astonishing ability to read the souls of the people before him. And clearly he had no understanding of what secrets in his own heart had made Cammon determine that he was worthy of the serlordship. Cammon would not have been dismayed at all to learn that Zellin Banlish was eager to get home and begin rebuilding—he would have been pleased to know that Banlish felt such great dedication and devotion to his land. Zellin Banlish was bullheaded and unpleasant, but he possessed traits that would serve a serlord well, and those were the only traits Cammon had cared about.

"What did you say when he asked if you had supported Rayson in the war?" Jasper asked curiously.

"The truth! That I thought the man mad. I wouldn't give

him a copper except what he managed to tax from all of his vassals, and I rode my estates every day, forbidding the young men to sign up as soldiers. Half of them did it, anyway, of course, but I think I kept a few out of his army."

"Cammon was probably very glad to hear that."

Zellin shrugged. He had finally decided where to station the bulk of his army, and he was busy arranging shields. "He was such a strange and wide-eyed thing. I'm not sure he really understood a word I said."

"If the stories they tell of him are true, he understood everything you said and did not say," Jasper replied. "It's said he reads minds."

"And credulous fools believe it," was Zellin's sneering answer.

"You don't fear mystics?" Jasper asked.

"Don't fear them, don't hate them, don't think about them one way or the other," Zellin said. "A man who can read minds—ridiculous! They say that Senneth Brassenthwaite can start a fire with her bare hands, and Kirra Danalustrous can take any shape she chooses, but *I've* never seen anyone do such things. I think all this outcry over mystics is nothing more than people indulging themselves with a little hysteria."

Wen slanted a look over at Moss, whose face bore the faintest smile.

"Well, it's true we haven't had many mystics to marvel over here in Fortunalt, since Rayson drove them all off," Jasper replied. He was lining up his own shields, though Wen couldn't tell much of his strategy from this angle. "Still, I believe their powers are sometimes great—and that Cammon's are remarkable." His arrangements done, he sat back in his chair. "Which leads me to wonder what he read in the Tilt and Gisseltess candidates that made him refuse to ratify their appointments."

Zellin shrugged. "Not my land. Not my business."

Jasper steepled his hands. "I wonder if it *is* your business—if perhaps he meant to send a message to the new serlords that the crown was going to stay involved in the lives of the nobility. Perhaps those rejected lords were sacrificed to the crown's desire to show it was retaining its power."

Zellin was concentrating on the board. "I read the charter.

All of us did—the new serlords, I mean. The titles are irrevocable. Even if Amalie doesn't like what we do, she can't take away our lands now."

"No, you misunderstand," Jasper said, very gently. "The rules for governance are based on the charter for the marlords."

"Yes, of course," Zellin said impatiently. "The queen can't take away their status, either."

"She can't abolish the title," Jasper corrected. "But she can remove the man."

Now Zellin looked up from the board. "What are you talking about?"

Jasper was still leaning back at ease in his chair, his fingertips still placed precisely together in the way that meant he was prepared to deliver a lecture. "If Malcolm Danalustrous were suddenly to go on a rampage and start murdering tenants and torturing children, you can believe that Amalie would send her Riders to Danan Hall immediately to take him into custody. She would strip the title of marlord from him—she is within her legal rights to do so. But she cannot vacate the title itself, and she cannot dictate the next heir. Malcolm can be seized, but not the House. His daughter would instantly take the title. And if his daughter was unfit, the next heir would be found, and so on down the line until there was one the crown deemed suitable."

Zellin stared. "That's not true."

"I assure you, it is."

"Then why didn't Baryn strip Rayson and Halchon of their marlordships before they took Fortunalt and Gisseltess into battle against him?"

"I never had the honor of a conversation with Baryn, but I have to assume that by the time he realized they were planning such an assault, they already had too much power for him to be able to enforce such mandates."

"So you're telling me I'm not secure in my new title," Zellin said with a great deal of dissatisfaction. "Then what did the Thirteenth House lords fight for? Why all these summits and all these petitions to the crown if we are not going to be able to command our own destinies after all?"

"But you are," Jasper said. "As long as you mind your land

and behave with honor, you are in no danger of losing your Manor."

"I don't like it," Zellin said, still displeased. "I'll feel like I'm being watched and judged every moment."

"All of us are watched and judged every moment," Jasper said lightly. "Titled or not, we have to earn—and continue to earn—our place in the world on a daily basis."

Zellin made an indeterminate sound to indicate his impatience with such fancy reasoning. "Stupid talk," he said. "Make your play."

Jasper sat forward, quickly moved a line of shields, and leaned back again. "I'm sorry you find my conversation tiresome," he said pleasantly. "I confess Karryn finds me bewildering as well."

Zellin was scowling; Wen guessed Jasper's game strategy had surprised him. "And I still don't understand why you've been installed at Fortune," he said, harking back to his observation over dinner. "Obviously Serephette isn't fit to be a guardian for a serramarra, but you—" He shook his head.

Jasper said, very softly, "I was chosen by the royal consort."

That made Zellin look up again. "What?"

"Much like the serlords, a handful of Thirteenth House nobles from Fortunalt were summoned to Ghosenhall shortly after the war. Amalie had decided that the heirs of Fortunalt and Gisseltess needed someone to tend them until they turned twenty-one since their fathers had died in the conflict. In Gisseltess, of course, the young serramar had their mother to guide them—"

"And Nate Brassenthwaite," Zellin spit out. "Once the marlady was misguided enough to marry *him*."

"But, as you say, Serephette does not inspire people with the utmost confidence in her ability to manage an estate. The queen was looking for a guardian who could oversee the region until Karryn attains her majority." He paused for effect, though Zellin's attention was back on the board. "Cammon is the one who interviewed me. Like you, I was amazed at his youth and his boyish manner. But unlike you, I was impressed at his thoughtfulness and insights. I thought him an extraordinary young man, to tell you the truth. I would not like him to make a judgment against me—I imagine it would be implacable."

Zellin was ranging his soldiers along a previously undefended border. "Well, he judged in favor of you, I suppose, and here you are," he said without interest.

"Yes," said Jasper. "Here I am."

Zellin studied his position for a moment, nodded, and said, "It's your turn."

Again, Jasper made a swift, unconsidered move, and Zellin gave him a look of bafflement.

"Have you ever *attempted* this game before?" the serlord demanded. "Your strategy is lunatic."

"I am trying a new style of play tonight," Jasper replied. "But I confess, I'm distracted by a raging thirst. Willa, could you see if Bryce is near enough to send for refreshments?"

Bryce, of course, was too young to be up this late *or* trusted with carrying trays full of delicate glassware, but Wen went to the door and found Bryce lurking outside. He was dressed in a small jacket that must have been cut down from a footman's discarded uniform, and a pearl-sewn sash made a bright slash across his chest. Nonetheless, he was yawning as he slumped against the wall, waiting to be called.

Wen repressed a smile and said, "My lord has asked you to bring refreshments."

That filled him with energy, and he dashed off. He returned moments later bearing a tray of wine and after-dinner sweets. Jasper had pulled up a second table near the cruxanno board and watched in some amusement as Bryce slowly lowered his burden, spilling nothing.

"Excellent, Bryce," Jasper said. "You will make a fine footman someday."

"Thank you, my lord," Bryce said.

"You can see he's an unusual boy," Jasper said, now addressing Zellin, who had not, in fact, shown any signs of noticing Bryce at all. "A mystic, though you profess not to believe in them."

That did make the serlord glance up, give Bryce one sweeping and unimpressed inspection, and return his attention to the game board. "He tells you that, I suppose."

"No, he proves it! Come, Bryce, let's show this skeptic what a reader like you is capable of."

"I am not interested in demonstrations, thank you all the same."

"Oh, this is very quick and most eye-opening, I assure you." Jasper picked up his small jeweled crown from the board—the most valuable piece in the game—and tossed it from hand to hand. "Look away," he commanded Bryce, who obediently turned around. "Really, Zellin, watch this. You'll be amazed. Which hand am I holding the crown in?"

"Your left."

Jasper switched hands. "And now?"

"Your right."

Jasper settled the crown in the middle of his graying brown hair. "And now?"

Bryce laughed. "It's on top of your head."

Jasper tilted his chin and caught the game piece as it slid off his forehead. "You see?" he said to Zellin. "He is never wrong."

"How can you possibly expect me to be impressed by such a bit of foolery?" Zellin demanded. "You could have rehearsed that before I arrived. That's hardly any proof of magic."

"You try it," Jasper said. He handed over his crown as carelessly as if it hadn't been the object of all Zellin's plotting for the last half hour. "Tell him when you're ready for him to speak."

Zellin sighed in irritation, closed his fingers over the crown and said, "Tell me, then."

"Your right hand, my lord."

"You see?" said Jasper.

"A lucky guess."

"Try it ten times over and see how lucky he is."

Grumbling and rolling his eyes, Zellin did so, and his frown actually grew blacker every time Bryce was correct. On the ninth try, he silently handed the game piece back to Jasper, then focused his suspicious eyes on Bryce's shoulders.

"Lord Jasper has it now," Bryce said confidently.

Jasper laughed and negligently flicked the piece up in the air, catching it in his right hand. "Enough of a demonstration for you?" he said. "It's a startling sort of magic, isn't it?

And, of course, Bryce's abilities are insignificant compared to Cammon's."

Zellin looked angry, but also a little discomfited. Wen imagined he was thinking back to his audience with Cammon and feeling just a little uneasy about what he might have revealed, all unknowing. "It doesn't matter," he said defiantly. "I have nothing to conceal."

Jasper nodded toward the door. "Thank you, Bryce. Off to bed with you now, I think." He waited until Wen had shut the door behind the boy, and then he turned back to Jasper. "Nothing to conceal?" he repeated in a pleasant voice. "I suppose your son does not confide in you, then."

Wen tensed and straightened, her hands moving closer to her weapons. After an evening of meandering and innocuous conversation, it appeared Jasper was suddenly ready to open battle with a heavy salvo.

"Tover?" Zellin said in blank surprise. "I suppose he has secrets from me, as any young man might, but— What are you saying, Paladar?"

"Karryn identified him as the man who abducted her, intent on marrying her to gain the title of marlord."

"That's a lie!" Zellin roared, coming to his feet with a dagger in his hand. Wen flew to his side, knocking him in the chest so hard that he tripped over his chair and fell heavily to the floor. His dagger skittered away to land against a bookcase near the far wall. Moss, as prearranged, had dashed over to defend Jasper. Wen stood over Zellin, her own knife drawn, ready to inflict real damage if he made another offensive move.

"Call off your guard," Zellin snarled, giving Wen an ugly look but making no effort to rise. "But if you don't withdraw your accusation against my son, I'll have your blood. And I mean it."

"Willa, let him get up and take his chair," Jasper said. He waited until Zellin was seated, Wen hovering mere inches away, before he added, "But I do not recant my statement. Tover kidnapped Karryn. He was assisted by a large, bald, brutish man named Darvis— I see by your expression that you recognize the description. They appeared to be carrying her northwest from Forten City. You have property in that corner of the region, do you not?"

"You lie," Zellin said. But Wen thought he was shaken. "Your ward has set herself to ruin my son. If you publicly accuse him, I will ruin *you*. Don't think I can't."

"I have very little that you can take away from me, so I am not particularly worried," Jasper replied. "But you might notice that I have not, so far, said a word against your son to anyone, not even Karryn's mother. I have no desire to cast aspersions on the whole rank of serlords, so new to their positions and fighting so hard for acceptance from both the Twelfth and Thirteenth Houses. I will not embarrass you by calling him to account—but I require you to do so."

"What do you expect of me?" Zellin said gruffly.

"Cast him off," Jasper said. "I do not know who your next heir is, but there should be a formal announcement that Tover is passed over—though you need not name the reasons."

Zellin stiffened in his chair. "I will not do it," he said. "Not on so little evidence. I will ask him, and if he admits it, then I will consider what you say, but I—"

"I will take my case to Ghosenhall," Jasper said calmly. "I will lay the matter before Cammon and ask him to adjudicate. No doubt he will summon you and your son immediately to the royal city." He gestured at the door. "You saw how easily Bryce was able to read your actions, and he is just a small boy with a modest amount of magic. Cammon will be able to read your soul—and your son's soul. Tover is no longer your heir, Zellin. Either you make that decision, for reasons you need not disclose, or the crown will make it, and possibly publish the reason. Those are your only two options."

Very neatly done! Wen thought with real admiration. It reminded her irresistibly of the game strategy she had employed in her own cruxanno competition with Jasper. Spin out the game interminably, lay out all the pieces in a manner that seemed completely random, and then, with a single move, destroy the unprepared opponent. Zellin could fight and lose, or he could surrender and save some dignity. He could not win.

"I will speak to my son," Zellin ground out. His hands were clenched upon the armrests of the chair; Wen saw his nails bite through the tapestried fabric. "If he admits what you tell me is true—then I will disinherit him. But if you speak of this to another living soul—"

"Only the crown," Jasper said. "And only if necessary." He seemed to be struck by a new thought. "Oh—and if Tover attempts any such course of action again, with my ward or any young woman, I will, of course, be compelled to speak up." He smiled at Zellin. "But I am sure you have ways to ensure that Tover never has the liberty or means to behave in such a fashion again."

"Yes," Zellin snapped, "you can be sure I know how to control my son."

"Well, then," Jasper said, reaching for one of the bottles of wine. "Shall we refresh ourselves? All this talk has made me thirsty."

Keeping a wary eye on Wen, Zellin came slowly to his feet. "No wine for me, Paladar," he said. "And no more cruxanno, either. It is too late to call for my carriage, or I would not even spend the rest of this night under your roof. I will be gone in the morning before you rise and I hope not to see you again anytime in the near future. You *or* your ward," he added.

Without another word, he stalked straight for the door. Wen had to follow him, of course, for it was clear to her that he could not be left unguarded for the rest of his stay in the house; no doubt she would be spending the night dozing in the hall outside his bedroom. But at the door, she briefly turned to give Jasper one quick, appraising look, all her wonder and admiration visible on her face. He caught her expression and grinned, exultant as a boy who had won his first game of skill against a much older and more seasoned opponent.

Chapter

15

THEY WERE A HALF DAY'S JOURNEY OUTSIDE OF Gissel Plain when dark found them still on the road. Senneth sighed at the prospect of spending another night at a roadside inn. Not that she was eager to arrive at Gissel Plain and whatever hospitality her brother might provide, but she was wearying of the travel.

Tayse, of course, had foreseen by noon that they wouldn't make it to journey's end by nightfall, so he'd sent on ahead to arrange for their lodging for the night. Sunset found them in a good-sized town with a commodious inn clearly designed to appeal to the wealthy. Tayse and Justin disappeared to settle the royal troops for the night, while the other Riders followed Cammon.

A tall, gaunt woman of indeterminate years led Cammon and his entourage to the second floor, pointing out the chambers that had been reserved for the Riders and then unlocking the door for royalty. After the Riders had inspected it for hazards and withdrawn, Senneth took one quick look around at the luxurious furnishings. The canopied bed in the middle of the room was enormous; she rather thought all nine Riders

could sleep alongside Cammon and none of them would feel
particularly crowded.

"Water will be brought immediately for your bath," the
haggard woman said in a sepulchral voice. "Would you like
dinner in your chambers or in a private room?"

"Oh, in the taproom, please," Cammon said.

The proprietress gave him a look of horror. "Among the
common people? Grubby and uncivilized?"

Cammon laughed. He seemed to find something about her,
invisible to Senneth, charming in the extreme, for he was giving her his brightest smile. "They're *my* people, after all," he
said.

"Highness, you might reconsider," the woman urged.

Senneth wished he would, too, but she didn't like strangers
trying to give Cammon advice. "He knows very well where he
would like to eat," she said sharply. "Now, perhaps you could
show me where I'm staying tonight?"

The woman gave Senneth one long, comprehensive
appraisal. "Aren't you one of the Queen's Riders?" she said.
"Won't you be sleeping with them?"

In fact, considering she lived with a Rider, she was usually
sleeping with one, and the gods knew she had had billets far
more rough than an inn room with a half dozen soldiers. But
the woman's haughty tone infuriated her. To be three weeks
on the road, tired to the bone, and have to contend with the
insults of innkeepers! Her temper rose.

"I am advisor to the crown," she said, her voice edged with
ice and anger. "I require my own chamber *and* a bath *and* a
certain level of courtesy, if you please."

The woman replied, "I can send for the bathwater, but I'm
afraid courtesy is out of the question."

For a second, Senneth was too astonished to speak, but
Cammon's choking fit of laughter clued her in. "Kirra, you
wretched girl!" she exclaimed. "How many times will I fall
for your—oh, you're impossible!" But she was laughing, too.
First she gave Kirra a hard shove on the shoulder, and then
she drew her into a quick embrace. When she pulled back,
Kirra was herself, all tumbling gold hair and mischievous
blue eyes.

"It's too hard to do that when Cammon's in the room,"

Kirra said, fanning herself with her hand as if overheated from effort. "I can't even look at him because he's trying so hard not to laugh."

Cammon hugged her in turn. "Where's Donnal?" he asked.

"I have no idea. I assume he was waiting for Tayse and Justin down near the field where they were going to put the soldiers. He was in the shape of a black dog last time I saw him, but Tayse and Justin will probably recognize him sooner than my closest friend recognized *me*."

"*I'm* your closest friend?" Senneth said incredulously, though she knew it to be true. "Imagine how well you treat the people you dislike."

"I don't bother dealing with those people at all."

"So *is* there a room for me?" Senneth asked. "How do you come to be escorting us around the inn, anyway? Did you take a job here? Are you low on funds?"

It was a joke, of course; as serramarra of Danalustrous, Kirra could never want for money. Of course, Senneth was a serramarra of Brassenthwaite and there had been plenty of times when she'd been penniless; but Kirra had always had a far better relationship with her family than Senneth had had with hers.

"No, I just skulked around the inn all day, waiting for your arrival, so I knew where your rooms were. Cammon let me know you were coming here, of course," she added.

"Of course."

"And the innkeeper's wife had conveniently stepped out to run an errand when I saw you pull up. I couldn't resist taking on her appearance."

"I hope she's nicer than you were," Senneth said.

"She does seem to be," Kirra said, moving uninvited toward the great bed, and curling up on top of the coverlet. "So tell me about your trip! Any adventures so far?"

Cammon, never a stickler for propriety, sprawled next to her. Senneth gave up any attempt at decorum and climbed up beside them. Feather mattress, or maybe two; she hoped her own bed was as soft.

"None to speak of," Cammon answered. "If you mean sword fights and people trying to kill us."

"Yes, that's what I mean," Kirra said. "Like our *usual* trips."

"Well, I hear there are brigands on the roads near the southern Houses, but none of them have been misguided enough to assault us," Senneth said. "Did you see? We have nine Riders and seventy soldiers in our party! Enough to go to war, practically."

Kirra grinned. "Will Nate feel threatened when you arrive at Gissel Plain with so many soldiers at your back?"

"Tayse thinks he'll feel honored instead by all the pomp."

Kirra lolled back on the bed. "I haven't seen Nate since his wedding," Kirra said. "I can't suppose he's improved much."

Senneth bit back a laugh. "He's Nate, as always," she said. "Very proper and pompous and strict. But he does seem— maybe the right word is gentler. Happier, anyway. To think he loved Sabina all those years while she was married to Halchon." She shook her head. "To think she loved *him* all that time. That's what's so surprising."

"Still, love doesn't make all your problems disappear, and they can't have had an easy time of it," Kirra said. "Taking over Gisseltess after the war! The people who supported Halchon would despise both Nate and Sabina, and the people who hated Halchon would be demanding wholesale reforms, I imagine. These must have been two very rocky years."

"Better than you'd expect," Cammon said. "I think the very things Senneth hates about him are the things that have made Nate a good administrator in such hard times. He has a passion for rules and order, and Gisseltess has benefited from both."

Kirra stared at him, then turned her eyes to Senneth. "Was that *Cammon* talking?" she demanded. "About political strategy?"

"Yes, our little vagabond has become quite the savvy king," Senneth said.

"I'm *not* the king."

"It's like having one of my father's dogs sit up and start explaining higher mathematics to me," Kirra said. "I can't quite take it in."

"It's easier when you see him every day," Senneth said. "But not much."

"I haven't really changed," Cammon said.

Kirra patted his head as affectionately as she would have if he really were one of her father's hounds. "Speaking as someone who remakes herself hour by hour and day by day," she said, "change is not such a terrible thing."

There was a knock on the door, then Justin pushed it open before Cammon could issue an invitation to enter. "Look who we found down in the stables!" Justin said, striding into the room behind a sleek black dog. Tayse stepped in last. "I figure it has to be Donnal, because he followed us all over town as we were getting the soldiers settled. Wasn't even tempted by a strip of jerky that one of the guards offered him."

"He knows better than to take food from a stranger's hand," Kirra said. Donnal put his paws up on the bed and uttered a sharp bark—a hello to Cammon, Senneth supposed—and then he settled back down on his haunches to watch them all.

Tayse nodded a greeting to Kirra, then pulled up a chair, reversed it, and sat. "Are you coming with us to Gissel Plain?" he inquired. He was always exceedingly blunt with Kirra, which sometimes seemed rude and sometimes seemed the only way to deal with the flighty serramarra. "And if so, why?"

"Well, that's not very welcoming!" Kirra said, sitting up. "Yes, I thought I'd join you. Don't I always lend an air of respectability to any gathering?"

"Maybe if the gathering was thieves and criminals," Justin said.

"Oh—you mean, *your* typical friends?" she replied sweetly.

Such byplay was what passed for casual conversation between Justin and Kirra, and Tayse ignored them. "Any reason why you want to join us?" he repeated.

"Of course I miss you all," she said in a soulful manner. Then, more briskly, "But, truly, no, I just happened to be in the area and Cammon let me know that you would be passing through. We can stay for dinner and be gone in the morning, if you like."

"Oh, come with us to Gissel Plain," Cammon said. "It's such a treat to have just the six of us together for a little while. Let's stretch it out as long as we can."

That was when Senneth, startled, looked around the room

and realized he was right. By Justin's smirk, it was clear he had noticed this wondrous fact already. Just the six of them, as it had been three years ago when they first came together on a mission for the king. Some of them strangers then, and a few of them filled with distrust and suspicion. Hardly the group you would have expected to forge such unshakable bonds. Now with the changes in their lives—Justin's marriage to Ellynor, the birth of his daughter; Cammon's marriage to Amalie and astonishing elevation in rank—it was rare for the six of them to find themselves together and unencumbered by other responsibilities.

"We couldn't have managed this if we'd tried to," Justin said with a laugh.

"Then I bow to the fates," Tayse said, suiting action to words. "Travel with us as long as you like."

KIRRA persuaded Cammon to forgo the meal in the taproom so that the six of them could catch up on their lives. Donnal even took human shape for dinner and entertained them with an account of an unfortunate hunting incident in Coravann during which Kirra almost ended up in someone's supper pot.

"But when she transmogrified from a quail to a lioness, he threw down his bow and went screaming back through the forest. So she survived," he ended. "Though I expect the poor man might be mad the rest of his days, gibbering to all his friends about impossible apparitions in the woods."

"They must be familiar with mystics in Coravann," Senneth commented once they'd all stopped laughing. "Marlord Heffel never persecuted them, at any rate, not that I ever heard."

"It's one thing to understand there might be shape-shifters in the world, and another to watch Kirra transform herself," Donnal said. "Especially when you were just thinking how tasty she would be."

"Well, I would have thought that Coravann and Helven and Nocklyn were all practically emptied of mystics by the time Coralinda Gisseltess got through hunting them down," Kirra said. "Maybe some are starting to drift back now, but

I'd wager very few of your ordinary citizens have seen much magic up close."

"And the Lumanen Convent still does have some influence in this area," Senneth said. Coralinda Gisseltess had headed the convent and led the drive to extinguish mystics from Gillengaria. "I believe they have softened their stance somewhat—and they certainly aren't burning mystics alive anymore!—but they still preach that magic is an abomination."

Kirra frowned at Cammon. "Why don't you shut that place down and send all the novices home?"

He shook his head. "Amalie feels we will be unable to expect tolerance for mystics if we show intolerance for a group that despises them. She says as long as they offer no violence, they can be allowed to speak. I have to say I agree with her."

"But you've also stationed permanent overseers near the convent to enforce her doctrine of coexistence," Tayse said.

"Well," Cammon said, "yes."

Justin lifted his right hand, which, through some invisible flick of the wrist, held his wicked dagger instead of his butter knife. "Welcome peace, but back it up with a blade," he said.

Cammon nodded. "That seems to be the underlying principle of the reign so far."

THEY talked late into the night, and consequently did not get a particularly early start. Then, too, Cammon felt compelled to breakfast in the common room to satisfy all the barmaids and shopkeepers and visiting merchants who had hoped for a glimpse of him before he moved on. So it was close to noon before their caravan finally set out, and close to sunset before they pulled in sight of Gissel Plain.

The city itself spread like a broad, flat valley all around the central feature of the marlord's mansion. It was, Senneth had to admit, an impressive sight, the central building being almost as big as the palace at Ghosenhall. While it had been expanded over the centuries as proud marlords added wings and annexed acres, each successive generation had made an attempt to harmonize the whole. The entire structure was built of a pleasant sand-colored stone that allowed for towers, crenellations, buttresses, arches, and connecting walkways. It was ringed with a wall of a somewhat darker stone that set it off from the surrounding city and made it easy to defend. And it probably, Senneth thought, offered all sorts of hidden passageways and secret exits that only a lifelong resident would ever discover. Certainly Halchon Gisseltess had seemed to come and go with ease during the time he was theoretically under arrest at this estate.

Had she married Halchon Gisseltess, as her father had intended, she would have been mistress of this House. Of course, she would have been mad or dead by her own hand within a week of arriving, so she could hardly look at the estate with any real regret. She still found it strange that it was her brother who sat here now. Perhaps the gods had always intended someone with Brassenthwaite blood to rule over Gissel Plain. Perhaps they had not particularly cared which individual it was.

Three flags waved from the highest tower. The Gisseltess banner showed a black hawk clutching a red flower, and beside it streamed a standard of Brassenthwaite blue. For the third flag, Senneth was pleased to note, someone had thoughtfully commissioned the design that had become Amalie's personal emblem: the royal gold lion interspersed with the fierce red raelynx, both sewn onto a field of pure black. The Queen's Riders wore sashes that boasted both lion and raelynx, though Baryn's men had only sported black-and-gold. It had been easy to see who in Gillengaria was most eager to embrace change by noting who had made a point of flying the new colors.

"Well," Senneth said, under her breath, "here we are."

DESPITE the lack of love between Senneth and Nate, the first evening the royal entourage spent at Gissel Plain passed civilly enough. Nate hailed them with his usual mix of pride and reserve, but Sabina hugged the women and greeted Cammon with affection. He had accompanied the marlady on a memorable journey before the war and it was clear she felt some fondness for him still.

Or maybe she was just so much happier with her life, now

that her first husband was dead, that she felt a fondness for
anyone who was alive and walking through her transformed
world. Certainly Sabina herself had changed almost past recognition. She was still small and delicately formed, though
perhaps not quite as slender as she had been two years ago,
but her thin blond hair had been styled into a froth of curls and
her expression was joyful. *Released from red and silver hell,*
Senneth thought. She didn't know how Sabina had endured
being married to Halchon for fifteen years.

After warmly greeting the general party and inquiring
how they had fared on their trip, Sabina asked, "Are you hungry? We weren't sure when you were arriving, so tonight's
meal will be simply family. Later in the week, we have invited
some of the vassals in to dine." She glanced at Nate and then
at Senneth; Senneth knew what was coming before she spoke
again. "Tayse is invited to sit at the table with us, of course, at
least when it's just family."

Nate could hardly get past the fact that his sister had married a Rider, and he must have grumbled to Sabina before they
arrived about the necessity of treating the soldier as kin. Senneth knew that Tayse would be just as happy to be spared the
honor of dining with the nobles, but by the Bright Mother's
red eye, he was her husband and she wanted him at her side.
She made her tone surprised and her face blank. "Oh—of
course," she said, as if she couldn't imagine there had been
any question on the topic at all.

Sabina glanced at Nate again. "And we expect he will stay
in your room as well."

"Naturally."

"I assume Tayse will want at least half the Riders within
call, so I hope you have set aside a room for them close to
mine," Cammon said practically.

"Not that anyone expects trouble here at Gissel Plain,"
Senneth said. "Tayse is always overcautious."

This didn't offend Nate in the slightest. "Of course. I expect
him to treat the consort's safety with utmost seriousness. *Two*
rooms have been commandeered for the Riders."

After a little more conversation, the members of the royal
party were all escorted to their chambers, and Senneth found
hers to be very attractive, though a little dark. She was inspect-

ing the burgundy drapes and cherrywood furniture when she overheard Kirra's voice from the hall.

"And my dog may stay in the room with me? You don't mind?"

"I'm very fond of dogs," Nate replied. "As long as he's well-mannered."

"Most excellently behaved, I assure you."

Senneth had to smother a laugh.

DINNER went smoothly enough, though the numbers were uneven and three of the people at the meal scarcely spoke at all. Present besides Senneth, Kirra, Tayse, and Cammon were their hosts and Sabina's two sons. Tayse she had expected to remain mostly silent, but until she sat down to the table, Senneth hadn't given any thought at all to Sabina's children by Halchon Gisseltess.

The youngest was perhaps twelve, with dark blond hair and his mother's delicate features. He had some of Halchon's height but none of his bulk; she supposed he would grow to be a supple, tall man with a certain grace of carriage. It was hard to tell what he was thinking. His eyes darted between the speakers and he seemed to listen intently to everything that was said, but he never once smiled or offered a comment of his own.

The older boy was, she thought, about sixteen, and clearly bore the Gisseltess stamp. He was blocky, strongly built, with dark hair, broad features and a sullen air. He spent most of the time staring down at his plate, unless someone made an observation he disagreed with, and then he would give the speaker one quick, contemptuous look. Most of the time, this look was directed at Nate, occasionally at Sabina. But his eyes nearly burned through Senneth once when she made the off-hand remark that Gisseltess was looking prosperous.

"Prosperous enough," Nate said, trying to keep the smug note from his voice. "There is still much rebuilding to do after that disastrous war. But we are making improvements."

The older boy gave Nate a hot look, then returned his attention to his plate. Senneth remembered now. Sabina had spoken with despair about her sons, how little they cared for her and how much they adored their father. Nate would not be anyone's notion of an ideal stepfather, she supposed, but he would be even harder to love for a boy who had idolized the arrogant Halchon Gisseltess.

She hoped neither boy realized that Tayse had been the one who sent their father to his death.

"What of your serlords?" Kirra asked. "Has that transition gone smoothly?"

Nate made an equivocating motion with his head. "Perhaps it could have gone better," he allowed. "The serlords have taken it upon themselves to question every decision Sabina and I have made that would have any widespread impact. So, for instance, projects to repair certain roads have been delayed because they were not willing to approve the order in which we specified construction. Many of the other vassal lords are siding with them—not out of conviction, I'm afraid, but simply to prove their independence from the House. I fear that unless we all pull together on common initiatives, *nothing* will be done, and no one will be better off."

Cammon, who had been looking over his shoulder as if listening to a conversation behind him, now directed his attention at Nate. "What of Seton Mayman? Has he been a disruptive force?"

Senneth couldn't think who Seton Mayman was, but she had a horrifying suspicion that Amalie's specter was hovering right behind Cammon, auditing this conversation. Kirra was watching him with a bright, inquisitive look, wondering how he had come up with that name. Fortunately Nate was not nearly as curious.

"Seton? Well, when you passed him over for serlord, he was furious, no mistake about that," Nate said. "I thought he might try to foment rebellion among the other lords, but instead he has decided to be obsequious to the House and to ally with Sabina and me, particularly when the serlords disagree with us. Sabina and I walk a very tricky line, for we want to accommodate many views, but we cannot cede all authority and still remain a strong House."

At that the oldest boy jumped to his feet. "*You* cannot keep Gisseltess a strong House! *You* can only destroy it!" he declared.

"Warren!" his mother cried.

"Of course the serlords flout you, and the vassals, too," he continued, throwing his napkin to the table. "They hate you! Almost as much as I do!" He spun on his heel and ran from the room.

Sabina's hand was over her mouth in humiliation. "I'm so sorry," she murmured, but Senneth wasn't sure if she was addressing Nate or the rest of the table.

Nate did not look particularly discomposed. "We have displays like that most every night," he said. "I had hoped he would manage to behave with more maturity with a royal guest in the House, but I see my expectations were too high."

"He mourns his father and he has not reconciled himself to my remarriage," Sabina said, dropping her hand and looking, for a moment, almost as sad as she had during the days when she was married to Halchon. "He does everything in his power to spite Nate—and Nate has been *so patient* with him. With both of them."

This caused Senneth, and everyone else at the table, to swing attention to the younger, fair-haired boy. Nate said, "Do you want to follow your brother out of the room? Just excuse yourself and you may go."

The boy's eyes made a quick circuit around the table. He looked even more tightly strung now that his brother had created such a scene, but he seemed excited rather than angry. "I don't want to go," he said. "I like hearing all the talk."

Nate nodded. "Then you're welcome to stay."

"Let's return to the topic of discussion," Senneth said, hoping to smooth things over.

"As I was saying," Nate resumed. "We spend much of our energy trying to strike a balance between fairness and strength."

Tayse spoke, for almost the first time. "Do you feel overmatched?" he asked. "Do you need royal soldiers in Gissel Plain to enforce your edicts?"

Nate bristled. "Indeed, no, we are quite capable of working out our issues without interference from the crown," he said. He glanced at Cammon. "Although—the strict limitations on the number of guards that can be deployed by the House does dilute any show of strength I might make."

Cammon glanced at Tayse, who remained expressionless. Then Cammon cocked his head, as if listening to someone whispering in his ear. *Bright Mother burn me*, Senneth
thought, but Amalie's comments were at least quick.

"I don't know that increasing your soldiery is the right
message to send at just this time," Cammon said. "But if you
think I would be of any use mediating disputes, I would be
happy to meet with your vassals and serlords while I'm here."

"In fact, the serlords and their ladies will be here tomorrow night," Sabina said. "We didn't invite Seton here to meet
you because his presence can be so disruptive. However, he
has begged us to extend to you an invitation to his house for
dinner. His estate is only a half-day's ride from here."

This time Cammon didn't bother glancing at the Rider for
a silent consultation. "Yes, I'd be happy to," he said blithely.
If he'd been close enough, Senneth would have hit him. Even
Kirra laid down her fork and looked astonished, then amused.
To have to guard royalty at the house of a disgruntled noble! It
was almost an impossible task.

Sabina was wreathed in smiles. "I'll send a note to him in
the morning."

"You might wait until we've worked out the logistical
details first," Senneth said pleasantly.

"Oh, all of you will come, of course," Cammon said to her.

She merely smiled at him. "Of course."

Tayse spoke up again. "What about traffic on the roads?"
he said. "I understand there have been reports of brigands."

Nate shrugged. "There will always be outlaws. We are no
more troubled by them than any other House."

Cammon looked unconvinced, but didn't bother to contradict Nate. Senneth said, "That's good to hear," and then there
was a moment of awkward silence.

Kirra was the one to break it. "So tell me," she said, "is
there any interesting gossip out of the southern or middle
Houses?"

Sabina leaned forward, animated again. "Heffel has confirmed that his daughter, Lauren, will be his heir," she said.
"She is the eldest, of course, but many marlords like to see a
son inherit."

"That's excellent news!" Senneth exclaimed. "I met her several times and liked her very much."

"And how's Mayva Nocklyn?" Kirra asked. "I heard that Lowell died in prison, so she would be free to marry again if she wanted."

"If she wanted," Sabina agreed. "She told me most emphatically that she is done with husbands." She smiled at Nate. "I told her she just hasn't found the proper one. Anyone can be wrong the first time."

Senneth had to cast her eyes down to keep from looking at Kirra, who was smiling in unholy amusement, or Tayse, who could hardly keep the sardonic look from his face. It was just so impossible to believe that even someone who had suffered at Halchon's hands for fifteen years would find Nate an attractive alternative.

"Well," Kirra said merrily, "husband-hunting for Mayva! That sounds like a most intriguing challenge! I'll have to start thinking about some of the eligible men I know."

"You yourself could think of taking a husband, serra," Nate said to her.

That caused Senneth to look up and become the one smirking across the table. Kirra wasn't married to Donnal, of course, but she might as well be; she loved him enough. "Oh, I'm much too unpredictable to settle down in such a conventional way," Kirra said, waving a hand. "If I were to wed, I would no doubt choose someone entirely inappropriate, and bring consternation upon my House. Surely it is better for everyone that I remain as I am." She gave Senneth a limpid smile—the last words had clearly been added for Senneth's benefit.

"Perhaps you're right," Nate said. Senneth gave him great credit for managing not to look at Tayse as he spoke. "And your sister married respectably—into the best of Houses!— and is already prepared to produce heirs for Danalustrous. So all is well."

Now Kirra was openly laughing. "All is well indeed."

Chapter
16

A FINE DESSERT FINISHED OFF THE MEAL, AND soon the travelers were all excusing themselves to seek their beds. First, of course, they all convened in the suite set aside for royalty to discuss what they'd learned since their arrival.

"You cannot possibly go to the house of this scheming vassal lord," Senneth said the instant she'd shut the door behind them. As she'd expected, Justin and Donnal were already present, sitting before the fireplace, halfway through a game of cards.

"Why not?" Cammon asked.

Kirra chimed in as she perched on the bed. "Because kings just don't go and visit small out-of-the-way estates, that's why," she said. "Those houses aren't designed with security in mind, the way a marlord's estate is, or a royal palace."

"I'm not the king," he said, settling in a chair near the bed.

Everyone ignored this. "It would be unsafe even if you believed the man to be friendly to the marlord and friendly to the crown!" Senneth said. "But a man who bears you ill will already—you cannot give him opportunities to assault you."

"You can't seriously think there's a risk of that," Cammon said.

"Liege, I agree with her," Tayse spoke up. "It would be difficult, although not impossible, to defend you from physical assault in a structure not built for defense, but I would think there is the possibility that someone in the house would attempt to poison you. The risk may be small, but it is still unacceptable."

"That's just ridiculous," Cammon said.

"One of us could be his royal taster," Justin suggested, clearly not serious. He slapped a hand against his thigh and pointed at Donnal. "Change him back into a dog shape and pretend you're feeding him scraps of meat just because he's your favorite hound. If he dies, of course, you stop eating."

"Why do you think anyone would want to poison me?" Cammon asked. "I think they're more likely to want to poison Nate."

Senneth gave a strangled laugh and dropped to the bed beside Kirra. "I'd save them the trouble and do it myself, except Sabina looks so *happy* with him," she said. "But he truly is the most annoying man."

"I know you don't like him, but I walked the defenses for a couple hours tonight, and the House is in excellent shape," Justin said. "The guard is small, but well-ordered, and none of the soldiers had anything but praise for your brother."

"The Thirteenth House sounds like it might be in a revolt, though," Tayse observed. He directed his question at Kirra. "How much of that is to be expected, and how much can be attributed to the fact that he is in some sense acting as regent and has no authority that will last past Warren's twenty-first birthday?"

"A little of both, I would think," Kirra said. "To some extent, his hands are tied, and the lesser lords know that. They will be trying what they can now to amass power. But the same thing goes on in Danalustrous and Rappengrass and any of the Houses. It is just a matter of degree."

"He was lying about something, though," Cammon said. "I think there is more thievery on the roads than he wants to admit. I think he's worried about it, too."

"I'm sure that's an important matter, but it's not the issue at hand right now," Senneth said. "You *cannot* go to a dinner at this vassal's house. Blame me if you like, but tell Sabina in the morning that you've changed your mind."

Cammon looked surprised. "But we just settled that! Donnal will go as my taster. And if he looks like he's been poisoned," he added, "Kirra will just have to use her healing magic to save his life."

"Meanwhile, the servants are all tripping over Riders every time they enter or leave the room, because we'll be nine deep around the table glaring at everyone in turn," Justin added with a grin.

"Liege, I agree with Senneth," Tayse said in his serious way. "Such an outing poses many risks."

"But Nate said Seton Mayman has become his ally in the council, and it seems like Nate needs allies," Cammon said stubbornly. "We don't want to give Gisseltess the power to raise more troops. But shouldn't we do what we can to make the House internally strong? By simple political measures with no cost attached?"

There was a short silence. Kirra rolled over onto her stomach, which put her face close to Senneth's. "When did Cammon start talking like a strategist?" she said. "I find it very peculiar. Is it possible that I'm just dreaming this conversation? Though I have to say, my dreams are usually much more interesting than this."

Senneth sighed and fell back on the bed so she was staring up at the gathered folds of the canopy. "So if we decide it's worthwhile to send him to this vassal's house, how do we make sure he survives the visit?"

"Do you really think there's a risk of poison?" Justin asked.

"Small," Senneth answered, still on her back. "But possible." She turned her head to look at Kirra, who was much more conversant with the rules of society than Senneth was. "Do we insult the lord if we bring in a taster? We cannot let him go shaped as a dog, of course. But as Donnal?"

Kirra tapped her mouth. "I think it will be acceptable if we're apologetic but firm. 'We feel we must go to extreme measures to safeguard the health of the royal consort. If we observe this course at every small estate, no one is singled out, and yet he is protected.' Something like that."

"Yet a taster really cannot guarantee anyone's safety," Tayse said. "If the venom is designed to act slowly, both Donnal and Cammon could seem perfectly healthy through the whole meal, only to succumb some hours later."

Kirra was practically bouncing on the bed. "I know! *I* will be the taster. But as I handle every dish, I'll change its composition, so there is no chance of any poison making its way into Cammon's mouth."

"Now that's an interesting idea," Senneth said.

"That'll be the blandest meal Cammon's ever eaten," Justin said. "What will you change his food to? Since you can't actually cook a decent meal."

"Just because I wouldn't mind if *you* starved to death doesn't mean I can't prepare a meal if I have to," Kirra returned.

"Won't this vassal lord be expecting to see Kirra as well?" Tayse asked.

Kirra's face was alight with deviltry. "Donnal can go as me," she said. "You've seen how well he can counterfeit my shape."

To prove it, Donnal underwent one of his amazingly fast transformations, and it suddenly looked for all the world as if Kirra was sitting at the hearth holding an assortment of cards. "I can copy her voice as well, though I don't think I would know what to *say*," Donnal said, sounding exactly like Kirra.

"Just talk nonsense," Justin advised. "No one will be able to tell the difference."

Kirra snatched up one of the pillows from the bed and threw it at him. Grinning broadly, he batted it aside to keep it from going into the fire.

"I suppose it could work," Senneth said slowly. "Tayse, what do you think?"

"It will serve," Tayse said.

"Good," Cammon said. "Now let's play cards."

How could you resist a ruler who was so wise one moment, so boyish the next? Senneth joined him at the table, ruffling his hair as she sat beside him, and the others all regrouped around them. Tayse dealt, while Senneth and Kirra filled Donnal and Justin in on the conversation over dinner.

"Not that I blame those boys for hating Nate, but *that's* a situation that won't get better anytime soon," Senneth said, describing Warren's exit.

"Has Nate given any thought to what will happen once Warren becomes marlord?" Kirra asked. "I'd think he'd find it uncomfortable to live here, unless relations dramatically improve."

"Is it certain Warren will be marlord?" Cammon asked. They all looked at him. "What?" he said. "Sometimes it's not the oldest child who's the heir."

"As we all know," Kirra said dryly. Her own younger sister would inherit Danalustrous from their father.

"Would the younger boy be a better choice?" Senneth asked. "Could you tell enough about their personalities to judge that?"

Cammon was rearranging his cards. "Actually, if you want the truth, I preferred Warren. There's a slyness to his brother. He's devious. Warren at least is honest."

"It might be worth giving Nate that piece of advice. Nurture the older boy, and be wary of the younger," Kirra said.

"Certainly. *You* tell Nate that," Senneth said. "He's always so willing to listen to someone else's opinion."

Justin tossed down three cards and took the hand, as everyone else groaned. "The oldest boy was hanging around the soldiers this afternoon," Justin said. "Looked like he would have liked to join the workouts but didn't quite have the nerve. If he shows up tomorrow, I'll offer to teach him some Rider tricks."

"Oh, that answers perfectly!" Kirra said. "Because you're just the man to give anyone else's self-confidence a boost. And, of course, it's an excellent idea to help a young malcontent learn fighting techniques that no one will be able to fend off."

Even Tayse was laughing. Justin grinned, unrepentant. "I think I know something about violent young men who need a little direction," he said.

"I'm so glad," Kirra said, "since you know nothing else."

Senneth laid down her cards and yawned widely. "Enough

pleasantries for the day, I think," she said. "I'm off to bed. I'll see you all in the morning."

SENNETH slept late, even though Tayse was stirring and out the door by dawn. When she finally went down to breakfast, she found Sabina alone at the table, working on correspondence.

"Nate has taken Cammon on a ride around the grounds, trailed by a half dozen Riders," Sabina said. "Is Justin with your party? I didn't see him this morning."

It took Senneth a moment to remember why Sabina would know to ask for Justin by name, but of course, they had shared an adventure about six months before the war. Sabina had grown convinced that Halchon meant to kill her and slipped away from him one winter afternoon. It was only by the sheerest good fortune that she had happened upon Justin, who had sheltered her until he could turn her over to Senneth. Who had ultimately turned Sabina over to Nate. Senneth still found the workings of the human heart to be entirely mysterious.

"He *is* with us, and I'm sure he would be delighted if you sought him out," Senneth replied. "Justin's married now, too—to a Lirren girl—and has a baby daughter. Still as fierce as he ever was, though."

"He saved my life," Sabina said.

"Yes," Senneth said. "I was never so proud of him."

They were silent while a servant brought food and hot tea for Senneth, but as soon as the girl left, Sabina gestured to a letter open on the table. "Seton Mayman sent a note this morning," she said. "Asking again that we all come to dinner at his house in a few days. May I tell him we will?"

"Making it clear that there will be nine Riders in our party, in the room with Cammon at all times. Oh, and a man to taste Cammon's food."

"A taster?" Sabina said uncertainly. "Did he have one last night?"

"No, but you might not tell Seton Mayman that. As long as he agrees to the rings of protection that we consider essential, we will be happy to accompany Cammon to his house."

"I'm sure he will," Sabina said, giving the smile that made

her look so pretty. "I will write instantly and let him know we have accepted."

AFTER the late breakfast, Senneth let Sabina get back to her household duties while she wandered the grounds. The day was sunny and considerably warmer than it would have been farther north in Ghosenhall, and she enjoyed the stroll through the unpretentious and well-maintained acres. At the back of the property, she came across a small practice yard where about a dozen men in Gisseltess colors were working out. Most of them weren't paying much attention to their opponents because they kept sneaking looks to watch two Riders in combat.

Senneth settled against the fence to take in the sight. It was Justin pitted against Janni, a mismatch in the general sense. These days only Tayse could reliably defeat Justin; and even so, Justin bested the older Rider every third or fourth outing. At a year or so shy of thirty, Justin was in superb physical condition, burly enough to put real power into his swings but lithe enough to move with astonishing quickness. Tayse was bigger, older, sometimes a step slower, but so experienced that his guile usually made up for any loss of prowess.

Janni, a sunny-tempered woman with curly dark hair and a blinding smile, obviously didn't have Justin's strength, but she was faster and completely fearless. She attacked him with lightning strokes and danced back out of reach, making him work hard to counter her agility with his brute power. Still, it was no real surprise when Justin eventually battered her down with a series of ringing blows. They were using practice blades, but Senneth, who was a decent swordswoman herself, knew that Janni would come out of this encounter covered with bruises.

"Dead," Justin announced, pulling back his sword and helping Janni to her feet. "But not without crippling me severely. Good job."

Janni was panting but cheerful. "I think you've got a gut wound that'll lay you up for a month. Maybe it'll get infected and you'll die."

"I have mystic friends," Justin retorted. "They'll heal me."

One of the Gisseltess soldiers stopped making any pretense of fighting his own battle and came a few steps closer to the Riders. That's when Senneth realized it was Warren. "How'd you learn to fight like that?" the boy asked. His face was alight with excitement, making him almost unrecognizable from the sullen serramar of the night before.

Justin pulled a dagger, flipped it, caught it, and sheathed it again. He didn't usually indulge in showy tricks, so Senneth assumed he was making a point about basic coordination. "Practiced every day, all day, till my hands were bleeding and I couldn't feel my feet," Justin said. "Never bothered doing anything else."

"I've never seen anybody that good," Warren said.

Justin looked him over deliberately, assessing height, reach, muscle tone. "You've got the right build," he said. "You could probably do some damage if you were properly taught."

Warren's sudden eagerness propelled him a step closer. "Would you teach me? Now? Show me how a Rider fights?"

Justin didn't even glance back at Senneth, though he had to know she was there. Justin always knew who was within a fifty-foot radius of him. "Why not?" he drawled. "I've got a little time. But you can't moan if you get hurt. This is a hard business, and you have to be hard yourself."

"I will be. I am," Warren promised. He was rebuckling his protective vest and hefting his practice sword.

"Weapons up," Justin said, and lunged for him.

Senneth only stayed for another twenty minutes to watch the demonstration, but it was clear Justin knew exactly what he was doing. He never let Warren land a blow or indulge any thought of besting the Rider, but he slowly and methodically demonstrated some of his own most lethal moves, then walked the boy through them over and over. Warren was all rapt attention and boundless effort, and he watched Justin as if one of the gods themselves had dropped down to give him a fencing lesson. "Good," Senneth heard Justin say as she walked away. "You've almost got it. More power in the swing. No, balance your weight on your left foot. . . ."

Justin a hero to Halchon Gisseltess's son. Surely, the world was so strange Senneth would never be able to comprehend it.

*   *   *

DINNER that evening was disagreeably formal. To please Nate and honor her royal charge, Senneth had worn a dress ever since she arrived in Gissel Plain, eschewing her usual trousers and plain attire. Tonight, of course, she must not just wear a dress; she must wear a gown and style her hair and try to look every inch the serramarra. She choose a dress of Brassenthwaite blue in striking lines, accenting it with the gold necklace Tayse had given her as a wedding gift. It lay just so it covered the Brassenthwaite housemark burned into her skin.

She used to wear a moonstone bracelet as well, but she had given that up when she almost lost her magic. Moonstones leached power away from a mystic, and these days Senneth didn't feel she had any to spare.

She collected Kirra and they headed down to dinner. Tonight, of course, Tayse had not been invited to join them and Sabina had taken great care with the table arrangements. The two serlords were seated closest to Cammon, and a bejeweled array of other vassal lords and ladies spread from his central presence like an army outfitted from a treasure house.

Senneth was seated among the lesser lords, and she spent most of the meal making laborious conversation with the man on her right. During lulls in conversation, she tried to listen to the rest of the talk around the table. The men sitting on either side of Kirra appeared to be having a much more lighthearted time of it, while those clustered close to Cammon wore looks of polite bafflement. She wasn't surprised so many people didn't know what to make of the royal consort.

Cammon himself appeared entirely at ease, asking his usual artless questions and listening with his usual close attention. Every once in a while, Senneth saw him tilt his head sideways and a little back. *Bright Mother burn me,* she thought. *Amalie's in the room with us and Cammon's listening to her.*

The lords who were puzzled by Cammon now would be even more stunned to think he was choosing his conversational subjects on the advice of disembodied voices. Despite herself, Senneth felt an unregenerate amusement. She caught Kirra's eye and directed her attention to Cammon. Kirra broke into a delightful laugh and then turned to make some airy comment to her dinner partner. But she, too, kept half of her attention on the royal consort.

So both of them were listening when Cammon leaned forward to address the serlord sitting across the table from him. "What do you think explains the higher incidence of banditry along the roads?"

The serlord sat up, affronted and taken by surprise, and all around them the other conversations gradually stuttered to a halt. "I'm sure I have no idea what you refer to."

"Outlaws. Brigands," Cammon expanded. "The roads around Gissel Plain are safe enough, but too far out in the country, and a small party is open to attack. Was this the case when Halchon Gisseltess sat in the House?"

That drew a glare from Nate to add to the scowls of the serlords and vassals. Cammon ignored them all and just sat there waiting, wearing a look of courteous inquiry.

"There have been incidents," the serlord said stiffly. He was large and round in contour, but his eyes were narrow and sharp; intelligence shaped his whole face. "We assume that many of the raiders are soldiers who came back from the war too bitter or too broken to return to their old lives."

Cammon seemed to listen for a beat, and then he said, "Have there been any policies in place to try to help such men rebuild? In Merrenstow, for instance, the marlord has set aside gold for former soldiers to borrow at a low rate of return, to help them put their farms back in order or to hire help if they have been too wounded to work."

"In Merrenstow, the region has not been beggared by the costs of an ill-conceived war," the serlord snapped.

Cammon steadily returned his gaze. "Most of the war was fought in the northeastern part of the country," he said. "Property damage was considerable. And the northern Houses paid a lot for this war, too, you know—and it wasn't their idea, either."

The serlord lowered his eyes. "I beg pardon," he said. "I know the entire country suffered."

The second serlord leaned forward over the table. He was thin and intense, with a pinched, scowling face. "What's needed is not charity but force," he said. "Gisseltess is ham-

strung by limitations on its fighting strength. Even a marlord
may not have more than fifty guards at his disposal! Give us
leave to raise troops and you will see our roads become safe
again."

Cammon sipped from his wine as if thinking this over, but
Senneth was certain he was listening to Amalie again. "You
could pool your resources," he suggested finally. "If the marlord can raise fifty men, and each serlord can raise thirty-five,
and every vassal lord has his own small guard of fifteen or
twenty, you could all contribute one or two soldiers to the
common cause." He drank a little more wine. "And the crown
would be willing to send troops as well to boost your numbers. You should be able to patrol the roads effectively with
such a force."

There was a small silence. "A generous offer indeed," Nate
said. His voice was very formal; Senneth couldn't tell if he
was angry or pleased. No marlord wanted interference from
the royal court—but no marlord wanted to risk losing all his
trade because of unsafe travel through his lands.

The small scrappy serlord was plainer. "Gisseltess can
solve its own problems without pressure from Ghosenhall,"
he said.

"If it can, then why hasn't it?" Cammon replied in a quiet
voice.

This brought another silence, this one even longer and
crackling with anger. Cammon looked around the table, seeming to give each individual a thorough inspection in one brief
glance. "Look at all of you," he said. "You are full of jeal-
ousy and spite—toward your neighbors, toward your House,
toward your queen. You are each fighting for the prestige of
your own small properties, but you don't seem to understand
that none of you will prosper if you don't all work together.
Gisseltess will never heal itself if you continue this way. I
know you don't like Nate Brassenthwaite leading the House,
but I can sense from none of you a willingness to change when
a true Gisseltess man is back in charge. By the time Warren is
twenty-one, you will all have become so steeped in hatred that
you won't be able to support him, either, and Gisseltess will
never again be the proud, strong House it used to be—at least,
not while any of *you* are still alive."

It was a remarkable speech, all the more so because it was delivered in Cammon's usual pleasant voice, and he displayed no scorn, no wrath, no malice. Just implacable honesty with no room for subterfuge. Everyone was staring at him; the table was so still there wasn't even the sound of rustling clothing or silverware striking against china.

"Hold a council. Figure out what each of you can do, and what kind of assistance you would like from the crown," Cammon continued. "Amalie and I would be glad to see this resolved."

Nate drew a long breath. "Thank you, liege," he said, and again his voice was unreadable. But Senneth rather thought he was impressed. "We will confer, and we will send a delegate to Ghosenhall."

Sabina was the next to speak, her light voice just very slightly quavering. "I hope you're all still hungry," she said. "The cook has made what looks to be a most delicious confection to end the meal."

SO *that* was a lesson in the sort of political acumen that Cammon and Amalie possessed between them, and made the dinner one that would be talked of for at least a decade, Senneth thought. She was hopeful that the meal at Seton Mayman's house a few days later would be less momentous, but in its way it was even more eventful. Though the entire tenor of the two meals was different. Dinner at Gissel Plain was tense; dinner at the Mayman house was farcical.

First, of course, there was simply the cast of characters: Cammon, relaxed and cheerful as always; Senneth, disgruntled at having to don a fancy dress for a second night; Kirra, in the form of a slim, silent, watchful young man dressed in royal black and gold; Donnal, shaped like Kirra and wearing a resplendent gown; and all nine of the Riders. Accompanying them were Nate, who spent the entire length of the journey giving them Seton Mayman's personal history, and Sabina, who fussed over Donnal. Donnal was pretending to nurse a cold so that he would not have to do much talking as Kirra. The six guests of honor rode in a single cramped carriage, so there was no way to avoid any of the personality quirks. Nate and Sabina carried most of the conversation, helped by Cammon. Senneth was too annoyed to speak, and of course the "taster" was expected to be largely invisible. Every once in a while, Donnal would offer a consumptive cough and then pat his throat with a dainty hand.

"I'm so sorry," he would whisper, batting those big blue eyes. "Perhaps I shouldn't have come."

Sabina would pat his arm and say, "No, no, I'm sure no one minds as long as *you* aren't too uncomfortable."

Once they arrived at the estate—a rather pretty place of white stone and black trim—the pomp was excessive. At least twenty footmen lined the hall leading to the dining room, but they had to press back to make room for the Riders, who paced around Cammon, solemn as funeral mourners. There was a general jostle in the dining room itself as the Riders stationed themselves at strategic points along the walls, and the servants and the other guests tried to make their way around them. Their host and his wife wore clothing that wouldn't have been out of place for an audience at Ghosenhall, and their nineteen or twenty guests were in similarly opulent attire.

When the whole group was finally settled around the table, there was one empty chair. Seton explained that this belonged to a young lord named Chelten, who would be arriving later. "He is most eager to renew his acquaintance with serra Kirra, of whom he has the warmest memories," Seton said, smiling at Donnal.

Donnal covered his mouth with a handkerchief for a discreet cough, managing to give Kirra a quick look and receive her slight nod in return. "Oh, it's good to be remembered so fondly," he said with a light laugh. "Not everyone finds me charming."

"Nonsense," Seton said. "I imagine you win hearts everywhere you go."

The first course was served, then successive courses, each one an amazing challenge in logistics. Kirra was perched on a stool right up against Cammon's chair, although everyone in the room pretended she wasn't there. So the servants presented each dish to Cammon with an elegant flourish. He would hand the item to Kirra, and she would work her invisible alchemy on it while managing to get the occasional forkful to her mouth. The plate with its altered contents would be handed back to Cammon, who would have to take his first bite before anyone else dared to eat.

"Delicious," he would say, or, "Oh, I like this very much." Senneth could tell by his polite tone that most of it was perfectly tasteless, and nothing like the feast the rest of them were enjoying.

The conversation was equally insipid, centering on weather and travel and a few morsels of mild scandal. Topics such as business and trade crept in among the men, and the women talked fashion. Senneth's dinner partners were planning a trip to Ghosenhall; could she recommend inns along the way? All very civilized, and she started to relax.

The hostess had a moment of mortification when the fireplace began to smoke late in the third course. "When the wind blows from the south, the chimney simply doesn't draw," she explained, fanning the air as if to dissipate the smoke with her hands. "I was so hoping for an absolutely calm day!"

"The chimneys at Brassen Court don't like a northern wind," Nate said. "I feel quite at home."

It was too chilly to douse the fire entirely. Besides, the dining hall at the Mayman house was an interior room, and the only illumination came from the fireplace, the wall sconces, and the candelabra liberally spaced along the table.

"I'm sure there are odd little quirks at Danan Hall, aren't there, Kirra?" Cammon asked, looking straight at his taster.

"Plenty of them," Donnal replied, raising his voice slightly, but keeping Kirra's lilting tone. "But my father is immune to inconvenience, so he never lets them bother him. And Casserah is much the same."

Cammon started, blushed, and struggled not to laugh. "I've never found too much wrong with Ghosenhall, though," he said a little breathlessly.

Senneth was not particularly good at social discourse, but someone had to redirect the conversation. "This is a very nice property, Lord Seton," she said. "How long has it been in your family?"

So they were rescued by genealogy, and then the servants came through with the final course. It looked to be some kind of cobbler, bubbling with fruit and sugar. Kirra had just tasted it and handed it back to Cammon when there was a sound in the hall and the door burst open.

Instantly, three Riders were gathered around Cammon and two had leapt for the door to block the intruder.

"Whoa!" the newcomer exclaimed, finding his way barred by a pair of crossed swords. He flung his hands in the air to indicate submission. "Seton, call off your men! I'm perfectly harmless."

Seton was on his feet. "My apologies, Chelten. You see that Queen's Riders have come here to defend the consort, and your abrupt entry must have startled them."

Tayse and Hammond dropped their weapons, gave brief nods to the young lord, and resumed their places against the wall, while the other three Riders also moved back into position. For another moment, Chelten stood where he had halted, elaborately adjusting the sleeves of his jacket, but appearing good-humored about the incident.

"I shall know what to expect if I ever go visiting royalty at Ghosenhall!" he said. "I will creep around the castle most carefully so I don't excite any alarm."

"Actually, that's likely to make everyone even more suspicious," Cammon said. "But it's not a good idea to jump through doors, either."

Chelten turned his eyes toward Cammon, obviously identified him as the royal personage, and sank to his knees right there on the threshold. "I beg pardon for disrupting your meal and thank you most sincerely for offering me this chance to meet you," he said. "I apologize also for arriving late, but I'm afraid that couldn't be helped."

"Well, we're glad you're here now," Cammon said.

"Yes, do sit down," Seton said. "You're in time for cobbler."

Chelten was on his feet again and scanning the table. "I've eaten, thank you, but I wanted to see—yes! Kirra! You *are* here! Let me give you a kiss!"

He dove headlong across the room with his arms outstretched. Donnal leapt to his feet, his skirts swirling around him, and Kirra loosed a squeak of horror. Oh, this was so funny Senneth almost let the situation unfold, but she wasn't sure Donnal would be able to stay in character if he were mauled affectionately by a lord. So she sucked in a hard breath and clenched her fists, and every flame in the room went out.

In total darkness, there were sudden cries of bewilderment, the stamping sounds of heavy bodies in motion, the flit and rustle of clothing as guests shifted position. "Bring us a candle!" Seton was shouting, and in less than a minute, servants were hurrying back into the room with lit tapers. The fresh light revealed all of the Riders converging around Cammon, who was perfectly unharmed, while Chelten had again frozen in mid-stride. Kirra was still on her feet, but looking much more serene—because now she really *was* Kirra, while Donnal had taken her place as taster at Cammon's side.

"What kind of madness has taken possession of your house, Seton?" Chelten demanded.

"It's the southern wind," the hostess said with a little moan. "It just blew out all the fires."

Kirra laughed and flung her hands out. "Don't be stopped by a few theatrics, Chelten," she said, her ailment all of a sudden forgotten. "Come give me a kiss, after all."

NATE and Sabina were in the coach on the way home, so naturally the rest of them couldn't discuss the hilarity of the dinner then; and once they pulled up at Gissel Plain, Kirra and Donnal melted away before Senneth had even disembarked. The Riders had already dispersed, and Nate drew Cammon aside, so Senneth was left to go upstairs all by herself, still trying to smother her grin.

When Tayse returned to their room a couple hours later, he locked the door, turned to her, and held out his arms. She collapsed against him, and felt him convulsed with silent laughter. She giggled, then she laughed, and then she was almost howling, clinging to his shoulders because she absolutely could not stand. They fell to the bed, still entwined, still helpless with laughter, and quite unable to speak.

Chapter
17

 AT WEN'S INVITATION, KARRYN HAD BEGUN TO visit the training yard in the mornings to watch the guards work out. It had taken a little persuading, though Karryn's reasons for hesitating had surprised Wen.

"Won't they think it's odd that I'm there?" Karryn had said. "I mean, don't they think I'm just a silly girl?"

"They might think you're a silly girl, but they've pledged their lives to protect you," Wen replied. "If you give them reasons to like you, they'll undergo that task with even more of a will. But they can't get to like you if they don't know you."

Karryn looked doubtful. "What if they get to know me and they *don't* like me? Then maybe they won't fight so hard for me after all."

That gave Wen pause—but, after all, *she* rather liked Karryn, and she was a difficult one to please. "Here's the secret to winning the hearts of your soldiers. Feed them well, pay them on time, never put them in unnecessary danger, and treat them with respect. If you simply learn and remember their names, that will please them. Not throwing a tantrum in front of them will help a little," she couldn't help adding, "but it's the respect and the money that will win them over first."

Karryn showed her true maturity by sticking her tongue out, but Wen grinned in response. Her comment had been deliberately provocative. "Anyway, you're an attractive young woman and most of them are men. They're predisposed to like you. That's the way of the world."

So Karryn had come down to the training yard the very next morning, wearing a flattering dress and a shy smile. As Wen had expected, the younger men were particularly eager to introduce themselves and proclaim themselves happy to be in her service, but even the old veterans like Eggles seemed pleased to meet the serramarra. Wen was impressed at how quickly Karryn was able to memorize and parrot back their names—even more impressed when Karryn proved she had actually noticed some of them before.

"You were with us when we went out on Coren Bauler's boat, weren't you, Amie? And, Moss, I think you accompanied me to Lindy Coverroe's house, didn't you? Orson—oh, I've met you a couple of times already! And one of those times, you saw me in a temper. Let me apologize now."

It was a charming performance, and it won over every single member of the guard. Even Wen, who hadn't particularly needed convincing. Davey, the youngest guard, perched on the top rail of the fence the whole time she was present, making no attempt to hide his admiration. Wen practically had to shove him back into the yard.

"Why don't you all show the serramarra some of the moves you've been practicing, so she understands why she pays you such a handsome salary?" Wen said. That sent them all scurrying off to find their shields and blades, and within minutes the yard was ringing with combat. Wen hadn't even had to pair off partners.

Karryn was unprepared for the violence; her eyes were huge as she watched. "Aren't they going to hurt each other?" she demanded, looking pale.

"They'll get banged up a little," Wen admitted. "Nothing like in a real battle, of course. Now and then someone's careless, and you'll get a serious injury. That's why we mostly use practice swords."

Karryn's eyes were fixed on the scene. "Are they very good? They look so ferocious!"

Wen felt a strange and wholly unexpected surge of pride. *I picked them. I trained them. These are my troops.* "They're getting better," she said coolly. "Orson's the best, probably always will be. Eggles is not quite his equal. You remember which ones they are?"

Karryn nodded and pointed, correctly identifying the men.

"So they'll probably win their contests," Wen went on. "But my goal is to get everyone as close to Eggles's level as I can before I—" Her mouth snapped shut.

But Karryn, always wayward, always noticed what you most hoped she'd overlook. She transferred the attention of her big brown eyes to Wen's face. "Before you leave? Is that what you were going to say?"

"Serra, you know I never planned to stay here long."

"I thought you might change your mind." Karryn watched her a moment. "Don't I pay you enough, Willa? Show you enough respect?"

Wen felt her mouth form a bitter smile. "That's what it takes to win over most soldiers. Things are a little different for me."

"Right, you're worried about saving everybody else's life," Karryn said. "But what if you leave and I get attacked and no one else is as good as you are and I *die*? Won't you feel awful then?"

Wen stared at her. The little brat. Straight for the gut with an underhanded blow. She said stiffly, "Maybe by that time I'll be so far away from Fortunalt that I won't hear the news."

"I'm a serramarra," Karryn said. "Everyone would hear that news."

Wen almost laughed. "You're a mean and manipulative child. Did anyone ever tell you that?"

"Jasper says it all the time."

"I won't leave until I can trust them to care for you. Is that good enough? In return, you must treat them all well even after I'm gone. Today was a very good start."

"I liked them," Karryn said. "I was a little afraid of them, but now I'm not."

"The head of your guard can turn out to be your very best friend. Many a marlord has a close relationship with his captain."

Karryn was nodding. "Mayva Nocklyn's captain helped her imprison her husband after it turned out he was poisoning Mayva's father. She says the captain was the only man she could trust."

Which made Wen wonder if she was encouraging *too* much intimacy between the soldiers and the serramarra. She wasn't up to giving Karryn a lecture on keeping a proper place, though; she'd just have to deliver that to the men. "You see? So take care to build a strong relationship with your guard, and they will gladly fight for you when the situation arises."

WHEN she made her report to Jasper Paladar that night, Wen made a point of praising Karryn's appearance at the training yard. It turned out he already knew of it.

"Yes, Karryn was quite full of Orson and Eggles and Davey and Moss," he said. They were still meeting in the library, still sitting at the little table, but they had not started another cruxanno game, for which Wen thanked the gods. She had, at Jasper's request, brought a deck of cards, but for the past three nights they had not bothered to play. They merely talked. Of course, none of these recent visits had lasted very long, either, and that made Wen a little sorry. She liked hearing Jasper Paladar's views of the world. "They say the queen knows every Rider by name," he continued. "No reason a serramarra cannot do the same."

Who would have expected him to bring up Riders in any conversation? Wen waited till she'd gotten her breath back, and replied, "And they say a Rider can walk into any room at the palace and interrupt royalty no matter what the occasion. I don't know that Karryn's guards should ever feel quite so unrestricted, but her captain should certainly have leave to come to her no matter what the time or situation."

He gave her a curious look, accompanied by a curious smile. "You feel free to come and go in the house, do you not, Willa?"

"If the danger were great enough, I would burst in on you

in the bath or in the bed," she replied, smiling back. "Any of you."

He laughed. "Well, then, I shall take certain safeguards that neither eventuality will leave either of us embarrassed."

That made her laugh in turn. "But I feel Karryn is safe enough behind the hedge," Wen said. "If nothing else, I have instilled in your soldiers the importance of a constant patrol. I think they are actually disappointed that no one has tried to breach the wall while they were defending it. It is when she leaves the House that I expect danger to strike—if it ever does."

"I doubt Tover Banlish poses a risk any longer. Did you hear the news? It arrived yesterday morning. He has been disinherited in favor of his younger sister."

Wen was pleased. "Excellent! Though I suppose this might make him an even greater risk than before. Now he will be nothing unless he marries a title."

"A man like that is nothing *with* a title, either," Jasper said.

Wen considered. "I don't know anything about how the marlords arrange their affairs," she said. "But does Karryn's mother think about planning a marriage for her?"

"Oh, Serephette started brooding over potential alliances while Karryn was still in the cradle. But Rayson's ambition threw all that out the window. There are some Houses now that wouldn't mate with Fortunalt for all the gold in Gillengaria. And—in case you hadn't noticed—Karryn's a headstrong girl. She says that Amalie married for love and she will as well. It doesn't matter how often we remind her that Cammon is Ariane Rappengrass's son—a bastard, maybe, but noble enough to placate the Twelve Houses! She won't hear of a political liaison unless she cares for the man in question."

"I have to say my sympathies are with Karryn," Wen said. "But surely there are some noble young men who are handsome and young? I don't know which marlords have sons and which ones don't—"

Jasper did, of course. She wasn't surprised. "There are the two Gisseltess boys, but even if Karryn desperately loved one of *them*, no one would allow them to marry," he said. "Another alliance between Fortunalt and Gisseltess? Out of the question! The same is true for Storian and Tilt, although Gregory

Tilton, at least, did the crown some favors during the war. Ariane has no unmarried sons and her grandsons are too young to consider. Malcolm Danalustrous has no boys. Kiernan Brassenthwaite has several, but I'll be damned if I let him sew up all four corners of Gillengaria. He has one brother in Gisseltess already and another in Danalustrous, and his sister sitting in Ghosenhall advising the queen. So Karryn must look outside of Brassenthwaite for a groom. But she is only sixteen, after all. There is plenty of time to find her a husband."

"Will you stay?" Wen asked. "After Karryn is married?"

He looked undecided. "I agreed to watch over her until she turned twenty-one—seven years, and it sounded like a lifetime two years ago! But I have become attached to Karryn and invested in the House. I will find it hard to leave unless I am convinced she no longer needs me. I suppose it all depends."

"And if you did leave? What would you do? Go back to your own house?"

He nodded. "For a time, at least. I have thought about going to live near my daughter so that we could work on a book together, but who knows what her life might hold in five years?" He shrugged and then surprised her by turning the conversation. "What about you? When you leave us, where will you go?"

"I don't know," she said. "I've never followed much of a plan. I might head east, though. I've seen very little of Gisseltess or Coravann, and I've never crossed the Lireth Mountains. Maybe I'll try that next."

"Oh, the men of the Lirrens wouldn't have any idea what to make of you! They prefer their women sweet and submissive."

Wen thought of Justin's wife, Ellynor. To look at her, you would think she exactly fit that description, for she was quiet and mild. But she had practically fought the gods to save Justin's life, and she had used her strange dark magic to aid the royal soldiers in the war. Wen hated her, of course, because Justin loved her, but she had to admit to a certain grudging admiration as well.

"I think I would manage just fine in the Lirrens," she said. "I seem to do all right wherever I go."

* * *

FOR the next three mornings, Karryn made a point of traipsing down to the training yard to watch her soldiers work out. Wen was pleased, of course, though the serramarra's visits tended to distract the guards more than she liked, and Davey was concentrating so much on Karryn instead of his opponent that he sprained his wrist fighting off a blow he really should have been able to deflect. Wen didn't tell Karryn this; she just splinted Davey's arm, lectured him sternly, and set him to doing small tasks around the barracks that could be accomplished by a one-handed man.

The fourth morning, Karryn didn't come down, but she'd already warned Wen that she was expecting company. Wen and two of the younger guards were on duty in the house when the Coverroe carriage arrived and Lindy went running upstairs with some kind of news for Karryn.

Five minutes later both girls were back downstairs, Karryn tying on a light cloak. It was finally spring, but the weather could be capricious—warm one day and full of chill the next. Today was sunny but cool, at least so far.

"Willa, Lindy has invited me to ride with her to a house just outside the city," Karryn said. "How quickly can you call together a guard?"

"Give me fifteen minutes," Wen said.

"We're only going to Mereton," Lindy said. "Our old housekeeper lives there, and she's sick, and my mother promised to send her a basket of food. And then she said it would be very nice of *me* to take the basket to her."

"I don't know where Mereton is," Wen said, preserving her calm.

"Oh! It's on the north road, just an hour outside of town. That's where our old house is," Lindy answered.

What did that mean, precisely? The house the Coverroes had owned before they spent all their money on the town mansion with the preposterous gold doors? "Even if Karryn's only gone a couple of hours, she needs an escort," Wen said.

She didn't miss the look Lindy gave Karryn—a roll of her eyes and a shake of her blond hair. But she didn't miss

Karryn's expression, either. A little smug, a little pleased. Karryn was starting to like having an entourage.

Less than twenty minutes later, they were sweeping out the main gate, two guards on horseback before the carriage, two behind, and Eggles sitting on the seat with the driver. Wen had chosen to ride in the rear because she felt it gave her a greater command of the field. She could scan the roads ahead to see if trouble approached; she could bend her attention behind her to listen for calamity racing up from behind.

Navigating the crowded streets of Forten City was tricky, as always, and she kept the guards in a tight formation around the carriage. But once they won through the northern border of the city, the road opened up and the travel became enjoyable. The sun climbed higher toward noon and brought a welcome warmth to the air; the countryside lay all around them, fields and forests competing to offer the most saturated shade of green. Wen looked about her with satisfaction. A prettier land than Tilt, that was for certain, and gentler by far than the territory around Ghosenhall. However short her length of service for Karryn, Wen reflected, it would have one benefit: It would erase for her that deep, instinctive hatred of the very word *Fortunalt*.

They arrived without incident in Mereton, which was a tiny village clumped along the side of the northern road. The Coverroes' former housekeeper lived in a small cottage with a sagging fence and an untended garden. Lindy and Karryn were welcomed at the door by a small, frail woman whom Wen guessed to be the old servant herself.

It seemed ridiculous to follow Karryn into the little house, though at the same time it felt like a gross dereliction of duty not to do so. Wen compromised by having all the guards dismount and prowl the limited grounds, instantly within call if a cry was raised from inside. She herself made one circuit of the building to determine where she might most easily break in, if necessary, but a quick inspection led her to believe there would be no way to keep her *out*. The windows were loose, the back door flapped open, and the roof itself looked so thin Wen thought she could kick it in and jump down to the floor inside.

As it happened, none of these measures were necessary. After a visit of perhaps thirty minutes, the girls emerged from the front door, waving good-bye. Lindy paused to give the old woman a polite hug, and then both girls climbed into the coach.

They were only twenty yards down the road for the return trip when Lindy stuck her head out the side window and called to the coachman. "Turn around! Let's go by Covey Park while we're so close!"

The driver obligingly pulled to a halt and guided the horses in a circle, and they followed the road north for perhaps another mile, all the Fortunalt guards following. Wen would have missed the turnoff that he eventually took to the left, it was so overgrown with weeds and opportunistic shrubs. The horses picked their way carefully through the vegetation, which thickened to clusters of trees on either side of the drive.

When the woods finally opened up, they were in a small clearing that contained a stark, severe house, three stories high and constructed of powdery gray stone. Masses of old ivy covered the entire southern portion of the house, so thick that Wen couldn't imagine any light made it through some of the lower windows. A flower garden ran the length of the front of the house, haphazardly blooming under what must be its own impulses and not the care of a devoted gardener. The entire front lawn was heavy with uncut grasses bending over with the weight of their seeds.

Wen couldn't entirely blame Demaray Coverroe for wanting to move from Covey Park into Forten City, even though she showed such lamentable taste in decorating her town home.

As soon as the coach came to a halt before the front porch, the girls were scrambling through the door. Wen was out of the saddle so fast that her gelding stamped his feet and tossed his head in surprise. She was on the porch before them, Moss and Eggles only a few paces behind the girls.

Lindy was surprised enough to address Wen directly. "What, are you going to come in with us? There's no one here, I assure you. Two servants and maybe a few ghosts." She laughed.

"An abandoned house like this could attract any number of

thieves and squatters," Wen said. "You can go in alone if you like, but Karryn doesn't set foot inside unless some of us are with her."

"By the Pale Lady's silver eye," Lindy breathed, and gave Karryn a sideways look. "She's worse than another *mother*."

Karryn's face showed both embarrassment and a touch of pleasure. "Oh, I don't mind," she said breezily. "It makes me feel important to be so looked after."

"It would make me feel suffocated," Lindy said.

Their arrival must have been noticed by someone because just at that moment, the front door swung open to reveal a woman who wasn't much older than Wen herself. Small, too, a little slatternly, wearing a much-mended dress that would have benefited from being much-cleaned as well. Her hair was dark and piled rather haphazardly on her head, and her expression was suspicious. But she recognized Lindy, for her face cleared immediately, and she dropped a slight curtsey.

"My lady didn't let me know she was coming to the house today," she said, sounding a little aggrieved. "There's nothing to serve you, if you were thinking of staying for a meal. Just some stewed rabbit and some dried apples."

"No, no, we're just here to look around," Lindy said. "I wanted to show the serramarra the old house. She says she's never seen it."

"It's a bit dusty," the housekeeper said, standing back from the door so they could file in. Wen allowed Lindy and Karryn to go first, but she was right behind them, and Moss and Eggles were on her heels. The servant looked even more doubtful.

"All of you? Tramping through? I hope you don't have mud on your shoes."

"I'm sure we don't. Not very much, anyway," Lindy said. She spread her arms to indicate the lower level. "This is the house," she said.

The first story was smallish, with a somewhat narrow stairway taking up the entire right wall. On the left, a pan-eled hallway opened to a series of rooms, and the girls peered through the doors one by one. Wen had been right; very little light penetrated the curtain of ivy on the southern side of the building. These rooms—a parlor, she guessed, a study, and a cramped library—were dark enough to seem spooky. None of them boasted much furniture, and the library offered no books at all, just a wall full of empty shelves and one lonely wingback chair.

"That was my father's favorite room," Lindy said. "He didn't like anyone else to go in there, so of course that's always where I wanted to be. I would wait till he was away on a trip, and then I would sneak in and creep around, looking for mysterious letters or treasure maps hidden behind the books. I was sure he must be hiding something exciting."

"Did you ever find anything?" Karryn asked.

"No, never! I suppose he just wanted to keep the place to himself because he got tired of dealing with my mother and me."

"Maybe something's been left behind," Karryn said, and stepped through the door.

Wen stepped right in after her.

The girls trailed their hands through the dust on the shelves and knocked experimentally on the wood that lined the wall. They tugged at the andirons to see if they might be connected to some secret spring, and Karryn tried to budge various stones that lined the grate. Nothing yielded up a secret.

"Well, if my father had any hidden treasure, it's still hidden," Lindy said, straightening up and brushing her hands together. "Come on upstairs. I'll show you my old room."

The sloppy housekeeper said, "Call out for me if you need me," and disappeared back toward what Wen assumed were the kitchens. Unescorted except by the guards, the girls flitted up the stairs, which took a sharp turn at the landing and delivered the whole party to the middle of the second story. Wen looked around with interest, automatically assessing the building. Rows of narrow windows at the front and back of this story allowed in bars of shaded light, but weren't wide enough for even someone as small as she was to force her way through. Good for defense; bad if there was a reason you needed to escape quickly.

"That was my parents' room, those two were guest rooms, that was the schoolroom, and here was my bedroom," Lindy said. She twisted the handle on the last door and stepped into the room. Karryn followed, the three guards right behind her.

It was the first place they'd seen at Covey Park that had some character and appeal, Wen thought. The room was high-ceilinged and painted white, so that it had a lighter and airier feel than the dreary spaces downstairs. What furnishings were left were also in very light hues—a spindly divan with white wood and soft blue cushions; a vanity table in white wood, set off by a tall rectangular mirror swathed in blue silk. Gauzy blue-and-white curtains fluttered at the windows, which were just as tall but not much wider than the ones in the hallway. There were more of them, though, so the light was better.

Lindy plopped down on the divan with a little puff of dust. More cautiously, Karryn sat beside her. The guards stayed motionless by the door, and both girls utterly ignored them.

"I was very sad when we left Covey Park two years ago," Lindy said. "I loved visiting the city, but I had lived here all my life and I didn't want to move."

"Why did your mother want to leave Covey Park?" Karryn asked.

"She says it's too far away from everything. Although I think the city is even farther! We have tenant farms another couple miles north of here, and my father would ride out to visit them every week. Now my mother sends someone to inspect them for her and come into the city every month to report."

"When did your father die?"

"Five years ago."

"Do you miss him?"

Lindy shook her fair head. "Not at all. We were never close. We scarcely even *spoke*. Sometimes I wondered if he would recognize me if he came across me somewhere outside of this house—if we met at a party in Gissel Plain, for instance. Would he have to be introduced to me? It's hard to miss someone you didn't even know."

"Well, I knew my father," Karryn said in a very dry voice. "And it's much better now that he's gone."

"But now that we live in the town house, I like it very much," Lindy said. "There's so much more to do in the city! So many more people to see! I never want to come back to Covey Park."

"Why would you?"

"My mother says the town house is very expensive, so if the farms ever have a bad year, we might not be able to afford it. And then we'd move back." Lindy sighed.

She could sell those gold doors and fund another couple years in town, Wen thought. Naturally, she did not allow the thought to bring even a small smile to her face.

"You could come stay at my house," Karryn said. "We'd go to all the parties together. It wouldn't be so bad."

"And maybe Coren would invite both of us to come out on his boat," Lindy said with a giggle.

That quickly, their conversation devolved from something that was almost interesting to a discussion of the more eligible young lords to be found in Forten City. Wen stopped listening until Lindy groaned and tossed a pillow in the air.

"And then next week my mother is making me travel with her to visit Deloden," Lindy said. "I can't bear it."

"Who's Deloden?" Karryn asked.

"My—oh, I can never get it right—my father's brother's first wife's brother?" Lindy said. "Somehow he and his family are related to us. They live on the southern coast, practically in Rappengrass. No one else there for *miles* around, nothing to do, and the most excruciating conversations imaginable! Deloden and his wife are bad enough, but they have two sons and they're just awful."

Karryn laughed. "What's so terrible about them?"

"Well, first, they're boring. They live at the edge of the *world* and they don't know anyone and they aren't interested in any of the things I have to say. One of them took me hunting one day, and then he *killed* things and swung them in my face—like I would want to see them! Birds and squirrels, all covered with blood, and it was *horrible*! I told my mother I never wanted to go back there again, but she insists that we visit once every year or two. She keeps saying she's going to invite them to come visit us, but so far she hasn't. Or if she has, they haven't accepted."

"There's no hunting in Forten City, so I don't know what they'd do here."

"They'd come visit *you* because I would bring them over every day!"

Karryn laced her hands in her lap. "My mother says the summer social season is starting and we should think about sending me to some of the balls," she said, her voice low and troubled. Wen's attention really picked up then; Jasper hadn't mentioned this before. If Karryn was going to be attending events at some of the other Houses, Wen was going to have an interesting time of it, trying to keep her safe.

Or more likely Orson. Wen wouldn't be staying long enough to trail behind the serramarra as she made the circuit of the Twelve Houses.

"Ohhhhh," Lindy breathed. "I'm so jealous. I would do anything to be invited to Rappengrass or Nocklyn! Or Brassenthwaite! It must be the wealthiest House in Gillengaria."

"I don't think my mother would send me so far," Karryn said. "But maybe to Nocklyn or Helven. Even Coravann, I suppose. But—"

"What?"

"But I don't know anyone at any of the other great Houses, and they would all hate me anyway," Karryn said in a rush. "I know I would be perfectly miserable. No one would dance with me, and I would just stay in my room all day and cry."

"Why do you think everyone would hate you?" Lindy exclaimed. "Everybody in Forten City likes you!"

Karryn pressed her lips together. "Because of my father. Because of the war. Because I'm Rayson Fortunalt's daughter."

"Ohhhhh," Lindy said again, this time on a long sigh. "It would be cruel and stupid for people to think the war was your fault—but people *are* cruel and stupid, much of the time."

"So I don't want to go."

"You could take me with you," Lindy suggested. "Then if no one asked you to dance I could sit next to you and watch everyone else and make spiteful comments."

Karryn giggled. "But people would ask *you* to dance!"

"I would tell them I would only dance with them if they asked you first," Lindy said firmly.

That was actually a much kinder promise than Wen would have expected from the shallow Lindy Coverroe. Karryn was moved, too, Wen could see, though she tried to act nonchalant.

"Well, that would be very sweet of you," she said. "It wouldn't be so bad to visit the other Houses if you could come along."

Lindy leaned forward, her expression suddenly mischievous. "And we don't even have to go to Coravann this summer, because Coravann is coming to us."

"What do you mean?"

"My mother says that Ryne Coravann is going to be in Forten City for two months! His father is sending him here to—to—help set up some port office? Something about trade, something about an uncle. But Ryne will be here for weeks and weeks! I'm so excited."

"I'm trying to think if I've ever met him," Karryn said, frowning.

"You'd remember if you had. He's very handsome but very careless—I'm not sure I've ever been with him when he wasn't drunk—and my mother says his father is ready to wash his hands of him. But charming! He was one of the lords who went to Ghosenhall to woo Amalie when she was trying to pick a husband. I can't imagine why she decided anyone else was better."

"Maybe my uncle will let me plan a dinner while he's here," Karryn said. "That would be fun!"

"I'm certain my mother will have at least one ball, or maybe a dozen," Lindy replied. "At any rate, I can't wait."

They were still on the fruitful topic of Ryne Coravann's many assets when there was a knock at the door and the slatternly housekeeper came in. "Were you wanting anything?" she asked. Wen had the impression that she wasn't so much offering to provide any service as checking to make sure her unexpected guests had not gotten into any trouble. "I could make some tea, I suppose."

Lindy came to her feet. "No, we'd better go," she said. "My mother will already be wondering what kept us so long on the road."

"Yes," said Karryn, standing beside her. "Time to go home."

THE return trip passed without incident, though the party didn't make it back to Fortune until evening had started to settle over the city. Wen spent a little time in the training yard trading blows with Amie, just to counter the sense that the day had been completely wasted. Amie was in her early twenties, a dark whippet of a girl who rarely talked and rarely smiled. But she was a natural fighter; she was the most improved of the raw recruits, and Wen expected her someday to be the equal of Eggles. After a quick meal in the barracks, Wen set off for the house to make her nightly report to Jasper Paladar.

The best part of the day.

Chapter
18

WEN FOUND JASPER IN THE LIBRARY, PORING over an untidy pile of papers. He looked completely rapt; she thought he might have a smudge of ink in his beard. She hesitated to speak, not wanting to disrupt his concentration.

But he had heard her come in, and he looked up with a smile. "Listen to this lovely little phrase," he said. "'The wakened blood careers / Through the body's weirs and frets.' Isn't that nice? I particularly like the internal rhyme."

"Very nice," Wen said, though she wasn't entirely sure what it meant and she had no idea what an internal rhyme was. "Is it from one of your books?"

"Mine? Sweet gods, no. Mine are very dry and precise. This man is a poet."

"So that was a poem? I don't think I've ever heard one before."

Jasper sat back in his chair, letting paper fall to the table. "That can't be right," he said. "Never heard a poem? In your entire life?"

"Well, if I did, I didn't notice it."

"But songs are poems, set to music—simple poems, it's true, but they meet all the criteria. They have meter, they have rhyme, they speak of deep emotions. Many of them are cathartic, and most of them create a mood. Any good poem will do the same."

He seemed to expect an answer, so after a moment she said, "Oh."

He was shaking his head. "Even in Tilt I didn't think they raised such savages."

She grinned. "It's not the House, it's the profession. Not many soldiers put much stock in poetry."

"Not even battle chants to get you fired up to fight?"

"Not the soldiers I know."

"But some of you do read, don't you? Now and then? A good story?"

"A few soldiers do," she allowed. "Especially to pass the time between deployments. But I never picked up the habit. I always thought books were boring."

He surprised her by jumping to his feet. "That's because you've never read the right ones," he said, crossing to one of the stacks of books on the floor and beginning to hunt. "I must have Antonin's *Rhapsody* here somewhere. Trust me, this is something the most bloodthirsty woman would find appealing."

She laughed. "That's an awful thing to say! I'm not bloodthirsty!"

"Well, you're certainly not a die-away romantic like so many authors expect women to be. I wouldn't give this book to Serephette, for instance, or Karryn or Demaray Coverroe! But it's one of the most brilliant character studies of our era, all wrapped in a tale of action and intrigue. You'll like it. Ha! Here it is."

His face was alight as he strode over to her with the book in his outstretched hands. Wen could just make out the title printed in gold on the worked blue leather of the cover. He held it out to her like an offering, but she made no move to take it.

"You expect me to read that?" she said.

"Yes, of course," he said impatiently. "It will only take a day or two—you see how short it is. Then we can discuss it."

"It would take me a month and I wouldn't enjoy a minute of it," she said.

He assimilated that and stood there a moment, looking down at her. She remembered again how tall he was. She had forgotten it somehow during all those days of playing crux-anno, when, seated across from each other, they had seemed more like equals. In stature, if nothing else.

"It would please me," he said at last.

She didn't answer that. She would like to please him—she would like to win the approval of any employer, of course—but this was a little like asking her to juggle cows. Even if she tried, she wouldn't be successful.

"Just read the first chapter," he said in a coaxing voice.

"I could say I would try, but I'm afraid I wouldn't get very far."

"Then—but I know!" he exclaimed. "I'll read it *to* you! Come, come, sit down. Just move those papers to the floor."

She followed him back across the room, but said helplessly, "My lord—"

He took a seat and waved her down, so she perched in the chair opposite him once she had cleared it of bits of manu-script. "It can't be any more tedious than playing cruxanno, can it?" he said. "You didn't enjoy that very much, and yet you indulged me."

"Well, at least I understand cruxanno," she said under her breath.

"You'll understand this, too. Just listen."

So she listened, but he didn't speak right away. He'd opened the book to its first page and studied it for a moment, as if savoring it, the way she had seen some men savor the scent of wine before taking the first sip. His face changed in a way she found difficult to describe—as if he was overhearing voices from a nearby room explaining mysteries that he had always wanted to learn. When he finally began reading, his voice was also subtly changed—more resonant, more deliberate.

I killed Maltis Fane with a single blow, the easiest strike I'd ever made to bring down a man. He had been focused on me for so long that it was a shock to see

*him lose interest in my face. He fell to his knees sound-
lessly, instantly, and his expression was already self-
absorbed; he was listening to internal conversations.
He no longer cared what I had to say.*

*Two more men in the house to kill and then I would
be on my way. But there was a noise in the hallway and
a voice lifted from outside. "Fane?" someone called.
"The girl is here if you still want her, but she's in pretty
bad shape." The girl, I thought. Then I'm not too late
after all.*

Jasper stopped reading and glanced up from the book.
"What girl?" Wen said.

He smiled. "That's the question, isn't it?"

"Is this a book about soldiers?"

"Not exactly. It's about a man who believes he has lost
his soul. And then believes he has found a way to regain
it—though that way involves about four more deaths on the
page and a handful that are only hinted at. It raises the question of whether violence can ever be the best resort—can, in
Antonin's words, be holy. But since the action sequences are
so exciting, many a young man has read the book for its story
and given not even a passing thought to its moral."

"Well, of course violence is sometimes the best resort.
Sometimes it's the *only* one," Wen said.

"Antonin agrees with you," he said. "Should I read a little
more?"

"Yes," she said, surprising herself with the swiftness of her
answer. "I like the way you make it sound."

In fact, he read for the next hour, and Wen sat there almost
unmoving for the entire time. Whoever this Antonin was,
he knew how to fight; as Jasper read a scene that described
a dangerous duel, she could perfectly picture the slashes and
parries. And he had gotten the rest of it right, too—the righteous elation when an unscrupulous man was beaten down,
the backlash of emotion when you realized a living, breathing
person had died at your hands. Oh yes, those were familiar
emotions as well.

She was startled when Jasper stopped speaking and closed the book. For a moment she felt like she had been jerked awake after a particularly gripping dream—to find herself in surroundings that suddenly seemed unfamiliar. Then the sensation faded.

"What did you think?" Jasper said.

"I think that I never knew there were books like that or I might have read one before."

He looked extraordinarily pleased. "So would you like to take it with you? Or would you like for us to read it together until it's done?"

"Oh, I want you to keep reading it!" she said. "I don't think it would be nearly as good if I wasn't hearing it."

"Yes, well, I am very vain of my ability to narrate, so you won't hear me protest, but I think you would find Antonin appealing even if you read him silently to yourself," he replied. "He's written a dozen books, you know. If you like this one, we'll try another, and so on through the canon."

"How many books have you read?" she asked.

"Too many to count! Well, let's see. If I am forty-five now and started reading in earnest when I was ten—let's say thirty books a year for thirty-five years—a thousand at least. Though I can't say every one of them was worth my time."

Wen couldn't imagine reading a hundred books in a lifetime, let alone a thousand. "Is that all you do during the day? Read?"

"That describes my perfect day, but no, in fact, it is not! Even when I lived in my own house, overseeing my own life and not Karryn's, I rarely could spend an entire day reading. But I probably manage an hour a day, at least, usually in the evenings." He surveyed her a moment. "Actually, I have read significantly less since you took up residence at the House. Between conversations and cruxanno games, you have absorbed much of the time I would ordinarily spend perusing a book."

Was that a complaint or merely a statement of fact? "I could come less often or stay more briefly," she said.

"No, no, your company has been a worthwhile trade for the loss of scholarship," he said with a smile. "A man like me sometimes needs to be forced to be social, to take part in the pageantry of the world. I vowed long ago that I would not allow myself to be swallowed up by words—either the ones

I wrote or the ones I read—that when I was offered a choice, I would take the interaction with the present human over the musings of the absent author." Her bafflement must have been obvious because he started to laugh. "I'd much rather talk to you than read a book," he summed up.

"Well, then," she said, because the statement pleased her but she didn't know how to react. "That's good. And when I come back tomorrow night, we can read together."

"The perfect compromise," he agreed.

She came to her feet. "Of course, if you're going to make me read books, I suppose it's only fair that I make you learn to wield a sword," she said.

He stood, too, leaving the book in the middle of the table among the welter of papers. "Horrifying thought," he said.

"I could at least teach you how to protect yourself from an assault by a lone attacker."

"I feel safe enough. It's Karryn I worry about."

"I am starting to feel that Karryn is well-protected," Wen said. "Orson and the others are coming together nicely. Pretty soon they'll make a fine guard."

As soon as she said it, she wished she hadn't, for his next logical question would be: *Then how soon will you be leaving?* The truth was, she wasn't quite ready to go yet. She knew she should; she was getting too comfortable, losing her sense of urgency. Some nights she lay awake thinking she would pack her bags in the morning and leave at first light. Other nights she just fell straight asleep, untroubled by dark thoughts. Those nights were the strangest, and the most unfamiliar.

Perhaps she could stay here just a little longer. Rest her soul just a few more weeks.

And Jasper did not ask the expected question; she sometimes had the sense that he hoped she would forget her plans to leave the city. "I'm glad to hear that they're improving," he said. "But I wouldn't think they're fully trained yet. I imagine it takes years before a group of disparate individuals really pulls together as a cohesive unit."

"Sometimes," she agreed, feeling oddly relieved.

"So you have more work to do, my Willa! I will see you tomorrow and you can tell me how much further you've progressed."

*   *   *

KARRYN was back at the training yard in the morning, greeting all the guards by name. They fought that morning as if performing for the queen herself, no one holding back. There would be some spectacular bruises in the barracks tonight, Wen thought, but no one would begrudge the manner of earning them.

Davey sauntered over after the first hour of the workout. With his right wrist splinted, he had been forced to practice bladework with his left hand, and he'd done fairly well at it, too.

"Does the serramarra care to take a little practice?" he asked Karryn, showing her his injured arm. "You see I'm hurt. You could probably take me on with no trouble."

"Davey," Wen said in a warning voice.

He gave her a look of injured innocence through a floppy fall of dark hair. "I think it would be an excellent idea for serra Karryn to learn to defend herself."

"Probably, but not from you," Wen replied.

Karryn looked between them, intrigued but uncertain. "Why not?"

"Because even injured, he could give a good accounting of himself against most men, and he'd certainly overpower *you*," Wen replied.

"I've never held a sword," Karryn said.

Quick as a flash, Davey had pulled his practice blade and offered it to her. She took it gingerly, obviously unprepared for its weight, and let the tip fall to the grass. "That's so heavy! How do you swing it around like that?"

Davey rolled back a sleeve to show off a pretty impressive array of muscles in his curled arm. "You build strength over the months and years," he said.

"I'd never be able to fight somebody with a sword," Karryn said.

Now Davey pulled a short blade from his belt, this one true metal. "Dagger, then," he said, offering it hilt first. "Can't use it except in close quarters, but you can certainly do some damage."

Karryn returned the sword and took the knife, examining

it with real interest. Davey's was plain but exceedingly sharp; Wen resigned herself to the fact that Karryn would cut herself, which she did almost instantly. But the sight of her own blood seemed to make her more intrigued, not less. "I might be able to learn how to use this," she said presently. "If someone showed me."

"I'd be happy to," Davey said.

Wen had a sudden intense, painful memory of a day spent at Ghosenhall. She and Janni were inside the palace, teaching the young princess how to hold a weapon. Both of them had relished the chance to get to know Amalie, who had always been so reclusive and shy. Not on that particular afternoon, though—Amalie had been friendly, determined to learn, and completely free of snobbery, and Janni and Wen had both found themselves delighted with their princess's openness. Cammon had been there, too, and they had laughed away the afternoon, despite the gloom that hung over Ghosenhall in those days. The princess needed to learn to fight because everyone was convinced that war was coming. They'd known they wouldn't have too many more carefree days.

"Willa?" Karryn asked, because clearly she had been silent too long. "Do you think it would be all right if he showed me how to handle a knife?"

"Of course it would," Wen said briskly. "Or someone! You don't have to take lessons from Davey if you think he's too forward." She gave him a heavy frown.

His expression was virtuous. "I will treat serra Karryn with the greatest respect!"

Karryn giggled. "I don't mind if Davey shows me. If he gets fresh, I'll just twist his hurt wrist."

"Serra!" he protested.

Wen reflected that Karryn probably could take care of herself after all.

"You might want to wear something a little less fancy," Wen said, indicating Karryn's dress. It was a simple enough style, but made of material that looked extremely expensive, and the lace at the throat would probably cost Wen her salary for the month. "Something old and tattered, if such a thing hangs in your closet."

Karryn glanced down as if to remind herself of her attire.

"Hmm. Maybe tomorrow morning, then. I'll find an old cast-off to wear."

She left soon afterward, and Wen took the first opportunity to crowd Davey against the fence. "If you touch her," she said in a pleasant voice. "If you make her nervous. If I look over and see the first sign of worry on her face. I will break your other hand. I will break your jaw. I will cut out your eyeballs with your own knife."

"Good," he said. "I was afraid you'd expel me from the guard."

She gave him a look of unspeakable disgust, and he laughed and poked her in the ribs. She was tempted to grab his arm, flip him to the ground, and batter his face just to underscore the seriousness of her threat. "You know I can kill you," she said.

"And you should know that I wouldn't give you any reason to," he replied, some of his laughter fading.

"She's just a girl."

"She's a pretty girl," he said. "She ought to get a chance to enjoy that."

Since Wen didn't know how to answer him—because she didn't know much about what it was like to be a pretty girl—she just gave him another darkling look and strode away. She took out some of her confusion and irritation in a hard bout against Eggles, but she was distracted. He bested her once when she made a careless mistake, and he almost caused her mock death until she beat him back with a sudden desperate frenzy. In the end, he was lying on the ground, winded and a little stunned, and she stood over him, breathing heavily and feeling like she had been pounded by rocks and hammers.

"I didn't think *you* ever had an off day," he observed from his position in the mud.

"Just want you to gain a little confidence with a near-win now and then," she said. His expression was skeptical, but he didn't bother to contradict her.

While they packed up the equipment after the morning's training session, Wen maneuvered a little to end up in the tack room along with Orson and Moss, the two guards she trusted the most. She laid out the situation—the serramarra interested in defense, the flirtatious young guard offering to be her tutor.

"Should I keep him away from her? She seemed pleased at the notion of learning from him, but—"

"Davey won't cross the line," Moss said, sounding certain. "Do you ever watch him with Ginny? He teases her and tells her she's pretty, but he never makes her uncomfortable."

"Ginny *is* pretty," Orson said in an admiring voice. "That hair alone! No wonder no one's ever late for dinner at the barracks."

Wen gave him a hard and level look. "If you touch her, I will cut your parts off," she said.

He burst out laughing and even Moss smiled. "I don't know how you ever find time to sleep," Orson said at last, "since you have to spend so much time taking care of everybody in the world."

"Not everybody, but Karryn, yes, it's my job, and Ginny certainly," Wen said grimly. "I'm the one who brought Ginny here and if something happens to her—"

Moss stopped her with a hand on her arm. With her other hand, she was brushing her pale hair away from her wide face. "Willa. He's just trying to get a reaction from you. If any of the men tried to seduce Ginny, Orson would kick them all the way through Forten City to the sea itself. He wouldn't let anyone hurt a young girl—and he's certainly not interested in one himself."

"Prefer me a mature woman," Orson said with a drawl. "One who knows a bit about pleasing a man."

Moss gave him a quick look accompanied by a faint flush and Wen thought, *What have I missed here?* Moss and Orson? They seemed an unlikely couple, she so odd and reserved, hardly any more feminine than Wen herself, and Orson so masculine and tough. Yet Wen had seen stranger pairings whenever women joined the ranks of soldiers. Throw men and women together in any situation, she supposed, and some kind of attraction would result.

"Well, we're not discussing Ginny anyway," Wen said shortly, since she didn't want to appear curious. "We're talking about Karryn. If you think Davey can be trusted to coach her, I don't see any reason she shouldn't learn a few moves. I doubt Karryn will ever be able to do much to defend herself—

but she's surprised me before. And it never hurts to be able to unsettle an attacker with a weapon he didn't think you had."

"I'll watch him," Orson said. "He's even more afraid of me than he is of you. He won't get out of line."

"She'll be back tomorrow morning," Wen said. "Ready to fight."

INDEED, Karryn was at the training yard the next day, garbed in a shapeless gray dress that she had to have borrowed from her abigail, since it had obviously never hung in her own closet. She was also wearing thick boots to protect herself from the mud, and she'd tied back her thick hair in a style that was unflattering but eminently practical. Wen was impressed. Karryn was here to do business.

She was accompanied by her guardian, which Wen noted in utter amazement. He had strolled down from the house with Karryn, and now he leaned against the fence, examining the yard with his usual curiosity. For a moment, he looked strange to her, and she wondered why. He wore the same loose-fitting jacket and unfashionable trousers that he always did; he had not trimmed his hair or his beard. It finally occurred to her that she had rarely seen him outdoors, in direct sunlight. This was an unfamiliar setting for him and she wondered if his behavior would change now that he was in it.

Almost immediately, something distracted his attention from the yard. "Gods, what a remarkable smell," he said, swinging his head to sniff the air. "Every year, I forget what a treat we are in for."

Indeed, the entire yard was heavily scented because, overnight, the hedge that surrounded Fortune had burst into ecstatic bloom. The gaudy white blossoms were so thickly clustered on the branches that it was difficult to see any green at all; standing beside the hedge was a little like leaning against a deeply perfumed cloud. Wen didn't wonder that Jasper was distracted. She herself had been drawing in deep lungfuls of air ever since she stepped outside.

"I've never smelled anything like it anywhere else," Wen said.

"And you won't," Jasper replied. "The story goes that Rintour Fortunalt—the man who built Fortune—imported seeds from some country whose name has been lost to memory. He planted them around his estate and coaxed the hedge to grow, but no one has ever been able to successfully transplant a cutting to any other patch of soil in Gillengaria."

"Is that true?" Karryn asked, looking pleased.

He smiled at her. "I don't know. But *I've* never encountered these blossoms anywhere except Fortune."

"No time to look at pretty flowers," Wen said briskly, because Orson and Davey had jogged up. "Is everyone ready?"

Karryn ducked between the railings of the fence to stand inside the yard. But she hovered close to Jasper, as if afraid of wandering too far into unknown territory. Still, her voice was firm when she said, "*I* am."

"Good. Let's get started."

They spent the morning showing Karryn various holds and moves that would frustrate an attacker and give her an advantage, however slight. Whenever Karryn didn't understand their instructions, Wen and Orson would demonstrate, and then Karryn and Davey would mimic their actions. Wen noticed that Davey didn't allow his injured arm to hamper him much, and she also noticed that he was very careful about where he placed his hands on Karryn's body. That might have been because Jasper, Orson, and Wen were all two paces away, watching intently. Or it might have been because he really would offer the serramarra no insult, even if he were alone with her. Just like Moss said.

Wen was proud of Karryn, who gamely tried any maneuver they described. Within fifteen minutes, the girl was spattered with dirt, and within half an hour, she'd been thrown to the ground and rolled in the mud. She had a smear on her cheek and her dark hair had come loose to hang in her face, but she just pushed it back impatiently and went to work again.

Wen tried not to spend too much of the morning glancing over her shoulder to gauge what Jasper thought of the whole engagement. She supposed that watching soldiers fight had never been the lord's idea of entertainment, and witnessing his ward trying to fend off an attacker could only make him shudder. Jasper Paladar was made for drawing rooms and libraries, not training yards and battlefields.

He was made to keep company with women who danced and read books, not women who scrapped and fought.

After about an hour and a half of a pretty vigorous work-out, Karryn pulled herself to her feet and shook her head. "I can't do any more, not today," she said. "I feel like my arms are breaking! And I just can't think clearly."

"I can't believe this is your first time trying to hold a knife," Davey said. Wen had noticed that the young guard flirted out-rageously only when he wasn't actually touching Karryn. With his hand on her back, he was very professional; with his arms crossed on his chest, his whole demeanor changed. "Girl as beautiful as you should be meek and helpless, but you'd have disemboweled me there if that knife was real."

Karryn was pleased. "I would have, wouldn't I? I wanted to!"

Jasper spoke up for almost the first time this morning. "It's still hard to believe that someone like Karryn could reason-ably fend off someone like—well, Orson here. She's so much smaller and more fragile."

"Karryn couldn't," Davey said. "But Willa could."

Jasper looked at Wen with his eyes narrowed, as if try-ing to judge whether that could possibly be true. Wen had the peculiar sensation that that had been his real question all along. *Can someone as little as Willa protect herself from the hazards of the world?* "Could she?" he said.

"You never saw her fight, but I did," Karryn said, climbing back through the fence rails and then leaning against them as if unable to support her own weight. "I don't know if Tover and Darvis were as good as Orson, though."

"They weren't." Wen laughed. "I'd have had a hard time fending off both of them if they were."

"He doesn't believe you," Orson said, glancing between Wen and Jasper. "Shall we give a demonstration?"

This was her punishment for tempting the gods the other night, Wen knew. *Oh, Lord Jasper, why don't you let me teach you to hold a sword?* And the gods had replied, *Even better. Why don't you let him watch you do the thing you do the very best?* No matter that now she was self-conscious and ill at ease. She would have to perform, and perform well, for the sake of her own pride and the honor of all women.

"Why not?" she said coolly.

Davey leaned back against the fence, close to Karryn. "Use knives," he suggested. "Show the serra how much damage you can do if you really know how to wield such a weapon."

Orson gave a wicked grin and drew his own knife, slim and deadly. "Excellent idea."

"Practice blades," Wen said firmly. When she and Orson worked out against each other, neither of them held back. The last thing she wanted was to give or receive a major wound while Jasper and Karryn watched.

"Afraid I'll hurt you?" Orson said in a taunting voice, but he tossed the knife aside and accepted the practice blade from Davey. Wen borrowed Karryn's weapon.

"Wouldn't want to completely embarrass you in front of the man who pays your wages," Wen responded. "I need you strong and confident, not whipped and hangdog."

Orson and Davey laughed. Jasper looked appalled. Wen didn't have long to fret over Jasper's expression, because Orson lunged straight for her with his blade extended.

She jumped back, ducked low, and bored in, right at his stomach. He spun away and hacked at her exposed neck, but she had anticipated the move and rolled aside. She managed to clip him pretty hard on his right knee, but he caught her shoulder with a glancing blow, spoiling her momentum and making her rethink her next two moves. And again, for he caught her from behind and sent her sprawling in the dirt. From her back, she bucked her hips and caught him in the groin with her heavy boots. Not enough impact; he staggered back, in pain but not incapacitated. She scrambled to her feet and attacked, slicing away at his ribs and his kidneys as he bent half-double and tried to fend her off with one hand. If she'd been wielding a real knife, he'd have been bleeding copiously by this time.

But he wouldn't have been dead, and there was plenty of fight left in him now. He straightened, whirled, and came right at her, trying to get in an underhanded strike that would allow him to rip his dagger from her belly up to her throat. He made contact. She could feel the tip of the blade through her protective vest, forcing a bruise right above her belly button. He closed the fingers of his free hand in the cloth at her neck and twisted, trying to strangle her enough to keep her from fighting off the motion of his knife hand. It was working; her breath caught and her vision darkened and she had that clear and frequent vision of what it would be like to die.

She dropped her blade, clasped both hands around the arm that was strangling her, and swung up her feet, kicking him in the gut with all her strength. He grunted and released her, wheezing for air. In a single motion, she fell to the ground, rolled, retrieved her weapon, and knocked Orson's feet out from under him. He tumbled heavily and she pounced, landing in a straddle across his back with her knife under his ear.

"If this was metal, I'd cut your throat," she said. She was breathing heavily and she felt his ribs working under her knees as he dragged in great gusts of air. "You're dead, my friend, and you'd better admit it."

She heard Davey's voice behind her, excited and admiring. "Did you see that? Did you see what she did with the dagger? She had to throw it away to make her move, but she knew exactly where it went, so she could snatch it up again as soon as her hand was free."

Orson took another deep shuddering breath and then lay still. For a moment, Wen knew, he had been considering how he could throw her off and continue the fight, but the reality of a knife to the throat had made him reconsider. "I'm dead," he agreed.

Wen heard Karryn clapping and cheering behind her. "Good for Willa! Does she always win?"

"Near enough," Davey said. "If Eggles and Orson take her on at the same time, she'll lose, but other than that, she's pretty much impossible to beat."

"How did she get to be so good?" Karryn asked.

Jasper spoke up. "I was wondering that myself."

Wen came easily to her feet and glanced over at Jasper; he was waiting for an answer. She had never seen his face look so severe.

"Told you," she said. "It's the only thing I ever wanted to be good at. So I am."

Orson laughed, coming to his feet and brushing at the dirt on his trousers. "Still doesn't really answer the question, does it?" he said. "It's the only thing I'm good at, too, and—" He shook his head.

"Well, I think Willa is marvelous," Karryn said warmly. "When should I come back? I want to be as good as she is."

That made all the guards laugh. "Come back any day you like," Wen said.

Jasper put an arm around Karryn's shoulders. "But for now I think you'd best go back to the house and clean up," Jasper said. "With any luck, before your mother sees you."

"My mother!" Karryn groaned, and allowed herself to be turned toward the house. She glanced back over her shoulder once to call out her thanks and promise to return as often as she could.

Jasper Paladar, on the other hand, did not look back once. Wen knew, because she watched him until he was out of sight.

Chapter
19

THAT NIGHT, WHEN SHE WENT TO MAKE HER report, Jasper was not in the library, though the Antonin book lay open on the table where they had left it the night before. Wen stepped back into the hall, considered, and then headed to the study where Jasper could often be found going over estate business. The door was closed, but a knock elicited a response, and she stepped inside.

Jasper was behind his desk, frowning over a paper. He looked up reluctantly to see who was standing at the door. His expression didn't change when he recognized his visitor. "Yes?"

His voice was cool, that of master to servant, and Wen took her cue from that. "Nothing special to report today, my lord," she said. "Davey's arm is better, no one got seriously injured in skirmishes. Amie has finally learned that maneuver from horseback that I've been trying to teach, but no one else has got it yet."

"Perhaps it's too difficult for ordinary soldiers to learn," he said.

As if Wen herself was not ordinary and that was the only

reason she'd been able to accomplish it. "No, it's a good trick. It just takes patience."

"Well, then," he said. "Thanks for checking in."

It was clearly a dismissal. Wen nodded and stepped back outside without another word. Her face was perfectly expressionless, but her mind was in chaos, and she stood outside the door a good five minutes, thinking.

Why could Jasper Paladar possibly be angry at her? She had offered no insult, been derelict in no duty, behaved in not the slightest detail differently than she had since the day she arrived. All that had changed was that she had helped Karryn learn to fight. Had he disapproved of the lessons? Had he thought it unladylike, inappropriate, for Karryn to be wrestling in the dirt, learning to strike and kick and bite members of her own guard? If so, he had had ample opportunity to say so. But Wen didn't think that was it. He had hugged Karryn after the practice, at any rate, treated her with the same casual affection he always showed her. It wasn't *Karryn* he thought shouldn't understand how to fight.

It was Wen.

She began slowly strolling through the corridors, head bent down, still trying to puzzle this out. Jasper Paladar had never seen Wen handle a weapon before—except in his library when she knocked Zellin Banlish to the ground. But that had hardly been a real struggle. It was mystifying. Jasper Paladar had *hired* Wen because of her ability to fight. The very first thing he'd ever learned of her was that she'd disabled two large men who were trying to kill her. He'd offered her money to impart her knowledge and abilities to others. So why would he be disconcerted—even distressed—even angry—to learn that Wen could destroy an opponent in fair and open combat?

Maybe he wasn't bothered by the knowledge itself. Maybe it was *seeing* her engage in full-out warfare, with no restraints, going for the kill—maybe that's what had bothered him. Maybe he had thought she was a more pristine creature; maybe he had thought battle itself was more dainty.

Maybe he thought that he could not waste his time talking about literature and philosophy with someone who scrabbled about in the mud and tried to cut out a fellow's intestines.

She started to feel resentful—enough so that she came to

a dead halt and considered striding back down the hallway to confront him. *What right do you have to judge me? I am exactly what I said I was, a soldier; I do exactly what I said I always wanted to do. How can you turn against me now? I didn't ask you to try to make me a friend. I didn't ask you to offer me books or read me poetry. How can you be angry that I am not the person you tried to turn me into? I am the person that I always was.*

Such a tirade would surely get her fired. Well, maybe it was time to be moving on. Time to change her fortune, as it were.

She was not ready to go, but maybe it was time anyway.

A voice inside her head then said the strangest thing. *I can't leave before I've heard the end of the Antonin story!* But who knew if Jasper Paladar would ever be willing to read her another chapter of that book? He might never recover from his unease—his disgust—with seeing Wen in her natural element. He might never invite her back into the library again.

She thought about it a moment, then she squared her shoulders and took up her customary stride again. Through the foyer, down the side hallway, back to the library. She picked up the book, marked the page, and carried it with her out of the room, into the hall, and out the front door. She nodded casually at Eggles, who was standing guard, and headed back to the barracks with the treasure in her arms.

Jasper Paladar didn't need her and she didn't need him. She could finish the story on her own.

THE unaccustomed coolness between Wen and Jasper continued for the next three days. Quickly enough, Wen got tired of the comments down at the barracks—"Oh, so suddenly we're good enough for you to sit with a while after dinner? What's the matter, the lord's company grown dull?"—so she engaged in a little subterfuge. She made her brief report to the lord, then she lurked in the back areas of the house for an hour or so before returning to the building she shared with the rest of the guard.

The very first night she tried this, she ended up in Fortune's formal kitchen. The cook, a large and forbidding woman, looked suspicious when Wen strolled in, though the rest of

the assistants and serving girls ignored her. Wen produced an
airy voice.

"I was looking for Bryce," she said.

The cook's face softened. "That little scamp," she said
affectionately. "He's here—I just sent him outside to throw
out the scraps."

A minute later, Bryce skipped back inside, an empty
bucket in his hand. "Hey, Willa," he said. "Were you looking
for me?"

"Just thought I'd check up on you. See if you were staying out
of trouble."

"He *is* trouble, just as any young boy is, but he's a good
one," the cook said. "Here, did you want the last of the bread
and jam? I saved it for you."

"Oh, *thank* you! Do you have any more chores for me?"

"No, you can go off with the captain if she needs you."

Wen and Bryce stepped out through the back door, she
grinning, he cramming the entire piece of bread in his mouth.
Night was starting to fall, lush with the perfume of the flow-
ered hedge and warm enough to be comfortable. "Ginny said
the cook liked you," Wen remarked. "But I didn't know you
were such a favorite."

"Women always like me," he said so matter-of-factly that
Wen had to laugh.

"Not me. I think you're a brat."

He grinned. "Then why did you come looking for me?"

"Just checking to make sure that you're all right. But I see
that you are."

He produced a deck of grubby cards from a back pocket.
"Because you're bored," he said. Wen sucked in her breath.
Damn the child for being able to read her mind! "Do you want
to play cards with me? Orson and Davey say I cheat."

They settled on a wooden bench near the vegetable garden.
The air was pungent with the green scent of growing things
mixed with the overpowering aroma of the hedge blossoms.
"Do you?"

"No, but sometimes—I can't help it!—I can tell what cards
they're looking for, and if I have those cards in my hand, I
don't play them."

Wen was grinning. "Well, this will be a challenge," she

remarked. "Sure, I'm good for a few hands with you. But I don't think I'll play for money."

She enjoyed the time with Bryce—and, the next night, the hour that Ginny joined them—but she couldn't escape a sense of things being askew. She could hardly confront Jasper Paladar, but she could fume at his unfair treatment. She didn't let herself think too long about why his coolness bothered her so much, when it would have been no more than she would have expected from any other employer.

There was no telling how long things might have stayed in this unsatisfying state if Demaray Coverroe hadn't arrived unannounced at Fortune on the fourth day. Wen was taking her turn patrolling the grounds when she saw the big coach turn in through the gate. She signaled Davey to send for her replacement, and she followed the noblewoman inside.

Probably nothing to fear from Demaray Coverroe. But Wen had made it a strict policy to allow no guests into the house without an armed guard within call, and she was not about to change her standards now.

The footman showed Demaray into the inviting parlor nearest the front door and dashed off to fetch refreshments. Wen wouldn't have liked to say she was trying to conceal herself, but she did take up a position that kept her somewhat in the shadow of the great staircase. It was entirely possible that Jasper didn't see her when he strode up the hallway and turned into the room. At any rate, he didn't close the door behind him. Wen edged close enough to overhear their conversation.

"Demaray. A pleasant surprise."

A slight laugh. "I'm afraid you might not think it so pleasant once I tell you my news."

"Please. Sit." There was the rustle of clothing, interrupted immediately by the return of the footman and the elaborate ritual of pouring drinks and selecting sweets. Finally Jasper spoke again.

"What's happened? You look upset."

"Lindy and I have been out of the city for a few days," Demaray said. Wen wondered if they had just returned from their visit to the so-boring Deloden and his loutish sons. "And we ran into trouble on the way home along the northwest road."

"What kind of trouble?" he asked sharply.

Demaray's voice trembled. "Our coach was stopped and bandits stole all of our valuables."

"No! Demaray, that's dreadful! What did you lose?"

"Some rings—some gold—everything in Lindy's trunk. She was terrified."

"But you weren't harmed?" he asked in an urgent voice.

"No—we were untouched, which I suppose was a mercy. But, Jasper, I had to warn you. Take extra care when anyone from your household goes a step outside the city limits."

"I'm sure our new guard can keep Karryn truly safe. But this is disheartening news, to say the least."

"I knew you would feel that way," she said very warmly. "And for that reason I hesitated to tell you at all. Jasper, this cannot be considered your fault!"

"Can it not?" he said wearily. "If Rayson Fortunalt were still alive, every citizen in the region would be shouting at the doorway, demanding that he do something to better patrol his roads."

"If Rayson Fortunalt were still alive, half the county would have been conscripted into his own personal army."

"My point is that the individual who sits in this House bears responsibility for the well-being of this corner of the realm. All this will fall to Karryn soon enough, and the gods know she is hardly equipped to grapple with problems of civil defense and troop deployment."

Give her a few more weeks of practice in the training yard, and she might do better than you think, Wen thought. Karryn was proving to have an aptitude for self-defense. She might well become a tactician if given enough instruction.

"In five years, many things will have changed," Demaray said. "The restrictions on the rebel Houses will have been lifted—the marlady will be able to command something of an army again. Then she'll be able to put enough soldiers on the roads to enforce order."

"There are days those five years stretch before me like an eternity," Jasper admitted.

Wen heard what sounded like furniture sliding across the floor. Had Demaray moved closer to Jasper Paladar? "You have been given an impossible task. I do not know how you manage it with such austere grace," she said. Her voice was even warmer than before, cozy and sympathetic.

He gave a slight laugh. "Most times I feel like I manage tolerably well, but then there are days . . . And I feel there is much Karryn needs to know that I have no idea how to teach."

"Is there anything I can do to help?" Demaray said. "You know I am always happy to have Karryn at my house. And I think she enjoys the chance to act like just an ordinary girl when she and Lindy are together."

"Yes, and we all appreciate how much you and Lindy both mean to Karryn."

"But is there something else I can do?" Demaray said, and her voice had dropped to a somewhat caressing tone. "For *you*, Jasper? I hate to see you so anxious and worried. If it will give you any pleasure or distraction, we would be happy to have you over just as often as Karryn comes. We'll send the girls to their rooms, and you and I could talk like rational adults. That might soothe your mind a little."

By the tone of his voice, Jasper was genuinely touched by this offer. "Why, thank you, Demaray. I might take you up on that someday soon. I often feel like I must lock myself in my office, going over accounts, answering petitions, making my reports to the queen. But I suppose I could slip away every now and then and spend my time on more frivolous pursuits."

"Exactly," she responded with a throaty laugh. "I can be entirely frivolous, if that's your mood, or entirely serious, if that serves you better."

There were footsteps down the hall; Wen quickly identified one of the footmen, who knocked respectfully on the open door. "My lady, your coachman wishes to know if you will be staying much longer, in which case he will have the horses stabled."

If Demaray was annoyed at the interruption, her voice did not show it. "Goodness, no, I meant to linger only a moment! I'm on my way. Jasper, don't forget anything I said."

"Bandits on the roads," he repeated.

"Yes. And a welcome at my house anytime."

"I'll remember," he said.

He escorted her to the door and gave her a shallow bow as she departed in the wake of the footman. Wen held her breath and pressed back into the shadows, observing him as he watched Demaray walk out of sight.

As soon as she was gone, he said, "I hope you found that edifying."

She was utterly silent for a moment, but it was clear he was speaking to her, so she finally replied. "My lord?"

"Demaray's conversation. I am aware that you audited the whole."

She felt her cheeks heat, but she didn't think he could see her all that clearly. "Most of it, I think."

"What did you make of it?"

"I think we need to double the guards who accompany Karryn anytime she leaves the compound."

"What did you think of her generous offer to keep me company on my darker days?"

Wen was suddenly furious. He had scarcely spoken to *her* for days, and now he suddenly wanted her interpretation of his conversation with another woman? "I thought you would be grateful for the opportunity to spend time with a lady who so obviously suits your notions of class and culture. Karryn goes to Lindy's from time to time, packing an overnight bag. Maybe you should do the same."

She was utterly astonished when he threw his head back and laughed. "Yes, I am aware that I deserved that," he said, still chuckling. "I have behaved very churlishly, I know."

She wasn't entirely certain what *churlish* meant, and she knew it was ridiculous for him to offer her an apology or for her to expect one. Still, it was what she wanted, and her reply was very stiff. "My lord has no need to explain his behavior to me."

"Don't I?" he said. He was gazing right at her, so perhaps the shadows were not as thick as she had thought, and his expression was thoughtful. "I think I do. I'm sorry I have treated you so badly these past few days, Willa. You mustn't think it was because of anything you did."

"That's not what I thought," she said, still coldly.

He sighed. "Men are strange creatures, and I suppose I am stranger than most," he said. "I operate so much on the theoretical plane. I do not always understand how my favorite theories and anecdotes translate into reality."

If this was an apology, it was one that made no sense. She didn't bother to answer in the pause he left. He came a step closer and expanded on his explanation.

"I love the tales of Rintour Fortunalt, but I'm afraid if I ever met him in person I would be disgusted by his rough ways and careless cruelty and probable body odor. I understand the man on the page, but I am not so certain I would understand him in person. I have for so much of my life been a man of abstractions."

She kept silent and he came yet another step nearer.

"In abstract, I understood that you could kill a man. But seeing you demonstrate the ability shook me to my core. There is nothing about you that is abstract at all. And nothing about battle that is poetic or pretty. I have made very few friends who had actual blood on their hands. I have spent the last few days trying to accustom myself to the notion."

"Men like you don't make friends with women like me," Wen replied in a hard voice. "You don't have to strain yourself trying to accept what I am."

He was now close enough that he could certainly see her face, even in the dimness of the corridor. At any rate, she could see his, familiar, curious, and rueful, wearing a half-smile as he peered down at her. "But we *are* friends, Willa, and I don't think either of us should bother trying to deny that. And friends are allowed to make mistakes with each other, and cry pardon, and forge on ahead, realizing that each misapprehension only leads to another level of better understanding. So will you let me say I'm sorry, and forgive me, and let us go back to the way we were before—changed a little, perhaps, but only for the better?"

It was an extraordinary speech for a lord to make to a person in his employ, but of course that was not the context in which he had delivered his apology. *We are friends, Willa, and I don't think either of us should bother trying to deny that.* Wen could not make friends—she could not be trusted to keep them alive—and every muscle of her body clenched against her conflicting desires to run from the building or drop to her knees and offer fealty.

You have a duty to this man and to this House, she told

herself sternly, but even she knew that that was not the reason she was able to convince herself to stay.

"Of course I forgive you," she said, but her voice was cool, mostly because otherwise she could not trust it at all. "And I would welcome the chance to spend the evenings with you, as we have in the past—any of the evenings you are not with Demaray Coverroe, that is," she couldn't help adding.

That surprised a laugh from him. "Demaray is a widow who is drawn to any man whom she perceives as powerful," he said, with more cynicism than he usually displayed. "My own power is reflected, but to her it is tangible enough, and she would like to bask in its source of light as closely as I will let her."

Whatever that meant. "Well, you don't want to disappoint a lady."

"No—and I don't want to disappoint you. Can you come by tonight after dinner? We had a few chapters of Antonin left to read."

"*You* did," Wen said somewhat rudely. "I finished the book without you last night."

That made him burst out laughing again. "Yes, I can see a man must be careful with you, mustn't he? He must never think you rely on him for anything at all, be it ever so esoteric. But I had thought with literature my hold on you was secure."

"You could pick out another book," she allowed. "I would like that."

"Most excellent! Then that is what I will do." He nodded at her, smiling carelessly. "Then I will expect you tonight at the usual time."

BACK in charity with Jasper Paladar, pleased with the progress her soldiers were making, and, for some unfathomable reason, not pushed by internal demons to move on. For a few days, Wen thought her life had finally achieved a balance of calm and purpose.

Then Ryne Coravann arrived in Forten City.

Chapter

20

THEY COULD NOT LEAVE GISSEL PLAIN SOON enough to please Senneth. But two nights after the wild dinner at Seton Mayman's, there was another formal dinner with even more Gisseltess vassals, and, of course, all of them had to be present for that. Senneth was interested to see that Warren was surprisingly well-behaved at that meal. Oh, he glowered at her brother whenever Nate said something particularly idiotic, but he responded to direct questions, he paid a little attention to the conversation, and he didn't fling himself out of the room after a furious outburst.

"Is any of that Justin's doing?" she wondered to Tayse that night as they were getting ready for bed. Well, she was packing clothes; he was lounging on the bed, watching her.

"Possibly," he replied. "One of the first things a Rider learns is to control his emotions. Anger can be productive, but it must be harnessed."

She carefully folded the blue gown, even though it would be impossibly wrinkled by the time they arrived in Rappengrass. "I'm not sure that's an improvement," she remarked. "Having Warren learn how to focus and direct his fury."

Tayse propped himself up on the pillows and grinned at her. "Oh, you must not have heard about this afternoon's conversation."

She looked at him with misgiving. "What?"

"Justin suggested that Cammon invite Warren to visit Ghosenhall—without Sabina and Nate, that is. Come see the city, live in the palace, get some society experience outside of Gissel Plain. Naturally, once he's installed, he would be invited to come down to the training yard and keep working out with Justin—or any of the Riders who showed an interest."

"Bright Mother burn me," Senneth said, and sat abruptly on the edge of the bed, the blue gown still in her hands. She thought it over. "I actually don't think I dislike that idea," she said cautiously. "Amalie and Cammon can be very winning. If he grows to like them, he might become an ally of the crown, instead of the malcontent his father was. I don't know about continuing his education at Justin's hands, but the rest of it might serve."

"Yes, and Amalie said—"

Senneth groaned. "Oh, she was present at this conversation, too?"

"Apparently so. She said she thought it was a wonderful idea, and she might begin inviting *all* the young serramar and serramarra to Ghosenhall in turn. Kirra said she thought that *you* would be happy to participate in their social education, drilling them on appropriate topics to introduce at a royal dinner table, for instance. Cammon replied in all seriousness that he thought you would do better to discuss Gillengaria history with them, and maybe talk about the gods and how they relate to magic. At which point," Tayse finished up, "Kirra couldn't keep a straight face anymore. So I don't think he would really expect you to participate in this plan."

She lay back on the bed, her feet still on the floor and her head somewhere near the region of his hip, and let the pretty gown fall over her like a coverlet of silk. "How is it possible that my life has come to this?" she demanded. "Playing older sister to the strangest king and queen in the history of the realm? Never did I dream about such a life when I was a girl growing up in Brassenthwaite."

He pushed the dress aside and tugged her up so she was

lying next to him, face-to-face on the pillows, and he stroked a hand through her flyaway hair. "No, when you were a girl growing up, you were dreaming about marrying a fine, noble lord and raising his fine, noble children—if you could figure out how to conceal from your cruel father how much magic ran in your veins."

She sighed. "Actually, from the time I was about twelve years old, I was trying to figure out how to get out of marrying Halchon Gisseltess, since it was clear from about that time that my father planned such a union for me."

He leaned in to kiss her on the forehead. "I cannot think that the life you have now is much worse than the one that had been laid out for you. Despite the fact that you have married below your station and you are forced to call the royal consort one of your closest friends."

"I suppose it's not so terrible," she allowed. "Though I could wish you were a little less respectable than a Queen's Rider. Marrying you was hardly enough of an affront to my family. I should have held out for a common soldier, I think, or perhaps a thief newly released from prison."

He drew her closer. "Even to win your love, I wouldn't agree to turn criminal," he said. "You must set me some other impossible task to let me prove my affection."

She put her hand on his cheek and smiled against his mouth. "Only one thing occurs to me at the moment," she said. "But I'll keep thinking."

THEY set out the next day for what would surely be a very slow trip to Rappengrass. The spring weather was damp and gray, so Senneth was happy to keep Cammon company in the coach, where Kirra promptly joined them.

"So you're coming with us to Rappen Manor," Senneth said to her. "And then to Fortune as well?"

"I plan to leave you at Rappengrass. I never really like going to Fortunalt."

"They say it's better now, with Rayson gone," Senneth said.

"Yes, but who runs the place these days?" Kirra said. "Rayson only had the one child and she's scarcely out of the schoolroom."

"Karryn," Cammon confirmed. "She's sixteen."

"But Rayson had a wife, didn't he?" Senneth said. "I'm sure *I* was never introduced to the woman, but I can't think her life was much happier than Sabina's."

"I met her a number of times, though I can't recall her name—Serephette! That's it," Kirra said. "She was a Fortunalt girl, Thirteenth House. When I was younger, I always thought she acted like a queen. She was tall and regal and haughty. When I was a little older," Kirra added, "I began to think she was insane. Abrupt and unpredictable and strange as they come."

"And she's raising Rayson's sixteen-year-old daughter?" Senneth said. "I don't envy Karryn."

"There's an uncle there, or maybe he's a second cousin," Cammon said. "He's acting as her guardian."

"Let's hope he's not some lecherous or power-mad old man trying to manipulate her into doing what he wants," Kirra said cynically.

"He's not," Cammon said.

"You've met him?" Senneth asked.

"I picked him."

Kirra started laughing. "Oh, well, then! I take it all back! He's gentle and wise and patient and good."

"I think so, yes."

Senneth said, "Will we meet him in Forten City? I must confess, you've piqued my curiosity."

"As we plan on staying at Fortune, I believe we will."

Senneth glanced at Kirra. "You'll have to continue on with us now. To meet the paragon."

"I really think Donnal and I will head back to Danalustrous after we've visited a bit with Ariane. I want to be there if Casserah needs me."

"My mother will be delighted to see you again," Cammon said.

Kirra looked at him, looked at Senneth, and back at Cammon. "Did you just call Ariane Rappengrass your mother?"

"He always does," Senneth said.

Kirra glanced elaborately around the coach, empty except for the three of them. There were Riders ringed all about the vehicle, of course, but none of them could overhear the quiet conversation inside. "You realize you're not *really* her son," she said.

He was grinning. "Since we went to a great deal of trouble to convince the Twelve Houses that I am—"

"Right, but Senneth and I know the truth. There's no need to pretend with *us*."

"It's not pretending, exactly," he said. "I never know when there might be another mystic nearby, someone who can read thoughts as clearly as I can. So I always think of her as my mother. I always refer to her that way. Even when I'm talking to Amalie. Sometimes I actually believe it," he added. "Or maybe I just like her so much that I want to believe it."

Senneth yawned and settled back against the cushions. "Well, she's not the most maternal woman I've ever met, but I'd have taken Ariane over my own mother any day."

Mischief lit Kirra's face. "As would I! Let's tell her we want her to adopt both of us. She already has five children—six, of course, including Cammon—surely two more wouldn't be any bother? And we're both old enough to take care of ourselves. I can't see why she would refuse."

"Because you're a hellion and no one would want to take *you* on," Senneth said promptly. "And I suppose I could hardly renounce Brassenthwaite again, now that I've finally reconciled with my relatives. So perhaps it's not such a good idea after all."

Cammon was peering out the window. "I hope you're not getting too comfortable," he said. "Looks like we're stopping here."

Senneth sat up. "Why?"

"There are people waiting for us. Oh, look, it's a little town, and they've put banners up to welcome me! And do you see that? Flower petals strewn all along the road. I'm going to have to get out and walk for a while and say hello to everyone."

The driver apparently had come to the same conclusion, for the carriage was already slowing to a halt. Senneth could see Janni nudging her mount over so she would be right at the door when Cammon stepped out. Senneth grinned over at Kirra.

"Oh, joyful day. A chance to mingle with the eager populace of Gillengaria. If I were a betting woman, I'd wager we only get another five miles before the day ends."

Kirra was laughing. "We may not make it beyond this village."

A small black bird swooped in through the open window and settled on Cammon's shoulder, calling out softly in his ear.

"Looks like Tayse thought I needed a little extra protection," Cammon said. "Donnal's going to ride on my shoulder and be ready to claw people's eyes out if they get too close."

"I thought you couldn't understand what he was saying when he was in animal form," Kirra said.

"I could tell what Tayse was thinking," Cammon replied. He twisted the handle and opened the door. "Ready?"

Senneth slid over on the seat, closer to the door. "Always ready to serve you, liege."

Chapter
21

TWO DAYS AFTER GOOD RELATIONS HAD BEEN restored with Jasper Paladar, Wen spent the morning watching Karryn fight a few rounds with Davey in the training yard. When the bout was over, Karryn was covered in mud and wiping a blade against the trousers she had begun to wear for these sessions. And then, in one of those transformations that Wen was beginning to expect of the serramarra, she skipped in a circle and performed a few dance steps.

"Willa, I hope someone told you. I'm going to Lindy's tonight. Demaray is having a dinner to welcome Ryne Coravann to the city. There will be dozens of people there, and maybe a little dancing. It will be utterly delightful!" She sobered immediately. "But I know some of you must come with me, and I promise to behave very well."

Wen was amused. "Yes, indeed, your uncle told me, for he and your mother are going, too. He said your mother was even planning to host some of her own events, so she must consider the serramar very special."

"Well, it's been so long since anyone from the other Houses has come to visit us," Karryn said frankly. "It's quite exciting."

"We'll be ready to go when you're ready to leave."

Davey climbed to the top of the railing and watched Karryn hurry back toward the house. "And who gets the honor of escorting serra Karryn to this grand party?" he asked.

She looked him over. He was still wearing the splint on his wrist, but it didn't seem to be slowing him down any, and this was the sort of outing that appealed to him. Davey liked people; he liked the color and excitement of any big event, even if he was only stationed on the outskirts. "You can, if you like," she said. "If Jasper and Serephette and Karryn are all going, we'll need at least six of us to watch them."

He nodded. Two guards to a subject as a bare minimum; that was the rule she had drilled into them so relentlessly that all of them accepted it now as unquestionable truth. At the same time, she would never allow them to empty out the compound. Someone must be left behind to patrol the grounds to prevent trouble from breaking in while the residents were merrymaking elsewhere.

"Glad to go," he said. "You?"

She hesitated. With Jasper gone, she would have the evening entirely to herself, except for what portion she spent taking her turn walking the perimeter. But what would she do with herself on a night completely free of distractions? Play cards in the barracks? Pick out another book from the library and read? "Probably," she said. "I like to keep my eye on Karryn. But you can round up the others."

"Best uniforms, I suppose," he said.

For these had finally arrived, handsome gray outfits set off by black trim, black cuffs, and black sashes sewn with mock pearls. They had all pretended to laugh at the extravagance of the material—high-quality wool, with piping of satin—but all of them were secretly pleased to own such fine sets of clothing. Karryn and Serephette had ordered new boots for the lot of them as well, polished black leather with tough soles. Very smart and very practical. The guards loved these, too.

"Outings like this one are the reason we got the uniforms in the first place," Wen said.

"Good. I'll be ready to go in ten minutes."

Of course, it was closer to six hours before the small caravan was ready to depart from Fortune and make the short trip to the Coverroe place. Serephette and Jasper climbed straight into the coach, but Karryn paused to show off her dress to the guards. It was a very dark burgundy, full in the skirts and the sleeves, tight at the bodice and the cuffs, and its dramatic color flattered her skin and her dark hair. Its primary ornamentation appeared to be ribbons, for long thin streamers of burgundy fluttered from each wrist and were woven into the braids that formed part of her coiffure. Another ribbon was tied around her throat and supported a great dewdrop pearl that fell just where her housemark was branded into her flesh.

"Don't you simply love this dress?" she demanded, dipping into a curtsey for them, to demonstrate how the skirt belled out around her.

"It's lovely, serra," Moss replied, managing to keep her voice serious.

"I'd trip over the hem before I took three steps, but it is beautiful," Wen agreed.

"Can't imagine anyone will look prettier than you do," Davey said.

Serephette called from the coach. "Karryn! What can be taking you so long? Get in the carriage right now."

Davey stepped up to lend her a hand, and Karryn smiled at him and climbed inside.

The trip was short, but the way was crowded. Wen preferred open road to a crowded thoroughfare any day, because you could see your probable hazards and had room to maneuver. She rode behind the carriage and spent the whole journey restlessly scanning the buildings they passed, gauging the striking distance of a weapon thrown from one of the windows, and eyeing the clumps of vegetation, wondering if they harbored assassins. She was pleased, when she glanced at Malton next to her, to note that he was doing the same. Not a skill most of these soldiers had practiced much before they came under her tutelage. Before she was done with them, any one of them would be good enough to ride to Ghosenhall and offer to serve the queen.

She could not decide if she would be filled with satisfaction or despair if Amalie completed the ranks of the Riders with someone Wen had trained.

The coach made it to the Coverroes' house without incident

and deposited its passengers at the front door. Wen waited until the Fortunalt party was safely inside, then nodded to her guards. Four of them melted into the shadows to patrol the grounds as long as the dinner lasted. Wen and Davey made their way around back to enter the house through the kitchens. The staff was familiar with them by now, and few of them even looked up when Wen and Davey stepped in.

"You'd just better keep out of the way," the head cook said, ladling gravy over a platter of meat. "If any of my girls trip over you while they're serving, I'll have plenty to say to Lady Demaray."

"You'll forget we're here," Wen said, and pushed through the door into the service hall.

Dozens of visits to the Coverroe house during the past six weeks had familiarized Wen with its basic layout, so she led Davey through the dark corridors that ran parallel to the main rooms until they came to a door that overlooked the dining hall. She didn't like it that Karryn was out of her sight for a short period of time while all the guests gathered in a small salon, but soon enough a door across the room opened, and the brightly colored crowd began to file in. Wen first picked out the people she was here to care for—and didn't Jasper Paladar look handsome in his finely tailored coat with the burgundy waistcoat embroidered all over with pearls—and then began assessing the rest of the company. Demaray was dressed in a springlike yellow that made her hair seem fairer, while Lindy was in a rose-pink dress that gave her an ethereal air, much in contrast to Karryn's striking darkness. Wen recognized Edwin Seiles and his wife, Katlin; the disreputable Coren Bauler; and a handful of other Fortunalt nobles. But there were plenty of strangers present also, and she made a point of examining each one thoroughly.

It was quickly obvious which one must be the much-anticipated Ryne Coravann. He was seated at Demaray's right, in the place of honor, and Karryn had been given the prime position of the chair right next to him. Wen had to admit that he *was* a most attractive young man, with an air of rakish charm. He couldn't have been more than twenty and was slimly built, with rich black hair that fell across his face in a careless fashion. He was finely dressed, of course, but his jacket was unbuttoned and the collar points of his shirt were uneven. A young woman across the table was speaking to him as she sat down, and he slouched into his own chair and gave her a devastating smile.

"Oh, I remember you from Helven last spring," he drawled, and the girl blushed pink and smiled and looked as if she had just been named princess of the realm.

Well, there wouldn't be much Wen could do if danger came stalking Karryn in the person of Ryne Coravann. He wasn't the sort who employed swords and daggers; he would do his work with flattery and laughter, and there was no defense for a girl's heart against weapons like those.

Servants brushed by Wen and Davey to carry in the meal. Wen flattened herself against the wall and continued to watch. Ryne had brought a wineglass in with him and emptied it in a final gulp; now he picked up a second glass already on the table, and finished that while servants were still making the rounds of the table. He turned to Karryn and gave her that rogue's grin.

"I can't believe I never met you before tonight," he said. "I go to all the summer balls, and I've never once seen you at any of them."

Karryn was making no attempt to hide her delight at his attention. For a girl who could be so self-conscious, she was responding with remarkable ease. She tossed her beribboned hair and said, "My mother thought I was too young to go out in society much, but that's going to change this summer. You might be seeing quite a lot of me."

"Oh, I hope so," he said, his long fingers playing with the stem of his glass. "Where will you go? Helven? Nocklyn? Farther north? Eloise Kianlever has some of the best parties. Brassenthwaite isn't much fun, but of course everyone goes whenever Kiernan entertains because he almost never does. Kiernan wants everyone to know he runs the wealthiest House in Gillengaria, so he doesn't stint with anything."

Wen missed Karryn's response—as more servants arrived, carrying more platters, the clatter of eating and drinking and general conversation made it impossible for her to hear any more individual interactions. She thought she had gotten a fair measure of Ryne Coravann in those few minutes, though, particularly when she added in the comments Lindy Coverroe had made about him earlier. A charming wastrel, addicted to good food, good wine, and good company. Unlikely to turn to violence, but a dangerous man in his own way.

Wen withdrew her attention from Karryn for the moment and glanced around the table again. Serephette was seated between Edwin Seiles and an older gentleman who appeared to be listening to her conversation with gravest interest, and she looked quite animated as she talked to him. The evening was young yet, of course, but Serephette appeared to be enjoying herself. Perhaps she would not find any occasion to sweep to her feet and go stalking from the room.

Jasper Paladar also seemed most felicitously placed, between two women who were close to his age or a little younger. Both had that indefinable air of breeding that, in Wen's experience, always marked a member of the nobility. While Wen watched him, he smoothly divided his conversation between the two of them, making first one smile and then the other laugh. The woman on his right wore a chaste dress with a neckline too high to show off a housemark, if she had one; but the woman on his left was not afraid to display her cleavage, and she leaned forward a little every time she spoke to him, as if to make sure he didn't manage to overlook it.

Wen tried to remember the last time she had worn a dress, let alone something that emphasized her figure. She thought maybe she never had.

Not that she would be displaying herself to Jasper Paladar even if she were to wear such a thing.

Nothing much of interest happened during the meal, except Ryne Coravann continued to drink wine and flirt with Karryn. He must imbibe on a fairly regular basis, Wen thought, for he showed no overt signs of inebriation and Karryn continued to look as though she was enjoying his company. Not exactly a point in his favor.

"I'd be on the floor heaving my guts out if I'd downed half of what *he's* been drinking," Davey muttered in her ear.

She silently agreed, but all she said was, "Nobles are different."

Davey made a rude noise. "Not that different."

Once the meal ended, Demaray shepherded everyone into

another room to pass the rest of the evening in casual conversation. Wen and Davey followed servants' hallways till they
were outside this new venue—a parlor of sorts, comfortably
set up with groupings of chairs and small tables. Footmen circled the room, offering trays holding sweets and wine. Ryne
Coravann disdained the comfits but he snagged two glasses of
wine, offering one to Karryn.

Karryn smiled at him, took the goblet from his hand, and
sipped at it. She must have told Ryne that she didn't like the
taste of this particular vintage, for he made a great show of
taking her glass from her hands, drinking from it, and utter-
ing a pronouncement that had her laughing. Then he held his
own glass to her mouth and encouraged her to try the contents,
and when she did, he gazed down at her with a lazy smile. She
nodded and kept hold of his glass, while he emptied hers in a
couple of swallows.

That was the end of their tête-à-tête, though. Lindy Coverroe descended upon them in a swirl of pink and the other
young women of the party crowded close behind her. Soon
the laughing Ryne Coravann was surrounded by a bevy of
girls, all of them giggling and blushing. Wen cast a quick
glance around the room to see the other young men looking
somewhat disgruntled, while the older adults seemed either
amused or completely oblivious. Serephette fell into the latter
category. She was seated on a small divan against the wall,
engrossed in her discussion with the man who had been her
partner at dinner.

Jasper was also among the visitors seeming to pay no
attention to the guest of honor. For he was standing on the far
side of the room in a small alcove created by the edge of the
great fireplace, and he, too, was deep in conversation. Demaray Coverroe stood so close to him that she was able to rest her
hand upon his arm. She was gazing up at him as if she were
Ryne Coravann and Jasper Paladar a freshly broached bottle
of the sweetest wine she was ready to gulp down in a single
swallow.

Well. None of Wen's concern if Jasper Paladar allowed
himself to be consumed by the Coverroe widow.

Wen spent much of the rest of the evening keeping her
attention studiously on Karryn. Finding the rest of the girls

at the party keeping a determined ring around Ryne Coravann, Karryn made her way to other groups—the young
married couples, the older dowagers, even the middle-
aged men, who tended to stand together to discuss matters of
absolutely no interest to girls Karryn's age. She did not look
particularly at ease as she circled the room—indeed, twice
Wen saw her pause to take a deep breath before approaching
some knot of individuals—and she realized that Serephette
or, more probably, Jasper had coached her on a serramarra's
social duties. But this was a forgiving crowd. No one met her
with anything but welcome, and Wen could actually see her
confidence growing as the evening progressed.

She'll do just fine at a ball in Helven, Wen thought, feeling
a small surge of pride. *If she's allowed to go.*

Who would have thought Wen would ever have cared about
the success of any serramarra at any ball across the Twelve
Houses?

It was well past midnight when the dinner guests began
dispersing. Ryne Coravann was sprawled on a sofa—still conscious, still engaged in conversation, but a little disheveled
and clearly, by this time, too drunk to stand. That didn't
seem to bother Lindy Coverroe, who perched beside him and
laughed immoderately at whatever he was saying, or the other
two girls who stood behind the furniture, giggling. But Wen
saw Serephette and a few of the older women give him looks
that ranged from concern to disgust.

A beautiful, dissolute boy. Well on his way to becoming a
ruined, polluted man.

Not Wen's problem, unless he involved Karryn in any of
his pursuits.

And then, only Wen's problem for as long as she stayed.

Chapter
22

OVER THE NEXT TWO WEEKS, WEN HAD MANY opportunities to view Ryne Coravann in a number of settings. Whatever reason he had had for coming to Forten City, it didn't seem to take up much of his time, for he was available for morning teas at Edwin Seiles's mansion, afternoon cruises on Coren Bauler's boat, and dinner parties at Demaray Coverroe's house. During that stretch of time, Wen didn't think more than two days in succession went by without some social event that involved Ryne Coravann—and, of course, Karryn simply had to attend them all.

It quickly became clear that a fondness for wine was not the young man's only vice. He was reckless, too, and absolutely impossible to restrain. During the nautical expedition, when they were an appreciable distance from land, he stripped off his jacket, kicked off his shoes, and dove straight into the ocean from the stern of the ship. All the girls who had been clustered around him shrieked with alarm, and Coren came running over, pale with horror.

Wen and Orson had crowded against the railing, trying to figure out how to effect a rescue. Wen didn't swim, so she wasn't about to jump in, but surely there was a rope they could throw him? It was a long, tense moment before Ryne's sleek head surfaced, and when it did, his face was alive with laughter.

"Sweet gods, but it's cold in the water!" he called. "Anyone want to join me?"

Coren was leaning over the rail. "Ryne! Are you mad? You'll freeze to death or drown!"

Coravann was landlocked, Wen knew, but somewhere the serramar had learned to swim, for she could see his arms and legs moving effortlessly under the water. "It certainly is colder than I thought! How do I get back aboard?"

At that very moment, some of Coren's sailors arrived and secured a rope ladder to the railing, tossing the other end to Ryne. He swam over and climbed up without any apparent difficulty, then shook himself like a dog once he was safely on deck. The girls squealed and jumped back.

"You'd better go below and warm up," Coren said frostily. "There's a fire in the galley. I don't know that I have a change of clothes for you, though."

"I'm fine," Ryne said, though Wen thought he looked pale and chilled.

It was Karryn, of all people, who stepped forward. "Coren's right," she said in a severe voice. She took hold of his wet sleeve and tugged him toward the stairs. "If you stand about in wet clothes for the next hour, you'll contract a lung ailment or something. Let's at least find you a blanket."

"You sound like my sister, always fussing," he said, amused, but he allowed her to lead him away.

Two days later, he almost came to grief on horseback. Karryn wasn't present at this event, however, so Wen wasn't, either; they only heard about it secondhand. Apparently Ryne had challenged Edwin's brother to a race through the crowded streets of Forten City, and he had run afoul of a small wagon being driven by an old man. Ryne's horse had sustained a nasty gash on one leg and the wagon had been overturned.

"But Ryne pulled out his wallet right there, and paid the old man at least twice what the wagon was worth, so there was no harm done," Lindy told Karryn while Wen was close enough to hear.

"What about his horse?" Karryn asked.

Lindy, who had seemed to think the rest of the story quite funny, grew serious at that. "I don't know. He let me take it home to our head groom, but Tom doesn't know if the horse will make it through. It would be awful if it had to be destroyed! Just because Ryne was having a little fun!"

"Yes," Karryn said, her face downcast, "that would be dreadful."

Wen herself didn't have any direct contact with the wild serramar until about ten days after the Coverroe ball. He had dropped by Fortune around the noon hour and been invited to stay for the meal. Wen didn't stand outside the dining hall and eavesdrop, but she followed her own rule and roamed the house as long as he was inside it.

On her second pass through the kitchens, she found Bryce there, sampling one of the little cakes the cook had made for dessert. Wen was seized with inspiration.

"Put that down and come with me for a few minutes," she ordered. Instead, he crammed the last of it in his mouth and followed her down the hall, licking his fingers.

When they were outside the dining room, Wen pointed at Ryne Coravann. "What can you tell me about the serramar?" she asked. "Good man, bad man, crazy, kind, dangerous?"

Obligingly, Bryce peered into the room and studied Ryne's handsome face for a few minutes. Wen was disappointed when he shook his head. "I can't read him," he said. "It's like his mind has shadows over it."

"Shadows?" she said sharply. "As if he's plotting something dark and secret?"

"No—more like—he's behind a curtain. It's very strange. I've never met someone who could just hide inside his own head like that. I can't tell *anything*."

Then Wen remembered. Ryne Coravann was half-Lirren, and even Cammon was unable to pierce the veils Lirrenfolk could draw around themselves. Cammon had never been able to read Amalie's stepmother, Valri, or Justin's Lirren wife. . . .

Just the person she wanted to be thinking of right now. Wen's mouth made a bitter twist, but she kept her voice gentle as she said, "Thanks anyway for trying. Now go back and get another one of those cakes."

Grinning, Bryce departed. Wen stepped back from the doorway so she could no longer see into the dining room, but she lingered in the hallway. From the tone of conversation inside, she guessed the meal was almost over and the guests would start to disperse soon. She wanted to keep track of the unreadable Ryne Coravann once he left the table.

But he was not among the people who filed into the hallway a few minutes later—and neither was Karryn. It only took Wen a second to realize they must have slipped out by the servants' entrance. Through the kitchens, out the door that led to the vegetable gardens, and from there, to any part of the grounds. Obviously they were trying to escape Wen's scrutiny. Would they attempt to sneak out the front entrance? Surely not—Karryn was aware that there was always a guard posted at the gate. Wen knew there was no second exit, because she had walked every inch of the fence herself, but there *were* portions of the hedge that were a little more bare than others. A man might push his way through if he didn't mind ripping his clothes up—he might then shimmy up the wrought iron reinforcing pole and heave himself over—

Wen spat a single nasty word and sped toward the front door, out into the warm spring air, and around the eastern edge of the house. She knew exactly where they were going, and *she* didn't have to move with stealth, trying to elude a patrol, so she actually made it to the break in the hedge just as Ryne Coravann was attempting to wriggle through.

Karryn saw her arrive and jumped back a pace at the fury in Wen's eyes. She uttered a little squeak, but that was all the warning Ryne got before Wen grabbed his wrist and yanked him free of the shrubbery.

"Ow!" he exclaimed, for she didn't mind if she hurt him a little, and then, "Ow! Ow!" as the sharp thorns of the hedge gouged his arms and face. He jerked free and put a hand up to his bleeding cheek, staring at her with more curiosity than anger. "Who are *you*?"

"It's Willa," Karryn said nervously. "She's the captain of the guard."

"Well, why does she think—" he started, but that was all the farther he got. Wen shoved him, hard, in the middle of the chest, so he landed heavily against the shrubbery and got a few more scratches on his back through his light shirt. "Hey," he said, and started forward, his hands balled into fists, and then she pushed him with such force that he tumbled to the ground.

"The serramarra," Wen said, carefully choosing to use Karryn's title, "is not to leave the grounds without at least two guards beside her at all times. I suspect you know that, or you wouldn't have tried to sneak off in this stupid and irresponsible fashion."

He shrugged but made no move to stand, still rubbing his cheek and eyeing her warily. "We thought it would be fun to see if we could outwit the guard."

"*You* thought it would be fun," Wen said in a dangerous voice. "The serramarra knows better. But she wanted to please you, so she agreed to try. That makes you a bully as well as an irresponsible boy."

Now he was starting to get angry. "It was just a little lark. A game. We were going to come right back in through the front gate."

By the way Karryn looked swiftly over at him, Wen suspected that had not been the original plan. "Were you? Or were you going to take her down to a tavern on one of the dockside streets? Introduce her to a few colorful sailors and buy her some rotgut wine? Give her an adventure right here in her own city?"

He shrugged again. "It would have been fun. Karryn never has any fun."

"The serramarra was kidnapped two months ago," Wen said. "That wasn't much fun for her."

Now he scrambled to his feet, staring over at Karryn. "I didn't know that! What happened?"

"Willa," Karryn whined. She hated anyone to talk about that misadventure.

"She was taken against her will by a young man of respectable family who had designs on her virtue," Wen said coldly. "You can see why I don't consider it much of a *lark* when a serramar wants to spirit her away for an afternoon's entertainment."

"Well, I'm sorry, but I didn't know," he said sullenly.

"Even if you didn't know, you should have respected the

wishes of her family—and of the serramarra herself," Wen
said. "She must have told you she was not allowed to leave
without an escort. It was cruel and stupid and selfish of you to
try to make her break her own rules, even if you didn't think
you were putting her in danger."

Clearly he was not used to being reprimanded, certainly
not by anyone so far below his own rank. His handsome face
darkened. "How dare you talk to me that way, you—" he
began, his hand going to the slim dagger at his waist.

Wen had him backed up against the fence so fast, her fore-
arm against his throat and her other hand buried in his stomach, that he was almost more surprised than in pain, though
he was quickly finding it hard to breathe. She was five inches
shorter than he was so she had to stare up into his contorted
face. "You cannot possibly hurt me," she snarled, at the edge
of her temper. "And you cannot possibly sneak Karryn out of
here without me finding you, and stopping you, and making
you sorry you tried. And if you ever, *ever* do anything to hurt
Karryn, I will find you, and I will kill you—serramar or no."

He was goggling, and his hands had come up to claw at
her arm, so she released him. He sagged against the hedge,
coughing and clutching at his throat. She spun on her heel,
prepared to stalk off without another word, but Karryn caught
at her arm. "Willa—"

Wen rounded on her. "I thought *you* had more sense! You
know the lengths we have gone to in order to keep you safe!
You know the guards are not stationed here merely to give you
consequence. They are here to protect your life with their own.
And then for you to throw away all that effort on a whim—"

"I'm sorry," Karryn said, wringing her hands. She looked
to be on the verge of tears. "But it seemed so harmless—just
to go away with Ryne—"

"He is not the last handsome scoundrel who will try to
make you compromise your principles," Wen said, giving
Ryne a hard look. He seemed mostly recovered; his breathing was even again, at any rate, but he was staring at her with
close, confused attention. "The gods alone know what some
of the other attractive rogues might ask you to do! Will you
go along with all of them because you want them to like you?
That's the surest way to ruin there is."

"No, I won't, it was just—I'm sorry! Don't be angry with me!"

"I *am* angry," Wen said. "Too angry to talk about this any longer." She cast one last glance back at Ryne, who seemed to have completely regained his insouciance. He even grinned, which incensed her. "I'm going to tell the guards at the front gate to come back here and make sure the two of you don't slip out after all."

Karryn blanched, but Ryne laughed. She didn't stay to hear what he said to Karryn or what Karryn replied. She caught the attention of the passing patrol and sent Eggles to guard the hedge until Ryne was gone from the grounds. She thought Karryn was properly chastised, but the serramar did not look to be easily cowed. She wouldn't put it past him to try to escape undetected, just to prove he could.

Furious as she was, she couldn't quite blame Karryn. It was that last light laugh that did it. If she'd been younger and stupider herself, Wen would have found Ryne Coravann equally irresistible. She had always fallen for the reckless boys, the ones full of careless deviltry. Justin, for instance. If he'd been born into the Twelfth House, all his considerable energy given no productive outlet, wouldn't he have turned idleness into chaos, just to churn up some excitement?

If this Ryne Coravann had had to fight his way into respectability, as Justin had, would he have turned into one of the most skilled and passionate of the Queen's Riders?

Impossible to know, of course. And it scarcely mattered who Ryne Coravann was or what he might become. All that mattered was that he not be allowed to put Karryn in danger. Wen was fairly certain she had managed to achieve that for the day at least.

JASPER found the whole Coravann Affair, as he called it, rather amusing. "You assaulted a serramar of the realm," he said, as they sat in the library that evening trading their stories of the day. "By my count, you've also engaged in battle with a devvaser, and knocked a serlord to the floor. What's next, a marlord? The queen? Have you no respect for rank or class?"

"Not when there's danger to the person I'm paid to protect."

Jasper leaned back in his chair. "You didn't seriously think Ryne Coravann posed a threat to Karryn, did you?"

"Did I think he was going to spirit her through the streets of Forten City, throw her aboard a rented ship, and carry her off? No. But I wouldn't have put it past him to take her down to the docks and get her drunk on bad wine. *That* would be bad enough, but if anyone truly wanted to do her harm, that would be the part of the city where she would be most at risk."

He sighed. "Well, you're right, of course. All in all, I am not sorry you were so harsh with the young serramar. It does no harm for others to realize how valuable we consider Karryn—and I think it is good for Karryn to realize it as well."

Wen made a face. "She's probably angry with me. I think I embarrassed her in front of a man she would like to impress."

He laughed softly. "In fact, I think Karryn is more worried that *you* are angry with *her.* She may not show it on a daily basis, or indeed, ever," he added, "but she greatly looks up to you and wants to please you."

That would make for a nice change, Wen thought, but didn't say so aloud. "Then she needs to try a little harder," was what she actually replied.

"I'm sure she will. Meanwhile, what do we do about Ryne Coravann? Forbid him access to the House? That seems pointless, since she will no doubt run into him at every social event from now until the end of the month."

"I don't think we can do anything about him at all," Wen said. "I would think we should focus on Karryn instead. Make *her* understand why slipping away with Ryne would be so disastrous."

"I think she has learned that lesson," he said.

Wen replied, "I thought she had learned it before."

"And there is to be another challenge to your guards and their defensive abilities," he said. "For Serephette has decided she must entertain next week. Partially in Ryne Coravann's honor, of course, but partially because Fortune has been something of a mausoleum these past few years, and it really is time it was opened up to company again. Do you think you can bear it? More truly, I suppose, the question is: Do you feel you can protect Karryn if we invite fifty or a hundred guests to the House?"

Wen nodded. "It's unrealistic to expect Karryn to spend her whole life secluded, or restricted to a few locations that I consider safe," she said. "We can guard her when you entertain—but we might be a little more obtrusive than she likes. By that I mean, some of us will actually be in the dining hall if you have a meal, and in the ballroom if you have a dance."

"I believe we are planning both a dinner and a dance," he said. "It will be an abysmal amount of work and trouble, but Karryn is very excited, and even Serephette appears to be intrigued. So little engages her attention, you know, that I am happy to see her getting caught up in the notion of entertaining."

Wen considered how to frame her next questions. "What was she like, before she married Rayson Fortunalt?" she asked finally. "And why did she marry him?"

Jasper sighed and leaned back in his chair, steepling his hands. "She married him because he was the serramar, and any girl in the region would have accepted him if he'd proposed. Did you ever meet him?" When Wen shook her head, he continued, "He aged badly, but when he was a young man, he was attractive in a sort of bold and energetic way. He used to *storm* into the room, even if he was just coming to ask when dinner would be served. Some girls consider that sort of energy romantic. I suppose Serephette did. At any rate, she was happy enough to marry him, or so I thought at the beginning."

"And what was *she* like?"

"Much more *present* than she is now, if you understand what I mean. She was never particularly warm, but she was always extremely intelligent—as a young woman, she could offer a spirited argument on any topic that happened to come up. If she'd married someone suited to her, I imagine she might have become quite remarkable. A scholar, perhaps, or a trader in exotic jewels. Someone who specialized in some obscure but fascinating field and threw her whole life into it. Instead, she married Rayson and basically withdrew from the world, bit by bit. What portion of herself she could not shield from

Rayson was systematically humiliated or brutalized, or so I've often surmised. The face that she shows the world today is the face that was shaped by marriage to Rayson Fortunalt. If there is another side to Serephette anymore, she keeps it deeply hidden. I hope that, the longer he is dead, the more she finds herself willing to emerge from her self-imposed seclusion. But so far we haven't seen much except the Serephette that Rayson left behind."

"I think Rayson Fortunalt did some damage to Karryn as well," Wen remarked.

"Unquestionably. He has left her unsure of herself, extremely self-conscious, and convinced no one will have a reason to love her—but I have always thought he could have done worse to her, and might have if he'd lived longer. I am glad he is dead. And not just because he tried to destroy the kingdom."

Wen had been on the battlefield the day after Rayson was killed. They had thought his death would signal the end of the war—it hadn't, but it had been an important step. She had joined with the others in celebrating the good news, but at the time she had viewed him less as a man, and more as an almost formless representation of evil. The more she knew of Karryn and the household Rayson had run, the more she was beginning to understand him as an individual.

None of that new knowledge made *her* sorry he was dead, either.

She pushed herself to her feet. "Well, he has left a mess behind him," she said. "But maybe everything will heal over in time, as you say. At any rate, Serephette and Karryn cannot be worse off now that he is gone, even if they never get any better."

After a few more words of conversation, she left him in the library, with his head already bent over a book. She was passing the great central stairwell when she came upon Karryn sitting on the steps, looking woebegone. The girl rose to her feet, standing on the third step, as Wen came to a halt. It was obvious Karryn had been waiting for her.

"Well?" Wen said. Her voice was stern, but not as cold as it should have been; Jasper's comments about Karryn's vulnerabilities had touched her heart.

Karryn laced her hands in front of her. "I just wanted to say—again—I'm so sorry, and I won't ever be stupid again. I promise you."

Wen nodded. "Apology accepted. But it is not for *my* sake that I wish you to behave with some caution. It is for your own. You are too valuable to take pointless risks."

Karryn came down the last few steps. "I suppose I'm not used to thinking of myself as valuable," she said. "Mostly I always just thought I was in everybody's way."

Which was as sad a remark as Karryn could have made. Wen said gravely, "Even if you never had a sense of your importance as serramarra, one day to be marlady, there is the value your mere existence has for the people who love you."

Karryn gave a hollow laugh. "There aren't too many of those people."

"Your mother—your uncle—your friends," Wen said, realizing the roster was shorter than it should have been. *But who has dozens of people on the list of those who love them?* Wen thought. *I have parents and siblings who will mourn my passing, but none of my friends even know if I am still alive.*

She closed her mind to the thought of those friends and forced herself to go on. "And someday, if you are a very good marlady, your vassal lords and all the people of Fortunalt will love you." She offered a smile. "I don't imagine it will take much effort on your part to do a better job than your father did, so it ought to be easy to win them over."

Karryn smiled in return, though she looked just a touch anxious. "I'm not sure I know how to be a good marlady," she said.

"You have time to figure it out," Wen said. She nodded a farewell and turned toward the door. "Goodnight, Karryn."

"Goodnight," Karryn said. And then, when Wen was ten steps away, she called softly, "Willa?"

Wen made a half-turn back to face her. Karryn hadn't moved a pace from the newel post. "Yes?"

"Would you really kill someone to protect me?"

Wen studied her a moment. Karryn tried to keep a casual expression on her face, but Wen suspected this, and not the apology, was the real reason Karryn had sat here waiting for her. *I'm not used to thinking of myself as valuable,* she had said. Karryn would never make her own safety a priority if she didn't think she was worth defending.

"Yes," Wen said. "If your life was at stake, I would take a life—or two, or three."

"Because I'm the serramarra," Karryn said, "one day to be marlady. Because it is your job to keep me safe."

Wen looked at her even longer this time. "Because you're my friend and I care about you," she said at last. "Because you are a serramarra, you are exposed to more dangers than an ordinary woman. But I would fight for you if you were just a girl I had found in the streets. As I would fight for Ginny, or Bryce, or your uncle, or your mother. I would not let harm come to any of them. It is you I would defend, and not just your title."

She had guessed correctly; Karryn's smile was utterly radiant. "I am surprised you have not left a trail of corpses behind you, if that is how you feel about all your friends!" Karryn said.

You don't want to ask me about the corpses, Wen thought. She gave a small smile and said, "I have fewer friends these days, so fewer causes to fight."

"I think that must be by your own choice," Karryn said.

"I suppose all of us live lives bound to some extent by choices we have made," Wen replied.

Karryn took a deep breath. "Well, I'm glad you have chosen to take your place at Fortune," she said. "I do feel very safe with you to guard me—and I promise to give you no more cause to worry about me."

Wen nodded. "Then goodnight, serra. I will see you in the morning."

Chapter
23

THE NEXT FEW DAYS WERE WRAPPED IN A BUZZ-ing layer of excitement as Karryn and Serephette began preparations for their ball. Tradesmen came to the door every hour, so naturally members of the guard had to be stationed inside the house to make sure none of the merchants offered any harm to the inhabitants. But much of the shopping had to be done on-site, so Karryn and Serephette often set out for the commercial districts of Forten City to visit florists, bakers, dressmakers, and jewelers. Each time, they were accompanied by a cadre of guards, and sometimes by Lindy or Demaray Coverroe—and more than once by Bryce.

This seemed so unlikely that Wen taxed Karryn with it after the second time Bryce had ridden along with them to the city boutiques. Karryn was laughing. "It's my mother's idea," she said. "She loves to bargain, you know, and she absolutely hates to pay a single copper more than she has to. She likes to bring Bryce with her because he can tell her when a vendor has reached his lowest price. Whenever he saves her a signifi-cant amount of money, she gives some of it to Bryce. I think they're both delighted with the arrangement."

Wen was grinning. "I guess you just never know when magic's going to come in handy."

Nothing untoward happened on any of these excursions, or at the House, despite the increased activity. Karryn was so busy making plans for the ball that she had less time to spend at the Coverroe house, which Wen thought was no bad thing, but from time to time Lindy dropped by to check on Karryn. Two days before the ball, and four days after he had run afoul of Wen, Ryne Coravann returned to Fortune for a casual visit.

Wen happened to be the one closest to the house when he rode up on his ill-mannered stallion. She considered calling for Moss or Eggles to follow him inside and make sure he got into no mischief, but then she shrugged and ducked through the door. What did she care if her presence made him uncomfortable? Particularly if it also made him more circumspect?

Wen loitered outside the parlor where Ryne made polite conversation with Jasper and Serephette while they shared afternoon refreshments. Once the plates were cleared away, Ryne turned to Karryn and said, "The day is too beautiful to sit inside. Can we go for a ride?"

Karryn was clearly torn. "Oh—I would—but I can't! The dressmaker is arriving in less than an hour to do my final fitting, and I *must* be here."

"Couldn't disappoint the seamstress," Jasper said.

"At the price of this dress, you wouldn't want to," Serephette said dryly.

Ryne stood. "Then let's just walk around outside until she comes."

Karryn jumped to her feet. "Yes, let's do that!"

Naturally, Wen trailed behind them at a discreet distance, far enough back that she couldn't catch what they said. Fortune wasn't nearly the size of the queen's palace; there wasn't that much ground to cover, nor were there as many gardens and nooks to get lost in. Wen wasn't surprised when Ryne and Karryn ended up sitting in a small gazebo set on the eastern edge of the property, close enough to the surrounding hedge to fall under its shadow at certain times of the day.

Close enough to the hedge to try to break through it if Ryne decided to test Wen's vigilance. No help for it; she had to be in a position to stop him if he tried to smuggle Karryn off of

the estate. That meant she had to be in a position to overhear
much of their conversation.

At first they talked about the ball and who might come.
Then he related some recent adventure that seemed to involve
a race, a bet, and a certain amount of alcohol. A clatter of carriage wheels on the other side of the hedge made her miss the
segue, but when it was quiet enough for Wen to hear again,
they were discussing their inheritances.

"Do you mind?" Karryn was asking.

At some point during their promenade, Ryne had broken
off a switch from an ornamental shrub, and now he ran it back
and forth along the stone slats of the gazebo. "Oh, I always
knew Lauren would be the heir," he said. "She's the oldest,
of course, and she's always been so *good*. You just look at her
and know that she's thoughtful and responsible and kind."
Wen could see the smile he gave Karryn. "Which is one of the
reasons I've always been so foolish and careless and wicked. I
could never compete with Lauren, so I had to be different."

"Do you dislike her?"

"No, I love her as much as everyone else does."

"So will you stay in Coravann Keep or will you find someplace else to live? Eventually, I mean."

He tapped at the slats again. "I don't know. I might travel
for a while. I've thought about going to the Lirrens someday."

"The Lirrens! Why? Isn't it full of strange, uncivilized
people who are always fighting with each other?"

He grinned. "Well, you could say that the people of Gillengaria are always fighting with each other, too, and some of
them are fairly strange, wouldn't you agree?"

"You know what I mean. The people there are different."

"That they are," he agreed. "Suspicious of strangers and
full of violence, as you said. But I'm curious about them. And
I could live with one of the families in the Lahja clan, I think,
since I could claim kinship."

"What do you mean?"

"My mother was from the Lirrens," he said. "Apparently
there's some terribly romantic story about how my father met
and wooed her, since Lirren girls aren't allowed to marry out-
siders. So I have uncles and cousins who've been coming to

visit the Keep ever since I can remember. I'm sure they'd let me cross the mountains and visit with them in turn."

"But what would you do there?" Karryn asked, clearly bewildered. "How would you pass the time?"

He laughed. "First I'd see if my cousin Torrin could teach me how to fight! He's amazing with a sword—or a knife—or his bare hands."

Wen felt a small shock of recognition when Ryne said Torrin's name. She'd remembered Ryne's Lirren blood, but she'd forgotten his specific family connections. Torrin had been among the Lirren men who joined the royal forces in the war. Senneth was somehow related to Torrin within the vast clan network that tied the Lirren families together. But Torrin had not come to fight for Senneth alone, or even for the king. He had come to support his sister Ellynor, who had married the Rider Justin. . . .

Yet another reason to dislike Ryne Coravann. Because he was cousin to the girl who had married the man who had broken Wen's heart.

How could it be that even the most remote and random strangers Wen encountered in territory as far from Ghosenhall as she could run would still somehow remind her of the man she wished she no longer loved? She would have to sail for Sovenfeld, that was all. She would have to leave Gillengaria altogether if she wanted to be certain she would never again hear Justin's name, or any name that reminded her of him.

Ryne was still speaking, and Wen gritted her teeth and continued to listen. "But sword fighting isn't what I'd really want to learn. They have this strange magic over in the Lirrens. Some of them can turn themselves invisible."

"That's not possible," Karryn protested.

"It's true, though. I've seen Torrin do it. The Lirrenfolk claim it's a power given to them by their goddess, and it allows them to slip through the darkness completely unobserved. I keep thinking that because I'm half-Lirren, I should be able to do it, too. Sometimes I practice."

Karryn was still unconvinced. "How?"

"I sit very still and I think about the way the sun shines and the shadows fall. I imagine being part of the shadow. I imagine the sunlight glancing away from me. I just imagine myself not there. . . ."

His voice trailed off. A moment of silence was interrupted by Karryn's urgent voice. "*Ryne!* Stop that! I don't like that. Come back right now!"

Her first word had jerked Wen's full attention to the gazebo and—*laughing gods and goddesses*—she could see that he had almost mastered the trick. His body had a dark and formless shape; he practically disappeared into an unexpected weave of shadows. It wasn't true invisibility—for she, too, had seen Torrin play that trick, and it was impressive as hell—but she didn't think it would take Ryne long to figure out the rest of it. And wouldn't the world be a risky place if Ryne Coravann could walk around completely undetectable, wreaking his endless mischief?

But laughter made him lose his concentration, and he was instantly his usual solid self. "I can think of *all* kinds of reasons I'd like to be able to completely disappear," he said. "And none of them are respectable."

"I'm not sure people like you should be allowed to have magic," Karryn told him.

"But you can see why I'd want to go to the Lirrens," he said. "So that's something I might do in the future."

If Karryn planned to answer him, she was instantly diverted by the arrival of a vehicle pulling up at the front gate. "Oh—there's the dressmaker," she said, jumping to her feet. "I have to go in now. Will I see you tomorrow at Lindy's?"

"Probably," he said, standing up to escort her back toward the door. "I've got nothing else planned, anyway."

"Good."

Wen followed them to the house and then loitered in the shadows while a groom went to fetch the serramar's horse. Moss had followed the seamstress inside; Wen would see Ryne Coravann off the property.

He surprised her by peering over his shoulder as if looking for someone. When he spotted her, he waved enthusiastically. His grin was such a patent invitation that she strolled forward to exchange a few words.

"Invisibility," she said. "You *would* choose magic like that."

He appeared delighted. "I knew you were listening."

"Was the whole demonstration for my benefit, then?"

"Mostly. But you don't have to worry. I'm not very good at it yet, as you could see."

"You *pretended* you weren't very good at it," she retorted.

This seemed to please him even more. "Oh, I wish that were true! I would sneak back in here tonight and start knocking over benches and flower boxes. Just to make you insane."

She didn't want to laugh, but she couldn't help it. "I've fought against magic before," she said. "Fought with it on my side, too. I confess I'd rather have magic as an ally than an enemy, but all it requires to defeat a mystic is a different kind of weapon."

He gave her that lazy, devastating smile. "Do you really think I'm your enemy? Or rather, Karryn's enemy?"

"Have you done anything to prove you're her friend?" Wen replied softly.

That snapped the smile right off his face, but then he gave a little laugh. The look on his face was appraising. "Maybe we define friendship differently."

"If you do anything to hurt her, you're not her friend," Wen said. "That seems like a pretty simple definition."

Now he was frowning. "I would never hurt Karryn. I know you don't like me, but I'm not cruel."

"You're thoughtless, and I think you don't know how cruel a thoughtless man can be," she replied coolly. "But you're wrong. I don't dislike you. I just don't trust you."

He jerked his head back, real anger now showing in his eyes. "I can't believe a guard has the nerve to say such things to a serramar!" he exclaimed. She had to think he was the kind of man who didn't trade often on his rank; she must have really galled him. "Aren't you afraid I'll complain to Jasper about you?"

The groom was leading his horse up—with some difficulty, as the animal fought and sidled all the way from the stables. "Go ahead and complain," Wen said. "I say what I want because I don't care what anyone thinks—you, Karryn, Jasper. Anyone."

"You'll care if you're released from your position," he said. He sounded curious, now, as opposed to threatening. He took the reins from the groom's hand but kept all his attention on Wen.

"It's a temporary position, anyway," she said. She allowed her smile to grow. "I'm already planning when I'll leave."

He swung himself into the saddle, letting the horse dance under him. "You're a strange one," he said. "But I admit you're interesting."

She was still grinning. "Ride with care," she said. "No more incidents in the marketplace."

"Not today, anyway," he said. He didn't bother with a farewell, but laughed, pulled the horse around, and trotted for the gate.

WEN recounted this entire incident to Jasper Paladar that night. "I don't know what to make of him," she summed up. "I don't honestly think he intends harm to Karryn, but I think he's careless enough that trouble follows him like a faithful dog, and Karryn could suffer for it."

"And yet, we have already agreed that it would be pointless to forbid him the house," Jasper said. "I see no reason to change our minds about that. Dangerous as he might be, she likes him. And I like to see her learning how to be at ease with a young man."

Wen grinned. "I suppose I can teach her to stick a knife in his ribs if he ever puts her in a truly risky situation."

Jasper leaned back in his chair. They had dealt out a card game, but after one halfhearted draw and discard, they had pretty much ignored their hands. "Is she still coming down to the training yard in the mornings?"

Wen laughed. "Yes! Even during all the excitement of the ball! Not only is she making real progress in her skills, but she's become a favorite with all the guards. Some of them would fight for her now even if they weren't taking home a salary for the privilege."

"Does that mean I can pay them less?" he inquired.

Wen shot him a doubtful look and he burst out laughing.

"A jest," he said. "Loyalty is more precious than skill. If anything, I should pay them more."

"Well, no one would object to that," she said.

Before he could answer, there was a knock on the door a scant moment before Serephette poked her head inside. "Jasper? Can I see you for a minute?"

He came gracefully to his feet. "Certainly."

They conferred just outside the doorway for a few minutes. Wen tried not to listen, but it was clear that Serephette wanted Jasper's opinion on a social invitation she had just received. Wen picked up her cards and sorted through them again, but she still didn't have much of a hand. It would be better to talk than to play.

Jasper was turning back into the room and his voice was a little louder. "I don't know," he said. "I'd have to ask Wen."

"Could you do that?" Serephette asked rather sharply. "As soon as possible?"

"I will," he said, and he closed the door. Returning to his chair, he picked up his cards without making any comment. Wen waited while he studied and rearranged his hand, but he seemed in no hurry to speak, so she finally said, "Ask me what?"

He looked up in surprise. "What?"

"What were you going to ask me? You said, 'I'd have to ask Wen.'"

He laid his cards on the table and studied her with sudden attention. "Serephette wanted to know if I'd be willing to visit the Flytens this week, and I said I'd have to ask *when* they wanted us to come."

Wen felt ridiculous. Not only had she been mistaken, she'd been caught eavesdropping. She could tell her face was heating, but she tried to sound nonchalant. "Oh. Sorry. I thought I heard my name."

"Which is interesting," he said, "because you've always told us your name is Willa."

Chapter
24

 WEN FELT HER FACE GO FROM RED TO WHITE, and her stomach closed into a hard ball of distress. She stared at him, unable to speak.

Jasper Paladar did not seem shocked or perturbed. In fact, he looked as if he had stumbled upon a most intriguing puzzle. "So that's your real name? Wen?" he said, trying out the sound of it. "Not very melodious. Wen. And yet it fits you, somehow. Brisk and to the point, though not at all harsh."

She had to explain—she had to apologize. No one enjoyed being lied to, particularly not a man who had hired you believing in your honor. This was grounds for immediate dismissal, and she should be spending her energy now arguing her way back into his good graces. Yet she could not think what to tell him, how much to give away. So she remained silent and merely watched him, though every nerve quivered with the need to dash from the room.

"I see by your stricken face that you think you're a moment away from being unceremoniously ejected from the grounds," he said, his voice still pleasant. "Will it make you feel less uneasy if I tell you that I am in no way surprised at this revelation? It was always clear to me that you had secrets, and your identity was certainly one of them. I am just sorry that circumstances have tripped you up. I was rather hoping you would confide in me one day of your own free will, because you had come to trust me."

"I do trust you," she said, almost forcing the words out.

He laid his fingertips together and leaned back in his chair. "And it was always clear that Willa could not possibly be your real name," he said, smiling a little. "I wonder why you chose it."

She took a breath and made two tries before she could answer. "It is—it is my name, or part of it," she said. "My family all call me Willa, but I tell my friends I am Wen. My true name is Willawendiss."

"Willawendiss! The tragic heroine of Danalustrous!" he exclaimed. "But that's a most romantic name—entirely unsuitable for you, of course, but with a glorious and heart-breaking story behind it. It was always my daughter's favorite tale. Someone in your family must have had a taste for the old folk stories."

"My mother," Wen said.

"Somewhere in the library I have a book called *Epics of the North*, and it has a couple versions of Willawendiss's story in it. I'll let you borrow it, now that we've done with Antonin. She was quite a popular girl a couple hundred years ago—she performed a singular act of sacrificial bravery and then threw herself into the northern sea out of grief and despair. But I thought you were from Tilt, where they have all sorts of brave heroines of their own. Elisa and Altaverra—"

Wen's mouth twisted. "Two of my sisters' names."

"So she called you after the doomed but noble girl, thinking you would become—what? Gloomy but honorable?"

Wen managed a smile. "I don't think she expected any of us to turn out like our names. She just liked the way they sounded."

He put a hand to his chest and declaimed, " 'Save us, save your loved ones, Willawendiss!' Never such a heartrending cry went so horribly unanswered! She had to choose, you see, between saving five members of her family and two hundred people in the village. Not an easy decision for anyone to make, but history generally concedes she chose correctly."

"She was real, then?"

"She was, as far as we can determine. Unlike Altaverra, who was probably an amalgam of two or three girls who lived at about the same time. And Elisa is thought to be an entirely fabricated woman, though her story is even more dashing. They're all covered in *Epics of the North*. You can be reading about your family for days."

Wen smiled tightly and did not answer.

Jasper dropped his hand and tilted his head to one side. "But I suppose the real question at hand is not 'how do you resemble your namesake?' but 'why bother concealing your true name at all?' You are not, forgive me, like Senneth Brassenthwaite, who disappeared for nearly twenty years and had a name that everyone in the Twelve Houses would recognize. I have not heard of Wen any more than I have heard of Willa. So why bother with the deception?"

She made a helpless gesture. "I wanted to leave myself behind. That meant leaving my name behind as well."

He watched her gravely. "Making sure that no one who might be looking for you would be able to trace you by your name."

She shrugged and was silent.

"*Is* anyone looking for you, Wen?" he asked gently.

That was a question that had haunted her nights ever since she walked out of Ghosenhall. *Were* they hunting for her, those friends who had been closer than siblings, those companions who had helped her discover her absolute limits and then pushed her to achieve more? She had had no contact with any of them; she had not answered the letters forwarded to her from her mother; she had changed her own address so frequently that even if her mother gave it out, it would have been hard for anyone to track her down. Not impossible, perhaps, but were they even trying? Most days she could not decide which would be worse—knowing they would not let her go, or knowing that they already had.

"If they are, it is because they miss me," she said at last, "and not because I harmed them."

"And if they miss you," he said, his voice gentler still, "should you not return to them and let them know you are well?"

She surged to her feet, unable to sit still. "I can't," she said. She wanted to pace—she wanted to run from the room—but she thought she might fall over if she tried. So she stood there, trembling, wringing her hands together to keep them from shaking. "I can't," she said. "That life is over. I can't go back to it."

More leisurely, he came to his feet on the other side of the table. Now he looked concerned and deeply sympathetic. "I wish you would tell me, Wen," he said, "what terrors that old life held."

"I told you," she said. "I failed to save someone I was sworn to protect."

"Who?" he said. "Who died?"

She shook her head in short, jerky motions. "It doesn't matter. If it was a boy in an alley or a marlady in her House. I was trusted but I failed. I am unreliable."

"You are utterly reliable," he said. "So much so that I am convinced it was impossible to save this person who so unfortunately met his demise. He willfully darted into the streets to be run over by a carriage, or flung himself from a turret, or swallowed poison, or buried a dagger in his heart. Or she, of course."

"He did none of those things," Wen whispered. "He wanted to live."

"Did you abandon him? Desert him in his hour of desperate need?"

"*No!* I fought beside him, but I—but he—he fell and I did not."

"Were you injured?"

Reluctantly she nodded.

"Severely?"

"Yes."

"So you both took blows, yet only his were fatal?"

"Others died defending him."

Jasper took a deep breath. "So you were in mortal battle, and everyone around you was in a brutal fight, and some lost their lives and some did not, and you yourself were badly hurt, and yet you believe it was *your* fault that this man died?"

"I should have died first!" she burst out. Now she found the power to move again; now she did break away and pace, feeling caged, feeling desperate. "I should have been dead before the sword went through his body!"

"So that is what haunts you," he said. "Not that you failed, but that you survived."

She whirled on him. "Because I failed, I don't deserve to live!"

"Then why do you?" he said. "You know how to take a life. Why haven't you taken your own?"

She stared back at him, motionless again. Shocked that he had spoken the words. But his expression wasn't severe; he had not meant them harshly. He had intended them as a hammer blow, aimed at her hard shell of self-loathing.

"That would have been another failure," she said at last. "I was prepared to lose my life, but I thought I should make it count. I thought I should sacrifice it on someone else's behalf. I am surprised it has taken me so long."

He nodded, as if that didn't surprise him, either. "So you went to Karryn's rescue, expecting to die. And you fought for Bryce and Ginny, expecting to die."

She felt a surge of irritation. "No. I wasn't even close to death either of those times. I knew I was better than my assailants."

"So even though you're worthless and you ought to be dead, you're good enough to save other people—strangers— although your actions won't bring you any closer to your ultimate goal of losing your own life."

She was jerked into motion again and strode angrily around the room. "You don't understand," she flung at him over her shoulder.

He pivoted just enough to watch her as she moved. "I'm trying to."

"As long as I live, I must turn my fighting ability to some kind of good. It is not enough to atone for what I have done wrong, but it improves the world by a small amount. And I will continue, day by day, trying to make up for that other loss, by using my sword to fight for anyone who needs protecting." She came to a sudden halt and swung around to face him. "But if I die in any of those attempts, that will be a relief to me. I don't really care about living. I only care about using what life I have left in a way that matters, at least a little."

"You're right," he said solemnly. "With an attitude like that, it's a surprise you aren't already dead."

"It will be hard to kill me. You don't really understand how good I am."

"And what kind of woman is such a skilled warrior that she is almost impossible to defeat?" he asked. "I think perhaps I shouldn't be asking for your true name, but your true profession. What position did you hold before, Wen, in whose household?"

She caught her breath. Just by knowing to pose the question, he would be able to deduce the answer. Perhaps he had known the answer all along—and perhaps it didn't matter. She was running from her own memories of Ghosenhall. What other people thought of her could hardly weigh her down more than those regrets.

Still, she did not reply aloud, but watched him with a wary gaze.

He nodded once, shortly, as if coming to an inevitable conclusion. "You're a Rider, aren't you? In service to Amalie."

"No," she said sharply. "I never swore my fealty to the queen."

"You must have been present when Baryn died."

She wheeled away from him, for it hurt to hear the words said aloud, hurt even to hear the king's name. "We were all there that day," she said, her voice very soft. "Assassins slipped over the palace walls—hundreds of them. Fifty Riders and assorted mystics held them off until the city guard could arrive. You never saw such slaughter in such a small space. You never saw soldiers fight so hard. Princess Amalie was spared. Queen Valri was spared. But the Rider Tir was killed, and Baryn after him, his body crumpling on top of Tir's. You could not tell their blood apart as it pooled there on the floor. *That* is the way a Rider should die."

She swung back to face him. She felt heavy, lost, oppressed with an old grief that never seemed to lose its sharpness. "Do you think Tayse would still be alive if the king was dead? Would Justin? No. Hammond fell guarding the princess, and only magic kept him alive long enough to recover. Four other Riders died that day. I should have, but I did not. I would not swear my oath to Amalie because I could not be trusted to keep her safe. Maybe you should not trust me with Karryn's life, either. I'm hard to kill, but death is not afraid to follow in my wake."

There was nothing more to be said. She shrugged, squared her shoulders, and headed for the door. But the geography of the room placed him closer to it, and, moving with surprising swiftness, he beat her to the exit. "Wen," he said, putting his back to the door. He lifted his hands as if to place them on her shoulders and physically restrain her. "You cannot leave while you're so distraught."

She was tempted to shove him aside so hard that he would have a better idea of her strength, but she halted a few steps away, not close enough for him to touch. "This is how I feel all day, every day," she said bitterly. "This minute is no different, except that you can see it."

"That's not true," he said softly. "I have watched you, you know. It was always obvious you were a soul in torment, but here at Fortune you seemed to have found a measure of peace. I am sorry that by my clumsy questioning I have wrought you up to a frenzy. That was not my intention. But I am not sorry to have learned the story behind your mask. Some of it I had guessed, and none of it surprises me. But it is a sad story even so, and I do not want to see you drown in it."

Half of what he said made no sense to her, but behind the flowery phrases she could read his real concern. "You don't have to worry that I will kill myself in the night because I have been made so wretched by this conversation," she said, her mouth twisting in what was almost a smile.

"That is only one of the things I fear," he said. "I am also afraid that you will slip away under cover of darkness, leaving us all behind because one of us now knows your secret."

It had been topmost in her thoughts, of course, the idea of abandoning Fortune and all its inhabitants. Her bones were all jangling; she thought she would not be able to sit still for a full day. It would be so much easier to run away, to expend her despair in motion. "I have not forgotten, even if you have, that my second month of service is up today," she said through stiff lips. "This conversation just makes it even clearer that it is time for me to go."

"But not tonight—not even this week," he said. "Karryn

still needs you. We have a ball to give in two days, don't you remember? The house will be full of strangers, and you are the only one who knows how to be truly watchful. You cannot walk away from us before then."

It was strange, she thought, how it was possible for her to passionately believe two contradictory things at the same time: that she could not be trusted to keep anyone safe, and that she was the only one good enough to reliably defend the House. *I would disappear tonight,* she told herself, *if not for this wretched ball. I cannot leave Karryn so much at risk. I will stay for the dance, and then I will go.*

She made her voice frosty. "Of course I would not desert you at such a time," she said. "But I can make no promises beyond that event. It is time for me to be moving on. I have been here too long."

"Have you?" he murmured. "I think you have not been here nearly long enough. Let us negotiate again once the event is over. Swear to me you will not leave without giving me a chance to convince you to stay."

She did not want to make such a vow, but his face was set. She did not think he would let her through the door without an argument or an act of physical aggression, and she was suddenly too weary to contemplate either.

"All right," she said ungraciously. "I will let you know when I am about to leave. But in return you must make me a promise."

"And that is?"

"Don't call me Wen in front of the others."

He raised his eyebrows. "You think Karryn and Serephette are conversant with all the names of the Riders who used to serve the king?"

She shook her head. "Not them, perhaps, but Orson and Eggles and some of the guards might recognize the name. Most soldiers idolize the Riders."

"Orson and Eggles might well have guessed your identity before this."

"Maybe. But it makes it easier for everyone if they don't have to know for sure."

"Then, Willawendiss, I agree to refer to you only by your common name when anyone is near enough to hear."

She almost smiled. "And *don't* call me Willawendiss."

"Ah, now, that is a promise I'm afraid I cannot make. The name is too sonorous and charming and inappropriate to be forsworn."

She rolled her eyes and then gave a ghost of a laugh. "You're the strangest man," she said. "Half the time I don't understand the things you say, and most of the time I don't understand what you're thinking."

He surveyed her with a small smile. "Don't you?" he said. "And yet I have never thought of myself as particularly opaque. I can be explicit, I suppose. I do not wish you to leave. I do not wish you to be grieving over a tragic but absolutely unavoidable incident in your past. I want you to be happy and at peace—and at Fortune. Is that plain enough?"

She nodded, but she felt a certain wariness come over her expression. "Most employers wouldn't care so much about one of their staff or servants."

Now his expression was grave. "Friends do, however," he said. "And I thought we had achieved a measure of friendship."

He had said virtually the same thing two weeks ago, and yet tonight it made her feel peculiar to hear the words again. Peculiar and yet delighted, filled with a buzzing warmth. Strange how that warmth served to combat the cold despair that had flooded her as she once more relived her memories of Baryn's death. "Friends of a sort," she amended, for true friendship was forged between equals, and they would never be that.

He was amused again. "Very well. So as almost-friends, we have managed a pact. I have promised not to give you away and you have promised not to leave without notice. I have expressed concern for your well-being and you have promised to care for yourself. I suppose those are the only pledges we need to make for tonight, at least."

"Then I am free to go?" she asked, for he still blocked the door.

He moved aside. "Free to go from this room," he said, smiling slightly. "But not much farther."

She was able to return the smile. "I won't stray past the hedge."

"Then goodnight, Willawendiss. May your dreams be peaceful."

She nodded, said nothing more, and paced out of the room. But she didn't think *peaceful* would describe any of her thoughts for the rest of the evening.

Chapter
25

TWO DAYS LATER, IT WAS TIME TO HOLD A BALL. There was so much cooking to be done that Ginny was called up from the barracks to help in the main house, so Orson and Eggles took over kitchen chores for the soldiers, to universal complaining. But the grumbling was almost rote. All the guards were alert and engaged, excited to be taking part in this event that would be a true test of their skills and how well they had come together as a company.

Wen was fairly certain they would pass that test without a misstep. She had laid out precise instructions about who was to patrol where at what hour during the day, and the soldiers met every checkpoint. Things would get trickier as the guests began pulling into the yard that night, but Wen felt fairly confident that she had set up safeguards that would see them all through the evening unscathed.

It was clear to her that this ball was even more a test for herself than her men. Ever since the harrowing conversation with Jasper Paladar, she had been edgy and unable to settle. All her instincts were at war, all her desires in conflict. Half of her wanted to flee this house, these responsibilities, the quiet regard of a certain noble scholar; half of her felt twisted with protest at the thought of leaving any one of them behind. Karryn was still so young, so prone to idiotic mistakes—how could Wen let her fend for herself, knowing the kind of trouble she might stumble into? And the twenty men and women of the House guard were showing such promise, such progress, and yet they were still so raw. There was so much more to teach them before they would truly function as a flawless unit.

And Jasper Paladar. Who knew her true name and had learned her most bitter secret. Who had wished her peace and called himself her friend. Who made her feel, when she was with him, like she was complex, intriguing, and valuable.

It was dangerous to believe such things were true. Dangerous to need someone else's affection and approbation. Dangerous to be so grateful that someone, anyone, cared if she lived or died. That way lay vulnerability and weakness, and Wen needed to armor herself in strength.

But she did not know how easily she would be able to tear herself away from Fortune, Karryn Fortunalt, and Jasper Paladar.

She told herself she would not think about her dilemma again until tomorrow morning. Today she had a ball to oversee.

She had given each guard his or her own commission to carry out once the festivities began. Eggles and Moss had been assigned to Karryn—they would know where she was every single minute, even if she slipped outside to tryst in the garden with Ryne. Four guards would be at the gate; twelve would patrol the grounds in a random, ceaseless pattern. Wen and Davey would be loose inside the house from the minute the first visitor arrived. Davey would stick close to the dining hall and the ballroom, but Wen would roam the corridors, trusting chance and instinct to guide her to any spot where there might be trouble. Twenty was a small number for such a concentrated initiative, but there had been only fifty Riders to patrol the palace at Ghosenhall.

Of course, these guards weren't Riders. But they would still fight for their charges with every ounce of their strength.

Accordingly, when the first carriage rolled through the gate in the hedge, all twenty guards were dressed in their best uniforms and ready at their stations. Wen thought the soldiers might be almost as excited as Karryn.

The Coverroes were the first to arrive, but Katlin and Edwin Seiles were right behind them, and soon enough the house was full. Wen peeked into the dining hall from time to time, to see Moss and Eggles standing at rigid attention on either side of the room, their eyes busily engaged in watching the diners. She stepped back into the kitchen, wheedled a scrap of meat from Ginny, and ducked outside to circle the house. No late arrivals galloping up the drive. No one scaling the walls, intent on breaking in through an upper-story window. She jogged to the gate, to confirm that all was quiet, then reentered the house through the main door, to rove the hallways and listen for anything out of the ordinary.

All indications were that Karryn's party was going smoothly.

Wen was in the hallway watching as the dinner ended and the guests slowly made the transition to the ballroom. This was a part of the house Wen had rarely been in until earlier in the week, when decorating began in earnest. From the complaints she'd overheard from the servants, the room had been closed up for so long that it was inches deep in dust, and every bit of crystal hanging from the chandeliers and the sconces had had to be taken down and wiped by hand. But now it looked sparkling and magical, filled with hundreds of candles and thousands of sweet-scented flower blossoms—all white to represent the pearl of Fortunalt. A murmur of approval went up from the guests as they stepped into the room and began scattering through it like jewels pouring from a spilled coffer.

Wen checked to make sure Moss and Eggles had followed Karryn into the room—yes—and then she began making her own unobtrusive circuit. The orchestra scraped through a brief disharmonic warm-up, but quickly enough offered the first skirling notes of an actual number. Wen paused to see who was partnering Karryn for the first dance. She was surprised and pleased to see Jasper, not Ryne, leading the serramarra to the dance floor.

They made a handsome pair. Karryn wore a gown of very dark red with great slashed sleeves that revealed a weave of pristine white. The crisscrosses of white fabric were repeated in a wide band around her waist, making her look much tinier than Wen knew her to be. Around her throat she wore a collar of pearls from which a single large pearl dangled, encircled by garnets to match her dress. She was both striking and vivid, and she was so happy that she was also beautiful.

Jasper, of course, was much more soberly dressed, in black with a bit of red trim. But his cufflinks were pearl, and so were the buttons on his waistcoat. His beard and his hair had been freshly trimmed, and their black-and-gray colors perfectly suited his severe attire. If he had not been smiling down at Karryn so affectionately, he might have seemed solemn indeed. He said something that made her laugh, and then they glided smoothly into the dance.

Wen supposed it was a waltz; she didn't know much about such things. At any rate, they were half-embraced as they moved with perfect timing through the deliberate rhythms of the music. All around them, other couples slipped onto the dance floor and mimicked those graceful movements. Ryne Coravann with Serephette Fortunalt. Coren Bauler with Lindy Coverroe. Edwin Seiles with his wife. Paired off, swirling around the room, the very embodiment of style and elegance.

Wen watched for the first dance only, then slipped out a side door. Time to check the rest of the house again.

For the next two hours, that was the routine she followed. Roam the house, upstairs and down, moving quiet as a rae-lynx through the empty corridors, and surprising more than one servant girl into nearly dropping her burden. Duck outside to circle the building and ascertain that it had not been breached. Return to the ballroom long enough to make sure no mischief had unfolded while she was not watching—and, just incidentally, note who was dancing with Karryn.

Sometimes, note who was dancing with Jasper.

Much of the time he stayed on the sidelines, acting the genial host. He was usually to be found in a conversation with some of the local men, discussing what looked like serious business, or laughingly enduring the interrogations of the older women. He only danced a few more times that Wen observed. Once with Katlin Seiles, who appeared to be a little in awe of him. Once with Serephette, who danced with the same majestic poise with which she did everything.

Once with Demaray Coverroe.

Wen stayed to watch the whole of that dance, which both participants seemed to be enjoying mightily. Demaray smiled up at him the entire time, except when she dissolved into laughter. Wen was not conversant with the rules governing social behavior in the highest circles, of course, but it seemed to her that Demaray clung a little more closely to Jasper than she really needed to. Even Edwin and Katlin were not hugging each other so obviously, and they, too, had paired up for this particular number.

Not that Jasper seemed to mind. He was gazing down at Demaray with that lurking smile that meant he was both interested and amused. Something she said made him throw back his head and laugh, loudly enough to cause others on the dance floor to look their way. When the music came to a dramatic conclusion, Jasper retained one of Demaray's hands and offered her a very deep bow, which she returned with a curtsey that brought her almost to the floor.

Well, she was a widow and he a widower, both Thirteenth House nobility with daughters of their own and each with a young girl to raise. They had a great deal in common—and they liked each other. Wen supposed there was hardly anything to be surprised about in that. No doubt he considered her at least as much a *friend* as he considered Wen—a more suitable one by any criteria. The thought did not make Wen feel especially cheerful.

The orchestra slid easily into another tune. Demaray surfaced gracefully from her curtsey and made an excited comment to Jasper. Wen guessed at the words. *Oh, I love this song! One more dance, please!* Whatever she said, Jasper smilingly acquiesced. Wen didn't stay to watch them perform. She already had a fairly good idea of how well they moved together.

Back through the lower levels of the house, back through the kitchen, back through the gardens and up to the front gate. All quiet, except for the muted strains of music drifting from the house.

"Is it as pretty inside as it sounds like from here?" asked Amie, one of those who had been stationed at the gate.

"Prettier," Wen said. "Go take a look. I'll keep your post here for a while."

That offer being accepted with alacrity, Wen then felt compelled to make the same bargain with the other guards so they could get a chance to see the nobility at play. It was another forty-five minutes before she returned to the house, and enough time had passed that she felt compelled to check on the ballroom again.

Karryn dancing with Ryne, Serephette dancing with an older gentleman, and Jasper standing with a knot of men, watching one of them tell a story that demanded a great deal of gesturing and explanation. Nothing here to be concerned about.

Wen headed upstairs to prowl through the corridors leading to the more private parts of the house. Everything fine on the second story; nothing disturbed on the third. She descended the back stairs and paused in the kitchen again to snatch a few more mouthfuls of food. Ginny was busy scrubbing pans, but she grinned at Wen and said, "It's good, isn't it?"

"Delicious," Wen replied.

After polishing off her hasty dinner, Wen stepped into the servants' hall to check the ballroom from a different vantage point. She had just arrived at the low, discreet door set into the wall when it opened, and Jasper Paladar stepped through.

"Ah, there you are, Willawendiss," he said. "Not watching us from the main door this time, but skulking around at the back."

The light was low—only a half dozen candles lit this whole snaking length of corridor—and his face was almost entirely in shadow. Still, she would have recognized his deep voice even in utter darkness.

"Were you looking for me?" she asked. She tried so hard not to sound shy that she sounded almost belligerent instead.

Nothing in his voice indicated that he felt self-conscious about this unlikely encounter. "Indeed, I was. I've caught sight of you a dozen times tonight, but never for long enough to come over and speak."

"I've been staying on the move," she said. "Is something wrong?"

"No, nothing's wrong. How about from your perspective? Any trouble?"

She shook her head. "Everything is calm. It appears to be a most well-behaved crowd."

"I hope you're not disappointed."

She laughed. "Of course not! Relieved."

"But all that effort wasted."

"All that effort is merely what you pay us to do," she said. "A guard spends far more time training to fight than actually fighting. The more well-prepared we are, the less likely we are to engage in real combat. Anytime your enemy knows you're strong, he hesitates to attack."

"Well, I'm glad we have no enemies here tonight," he said. He stepped back a little to survey her in the poor light. "Is this one of the new uniforms that Serephette and Karryn were so keen on designing? It looks very smart."

Wen raised her arms and did a half-turn from side to side as if to model some of the features of the outfit. It was nice to have him looking at her, even if he was only admiring her clothing. "Yes, all the guards are quite pleased with them. Functional and attractive. It is never a bad thing to instill a sense of pride in your regiment with such small things—easily overlooked, but they mean so much to the soldiers."

"I will remember that if, in the future, I have cause to outfit a troop," he said. He was looking down at her with the same half-smile he had given Demaray, warm and intimate. "But I must confess, I was wondering if you had ever had cause to wear something even more formal than this uniform."

Only another uniform, even more striking than this one, she thought. "More formal in what way?"

"I meant, perhaps, a dress?"

She grimaced. "I haven't worn a dress since I left home," she said.

"Even for fancy occasions? To attend a wedding, perhaps?"

Now she laughed. "I've only been to a handful of those," she said, "and everyone else was in uniform as well."

"None of your siblings married? Neither Elisa nor Altaverra asked you to stand up for her?"

Wen was silent a moment, momentarily taken aback by

the fact that he had remembered her sisters' names. But then, she imagined Jasper Paladar remembered most details of that conversation the other night. She certainly did.

"I've made it home for three out of the five weddings my brothers and sisters have had so far," she said at last. "And I wore my Rider uniform each time. No one, not even my mother, asked me to change into something else. You must not understand me very well if you think this is a persona I put on and take off as the mood strikes me. I'm a soldier. A fighter. All the time."

"Yes," he said, "I am beginning to realize that. Pure to the core."

She almost laughed. "I didn't say that."

"Pure in essence," he amended. "Unadulterated."

She let that pass, not entirely certain what he meant. He seemed to consider a moment, while, through the half-opened door behind him, the orchestra sidled into another melody, this one rather plaintive and slow. Jasper smiled.

"Well," he said, "I suppose a woman can waltz in trousers just as well as a man can. Will you dance with me, Wen?"

For an instant, she was both speechless and paralyzed. She found her voice at the same time she recovered the power of movement, for she stepped back from him and demanded, "Are you mad?"

His smile intensified. "I don't think so, no. Does that mean you won't?"

"Lords don't dance with members of their personal guard."

"You're Karryn's guard, not mine," he said.

"It's the same thing."

He came a step closer and, when she did not pull back, laid his right hand gently on her shoulder. "Here," he said. "In the hallway. One dance."

She forced the words out. "I don't know how to waltz," she said.

He leaned forward to pick up her right hand in his left one. "It's simple enough," he said. "A count of three. *Step*-step-step. *Step*-step-step. Let me guide you through the motions."

He waited, as if for a protest, but she was beyond the power to resist. The gods take pity on her, she *wanted* to dance with him—feel his hand sliding down from her shoulder to rest on the curve of her waist, pretend she was dressed in floating silks, imagine she was Demaray Coverroe, all fine skin and smiling fairness. It was not something that had even occurred to her to dream about, and yet here she was, suddenly convinced she would die if she did not tread out a few measures of music with this unpredictable man.

He tugged her a few inches closer and suddenly they were dancing, small, cautious steps this way and that in the close confines of the dark hallway. He was right; the beat was unmistakable, the motions simple enough to pick up with only a little concentration. She was used to mastering physical skills with a minimum of trouble. Dancing wasn't really that hard, if she wasn't expected to be showy. Jasper was smiling broadly, apparently pleased at her deftness, and he pulled her into a wider turn, a more energetic sequence of steps. She couldn't hold back a laugh; the motion of the dance was joyful enough to elicit that kind of response. He laughed back at her, but neither of them said a word. Around them, the music continued its jaunty swirling and Wen mentally counted out the beats. *One*-two-three-*one*-two-three-*one* . . .

The music ended with a flourish, catching both of them off guard, and they were left standing there, hands still clasped, staring at each other, in a world gone suddenly silent. Well, of course, there was the sound of voices from the ballroom, the more distant clatter of dishes from the kitchen, but in this hallway, between these two people, there was a deep and utter stillness.

Jasper broke it. "There, you see? Not so difficult at all."

"No," Wen replied, and could not think how to embroider her answer.

He dropped the hand that was at her waist, but kept his other one wrapped around her fingers, and now he drew this hand against his heart in a courtly gesture. "Thank you, Captain," he said. "I believe that was my favorite dance of the evening."

She could not drop a curtsey, so she bent in a creditable bow. "Thank *you*, my lord," she replied. "It was my favorite as well."

That made him laugh, and she was able to retrieve her

hand without seeming to be in any big hurry to pull it away from him. "It is a pity," he said, "but I fear I must return to my guests or be branded the most lax and unforgivable of hosts."

"And I should be circling the house again, making sure you have attracted no intruders."

"Then go," he said. "We will talk tomorrow."

But he made no move to retreat through the door and Wen found it impossible to leave first. He opened his mouth as if to speak again, shut it, then gave a sighing little laugh. "I never know what is calculated to frighten you away," he said. He kissed his fingers and laid them against her lips. "And that's even worse than *dancing* with your guard," he said.

She was so shocked she could not move, not to retreat, not to fling herself in his arms. He gave a crooked smile, offered another very slight bow, and pulled the door all the way open. She caught a brief bright glimpse of color and motion before he slipped across the threshold and shut the door behind him.

Wen was left standing in partial darkness, staring at an afterimage of revelry. Her body was motionless; her face was set like marble. Anyone looking at her might believe she had been bespelled by a mystic whose talent was turning flesh to stone. But she stayed so still merely to contain her inner riot—the clamor in her ears, the thrumming in her bones, the surging of her blood moving in a syncopated waltz of its very own.

Chapter
26

RAPPEN MANOR WAS ALL DECKED OUT TO receive the royal visitor. Flags from each of the Twelve Houses flew from the turrets of the mansion—which was more properly a fortress, Ariane Rappengrass always being prepared to defend her own. Interspersed among the House flags were two to represent Ghosenhall: the traditional black-and-gold banner and the modern version featuring the red raelynx nestled beside the gold lion. Danalustrous and Brassenthwaite flags had been given slightly greater prominence, indicating that someone had informed Ariane that Kirra was still riding with the entourage.

"Or that Ariane likes my father and your brother more than she likes the other marlords, which is just as likely," Kirra remarked as the coach pulled up in front of the splendid main doors of the fortress. "Gods! It will be good to stop traveling!"

They had been on the road nearly two weeks, though Senneth knew the trip between Gissel Plain and Rappen Manor could be made in less than half that time if the travelers were motivated to keep moving. Some days they had not covered more than ten miles, and most of that on foot as Cammon insisted on walking through some of the smaller towns. She couldn't imagine what the journey would be like if Amalie herself ever attempted to tour the country. It would take her a year just to make it from Ghosenhall to Forten City.

"It will be good to see Ariane again," Senneth remarked.

In fact, the marlady was waiting for them when Senneth followed Cammon and Kirra out of the coach. Ariane was in her sixties, Senneth supposed, a stern and formidable presence, with her imposing height, strict carriage, square face, and unmistakable intelligence. Just at the moment, her expression was softened by a rare blinding smile.

"Three of my favorite people in all of Gillengaria, arriving together!" she exclaimed, taking Cammon in a tight hug, then pulling back enough to scan his face. "All is well at the palace? How's Amalie?"

"She's fine and she sends her love," Cammon replied. "She wants you to come visit soon."

"Tell her to have my grandchild and I will be there so much she will banish me back to Rappengrass," Ariane said.

Senneth traded a look of amusement with Kirra. The whole country was obsessed with the notion that Amalie should produce an heir as soon as possible—preferably several—but only Ariane would phrase the idea so bluntly.

"You have plenty of grandchildren," Cammon said with mock sternness. "You don't need to be pestering Amalie on the subject."

Kirra pushed Cammon aside to bestow her own embrace on Ariane. "Indeed, do you give Darryn this kind of grief? He and Sosie haven't produced any offspring yet, either, as far as I know."

"Darryn's children, while I would love them greatly, might not be as essential to the well-being of the realm," Ariane said tartly. "How are you, Kirra? You look beautiful, as always."

"I'm a shiftling," Kirra replied. "I intend to look beautiful forever."

Ariane laughed and turned her attention to Senneth. "I must say, domesticity agrees with you," the marlady observed. "I never thought to see Senneth Brassenthwaite looking so settled."

Senneth laughed and hugged her. "Kirra is beautiful but I'm matronly?" she demanded. "What kind of insult is that? I should set your house on fire to teach you that I am not so tame."

"I understood that your power was not rebuilt to such an extent that I had anything to fear from you," Ariane replied.

Senneth offered her a fiery handshake and Ariane, unafraid of magic, instantly laid her palm in Senneth's. This was sorcerous flame, pretty but harmless. "I am recovering slowly," Senneth said. "I don't know that I will ever regain my full strength, but I could conjure up a fairly impressive blaze if I had a compelling reason."

"Then I take it back. You are looking utterly magnificent."

Footsteps came pounding up from the side of the house, but even the Riders were unalarmed at the sight of the individual who was racing toward the new arrivals. A dark-haired girl, maybe ten or eleven, with bright eyes and something of Ariane's determined expression.

"Uncle Cammon!" she cried, and flung herself into his arms. He laughed and swung her into the air.

"Look at you! At least two inches taller! Are you two inches smarter as well?"

"Is that Lyrie?" Kirra demanded. "Looks like she never had a day of ill health in her life."

"And she hasn't, since you healed her of red-horse fever," Ariane said. "The healthiest, most exuberant child you ever saw."

Lyrie was leading Cammon into the house, chattering as she went. Ariane gestured at the others to follow and glanced over her shoulder, where Tayse and Justin were conferring about how to deploy the Riders. This was Rappengrass, the most well-defended of the Houses. Senneth knew that here, if nowhere else outside of Ghosenhall, Tayse might be willing to relax his guard a little.

"Tayse," Ariane called. "We are just having a family dinner tonight. Please join us if you wish." She glanced at Kirra. "Donnal, too, if you like."

Kirra laughed. "If he comes, he will not sit at the table like a proper man but follow me to the room shaped as a dog, expecting me to feed him scraps from the table."

"He is welcome to do so. And bring any of the other Riders who would like to join us."

"I think this will be much more fun than the dinners at Gissel Plain," Kirra said.

Ariane made a noise that sounded suspiciously like a snort. "I would be offended if it were not."

Indeed, a couple of hours after they'd all settled into their rooms, cleaned off the grime of travel, and changed into somewhat less wrinkled clothing, they reconvened in the smaller of Rappen Manor's dining rooms for an extremely convivial meal. Both Justin and Donnal elected to skip it, but Senneth was pleased that Tayse joined them willingly. She knew he liked Ariane Rappengrass. The marlady was forthright, unapologetic, loyal, and smart. And she poured a lot of resources into her fortifications and her soldiery. Senneth supposed Tayse appreciated that most of all.

"Does everyone know everyone?" Ariane asked over the babble of voices as they all took seats anywhere they could find an open chair. For Ariane, "just family" meant four of her children, their spouses, and *their* children added to the visiting party, which meant more than twenty people were sitting down at the table. "That's Bella, that's Marco, Lyrie you met this afternoon, and, of course, you know Darryn and Sosie—"

Senneth didn't try to keep all of them straight, just smiled and addressed herself to her dinner. She had ended up beside Bella, Ariane's oldest daughter and heir, with whom she'd only exchanged a few words in her life. But, not at all to her surprise, she found Bella well-spoken and unpretentious, though often distracted by the antics of her children.

"And how were Nate and Sabina?" Bella asked. "Desti, sit down and finish your potatoes. Sit down *now*. Thank you. He must have been quite pleased at the prospect of entertaining such royal company."

Senneth was amused. "Indeed, Gisseltess vassals were lined up five deep to meet with Cammon at almost every meal."

"Well, you can expect some of that in Rappen Manor as well!"

"Cammon has spent the entire journey taking every opportunity to meet anyone who's shown any interest, from backwater farmers to highborn ladies, so I don't think he'll mind."

"Desti, do you want me to send you from the room? Then sit *down*. Well, no matter who he's talking to, I've never seen Cammon lose his sense of graciousness," Bella said. "Although that's not the right word."

"He genuinely connects with people," Senneth agreed. "He draws strength from their closeness. If you wanted to send Cammon into despair, you would lock him in a room far away from any other human presence. Although, since he's Cammon," she added, "he would probably be able to communicate over great distances with the people he loves the best, so it wouldn't be as much of a hardship on him now as it might have been once."

"Lyrie, could you show a little more decorum, please? You're a serramarra; you could try to act like one. I'm glad to hear you say that," Bella said, turning her attention back to Senneth, "because I've often had the sense that he and my mother really are in touch with each other—sharing thoughts, having actual conversations—while he's in Ghosenhall and she's here at Rappen Manor. She will just casually say, 'Oh, Cammon mentioned that he thought this might be a good idea,' and I'll say, 'Did he send you a letter? Can I read it?' And she'll get sort of vague. 'No, not a letter, exactly . . .' It's very strange. And I'm starting to think Lyrie is in touch with him, too."

Senneth toyed with her wineglass. "Cammon's abilities are remarkable," she said. "Is he having actual conversations with your daughter or your mother? Yes, I would guess he is. He has had them with me. On some of my darkest days, Cammon has been present in my mind. It is hard to feel abandoned when a friend is whispering reassurance."

Bella snapped her fingers at the rambunctious Desti, who straightened in her seat and stopped twisting her brother's arm, and then turned her head to thoughtfully survey the subject under discussion. "It was hard to know what to think when my mother came back after the war with the news that she had found him," Bella said. "I was the only one of my brothers and sisters who realized she was pregnant back when it happened, and I was only just old enough to understand what a scandal it was for an unmarried woman to be in such a state. She went away to have the baby, but she came back home without one, and she never talked about what happened. I just assumed the baby had died."

Senneth's mouth was dry. Such delicate lines here between truth and falsehood! How much did Bella know? "Apparently, that's what your mother was told by her friends and physicians."

"And then twenty years later, this stranger appears, and suddenly my mother is calling him her son," Bella said. "You have to realize, my siblings and I all assumed he was some adventurer who had stumbled upon an old secret and was blackmailing her in an attempt to win money or respectability."

"I've always thought your mother would be very hard to manipulate," Senneth said with a slight laugh. "She'd be more likely to publish some awful truth herself than to allow someone to use it against her."

Bella nodded. "Exactly. *No one* intimidates my mother. So what kind of hold could this young man have over her? As soon as I saw him, of course, I realized the truth."

"What truth?"

Bella spread her hands as if a gesture could convey unimaginable vastness. "She loved him. He belonged to her. She looked the way she looked when each of her grandchildren was born. I realized Cammon was part of her. And so it became very easy to welcome him, after all."

Senneth, listening closely, could not tell if Bella actually believed the tale of Cammon's parentage or if she had decided the truth didn't matter when balanced against her mother's happiness. "And I suppose there was no reason to fear he was after your inheritance," she said cautiously. "Since he was set to marry the princess and would have no need to be usurping Rappengrass."

Bella smiled. "I admit that made me easier in my mind. And I confess, I have not been reluctant to have my children be nieces and nephews to the queen and her consort. All in all, Cammon has proved to be a most satisfactory half-brother. I would fight very hard to keep him if someone tried to take him away from us."

And that, Senneth thought, was just as good as true conviction. "One thing I have discovered about Cammon," she said. "Once he has decided you are part of his life, it is no easy thing to dislodge him. So I think he would fight just as hard to stay, if someone tried to make him renounce all of you."

None too soon, their talk turned to less dicey topics like weather, travel, and Bella's children. "Lyrie is your oldest, isn't she?" Senneth asked. "She looks a great deal like your mother."

Bella nodded. "My oldest and my most spectacular. Oh, I love them all, of course, and I believe Desti will go on to do marvelous things in this world, if I don't kill her first, but there is something special about Lyrie. She's so interested and responsible and gifted. I am my mother's heir, you know, and I am already certain that Lyrie will be mine. Rappengrass has a long history of choosing marladies over marlords, and I see that continuing for another couple of generations at least."

Senneth took a meditative sip from her wine. "I find it interesting," she said, "how many of the next set of heirs will be women. Mayva is already marlady in Nocklyn. You will be running Rappengrass. Casserah is Malcolm's heir in Danalustrous. Rayson's girl, what's her name—Karryn—in Fortunalt. Lauren in Coravann. And, of course, there is a queen on the throne in Ghosenhall. What will it mean, I wonder, to have so many women wielding so much power?"

"What I hope it means is an end to violence," Bella said.

Senneth shook her head. "Coralinda Gisseltess marched beside her brother when he went to war two years ago. And you must admit your mother has always had an instinctive understanding of what is worth fighting for—and how to fight. I do not know that women can be counted on to be more peaceful than men."

"Perhaps not," Bella admitted, "though I like to believe we will first try collaboration over coercion. At any rate, I think women can work together to build a stronger Gillengaria. I hope we can, anyway."

"It is a good goal," Senneth said softly. "I hope you can, too."

*   *   *

AFTER the meal, all the children were sent up to their rooms while the adults regrouped in a pleasant salon and sampled a variety of sweet wines that some of Ariane's vassals had bottled. Senneth found Tayse deep in conversation with Bella's husband, Marco, discussing hypothetical battle maneuvers.

"Bella was right, after all," she said laughingly.

"She usually is," Marco said. "What did she say?"

"Oh, merely that men are more prone to violence than women."

Tayse smiled down at her. "I have seen women on the battlefield who acquitted themselves better than most men."

Ariane joined them, Kirra tripping along beside her. The marlady said in her astringent way, "There will always be aberrations, and your wife is one of them, but that does not mean they distort the general truth."

"I *can* fight," Senneth said. "But I don't particularly like to. In fact, the older I get, the less I like it."

"I rather enjoy it, but only if my opponent is truly evil," Kirra remarked. "Then I can feel justified in taking lioness form and eating his heart."

"But then, you're feral," Tayse said.

She made a face at him. "You might be the finest Rider of your generation," she said, "but I could probably claw your eyes out."

"I think we have refuted the proposition," Senneth said.

Cammon strolled up to their group, smiling widely enough that the topic of death naturally retreated. "It's so much quieter with the children gone!" he exclaimed. "I felt like I was shouting through the whole meal. But I miss them already."

"Well, you won't have to miss them for long," Ariane said. "I believe Desti and Moro plan to wake you up before sunrise tomorrow to go on some expedition."

Tayse looked at Cammon with his eyebrows raised. "Here at Rappen Manor, we had not planned to set guards outside your door, but if you want us to—"

Cammon was laughing. "No, I like being plain Uncle Cammon," he said. "I am enjoying the children so much! I can't believe how they've grown."

"You should visit more often," Ariane said. "You and your wife both. It's not good for you to be immured in that palace. Spend more time traveling Gillengaria."

Cammon tried to keep his face polite, though he could not help sending accusing looks at Tayse and Senneth. "Our advisors have cautioned us against going too far outside of Ghosenhall," he said.

"Well, if you want my opinion, I think that staying behind his palace walls so much was one of Baryn's few mistakes," Ariane said roundly. "Maybe if he'd been more accessible, there wouldn't have been so much dissent."

"I don't know about that," Kirra said. "Halchon and Rayson probably would have coveted the throne even if Baryn had come to see them every six months."

"Maybe," Ariane conceded. "But I don't know that Rafe Storian would have joined the rebellion if Baryn had been a more sociable king. I would like to see Amalie travel to every corner of the realm—and do it every year."

Senneth kept a wary eye on Tayse. "But Ariane, the prime issue is safety. How can we protect her if she's on the open road—or in a house that offers a poor setup for defense?"

"How can you protect anyone anywhere?" Ariane demanded. "Baryn died right there in his own palace, with Riders on either side of him! I'm not saying you should take foolish chances, but there's a different sort of risk involved in never letting her out of the city at all. She's a very lovable girl. Make her a lovable queen, and you will scotch any desire for another war anytime soon."

"I think that's very good advice," Cammon said, beaming.

Tayse offered a smart bow. "The marlady makes an excellent point."

Kirra seemed to be struck with a marvelous notion. "She can make the summer circuit!" she exclaimed. "Go to all the balls, just like she did three years ago."

"Oh yes, because there was *never* any excitement or danger when we traveled with her then," Senneth said.

"Well, she survived just fine, didn't she?" Ariane demanded. "And the two people who most wished her harm are now dead. It might be a very good idea. Anything to get her out of the palace."

"I could send for her right now," Cammon offered. "She could round up a dozen Riders and meet us in Fortunalt."

"I would rather be present for any expedition that includes

the queen," Tayse said, his voice respectful but unyielding. "Give us time to consider and plan."

"It's sounding more and more like she should travel the summer circuit," said the irrepressible Kirra. "I'll *have* to join you for that."

"Bright Mother burn me," Senneth said with a sigh. "And I swore I would never attend another dress ball." She cheered up as a thought occurred to her. "Though I don't suppose I'd have to come along."

"Of course you would," Kirra and Cammon said in unison. Kirra added, "I'll help you pick out your gowns. It will be fun."

"Aren't you glad you came to Rappengrass and asked my advice?" Ariane said.

"I don't actually recall asking it," Senneth said. "I think you volunteered your opinion."

Ariane's broad face was creased with a smug smile. "That's what mothers-in-law are for. To say the hard truths everyone else is afraid to voice. Now come try one of our new wines. There's a slight flavor of honey spice to it, imported, of course. Rappengrass would be happy to gift a few bottles to Ghosenhall, especially if you mentioned the vintner. We think very soon it will be all the rage."

WHEN the evening was finally over and they were back in their room, Senneth turned to Tayse as soon as the door shut behind them.

"I'm sorry Ariane said it in such a clumsy way," she said, "but she might have a point."

He smiled briefly, but behind the expression she could still read two years of buried pain. "Baryn *did* die with Riders on either side of him," he said. "It was no more than the truth."

She put her arms around him, leaning for a moment against his broad chest. As always, even when she wasn't aware of being particularly fatigued, she drew strength from him; she knew that, when he needed it, he could pull energy from her. Together they were a powerful combination. "But Riders kept Amalie safe that same day," she said. "Can you do so on the road?"

He kissed the top of her head. "I believe we can," he said. "When they work together, there is very little that Riders cannot do."

"And you will have mystics beside you," she said.

He kissed her again. "Ah, then, we will be impossible to defeat."

Chapter
27

WEN WAS THE FIRST ONE AWAKE IN THE BAR-
racks the morning after the ball, despite the fact that
she was almost certainly the last one to have fallen
asleep. Well, there was some possibility that she had not slept
at all. She got up and moved silently through the quiet building, pausing in the kitchen to make a cup of tea. Then she
sat on a bench outside in the weak dawn sunlight and tried to
think.

What had Jasper Paladar meant last night by his warm
smile, his pretty waltz, his proxy kiss? He was flirting with
her—yes, of course—Wen had had her share of enjoyable
encounters over the years, and she knew when a man was
sending a certain kind of signal. But to what end? He didn't
seem like the sort to take a tumble with his housemaid, and a
soldier was scarcely of a higher social caliber than a servant.
Was he only trying to keep her off balance and on edge? Did
he seriously hope to seduce her? And then—what? How awkward it would be to accept battle reports from the woman you
had just taken to your bed. How strange to discuss with her

troop strength and weapons requisitions in the morning if you had been making love the night before.

Of course, he knew that she did not plan to stay much longer. He might think a casual liaison would carry no penalties. She would be gone before he had time to tire of her.

Perhaps he had not even thought it through so methodically. He might simply have been intoxicated by the music, the company, a few glasses of wine. He might have been enflamed, perhaps, by the close embraces with Demaray Coverroe and the other fine ladies—women to whom he could hardly make bold advances without offering some kind of commitment in return. Perhaps he liked the idea of a woman in his bed but not a wife in his house. Someone like Wen would expect nothing from him except a little easy pleasure—the very thing he would hope to get from her. He could satisfy the cravings stirred up by those titled ladies without losing any of his independence.

She sipped her tea. That was not a particularly heartening notion, though she did think it made a great deal of sense. He had been a widower for five years. It would hardly be surprising if, from time to time, he looked for physical companionship. He might not be ready to marry again, but that didn't mean he didn't need gratification.

She drained the cup and set it on the bench, resting much of her weight on her hands as she leaned back. Well, she could use a little gratification, too. Since she had left Ghosenhall, she had only taken one man to bed, and they had only spent three nights together. She missed the casual delight of a lover's touch, the varied and sensual pleasures of intimacy. If Jasper Paladar wanted to invite her to his bed before she left Fortune, she would not refuse.

Though that might not have been what he intended at all. He had called himself her friend—he might have thought his *friend* might appreciate flirtatious attentions designed to make her feel feminine and desirable. For all she knew, he had brushed his lips against Demaray's cheek or touched his fingertips to some other woman's mouth, smiling all the while in that private fashion. Perhaps such gestures meant nothing, at least to the nobility, and Wen would be ridiculous to expect

Jasper to follow through with any kind of declaration, no matter how informal.

Very well. She would expect nothing, ask for nothing, require nothing. But if he offered her anything, she would take it. She would be leaving Fortunalt soon enough, and if any liaison with the serramarra's guardian proved to be uncomfortable, she would merely move up her departure date.

But she thought it would be a rare treat to lay her slim body next to Jasper Paladar's tall one. And she had not had many things to savor in the last two years of her life. She thought she deserved this much, if it was going to come her way.

THERE was little chance to pursue a romance during the next two days. While most guests had gone straight home after the ball, a few had stayed in Forten City. These were the lords and ladies who lived some distance from the city and were enjoying a chance to shop and dine and visit with friends. Serephette rather begrudgingly invited them back to Fortune for dinner the next two nights, and the men lingered in the library with Jasper long after the meals were over. Wen went by both nights to make a brief report, but she delivered it in the hallway while Jasper stood in the doorway, his attention half on the room behind him.

He did not make her feel like she was being a nuisance, however. Both nights, he seemed pleased to see her and interested in what she had to say. And there was that familiar smile at the back of his eyes. She found herself smiling back, as if at an unstated joke.

"Paladar! Come settle an argument!" one of the men called that second night as he lingered with her in the hall.

"In a minute," he replied, instantly returning his attention to Wen. "Did Serephette or Karryn tell you?" he asked. "We have been invited to a luncheon at the Flyten house tomorrow. It is something like a three-hour drive in each direction, so we shall have to leave in the morning. Karryn is not particularly eager to go, since it means she will miss some breakfast or another at the Coverroe place, but Douglas Flyten is a good man, so Serephette and I have insisted she accept the offer."

Wen nodded. "Karryn mentioned it this morning. I have already picked out the guards who will be your escort."

"And will you be among them?"

She nodded again. "I like to go along anytime Karryn is off the premises."

He was watching her closely. "We have not yet had time to discuss an extension of your contract," he said. "You promised to stay through the ball, but, of course, the ball is over. May I have your word that you will stay at least another week, or until we have time for negotiations?"

She met his gaze steadily. "I already promised that I would give you notice before I planned to leave. I won't renege on that. I will certainly accompany you to the Flytens' house."

"Good," he said. "I am sure we will be perfectly safe in the hands of Captain Willawendiss."

That made her smile again. Someone from the library called his name with impatience, so he shrugged and disappeared behind the door.

Wen sighed and returned to the barracks to prepare herself for the morning's travel.

THE weather the next day was utterly sublime. A languorous sun slowly climbed through a cloudless sky; a light wind kept the spring heat from becoming oppressive. It hadn't rained for at least three days, so all the roads were relatively dry. A finer day for travel it would have been difficult to order.

This was the longest journey Karryn had made since under Wen's care, and Wen hadn't forgotten the tales of bandits on the highways. She had taken extra precautions and enlisted more than the usual complement of guards. While they moved through Forten City, she kept the soldiers in a tight formation around the coach, but once they made it to open road, she spread them out the way Tayse would have deployed them. One guard galloped in advance of the coach to scout out the territory ahead. Two fell behind to make sure no trouble crept up from the rear. Two were perched on the back of the coach, clinging to specially made straps, while four rode horses immediately before and behind the conveyance. Excessive, perhaps, Wen thought—unless they actually saw combat. Then perhaps not enough.

She herself rode close to the coach, a few paces to the rear, though now and then she nudged her gelding near enough to exchange remarks with Moss and Eggles, who had taken the positions on the vehicle. Moss loved this mode of travel, Wen had learned to her surprise; she was smiling happily as the coach jounced along.

"Comfortable?" Wen called out to her over the noise of hooves and wheels.

"Extremely!" Moss called back. "What a beautiful day! It wouldn't be nearly as enjoyable in the rain."

"I think I'll trade with Davey for the trip back," Eggles shouted. Davey's wrist had finally healed, though Wen wasn't sure how much good it would do him to be clinging to a strap for three hours while the carriage plunged over ruts and road debris.

"As long as someone has every post, I don't care who rides where," Wen replied.

They stopped once at a roadside tavern for everyone to refresh themselves. Wen had to admit she rather enjoyed making a stir as she and Moss and Eggles and Davey stalked through the main room and the kitchens, checking for danger, before allowing the nobility to enter. The display certainly earned Karryn a little awe; the serramarra got excellent service, and even the guards were given sizable portions of ale and bread. Jasper seemed to appreciate the exhibition. Serephette didn't appear to notice.

They were on their way again soon enough, heading southeast along a route Wen had not traveled before. This part of Fortunalt roughened to a series of low hills through which the road made its twisted passage. Everything showed a green and gorgeous face—grass, shrubs, trees, all varieties of vegetation, which grew thicker the farther south they traveled.

Wen wasn't keen on the crowding of woods against the side of the road, especially when the trees covered the hillsides so densely. Plenty of places here for brigands to gather in shadow, awaiting a less well-defended party to pass by. She was starting to wish she'd brought twelve or fifteen guards instead of nine.

But they completed the journey with no trouble at all and pulled up at the Flyten house just when they were expected. Malton, who had ridden in the lead, was there ahead of them. "I checked the grounds and all is well," Malton reported to Wen as she swung out of the saddle. He was a big man, looked slow, but he was utterly steady and incredibly powerful.

"Good," she said. "Moss, you and I will accompany Karryn inside. Amie and Davey, you wait right outside the front door. Two of you at the back door; the rest of you roam the grounds. I understand we'll be here three or four hours, so spell each other now and then. Two patrolling at any one time should be enough."

Karryn didn't even seem to notice when Wen and Moss trailed her inside—that was how used she was by now to the notion of constant attendance. The Flyten footmen seemed taken aback at their presence, but no one made an effort to put them out of the house. Wen had decided she and Moss didn't actually have to be *in* the room with Karryn, but they would position themselves just outside the dining hall and be ready to fling themselves into motion at a moment's notice.

It seemed obvious almost immediately that there was nothing to fear from Lord Douglas Flyten and his wife, Tannis, both of whom appeared to be about eighty and employed servants who might have been with them since birth. Wen counted two footmen and a serving girl who looked to be younger than thirty; everyone else was, frankly, decrepit. Well, good. Easier to fend them off if they suddenly took it into their heads to attack the serramarra.

Wen fairly quickly lost interest in the parts of the conversation she could overhear. By her rather sullen tone of voice, Karryn wasn't much interested, either, but after a sharp comment from her mother, the serramarra began to make a little more effort. Even so, without Jasper and Lady Tannis doing their best, the whole table might have sat in dismal silence for the duration of the meal. Serephette had no talent for small talk, and Lord Douglas's conversation mostly consisted of, "What's that? Didn't hear you." Wen assumed he was deaf, or nearly so.

Still, it was clear that the vassal and his wife were delighted at the serramarra's presence, and from the number of courses carried in from the kitchen, the cook must have been slaving over hot ovens since well before dawn. Taking her cue from her uncle, Karryn began praising the more lavish dishes, and she seemed to genuinely like the confection that ended the meal. She happily accepted Lady Tannis's offer to have someone write down the recipe for the cooks at Fortune.

"I know you have a long drive ahead of you, but we were hoping you'd have time to walk the grounds with us before you go," Lady Tannis said. "I've imported some shrubs from Arberharst and they've taken to the climate spectacularly. They've just started to bloom down by the eastern wall—I think you'd enjoy seeing them."

"Well," Karryn said doubtfully, but Jasper spoke right over her.

"We'd be happy to see the gardens," he said.

That meant the whole lot of them had to parade across the lawn—the Flytens, the Fortunalts, Jasper Paladar, Wen, Moss, Eggles, Davey, and the two gardeners who apparently were needed to explain what special measures they'd taken to make sure the foreign shrubbery flourished. Wen had to admit that the bushes—low to the ground, dense with dark green leaves, and bursting with tiny purple flowers—were impressive. She didn't blame Karryn for bending down to take in an exaggerated breath of their heavy scent.

"We have a wonderful hedge around Fortune, but its flowers have already faded," Karryn said. "I wonder how long these will last? They're gorgeous."

"I've seen that hedge," Douglas said, after first asking his wife to repeat what Karryn had said. "Took a couple of cuttings from it, but never could get them to root."

"They say no one's ever been able to get a piece of that hedge to grow anywhere else in the country," Tannis added in her soft, quavering voice. "It's magnificent, but it can't be transplanted."

Karryn sniffed at the purple flowers again. "I suppose these bushes can't be, either."

"Oh, no, they take hold almost anywhere, as long as you treat them properly," Tannis said.

Then, of course, nothing would do but that the Flytens had to offer Karryn a cutting, and one of the gardeners had to run back to some shed to find shears and potting soil and a scrap of burlap to wrap it in, while the other solemnly repeated for Karryn all the details of its care. Wen was certain Karryn was sorry she'd said anything complimentary, but the girl made a creditable attempt to look grateful and didn't even shrink away when the muddy ball was laid in her hand.

"And now I really do think it's time for us to go," Jasper said to their hosts. "Thank you so much for having us to visit! It has been a most enjoyable day."

Karryn brightened immeasurably at the news they were leaving. "Yes—quite lovely," she said. "You've been so gracious."

Of course, it took another quarter hour before the coach was called for, the team was hitched, the guards were mounted, and everyone else had climbed inside the carriage. But they were finally on their way again, back through the undulating green countryside and the indolent sunshine. Wen estimated they had four hours or so of sunlight left; they should be back home before dark. Always better to travel by daylight unless you were on a mission of stealth.

As before, Wen stayed mostly to the rear of the carriage, back far enough to get a broad perspective of the upcoming view. Now and then she spurred the gelding close enough to exchange a few words with Moss and Eggles, who had kept his post on the coach after all. Malton had chosen to stick with the carriage for the return trip, and with him was a raw recruit named Cal, a young man with natural instincts but no battle experience. In the lead position Wen had sent a young man named Garth. He was blond and cheerful, older than Davey but just about as energetic. He was an excellent advance scout because he was too impatient to keep to the sedate pace of the carriage.

They'd been traveling about ninety minutes when Karryn put her head out the window. "I'm bored," she called to Wen. "My mother and Jasper are both sleeping. Can I ride while one of you sits in the carriage instead?"

Wen grinned and kept her horse at a trot alongside her. "I'd rather you stayed inside. Besides, you're not dressed for riding."

Karryn sighed. "I know. But I'd almost rather ruin a dress than sit here and be so dull."

"You could try sleeping, too."

"If I sleep, I'll muss my hair. My head rubs up against the back of the seat."

Wen laughed. "Are you expecting any company tonight who will care what your hair looks like?"

Karryn was scandalized. "*I* care! Even when no one can see me! Anyway, Lindy said she might come by later and tell me how the breakfast went. I wish I could have been there, but no, I had to see stupid Douglas Flyten."

"Is he a very important man?"

"His family members have been vassals to House Fortunalt since the very first marlord was named. They aren't the richest of our Thirteenth House lords, but they've been very faithful." Karryn brooded a moment. "He wouldn't raise any troops for the war. My father was going to divest him of his lands once he got back from Ghosenhall." She shrugged. "Of course, my father didn't come back."

"Who made the decision to let him keep his lands?"

Karryn looked surprised. "I suppose I did. I mean, everything was such a mess those first few months after the war. When Jasper first arrived he spent all his time trying to straighten out the accounts. He would call me or my mother into his study and ask all these questions. 'Who is Coren Bauler and why does he owe us this much money? Who is Demaray Coverroe and why should we accept an invitation to dinner at her house? Why is Douglas Flyten about to be banned from his Manor?' My mother said, 'The Flytens did not support the war,' and I said, 'Then we should support the Flytens!' And Jasper said, 'Well, good. That's one easy decision.' And then he picked up another piece of paper and asked about someone else."

Wen was smiling. "Then I suppose it's no secret why the lord is predisposed to like you."

Karryn laughed. "I don't think he knew he was so close to being dispossessed."

"He probably did. He had to know your father was fanatical about this war, and anyone who opposed him risked losing his lands—or his life. It took him some courage to resist. So he must be quite happy that the serramarra has allowed him to retain his property."

"I never thought about it like that," Karryn said. She was starting to look pleased with herself. "Well, I'm happy about it, too."

From the front of the coach, there was the softest soughing sound, and then a harsh cry of pain. The horses suddenly stumbled in the traces and the coach began lurching from side to side.

"What in the red hell—" Wen began, when there was a series of harder thumps and taps, as if rocks had been flung at the sides of the coach. *"Get down!"* she shouted at Karryn, wheeling her horse around. "Wake your uncle! Moss! Eggles! We're under attack!"

Wen leaned low over the saddle and raced to the front of the coach, where the confused horses were pulling in different directions, halfway between bolting and milling to a halt. Yes—an arrow had gone through the driver's throat, and his hands lay lax on the reins. He was dead. That meant their attackers wanted to stop them here so that they were vulnerable to another volley of arrows.

Or wanted the crazed horses to go stampeding down the road to the next stand of brush, where a second ambush might lie in wait.

They were not safe moving or standing still.

Davey had leapt from his horse onto the driver's bench and was wrestling the team to a standstill. "Run or halt?" he cried to Wen over the noise of the plunging horses.

"I don't know!" she called back. "Just get them under control! And cover your head!"

He nodded. He had brought his small travel shield with him as he transferred from the horse to the carriage, but it didn't provide much coverage. Still, he hunched himself into a small shape on the bench, the shield flung up with his left hand to protect his head while, with his right, he pulled on the reins.

Another sequence of bumps and knocks—another round of arrows hitting the coach. There was a shriek from inside but Wen thought that was only Serephette waking up and expressing fear; she didn't think any missiles had found a target inside the coach. Eggles had been nicked in the arm, but not badly. He hadn't even bothered to tie up his wound, but had crawled to the top of the coach and flattened himself on the roof. He had a bow of his own, the long curve hanging over the side of the coach, an arrow nocked and drawn. He was sighting toward a clump of trees lining the western edge of the road. When he let the shot fly, he was rewarded with a cry and the sound of a crashing body.

But Wen had seen arrows protruding from both sides of the coach. There were attackers on each side of the road—more than one, judging by the output. Three to a side, perhaps? Four? And two more ahead, lying in wait?

Moss had jumped from the back of the coach and swung herself onto Davey's horse. Cal and Malton were riding in a tight circle around the coach to distract the archers, moving in a jagged pattern to make themselves harder to hit. But the whole party was exposed and utterly vulnerable. Wen had just kicked the gelding forward to catch up with Cal when Eggles shouted warning of another volley coming. They all hunched in their saddles, shields up. Wen waited for the *rattle* and *thunk* of metal tips burying themselves in the wood of the carriage.

The sound didn't come. "Son of a *bitch*," Eggles said, and Wen flung up her head to see what had happened.

Arrows littered the ground on both sides of the coach, stopped in midair before they could find their targets. Wen stared around wildly till she caught sight of Moss, struggling to keep Davey's edgy beast under control, and smiling with a savage satisfaction.

"Moss! Yes!" Wen cried out, seized with battle jubilation. "Can you keep doing that? Even if arrows come from both sides at once?"

Moss nodded. "I think so!"

"Cal—you and I'll ride to the left. Eggles, swap with Moss and ride with Malton. Davey, hold us here. I think there's an ambush ahead—don't take us farther."

Eggles was on the ground and Moss was hauling herself up to the roof when Davey cried a warning. Moss flung out a hand, and this time the arrows fell even farther away from the roadside, halfway back to the line of trees. Wen could have sworn that, desperate as the situation was, Eggles chortled.

"Kill them or just stop them?" he inquired from horseback, hunkered down over the animal's neck.

"Stop them, but I don't care if you kill them," she replied grimly, and then she charged straight for the line of trees on her left.

Time to fight like a Rider.

Chapter
28

THE ARCHERS IN THE TREE WERE LOOSING more arrows as Wen and Cal galloped up, but Moss's magic was so disrupting their aim that they might as well have been flinging tinder to the winds. There was one body on the ground where Eggles's shot had hit home, but through the shivering leaves Wen could make out two men who were very much alive. As the gelding swept under the branches at a full-out run, she kicked her feet free of the stirrups, crouched in the saddle, and grabbed the lowest limb. Swinging herself up, she felt the springy surface sway and dance beneath her boots. One archer was a level above her, the other one even higher. She scrambled up till she was balancing on the lowest branch that held an enemy. One hand clinging to whippy switches, she drew her dagger for close fighting.

Neither of her enemies had expected her to bring the battle this close to their territory, and her extra weight was making the branch tilt ominously toward the ground. The man who was sharing this precarious perch with her let out a shout of alarm and began inching her way, closer to the trunk and a modicum of stability. The man higher in the tree—slim

enough to be a boy, and lightweight enough to have taken up
a spot on a thin limb—called out encouragement and began
working his way down toward Wen. Those were bad odds.
She took a hard grip on the bough above her and jumped up
and down, trying to break off the branch beneath her feet.
There was a loud *crack* and suddenly she was standing in
upthrust splinters—the branch had shattered, though it didn't
completely tear away. But it was enough. Her assailant let out
a horrified cry and went tumbling to the ground. She heard
Cal's shout of triumph and the sound of metal engaging.

No time to watch that fight. The second archer was almost
upon her, and, with the branch broken off so close to her feet,
she had practically no room to maneuver. The boy had a small,
short sword and was using it to slash at her fingers where she
clung to the bough above. He didn't seem to have much skill
with anything but a bow, but he didn't need much right now;
she was at a clear disadvantage. She let go of her stabilizing
grip and balanced on the stub, then had to duck low as he
swung again for her forehead. Gods and goddesses, unless she
could knock his feet out from under him, she couldn't possibly get close enough to kill him.

Retreat and regroup. She plunged back toward the trunk
and swung herself around to find purchase on a limb on the
other side. Swiftly she climbed another two levels, scrap-
ing her hands on the rough bark; her opponent matched her
branch for branch.

Now they were positioned on either side of the tree bole,
narrower here closer to the apex of the tree. The boy had his
short sword out again, and was stabbing it on either side of
the trunk. Wen had sheathed her dagger and pulled her own
sword, though fencing around a tree was a little like fencing
around a stone column in a palace—ridiculous—except here
there was no marble floor to take your weight.

However, on equal footing, the advantage now was clearly
hers. Wen waited for his sword tip to appear and then batted it away, hard, hoping to wrench the hilt from his hand,
but after a few tries it was obvious that wasn't going to work.
She edged as close as she dared to the trunk itself, holding on
to a thin bough behind her and thrusting her sword around
the tree to the full extent of her arm. She connected; she felt

the impact of bone a second before the boy's howl rent the air. She wrenched back so he couldn't rip the sword from her hands if his body toppled to the ground, but no such luck. He responded with a flurry of wild strokes, energetic enough to let her know she'd only wounded him.

Still. It had worked once, and he wasn't good enough to know how good a truly gifted fighter could be. She transferred the sword to her left hand, grabbed a fistful of tree with her right hand, and plunged the sword blindly in his direction. This time his cry was more of a gurgle; she'd caught him in the throat or belly. She pulled back just enough to make room for a second thrust in almost the exact same spot. This time his cry was fainter and sounded more like a cough. It was followed almost immediately by the noise of his body crashing through the lower tree limbs and landing with a sodden *thump* on the ground.

Wen sheathed her bloody sword so she could use both hands to shimmy down. Cal's own battle had devolved into what looked like a wrestling match, but the Fortunalt guard had the archer on the ground with his arm twisted behind him, so Wen didn't give him more than a passing glance. She spun around to assess the rest of the scene. The coach looked the same, marooned in the middle of the road, Moss perched on its roof swiveling her head to look for danger in all directions. Across the road, Eggles and Malton still engaged in their own fights—no, one attacker was down, and Eggles had turned to offer his help to the less-experienced Malton. All briefly under control except—

"Willa!" Moss called, waving both arms above her head. From her higher vantage point, she had spotted trouble first. "Coming from the east!"

Wen whirled around to see and—*Bright Mother burn me!*—she saw four riders cantering up from the spot she had considered the likely ambush. Four! She had expected only two more.

"Finish him off! We have more company," she called to Cal, racing for the gelding and throwing herself into the saddle. The horse was already running before she got her left foot secure in the stirrups.

"Hurry!" Moss was shouting, waving her arms even more frantically.

Wen almost called back, *I am!* but she heard the sound of
pounding hooves and realized Moss hadn't been addressing
her. She risked a glance over her shoulder—yes! Orson and
Amie arriving from the rear, and just when they were desperately needed.

No reason to hold back now. Wen kicked the gelding to a
higher speed and leaned low over his neck, holding the reins
with her left hand and pulling the sword again with her right.
The gelding was battle-hardened; he made no move to veer
away as she directed him straight at the oncoming assailants.
The lead rider didn't have the guts. At the last minute he tried
to pull his mount aside, and Wen and her horse plowed straight
into them. There was a wretched sound of slamming bodies
and screaming horse, and the attacker was practically knocked
from his saddle. Wen didn't hesitate. She half stood in her stirrups for greater leverage and swung her sword hard against his
chest. A gaping wound opened with clean and shocking sud-
denness. His face showed nothing but surprise as he relaxed
his fingers and dropped both reins and weapon. His falling
body twisted to one side of the saddle, and his maddened horse
bolted for open land, dragging the dead rider behind it.

There was a thunder of hooves and suddenly Wen was surrounded by comrades—Orson and Amie, Cal and Eggles—
and all around her was the deadly, exuberant clangor of blade
against blade. Suddenly her fear was gone. She knew they
had the numbers and the skill for victory, and she was seized
with battle euphoria. Her blade swung from her hand as if
weightless. Her eyes saw everything at once; her body moved
without receiving conscious commands. She was a conduit of
violence, a weapon sculpted from bone and skin. She struck;
she killed; she moved on.

Until there was no one left to strike, no enemy left standing. Wen drew a hard breath, took a last swift look around,
and slowly lowered her sword. With a jolt, her soul reentered her body. She was suddenly herself again, bloody and
exhausted, shoulder to shoulder with comrades on a field of
broken corpses.

"What's our damage?" she asked sharply.

"Malton is down," Eggles said, a pant in his voice. In addition to the wound he'd sustained at the beginning of the fight,

he'd taken a few cuts to his face and his legs, but he didn't sound hurt so much as winded. "Don't know how seriously he's injured."

"The rest of us have all taken some blows, but nothing bad," Orson said.

"Moss and Davey were fine when we passed them," Amie added.

Wen nodded. "I'm thinking Garth is dead," she said grimly. "He didn't ride back to check on us, and he should have when we didn't appear behind him."

She saw a look of grief and fury cross Orson's face, and then his expression shut down. "I'll go look for him."

"Be careful," she said. "I think we've accounted for all of them—but there were more than I expected."

Orson's gaze was directed downward at one of the dead men. "Not bandits," he said.

Wen shook her head. "I don't think so."

Now he looked at her, his eyes hard. The others crowded closer, their horses all whickering and shaking their manes. "Who, then?" Orson asked. "And why?"

Wen lifted her shoulders in a gesture of ignorance. "Someone who wanted to harm the serramarra."

"Kill her, you mean," Eggles said. "And everyone with her."

Wen nodded. "Looks that way."

Orson was still watching her. "Who'd want to kill a pretty girl like Karryn?"

She was suddenly so tired. Almost too tired to sit in the saddle. Tired of intrigue and ambition and bloody bids for power. "Who wanted to kill King Baryn?" she asked wearily. "Someone who wanted his throne."

"Someone wants House Fortunalt?" Cal asked, sounding dazed. Despite his inexperience, he'd fought hard. He'd been every bit as good as she'd hoped he'd be when she hired him.

"No matter what anyone has, someone else wants it," Wen said. "That's the lesson I've learned too many times to count." She nodded at Orson. "Go look for Garth. Cal, Eggles, search the bodies and see if you can find anything to identify them. Amie, see what you can do for Malton. I'm going to check on Karryn and the others."

They dispersed, not moving as crisply as Riders would have but, sweet gods, doing everything she asked of them. This had been their first test in battle and they had all responded magnificently. Protected their charge, defeated their enemy, taken orders when they could, thought for themselves when they had to. And survived to fight another day.

Most of them, anyway.

Wen turned the gelding's head and jogged slowly to the coach. Davey had the horses well under control—and his sword at the ready beside him on the bench. Behind him, Moss's head peered down from the roof. She braced herself with one hand, held a dagger in the other. Wen experienced a surge of pride so fierce that she felt a momentary pain deep in her chest.

"Captain?" Davey called. "What's the situation?"

At that salutation, Jasper Paladar immediately stuck his head out of the window. "Willa? What's happening?"

Karryn's head appeared right under his. "Willa? Thank the Silver Lady, you're alive! Who were those men? Are we safe now?"

She came close enough to answer them all. "I think we're safe—we've fended off *this* attack, at any rate. Our advance guard is missing and one of the others is down, so we might have lost two guards, and the coachman is dead as well. But we faced nine, so we gave a good accounting of ourselves."

Now Serephette's pale face poked between Jasper's and Karryn's. "Who were these people?" Serephette demanded. "What did they want from us?"

Wen met Jasper's eyes and he gave a slight shake of his head. "We don't know yet," she said. "Unfortunately, none of them are left alive, so we can't ask them. We'll search their bodies and see if we learn anything about their identities."

"You said two of the guards were injured or missing," Karryn asked. "Which ones?"

"Karryn, dear," Serephette said reprovingly, but Wen was glad Karryn asked.

"Malton's hurt and we don't know what happened to Garth."

"Should we put Malton in the coach?" Karryn said next.

This was cause for another "Karryn!" from Serephette, but

Wen liked the suggestion. "Maybe. Depends on how badly he's injured."

"I could ride his horse," Karryn offered. "To make room for him."

The suggestion actually made Wen smile, something she hadn't expected to do on this bleak day. "If nothing else, this little incident proved that you should stay safely inside the coach," Wen said. "All of you."

From the other side of the carriage, she heard Amie's voice raised in a call. "Captain?"

She nodded at Karryn and the others. "Stay inside," she repeated, and pulled the gelding around to check on Malton.

The big man was sitting up, though he looked woozy, and there was blood all over his face and chest. But she was so happy to see him more or less whole that she found herself grinning as she slid out of the saddle. Amie had bound up the more obvious wounds on his arm and shoulder, but there was a cut across his forehead that looked like it would need stitching when they got someplace they could fetch a physician.

"How are you feeling?" she asked.

"Like death came knocking," he replied in his slow voice.

She made her voice provocative. "The serramarra says if you're gravely injured, she'll give you her seat in the coach and ride your horse home."

At that, even his placid face showed alarm. "She can't ride! She'd be a target!"

"That's what I told her. But can you sit a horse?"

He hesitated. "I don't know."

"He could sit on the driver's bench next to Davey," Amie suggested.

Malton nodded. "I think I could manage that."

"What about the coachman?" Amie wanted to know.

"Dead," Wen replied.

"And Garth?" Malton asked.

"Orson's looking for him. But—" She shrugged expressively then came to her feet. "In any case, no use lingering here. Let's get going."

Amie was slim, but strong enough to help the much heavier Malton back to the coach. Wen remounted her gelding and joined Eggles and Cal, who had returned from inspecting the bodies. "Good swords, well-used, well-cared-for," Eggles said. "And plenty of gold in their pockets."

"Definitely not bandits," she said.

He was watching her. "And the archers were specialists," he said. "Excellent shots, but not very handy with a sword."

She nodded. "I noticed that."

"Hired to kill," he added, in case she hadn't put the pieces together.

"Right."

"They didn't have any insignia," Cal added. "No way to know who hired them."

"I'm hoping Karryn's uncle might be able to help us figure that out," Wen said.

"You mean you don't have a theory?" Eggles asked.

She shook her head. "I don't know how the gentry think," she said.

"But you've always believed Karryn was in danger," he prodded. "That's why you hired us. You're not surprised this happened. You've been expecting it."

She eyed him soberly. Orson hadn't come out and said it, but that was obviously what he'd been thinking, too. "Karryn's a vulnerable girl in a position that a lot of people covet," Wen said quietly. "I haven't been expecting anything specific. I just don't trust people in general, I suppose. I expect them to look around, and find a weaker opponent, and take what they want. I wanted to even the odds a little if it ever happened to Karryn." She took a deep breath. "I can't say I'm happy to have my worst fears realized. But *damn*, I'm happy that we were good enough to fight back. I'm happy we were strong enough to win."

"And stronger next time," Eggles said quietly. "It toughens a man up when he's in a real fight. You don't kill him right off, he'll beat you if he ever sees you again." He nodded at Cal, glanced over at Amie and Davey, all of them too young to have the depth of experience he and Orson and Wen had. "This lot will be even better next time someone tries to take them down."

And there's always a next time, when you're a soldier, Wen thought. *Anytime you're prepared to fight, there's always a fight in your future.* "Let's get everybody safely home before we start congratulating ourselves too much," she said.

"Orson's not back with Garth yet," Cal said.

"I know. Let's get the coach moving and go look for them."

The coachman's body was lashed to the roof and the soldiers were quickly redistributed. Malton sprawled next to Davey, Moss and Eggles mounted the extra horses, and they were on their way. Wen hated not to have a rear guard, especially since it had proved so useful in this particular fight, but everyone was so spooked that she wanted to keep them all together, riding as tightly around the coach as the terrain allowed. She dropped back just enough to be able to command a broader view of the oncoming road, unimpeded by the carriage. More risky territory ahead—more of those undulating curves through low hills and clumps of trees.

Surely if they were attacked again, it would not be by professionals focused on killing. It would be by starving outlaws desperate for food or money—easy enough to stave off or appease. Whoever had hired this particular troop had paid a high dollar for skilled men who would fight to the death; surely no one could afford to set up two such ambushes along the same lonely stretch of road.

But Wen kept watching, just in case.

About a mile later, they came across Orson kneeling at the side of the road beside a bundle of cloth and leather that had to be Garth. Wen felt a quickening of hope. If Garth had been dead, Orson wouldn't be so intent. She waved to the other guards to keep a close circle around the coach as it halted, but she and Moss spurred over and dismounted.

"He's alive?" she demanded, dropping to the dirt.

"Barely," Orson said. "Arrow through his chest, but high. Might have nicked a lung." He gave her a serious look and a shrug. "Don't know if he can be saved."

A voice spoke behind them, spinning Wen around on her knees. "Well, we can't leave him here to die."

"Karryn! Get back in the coach!" Wen exclaimed, springing to her feet.

But Karryn wore her intractable look. "Only if you put Garth in first."

Orson looked up at her, his expression unreadable. "Serra, he might die on the journey."

"If he dies because he was defending me, then I ought to be there to witness it," Karryn said. Her voice wavered, but her determination did not.

Orson nodded. "Let's wrap him in a blanket first."

It was an excruciating—and excruciatingly slow—exercise to bind the wounded man, bundle him into a blanket, and insert him into the vehicle without slamming his broken body against the doorjamb or the seat. Serephette was distressed and disapproving, though she didn't actively try to impede them. Jasper was sober and silent and helped when he could.

"I can't think he will survive the rest of the trip," Jasper said to Wen in a low voice.

Wen shook her head. "I can't either. But I am so impressed that Karryn wants to take him in."

Karryn, in fact, was receiving advice from Moss about what she might do to ease the hurt man if he gained consciousness or began bleeding through the rough bandages Orson had applied. Wen added, "She'll ruin her dress, of course. I wonder if she remembers that she's expecting Lindy to come over this afternoon."

Jasper, like Wen, was watching Karryn with a small, satisfied smile. "I wonder if she cares."

As soon as Garth was settled, the nobles climbed back into the carriage, the three of them crowding together on one seat. Wen waved the guards back to their places. "Move out! And keep a lookout. We aren't home yet."

Back on the road, Davey tried to compromise between speed and caution, guiding the carriage around the worst of the ruts and constantly apologizing to Malton for the roughness of the ride. Moss trotted right next to the carriage, calling advice to Karryn through the window. Wen figured as long as Moss was talking, Garth was still alive. She signaled Eggles to fall back to take the rear position and urged her horse past the coach so she could confer with Orson, riding point.

"That tavern we stopped at on the way out," she said. "Could we leave Garth there?"

His eyebrows rose. "Maybe. They had rooms to rent upstairs. We could leave Moss behind with him. She's had some training in the sickroom."

She met his eyes. "Then we'd be down to seven. Six if you discount Malton."

He held her gaze a long moment before returning his attention to the road ahead. "You expect a second attack?"

"I wasn't *expecting* a first one."

"No," he contradicted her. "You're always expecting one. You just don't know when it's going to come."

She acknowledged that with a shrug. Her life was one long series of contingencies. If and then. *If an attack comes from the right, then I will duck to the left. If a man tries to cleave my head open, then I will feint to the side. If an assassin attempts to kill the king . . .*

. . . Then my life is over.

"I can't decide about leaving Moss behind," she said. "Let's see what the situation is at the tavern. We might get lucky."

They did. Wen and Orson left the others with the coach when they stepped inside to inquire into amenities. The tavernkeeper remembered them from their earlier visit, and he was obsequiously eager to show honor to the serramarra and her entourage.

"Certainly—we would be extremely happy to keep the serra's guard!" the proprietor exclaimed. "How badly is he injured? My daughter-in-law is a healer—a mystic, you know." He then looked nervous at having let that secret slip, for mystics were still widely reviled in Fortunalt. "Unless the serra would prefer we practice no magic upon one of her men," he added hastily.

"The serra would prefer anything that keeps her men alive," Wen said. "In fact, she keeps two mystics in her employ. Times have changed since her father was marlord."

The tavernkeeper brightened even more at this news. Wen wondered if he had a grandchild or two who had also shown evidence of mystic blood. He might not feel much affection for a sorcerous daughter-in-law, but a grandson? A man could be expected to fight hard for his own flesh and blood.

"I will send for her right away," he said. "She can be here within the hour."

Wen nodded. "Good. Then we will bring our friend inside. And leave some funds with you to cover the cost of his care."

Naturally, it was just as tricky to move Garth out of the carriage as into it, and then they had to negotiate the narrow halls behind the taproom. Karryn, to Wen's admiration and dismay, insisted on accompanying the fallen soldier to his temporary infirmary and then personally thanking the proprietor, while handing over an impressive pile of coins.

"I will send someone back for him tomorrow," Karryn promised the tavernkeeper as Wen tried to encourage her toward the door. "Thank you again for your hospitality."

At last they were on the road again, moving at a somewhat more rapid pace. Malton had fallen into an uneasy sleep and sunset was less than an hour away. At this rate, full dark would arrive while they were still on the road.

"As fast as you can go without tiring the horses overmuch," Wen instructed Davey, and he urged them to somewhat greater speed.

She had a hard time remembering the last time she had so desperately wanted to be home.

Chapter
29

THREE HOURS LATER, THEY WERE SAFELY IN-
side Fortune's hedge. Karryn's mother had swept her
into the mansion without letting her pause to speak
to her guards again. Malton had been carried to the barracks,
where Eggles and Moss treated him rather more thoroughly
and expressed their opinion that he would be fine as long as
his wounds didn't get infected. The soldiers left behind had
been filled in on the events of the day, most of them expressing a little envy at having missed out on the excitement. Wen
reshuffled the planned watches, for those who had had escort
duty needed a break, but the house and grounds still needed
to be patrolled.

They all devoured Ginny's meal as if it was a banquet
served for the queen herself. "Who will go to look after
Garth?" Ginny asked as she sat beside Wen to join them for
the meal.

"Moss is going back tomorrow, and maybe Davey," Wen
said.

"I don't suppose you have any magic in you," Davey asked

Ginny, flirting a little. "Like your brother does. Only what we need right now is a healer, not a reader."

Ginny tossed back her red braid. "I don't. But I did a lot of the nursing back on my mother's farm."

"Good. Then you can come with us," he said.

Orson speared another slice of meat and dropped it on his plate. "From what I hear, Moss's magic is what saved us this afternoon," he said. "I'm sorry I was riding so far in the rear I missed *that*."

Moss made a small motion with her right hand, as if to brush aside her importance, but Wen could tell she was pleased. Moss was sitting beside Orson, and Wen thought her left hand might be resting on his thigh under the table. That was what a brush with death did for you—it made you want to draw closer to the people for whom you felt a strong affection. Moss said, "I didn't even think. I saw the arrows coming and I made them stop. I hadn't even realized I could do that."

Wen toasted Moss with her glass and the rest of the guards followed suit. "Orson's right. Without your magic, we'd have lost more than a coachman. We'd have seen three or four of the guards go down—maybe more."

"I wish I knew how to turn the arrows around and fling them right back at the archers," Moss said.

She sounded so bloodthirsty that Orson laughed. "Guess you ought to start practicing that very thing tomorrow morning," he said. "I'll help you out—I'm not bad with a bow. But you better not stick any arrows in *me*."

The rest of the meal passed in much the same way, a mix of banter, speculation, and analysis of what they had done right and wrong. After dinner, the whole group slowly dispersed, some going to bed, some going to patrol. Davey lingered to help Ginny clear the table and ask her again if she wanted to ride out with them in the morning. Wen stood at the door for a few moments, watching him doubtfully. Ginny was too young to be drawing the attention of men, but Davey was barely eighteen himself, scarcely four years older than she was. And he made her laugh. Twice while Wen listened, Ginny giggled in response to something the young guard said. She didn't look like she minded his attention. Wen hesitated a moment longer, then stepped outside.

Orson was a couple moments behind her. A little light spilled out from the windows but he was something of a blur in the dark of evening. "He doesn't mean her any harm," he said. He had obviously noticed her concern about Davey and Ginny. "And Moss won't let him try anything if Ginny goes with them tomorrow. Moss isn't much of one for tolerating bullies. But I don't think you have anything to worry about."

Wen gave him a tight smile. "Never thought I was the type to fret," she said.

She could just make out the amusement on Orson's face. "Really? And here I thought that's what you do best."

Now her expression was threatening. "Make fun of me and I'll show you what I do best," she said. "And you'll see it from the ground with your head bashed in."

His grin widened. "That's what I like about you," he said. "You prefer extreme solutions."

"I prefer solutions that work," she retorted. "I don't mind if they're extreme."

He nodded, instantly sobering. "You did good today," he said softly. "Holding off the attack, organizing the guards. All your training was for something like this. You passed the test."

"So did all of you."

"Yeah," he drawled, leaning back against the outer wall, "but it was your test. So now can you believe in yourself again?"

Her chin jerked up. She glared at him through the darkness. "What makes you think you can ask me a question like that?"

"Fought beside you," he said. "I can ask what I want."

She took a deep breath. "There aren't enough fights on enough roadsides in all of Gillengaria to make me believe in myself again," she said, turning away from him as she spoke. "But I'm more thankful than I can say that today's encounter ended up the way it did."

She was four steps away from him on her way to the house when she heard his soft voice behind her. "Then maybe what it takes is someone else believing in you." She kept walking. She had no intention of turning back to ask him what he'd meant.

* * *

SEREPHETTE was in the library with Jasper, pacing with her usual grand elegance. She was clearly agitated over Karryn's behavior. "And *then*! When I told her I thought she should spend tomorrow quietly at home, she informed me that she thought it was important that her people see that the serramarra was not frightened off by outlaws and bandits! *Her people!* When did Karryn begin to talk like that?"

Jasper started laughing. "Oh, but you have to give her credit!" he exclaimed. "She was very cool today. Not shrieking and shrinking back as Lindy Coverroe would have done."

Serephette gave him a reproving look out of her hollow eyes. "At least such conduct would be more ladylike than her current behavior."

Jasper motioned Wen deeper into the room. "I'll wager the captain has a different opinion."

Wen made a respectful bow in Serephette's direction. "Marlady, I have to confess I thought Karryn's behavior today was magnificent. She showed bravery. She showed that she cares for the men who risk their lives to keep her safe. And that means they will fight for her even harder next time."

Serephette frowned at her. "You want to remake my daughter. You want to turn her into some kind of—mannish woman. Playing at swords and calling the guardsmen her friends! A proper serramarra doesn't do such things."

"I don't think Karryn's ever going to be a conventional serramarra—or a conventional marlady," Wen said quietly. "She didn't love her father overmuch. Once it occurs to her that other men might not be much better, she might choose not to marry at all. She might decide to take on all the work of running Fortunalt herself. She's teaching herself a lot of things she'll need to know in that case. Running a guard is one of them."

"And it seems to me Karryn still spends plenty of her energy brooding about gowns, balls, and men," Jasper added. "I don't think we need to worry about Karryn losing *all* her superficial qualities."

Serephette bestowed a scathing look upon him and swept toward the door. "Of course *you* wouldn't understand," she shot out. "You both want Karryn to be *different*. You don't understand that being different just makes her life harder."

"I do understand," Jasper said soberly, as Serephette paused with one foot in the hall. "What you don't understand is that Karryn's life is already hard, and she's already different because of it."

"I see I have no allies here," Serephette said coldly, slamming the door behind her as she left.

Wen and Jasper were left to gaze at each other in reverberating silence.

"Well, I'm sorry she thinks I'm interfering in her daughter's education," Wen said. "But I have to say Karryn's behavior made me proud today. Reckless but splendid. She deserved every drop of blood shed for her."

"What about Garth? And Malton?"

"Malton's going to be fine, I think. We won't know about Garth for a while yet, but I'm hopeful that the tavernkeeper's mystic daughter-in-law will be able to save him."

"Magic again," Jasper said. He waved Wen over, and they sank into their customary chairs on either side of the small game table. "I thought Rayson had managed to banish it from Fortunalt, but since you've arrived, it rears its shy head everywhere."

She grinned. "Magic was always here. It was just in hiding. If Karryn shows that she's not afraid of it, it will flourish throughout Fortunalt. And I think you'll find that to be a good thing, on balance."

He leaned back in his chair and regarded her with a small smile. "I still think the credit goes to you. Are you sure you're not a mystic yourself?"

She laughed. "Pretty sure. I think I'd know by now." She shrugged. "Although—some people believe that magic is a gift from the gods, and one of the gods might watch over warriors. I wouldn't mind having sorcery like that."

His smile had vanished. "I think you must. I watched you from the coach, you know—feeling a mix of terror and exultation the whole time. You could have been killed a dozen times over. I was sure my heart would stop when you disappeared into that tree, and all we could see were these wildly waving branches. And yet you emerged victorious. You! Tiny thing that you are! And the men who attacked you fell dead. I was so afraid—and I was so amazed. If that's not a kind of magic, I don't know what is."

She was pleased and embarrassed. It occurred to her, suddenly and sharply, that she had not had a solitary conversation with this man since he had kissed his fingers and laid them against her lips. The memory made her suddenly hot and awkward. She tried to cover her discomfort with a solemn expression.

"I was glad my skill was equal to the task," she said. "But what I want to know is, why were we fighting? And who? Do you have any idea?"

Now his face was as sober as hers. "You don't think these were just outlaws stopping random carriages as they passed?"

She shook her head, regaining her composure now that they were talking about serious matters. "They were too well-fed, too well-organized, and too well-supplied," she said bluntly. "They were trying to kill us. More specifically, they were trying to kill Karryn."

He uttered a curse—shocking words from such a polished man—and came to his feet to stalk the room. Wen stood uncertainly but stayed where she was, watching him. "I was afraid you would say that," he said over his shoulder. "I had the same impression, but I hoped I was wrong."

"Do you have any theories about who would plan such a thing?"

He shook his head. "Tover Banlish comes most instantly to mind, but what would he have to gain?"

"She humiliated him and because of her, he's been disinherited," Wen suggested. "Those are pretty powerful motives."

"And yet, if his goal is to improve his lot—particularly through marriage—murder hardly helps his cause," Jasper pointed out. "He can scarcely marry Karryn if she's dead, and no one else would have him if they knew he'd killed her!"

"But if no one knew—"

He nodded, continuing to pace. "Yes, of course, and it certainly has to remain as a possibility. I will send an urgent letter to his father in the morning. But to me this doesn't seem like the work of a man as clumsy as Tover."

She had been strongly leaning toward the devvaser as a villain, but those words made her stop and consider. Tover was stupid and he was arrogant, and he had been the lead kidnapper in Karryn's abduction. Was he intelligent enough to locate and strike a deal with professional soldiers? Would he have been able to resist the thrill of working alongside them?

And was he really evil enough to sign Karryn's death warrant? A woman he had wanted to *marry* only a few months back?

"But if not Tover," she said slowly, "then who?"

"The question has haunted me all night," Jasper admitted. He had come to a halt across the room, and now he stared at her, his face grim. "What's the point of killing Karryn? Who benefits?"

She had said much the same thing to the guards at the site of the ambush. "If Karryn dies," she asked, "who becomes marlord of Fortunalt?"

Jasper looked thoughtful. "I don't actually know the answer to that. Rayson had no siblings—no cousins, either. The joke among the Thirteenth House was that no woman could endure the touch of any of the Fortunalt marlords for the last five generations. So they gave their husbands one heir apiece and then never allowed the men to touch them again. Rayson's own mother—Karryn's grandmother—ran off with the steward. It was a scandal, of course, but everyone who heard the story said, 'Good for her!' or words to that effect. You had cause to hate Rayson, but Reynold was even worse."

Wen smiled a little. "That's amusing, but that doesn't help us right now."

"Serephette is sure to know. We'll ask her in the morning," Jasper said. "I suppose Karryn's heir becomes the person most likely to want her dead."

Wen suddenly felt tired. "Or perhaps not. Perhaps there are feuds among the Houses that we know nothing about. Perhaps Ariane Rappengrass wants to see Fortunalt weak enough that she can invade the lands and take over some of the property."

"I've met Ariane, and I seriously doubt that," he murmured.

"Or perhaps a lesser lord with a great deal of money hated Rayson so much that he doesn't want to see anyone with Rayson's blood ascend to power in Fortunalt."

Jasper stared at her in dismay. "In that case, the possible suspects are virtually limitless."

"I know. It would have been better if we had kept one of our assailants alive to learn what we could in interrogation." She shrugged. "But at the time, I was more interested in keeping Karryn safe. So now she is alive but we are ignorant. I can't regret the bargain, but it does leave us with nothing but questions."

He came slowly toward her across the room. "And here's another question," he said. "Will there be another attack on Karryn's life? Should we no longer allow her outside of these protected walls?"

Wen felt her mouth tighten with dissent. "Lock her up to keep her safe," she said. "That's what King Baryn did with Amalie when she was young. I had been a Rider for years before I ever saw her to speak to. I don't think that's much of a life."

"Still, she survived to become queen," Jasper pointed out.

"And for the rest of her life there will be enemies who would like to see her dead," Wen replied. "What kind of queen will she be if she never leaves Ghosenhall? What kind of marlady will Karryn be if she never leaves these grounds?"

"Then what's the answer?"

"I'm the answer. You know that already. I am, and Orson, and Moss, and all the other guards we've assembled. We never let her out of our sight."

"But your contract is up," he said softly. "You'll be leaving soon."

The words hit her like a hard slap. She stiffened, caught unprepared. "Yes," she said at last, "but she will be safe with the others."

He had come to a halt only a couple feet away from her. "I don't believe Karryn will trust anyone as she trusts you."

"I wasn't the only one who fought today," Wen said. "And no one let her down."

"It would be better if you stayed," he said.

The words hung between them during a long silence. Then he added, "I believe you want to. Don't you? You just haven't allowed yourself to think you can."

Now she was the one agitated enough to pace, but he stood too close to her, hemming her against the chair. She clasped her hands together, hard, to keep them from clenching and unclenching with stress. "Sometimes it's not a matter of what I want or what I choose," she said in a low voice. "I feel a sense of—of—it might almost be panic, and the only way to make it fade is to get on my horse and ride out."

"And do you feel that sense of panic now?" he asked.

She gave a shaky laugh. "I didn't until you came to stand over me like that."

He smiled slightly. "So would you like me to back away?"

It was a long time before she answered. "No."

He reached out a hand and gently, gently touched his fingertips to her cheek. "You have accused me before of being obscure, so let me be forthright now," he said. "I want you to stay. For Karryn's sake, yes. Because I trust you to watch over her. For your sake. Because I think, in Fortunalt, you might find a place you can come to rest, if you can only convince yourself that you deserve to." His hand traveled upward, took a lock of her short hair between his fingers, tested it as if it was purest silk. "For my sake," he added. "Because I will miss you dreadfully if you go."

She was astonished at how much her skull tingled under his touch as his hand moved farther back, cupped itself around her ear, splayed at the back of her head. "Those are all reasons for me to linger," she said, focusing on her words as much as she would have if she were drunk. "But I don't know how long I could promise to stay even so."

"Another month?" he said, a whisper of a laugh in his voice. "Haven't we advanced our contract in such increments almost from the beginning?"

She met his eyes squarely. "A month might seem like a long time," she said, "if you seduced your captain and began to find her tiresome in a week."

That made him laugh out loud. "Oh, you are the most refreshingly direct woman!" he exclaimed. "Surely I would not find you tiresome for a year at least."

So he didn't deny that seduction was his intent. The news made her feel even more cheerful, and she had already thought she might be exhibiting a certain sparkle. "Well, I won't ask you for promises," she said. "So I don't think I have to make you promises in return."

"One or two promises I think I can make you," he said. He had lifted his other hand and placed it at her waist, and now he drew her closer to him, almost into an embrace. She could feel the heat of his body through his fine embroidered clothes. "I will never treat you with disrespect and never speak to you unkindly."

"You *have* to keep those types of promises," she said, letting her voice fill with mock scorn. "You know I'll cut your heart out if you don't treat me well."

He laughed out loud and swept her into his arms, bending his head to kiss her firmly on the mouth. This was a bedazzlement she hadn't expected; this was a richness. Jasper Paladar kissed the way he talked, with subtle shades of nuance and an extensive vocabulary. Clearly he enjoyed kissing. Most men Wen knew didn't bother too much with the preliminaries, so she was finding this a rare and enlightening experience. She let her hands creep up to lock around his neck and pressed herself against him with a purr of pleasure.

When he finally pulled back, he was still laughing, or laughing again. "If that is a prelude to the evening's delights, I see I am going to enjoy myself even more than I hoped to," he said. "But I am just now struck with consideration of logistics."

She felt her face crinkling into its own laugh. "How to get me up to your room so that nobody sees me."

"Not that I wish you to interpret that as my being ashamed of your company," he added hastily. "That was not intended to be disrespectful in the least."

She pretended to be offended. "I believe I am the one who has more of a reputation to lose," she said. "I'm sure Karryn would be disappointed to learn how lax my moral standards are."

He kissed her quickly. "I think we must go up separately. Do you know which room is mine?"

She nodded. "I know every room in the house, my lord."

For a moment he looked horrified. "You're not going to call me that, are you?"

Now she was laughing again. "No. Unless you like it."

"I mean—will you find it strange to call me Jasper? I use your own name quite freely, and yet I realize you almost never address me at all. Even by my title."

"In my mind, I have been calling you Jasper almost from the beginning," she said. "It might take a little while to get used to saying it out loud."

"You might practice," he suggested.

She tilted her face up. "I like it very much when you kiss me, Jasper."

He responded most satisfactorily, then said, "I think you will like it even more when I do more than kiss you."

Which made her dissolve into laughter again. "And I always thought lords and ladies were so reserved."

"Did you? I think you will be quite pleased to see that I have very few inhibitions at all."

"In that case, let's not waste any more time getting to your room!" she said. "You go first, and I'll follow. I'm pretty good at covering ground without being seen, but if I run into any-one I'll just say that I'm checking the house more thoroughly tonight after this afternoon's adventure."

"An excellent notion," he approved. He kissed her once more before releasing her. "Don't keep me waiting," he said, and left the room.

For a minute, Wen stared at the closed door and wondered if she was mad.

But her blood still shivered with excitement and her skin was flushed from contact. Gods and goddesses, she couldn't remember the last time she had been this eager to give her body to a man. No one would stop her, not even masked assailants who might come flowing over the outer hedge. She was gliding through the halls to spend the night beside Jasper Paladar.

Or what portion of the night she could spare before taking her turn to patrol.

Chapter
30

IT WAS A SIMPLE MATTER FOR WEN TO LEAVE the library and creep through the house to the servants' stairway so she had less chance of running into Karryn or Serephette. It was not that late, in fact; any number of people could still be up and roaming the halls. But Wen was careful and did not encounter a soul.

She gave the lightest tap on Jasper's door and it was instantly opened; he had obviously been awaiting her faintest signal. She slipped into the room and into his arms in a single motion. They paused for another exchange of kisses before she looked up to glance around. The room was not nearly as opulent as some of the bedrooms at Ghosenhall, but luxurious even so. It was spacious enough to sleep twenty soldiers, though, of course, there was not nearly enough furniture to do so—a few groupings of chairs and tables; various armoires and dressing tables; a large four-poster bed piled high with a maroon comforter and a dozen pillows. The dark curtains were pulled against the night, but a dozen candles offered plenty of illumination. Wen couldn't see any discarded clothing or cast-off shoes. Either Jasper Paladar was a very tidy man, or his valet was.

She did see books everywhere—open on the nightstand, piled on the dressers, stacked with papers on the smaller tables. No servant had been allowed to straighten up *those* essential items.

"Does my chamber meet with your approval?" he murmured, watching her appraise the space. "What are you thinking as you gaze around? Are you assessing the possibilities for attack through the windows?"

"Oh, I did that weeks ago," she retorted. "Second-story room, not hard to reach. There's a gutter that offers a handhold, but it's a little rickety, so someone who weighs too much would probably end up pulling it down, which would be loud enough to catch my attention—"

He was almost doubled over with laughter. "Enough—I see—I have underestimated you again," he finally said, practically gasping out the words. "So we may lose ourselves in love without worrying about being surprised by assassins."

"Well, there are four guards patrolling," she said. "They ought to minimize the chance of assassins as well."

"Willawendiss, Willawendiss," he said. "You *are* the most extraordinary girl."

"I'm glad you think so," she said, and she kissed him.

In no time at all, they had drifted over to the bed and collapsed on top of it. Wen lay on her back and stretched her arms as wide as they would go, and still couldn't touch both edges of the mattress. "I have *never* slept in a bed this big," she told him.

"Even when you were sleeping next to someone else?" he inquired. He was lying next to her, propped up on one elbow. With his free hand he was slowly untying the laces on her vest. They'd both already discarded their shoes, but the rest of the disrobing was going at a relaxed pace. Both of them were enjoying themselves too much to rush.

She grinned up at him. "Well, you know, if you had a few minutes of privacy in the barracks with someone, you never wasted it *sleeping*," she said. "And the beds in most of those quarters are about two feet wide and hard as iron. And if I happened to take a lover who had his own room somewhere, it was usually rented from some old lady, completely furnished, and not designed for extravagance."

"You need to upgrade your quality of bedmate," he said.

She made an equivocal motion with her head. "Let's see how well this goes," she said pessimistically. "I might find the gentry aren't worth the trouble."

That made him laugh, of course, and apply himself with a little more determination to her vest and shirt. All the while, she was helping him from his own clothes, though she couldn't help noticing the differences between their attire—his all silk and fine wool, well-made and almost new; hers leather and cotton, well-worn and broken in. They were both half naked, and his hand was moving in a slow, sensuous sweep along the slope of her ribs, when she realized that most of the laughter had gone out of him. She gave him an inquiring look.

"What's wrong?"

His fingers traveled lightly over the long, faded scar that cut its jagged way from her navel to her left breast. That was the worst of them, but he took a moment to touch the marks on her arm, her throat, her right shoulder. She thought that just now he probably couldn't see the two that crossed her back, and she shifted her weight a little so he'd have less of a chance to notice them.

"You look like you've been badly hurt," he said softly. "Over and over again."

She wasn't sure how to play this, so she chose her words cautiously and made them sound casual. "That's a soldier's life," she said. "You expect to receive wounds, and get them bound up, and go out to fight again. Any blow that doesn't kill you becomes a badge of honor. A symbol of your skill and determination."

He traced the longest scar again. "Well, I always knew you had plenty of both. But it troubles me to see the evidence written in such a brutal fashion."

"You find them repulsive?" she asked, because she wasn't sure what he meant. "We could blow out the candles so you don't have to see them."

He shook his head. "No. No, no, no. Not repulsive, and certainly quite honorable. I just—I don't like to think that at some point you were hurt and in pain."

She let that pass, because she didn't know how to answer. To her, pain had never seemed to be the point; surviving was the point. Instead, she flattened her hand against his chest, the unmarred flesh partly covered by a light sprinkling of curly gray hair. "And look at you," she said, her voice half teasing, half admiring. "Skin as smooth as a baby's. I never touched an aristocrat's body before. It's so clean! I think you must bathe every day and then cover yourself with scented oils."

"I have some of those very oils in that cabinet over there," he drawled. "Shall I fetch them? I think you might like the way they feel."

She laughed back at him. "I think I might."

He hooked his fingers in the loop of her trousers and began to pull down. "In a minute," he said, his voice a little husky. "First, let's see what else we'll find."

What he found was her ankle sheath strapped to her left leg, with the small, deadly dagger still in it. She snorted with laughter at the expression on his face. "You never know when you might need another weapon," she explained.

"Could you—do you think—take it off? Just for a while?" he asked.

She pretended to consider. "I don't usually. Not for any reason."

"Not even in situations such as this?"

She raised her eyebrows in a skeptical fashion. "When I'm sharing a bed with a new man for the first time? When I'm at my most vulnerable? That's the *last* time I'd want to give up all my protection."

"I assure you," he said solemnly, "I have no designs on your life. Only your virtue."

"And I could fend you off if you tried to overpower me," she said.

"I'm bigger and heavier than you are," he pointed out.

She gave him a derisive look. "You're weak and untrained," she said. "No conditioning."

His eyes gleamed in the candlelight. "And yet, I think you'll find my endurance remarkable."

She sat up just enough to unbuckle the sheath, though she very ostentatiously laid it on the nightstand within easy reach. "I hope so," she said. "Let's begin the demonstration."

* * *

WEN had thought she had enjoyed making love in the past, with partners who brought a range of passion to their encounters. Sometimes she had found the sex act to be a laughing romp, other times a brief and intense coupling, other times a clumsy and unsatisfying physical bout.

But Jasper Paladar made her laugh and made her gasp and made her feel cherished and then started all over again. She found she liked the sweet-scented oils. She liked the feel of the fine linen sheets against her skin. She liked the way the aristocracy considered lovemaking a leisurely pastime, as much to be savored as good wine or good food.

Or maybe that was just Jasper.

She was pretty sure not all Thirteenth House lords recited poetry to their bedmates once the lovemaking was over. He ran his fingers with a delicious lightness over the curves and surfaces of her body as he murmured verses about someone remembering a night of abandoned passion.

> *I am awake now, but then I was surely dreaming,*
> *Few hours come so laden with content.*
> *Few pass with such luxury, gorged and heavy-seeming,*
> *And I know this, and I will not repent—*
> *No, not though six days or sixty years pass by,*
> *Clamorous with struggle, tense with strife and plot,*
> *And holding no other treasures . . .*

She liked the words more than she would have expected. "Who wrote that?" she asked. "You?"

"Hardly. I have put my hand to a verse or two, but never with particularly felicitous results. That was by Martolin Brassenthwaite. Related in some distant fashion to the current marlord."

"Write it down for me," she said.

"I'll do better than that. I'll give you one of his books."

She was doubtful. "I don't know that I want to just sit around reading poetry. And, you know, I pack light. I don't keep too many unnecessary possessions."

"It's a very small volume," he assured her. "Illustrations on half the pages. Anyway, books *are* necessary possessions."

"Weapons are necessary possessions."

"Then I suppose you might give me a dagger to commemorate this night?"

"You ought to have one. Just in case. But since you don't know how to use it, I don't know that it would do you much good."

"You could give me private lessons."

"Oh no," she replied. "If you're going to learn to fight, you should learn it in the training yard like Karryn does."

He sighed. "You have such a soft and romantic way about you."

"I'm a practical girl," she said. "It's what you like about me."

"It's *one* of the things I like about you," he corrected. His hand continued its idle stroking, but she had the sense that his mind had moved on to another matter. Fair enough. She had matters of her own to attend to. She pushed off against the pillows and sat up.

"Where are you going?" he asked, sitting up beside her.

"You didn't expect me to stay the night, did you, and risk being seen leaving in the morning?"

His face was blank. "I hadn't thought about it at all," he said. "Though I would like it if you could stay a little longer."

"I could come back tomorrow night," she suggested.

His eyes widened. "Of course you can! I mean, I assumed you would! Must I issue an invitation every day, or will you understand that you are always welcome in my room?"

She wrinkled her nose. "I think, with all our restrictions, we will have to make sure we are both free any night we want to meet," she said. "There are people who are paying attention to my movements, even if they can't call me to account, and there's no end of people watching you."

"So we must accept the necessity for a certain degree of subterfuge."

"Yes," she said, grinning again, "but sometimes that's half the fun."

He didn't smile back. In fact, he looked a little worried. "I have something to tell you that you won't like," he said.

She casually reached for the dagger and began restrapping it to her ankle. She wondered if he was about to confess some long-standing betrothal or other commitment, something that would make it clear how very different their stations were, how transitory their relationship. "Yes?"

"Remember, though, that you promised you wouldn't leave for another month? At least?"

"I don't think I did make that promise."

"Well, make it now."

The sheath in place, she settled back on the bed facing him. She was quite comfortable being naked, and he didn't seem discomposed, either. At least by his nudity—something else was clearly on his mind. "This seems like a bad time to be making you promises," she said. "Just tell me what you're so worried about."

He took her hands in both of his, holding them rather tightly. "The royal consort will be arriving here sometime in the next week," he said. "Accompanied by a cohort of Riders."

She jerked back, feeling a hot spike of inchoate emotions— rage, fear, panic, resentment, longing, loss. It took only one fierce twist for her to free her hands, but he instantly caught hold of her again and this time she let him keep his grip. She was surprised to find that she was shivering. Less surprised to find her stomach a hard and bitter knot. She didn't meet his eyes. She wasn't sure what she wanted him to read on her face.

"Why is he coming here?" she asked at last.

"He has been touring the southern Houses. He will be leaving Rappengrass soon. But, Wen, I didn't mean to be concealing this from you. I have known for some time that Cammon was on his way, but it is only recently that I realized what such a visit might mean to you."

She shook her head as if to ask for silence, and he immediately stopped talking. It took her a moment to achieve calm, but she was determined to rein in her galloping heartbeat. If Cammon was coming to Forten City, he would be attended by a half dozen Riders at least. Some might be new recruits, but there was no chance he would have left the palace grounds without some of the most seasoned Riders at his back. Tayse, for a dead certainty. Justin, just as likely.

She could not face either of them. She could not face Janni or Hammond. Too many questions, not enough explanations, not enough peace in her heart. She would leave in the morning, she would slip outside the hedge this very night, pack her bags in stealth the minute she made it back to the barracks. Serephette would probably be glad to see her go, and Karryn would soon enough overcome her disappointment. . . .

But someone wanted Karryn dead.

Whoever had tried to kill her once would undoubtedly try again. The guards Wen had assembled were good, but were they good enough?

What if Wen left? What if another assault was made, and this one was successful? What if Karryn was murdered? Would that not be as unforgivable as allowing Baryn to die practically at her feet?

But I cannot stay here forever, Wen thought. Her fingers spasmed within Jasper's grasp, but he did not release her and she did not try to pull away. *Even if I stay until this present danger is past, some new threat will arise. A marlady is never completely safe.*

But if I wait until this crisis is resolved, I can ride away with a clear conscience, knowing that I have discharged my duty during my prescribed time.

But this crisis is very far from over.

I cannot leave her. I cannot leave Jasper. Not now. I cannot ride away tonight.

She took a deep breath and finally looked up at him. His face was creased with concern; his gray eyes were narrowed with a combination of hope and worry. "I can't be at Fortune while Cammon is here," she said flatly.

He nodded. "I know that. But—"

"But I am not ready to leave for good," she added. "I will stay on the grounds until just before he arrives. And I will take lodgings in the city while he and his entourage are here. If anyone needs me, I'll be easy to find. And I'll return when Cammon is gone. I don't think you can ask more of me than that."

He looked inexpressibly relieved. "No, indeed, that is quite generous," he said. "Now if you will only forgive me for concealing information from you, your generosity will be complete."

"I will think that over," she said darkly, and he sighed.

"Could you think it over from here?" he suggested, tugging her in his direction.

She snapped her wrists and broke his hold. "I have to check in at the barracks," she said. "They'll be wondering already where I am. But I'll be back tomorrow night with a better story in place to explain my absence."

"Then, Willawendiss, I bid you goodnight."

Once she was dressed, he escorted her to the door, a silly but charming formality, and kissed her good-bye before she slipped out into the hall. She made her way easily through the unlit corridors, across the dark length of the outer lawn, pausing twice to speak to the soldiers on patrol. The high moon was almost completely obscured by clouds, but Wen didn't need its light to see. The whole world seemed to bloom with a buried incandescence, lighting every banister, every doorway, every pathway, every tree. Or maybe she was the object alight with an internal fire; maybe she was the one whose blaze threw every detail of the landscape into shocked and exquisite relief.

THE following week was strange, both exhilarating and harrowing, as Wen balanced her delight in Jasper's attentions with her dread of Cammon's arrival and her determination to keep Karryn safe. Her absence had been idly remarked upon that first night, and she made the offhand comment that she was going to station herself in the house for a couple of hours every night just as an added measure of protection. Everyone seemed to accept that, for she had proved herself fanatical about security in the past. Well, Moss did send her a speculative look before she and Davey set out to fetch Garth, and Wen was pretty sure Orson also doubted her explanation, but no one asked her any questions. Neither Moss nor Orson wanted Wen to start making inquiries into *their* lives. True privacy was too hard to come by in a soldier's life, so one of the first rules of survival was to respect your fellows' secrets.

In any case, there were professional reasons to meet with Jasper Paladar these next few days as they tried to deduce who had attacked Karryn on the road. A note from Zellin Banlish arrived the morning after Wen's second night with Jasper, and he showed it to her that evening.

Paladar,

I was sorry to hear the shocking news about serra Karryn's encounter with brigands. Naturally one of your first suspects was my son, but I cannot believe he had the resources for such an attack, which I understand required a considerable outlay of money. I have cut off all his funds and make him apply to me even for such necessities as clothing and horseflesh. If you do not believe me, I will come to your house and speak my piece before that mystic boy of yours.

Banlish

"Not definitive," Jasper said after Wen had read it. "But it certainly makes Tover's involvement seem even less likely."

"I agree," she said. "Was Serephette able to supply the name of the next in line?"

"Instantly," he said, "but I remain even more puzzled than before. It would be a man named Maller who lives with his wife and adolescent sons on some remote corner of Fortunalt lands. I've made a few discreet inquiries, and I can't find evidence that any of them have set foot in Forten City for the last twenty years. Certainly they don't seem to be putting much energy into checking out their inheritance."

"I suppose they could have spies in Forten City, and a trusted agent who would hire mercenaries for them," Wen said doubtfully.

"Possible," Jasper said. "But at the moment, they seem unlikely suspects."

She stared at him. "Then who?"

He shook his head. "Perhaps the consort will have an idea. His powers of discernment are remarkable. We shall ask him when he arrives."

As always, Wen felt a thrill of terror at the thought that Riders would be momentarily at the gate. "And he will be arriving exactly when?"

Jasper shook his head. "Apparently he is on the way, but traveling slowly, according to the messages I am getting from his party."

"Make sure you give me plenty of warning before he appears," she said in a threatening way.

"I promise, Willawendiss, I promise."

But, as it happened, she learned of Cammon's approach from an entirely unexpected source.

Three days later, she was overseeing the morning workouts in the training yard, and she had pitted Karryn against Davey. He and Moss had returned the day before, a much-improved Garth between them. Moss was still supervising Garth's convalescence, but Davey had instantly returned to the training yard, and Wen wanted him to show Karryn some of the moves that he did particularly well. But Karryn was clumsy, or not paying attention, or worried about getting her hair dirty, and she kept botching the upthrust.

Impatiently, Wen grabbed the practice sword from Davey and shooed him away. "No, like *this*," she said, demonstrating again. "You're not turning your wrist when you need to."

Karryn tried again and failed again, and Wen eventually gave up. "I think we're just wasting our time today," Wen said, trying not to sound disapproving.

"I'm sorry, Willa, but I'm just so excited," Karryn said. Indeed, her brown eyes were bright and her face was flushed with eagerness. "The royal consort is only a day's ride from Forten City! It would be a half day, except he is moving so slowly," she added.

Wen felt her stomach tighten, but she spoke calmly. "Indeed? Did your uncle receive a message this morning?"

Karryn looked puzzled. "No, I—" Her forehead creased even more, as if she was trying to remember how she had obtained this particular piece of knowledge. "It's just that I—"

Wen laughed at her. "Did you dream it, perhaps? I've had a dream or two that seemed as real as life."

Karryn shook her head with emphasis. "*No*, I can tell you exactly where he is. About four hours south of us, near the little town called Pettis . . ." Her voice trailed off and her eyes got even bigger. "Willa. I don't know how I *know* that."

Wen beamed at her. "It's your marlady blood telling you," she said. "I've heard stories that say Malcolm Danalustrous is aware of it the minute anyone crosses the border onto his lands. It looks like you're developing the same skill."

Karryn looked as though her head had been knocked askew. "Could my father do that?"

"Who knows? Maybe it's only a skill that *good* marlords and marladies possess."

Karryn straightened. "I must go tell Jasper!"

"About Cammon's arrival?"

Karryn was already climbing over the fence. "About my ability to sense it! Won't he be proud of me!" And with a flip of her brown hair, she was gone.

And time for me to go, too, Wen thought. *If he's only four or five hours away, Cammon might actually be here by nightfall. I cannot be here when Riders sweep through that gate.*

An hour later she was packed and saddling her horse, reciting a detailed list of instructions to Orson. He must send someone every day to report to her at the inn where she would be staying. He must increase the patrols at the gate and on the grounds while Cammon was in residence, although the Riders would surely add their own formidable skills to the task of protecting royalty. He must make the Riders free of any equipment they wanted to borrow, any space they wanted to utilize, for their own practices.

"And if anybody asks after you?" Orson said. "I should tell them I don't know where you're staying in the city?"

She glared at him, but he gazed right back, his expression shrewd. "Why would Riders be asking after me?" she demanded.

"Why would you be running from Riders?" he shot back.

She swung into the saddle, tense and irritable. "You don't know what you're talking about," she said.

He shrugged and watched her go. "See you in a few days," he said.

She nodded and rode out without bothering to speak another word. Most of her was weak with relief that she was escaping before anyone from Ghosenhall could see her. Would they shout out their delight when they recognized her face? Pull her into their rough embraces, demand to know why she had run, beg her to return? Would they turn their backs on her, a flawed and useless comrade, one who had failed them in the most disastrous fashion possible? Would they love her or shun her? She didn't know. She couldn't bear to stay and learn.

But a tiny, sad, shivering corner of her heart longed to stay and find out.

Chapter
31

"I NEVER THOUGHT I'D BE GLAD TO BE ARRIVING in Forten City," Senneth remarked as their cavalcade crossed into the city limits late on a sunny afternoon. To hasten their progress on this leg of the journey, she had finally demanded that Cammon climb into the coach. She herself had locked the door, and now she sat with her back against it so that he couldn't unexpectedly exit and begin talking to the populace. "I like it only slightly better than I like Gissel Plain."

Cammon was peering over her head to watch the crowded streets roll past. "I don't remember it being such a terrible place when we were here three years ago," he said.

She made a dismissive sound. "You were just getting used to us then. You were still this wretched vagabond we'd picked up on the side of the road. You were so happy to have friends that you didn't care what we did or where we landed."

He grinned. "I wasn't *wretched*. I wasn't very well-groomed, maybe."

Her only answer was a disbelieving snort. He was hardly

well-groomed now, though at least he owned clothes that fit and he would sit still for a haircut now and then.

He looked out the window again. "Anyway, you only hated it because of Rayson Fortunalt. Now that he's gone, maybe you'll find it a charming place."

"Maybe," she said doubtfully. "But I can tell you right now that I'm getting eager to go home, so the shorter our visit, the happier I'll be."

Kirra and Donnal had left them already, Kirra saying frankly that the pace was driving her to madness. So far, Justin seemed content enough to dawdle on the road, but Senneth knew his impatience would begin to show once it was time for Ellynor to quit her sojourn in the Lirrens and head back to Ghosenhall. Tayse seemed to be the only one of them who didn't mind how long the journey lasted or where it took them. He was guarding royalty; thus, he must go wherever royalty went. Most of Tayse's choices were drastically simple.

"I think Fortunalt may end up being the most interesting part of our visit yet," Cammon said.

Senneth doubted that, but a few minutes later she had to admit their reception at Fortune was very hospitable. With Kirra gone, she was forced to play the role of grand serramarra, companion to royalty, so she tried for a regal graciousness as she introduced herself to the occupants of the house. It only took a couple minutes to write off the marlady as a borderline lunatic, but Karryn Fortunalt and her guardian went out of their way to be likable.

"We're so pleased to have the honor of entertaining the royal consort of Gillengaria and his companions," the young serramarra said in such a stilted fashion it was obvious she'd been rehearsing the phrase for days. But she smiled so brightly that the words rang true nonetheless. Karryn looked too much like her father to be pretty, and was too young and coltish to be elegant, but she was trying hard to be cordial, and Senneth allowed herself to be cautiously won over.

Cammon knew no such caution. He was responding to the serramarra's smile with an enthusiastic one of his own. "And I can't tell you how pleased I am to be here," he said.

"I hope your journey has been very pleasant," Karryn added.

"Trouble free, thank you," Senneth said.

"Unlike our *own* last trip through Fortunalt lands," Serephette said in a dark voice. "We were set upon by bandits while on a lonely stretch of road! Fortunately, no one was hurt."

"The coachman died and two of the guards were hurt," Karryn said swiftly, "though not severely."

Oh, this was surely news the attractive Jasper Paladar did not want shared with Cammon the minute he stepped through the door! Senneth caught the quick frown he sent Serephette's way, but the damage was already done.

"Yes," Jasper said smoothly, "I believe we are not alone among the southern Houses in seeing an increase of outlawry. I am glad to learn you made your trip unmolested."

"Well," said Cammon, "they would have to be pretty reckless outlaws to attack a party that included nine Riders and seventy soldiers. And a couple of mystics."

Now Senneth was the one who wanted to send a frowning look at her indiscreet companion. Did they really have to discuss magic while they were still standing in the hallway? But Karryn was instantly intrigued.

"Well, *you* are a mystic, or so everyone believes," she said. "But who else in your party has magic?"

Serephette actually lifted a hand and pointed straight at Senneth. "The Brassenthwaite girl," she said. "Thrown from her father's House when she was a young woman because he discovered sorcery in her veins. Everyone believed she was dead."

"Really?" Karryn breathed, clearly thrilled by what she perceived to be a romantic tale. "How dreadful for you!"

Senneth forced a light smile. "It was before you were born," she said. "Times were different then. These days, fewer people are afraid of magic."

"I like magic," Karryn announced. When her mother, clearly scandalized, hissed her name, the serra shook her head. "I do. I find it very useful."

"So do I," Cammon said.

They shared another smile, perfectly in charity with one another. Senneth happened to catch Jasper Paladar's expression and knew it closely mirrored her own. *What am I going to do with this ungovernable but wonderful child?* Involuntarily, she grinned at him, and he smiled back, his face relaxing.

"I'm sure you must be tired from your travels," he said. "We have planned no entertainments for tonight, but tomorrow and the evening after, there are a number of local lords and ladies who would very much appreciate the chance to meet you."

"Oh, yes," said Cammon. "Introduce me to as many people as you can."

"But first I would very much like to wash my face and change my clothes," Senneth said.

"Of course!" Karryn exclaimed. "Won't you follow me and I can show you to your chambers?"

DINNER that night was a reprise of that opening conversation, awkward but well-intentioned, except for Serephette's clear disregard for normal civilities. When, late in the meal, Serephette abruptly came to her feet and swept from the room, Senneth could tell by Jasper's expression that he was disappointed but unsurprised. Her absence actually made the rest of the meal go more smoothly, as Karryn and Cammon were quickly absorbed in conversation, and Senneth and Jasper found themselves quite at ease with each other.

"I'm sure you're thinking this is a most unconventional household," he said to her when it was clear Cammon and Karryn had no interest in anyone else's observations.

Senneth sipped her wine, which was almost as good as the honey-spice vintage Ariane had served. "The first night we dined at Gissel Plain, the heir to the House stormed out of the room after first announcing his hatred for his stepfather," she said. "I can't imagine the tension here is much higher than it is there. The war left behind more than unconventional households. I am surprised the realm has been put back together as well as it has."

He smiled slightly. "Graciously said," he responded. "And yet I hate to have the royal consort see us at our worst on his very first night."

Senneth watched Cammon, who appeared to be demonstrating for a captivated Karryn just how well he could pick up thoughts and memories from her head. "Cammon is somewhat eccentric himself," she murmured. "And it is useless to try to impress him with counterfeit displays of pomp and grandeur. He often does not even *notice* the outward displays if they don't match the interior soul. It is pointless to try to be anything except wholly genuine around him."

"I am not sure if that is comforting or terrifying," Jasper Paladar replied.

She laughed. "No," she agreed. "Many aspects of Cammon's personality present me with precisely that dilemma."

"And yet you appear to be fond of him."

She nodded. "Oh yes. I would protect him with my life. I was struck to the heart at Baryn's passing, but I believe that Cammon and Amalie may prove to be the strongest rulers the realm has ever seen. At any rate, I have pledged myself to them with what I am very sure will be a lifetime vow. As my husband has as well."

He lifted his eyebrows. She liked his face, intelligent and fine-featured and starting to show a little wear after forty or so years of living. She remembered that Cammon was the one who had chosen him for this position, and so she felt none of her usual impulse to wariness upon making a new acquaintance. She was ready to like him without reservation.

"Your husband?" he said. "Forgive me, I'm not as conversant with current events as I am with past history. I know you are Kiernan Brassenthwaite's sister, of course, but I don't know who you married."

Clearly Cammon hadn't given *all* his attention to Karryn. Senneth caught his small grin, but he didn't even look her way. She laughed ruefully. "I am so used to being notorious for my choices that I didn't expect to find anyone who didn't know my story," she said. "My husband is one of the Queen's Riders who accompanied us here today."

Now his face sharpened with sudden interest, though he didn't look horrified in the least. "Ah, now I understand your use of the word 'notorious,'" he said. "But I confess I am surprised. I didn't know Riders ever took wives—or husbands."

She acknowledged a moment of surprise in turn; not many

aristocrats realized that there were women among the Riders. "They rarely do," she admitted. "As you might imagine, their fanatical level of devotion to the crown rules out many other attachments. I believe it is only because I, too, had given my allegiance wholeheartedly to Ghosenhall that my husband allowed himself to fall in love with me."

Now Cammon spared her one quick, droll look, but she refused to meet his eyes. "And he is here with you on this trip?" Jasper asked.

"Yes, and eight other Riders."

Jasper gestured in the general direction of the stairs. "I would not be responsible for separating a husband and wife. If you wish him to join you in your room—"

She smiled. "I appreciate the courtesy and I will accept, although I would not have asked for such a favor. Tayse and I have enough strength of character to survive a few nights apart from each other without suffering emotional damage."

Jasper poured himself another glass of wine. "I know very little about the royal Riders," he said, "and I find myself suddenly and deeply curious. What can you tell me about your life among them? I am a historian, you know, so don't consider any detail too insignificant."

That was an enjoyable way to pass a half hour, Senneth found, describing her life at the palace as the wife of a Rider. In some ways, it was easy to sum up all Riders with a single sentence—*They never betray their monarch*—but in other ways, it was impossible to convey the intensity of the bond the Riders felt, to their ruler and to each other. They trusted each other as they trusted no one else, not families, not lovers; they could convey volumes of information with a single look. But what defined them more than anything was their unshakeable devotion to the throne.

"If a Rider has to choose between saving the queen and saving anyone else, he will choose to save the queen," Senneth said. "Tayse would give his life for Amalie even if I were in danger."

At that, Cammon apparently couldn't restrain himself. He looked over and said, "But Tayse knows you can protect yourself. So it's not like he would be abandoning you to certain death."

Less true these days than it once was, Senneth thought, but she nodded. "And perhaps that's the trick of it," she said. "Riders who want successful marriages must choose partners who can take care of themselves so they don't have to worry about dividing their loyalties."

Jasper Paladar sighed slightly at that pronouncement. "So they never marry fluttery young women who are slight and ornamental," he said in a sad voice.

"They do," Senneth said, "but generally everyone regrets it."

Cammon, for some reason, had become so fascinated by their conversation that he had momentarily left his own untended. Karryn listened politely, looking just a bit puzzled at the turn the talk had taken. "I wouldn't say Ellynor is fluttery and ornamental, but she's hardly a warrior like you are," Cammon said. "Ellynor married a Rider, too," he added to Jasper.

"And Ellynor is hardly helpless," Senneth reminded him. "If someone tried to harm her—well, Ellynor's a mystic. She has ways of escaping unscathed."

Cammon was watching Jasper. "My point is, I don't think a Rider necessarily has to marry someone who's a fighter," Cammon said. "Anyone who wants to be with a Rider has to be strong in his own way—has to have abilities and interests of his own—he can't just cling on and expect to be made happy. A Rider never makes another person his whole life, even if he invites another person into his life. You have to have some richness yourself if you're going to successfully love a Rider."

Why is he going on like this? Senneth wondered. *This cannot possibly be what Jasper Paladar meant when he said he wanted the smallest details.* "Well," she said, "since you yourself married a princess, I don't know that you're much of an authority on what a Rider wants."

Cammon gave her his most disarming smile. "I understand people better than you do," he said.

She couldn't help but laugh at that, and she made him a mocking half-bow from her chair. "Liege, I have to admit that's true. But I think we've bored our hosts long enough on this topic. Time to think of something else to say."

In fact, the meal came to a close a few minutes later as everyone admitted to fatigue. Senneth was amused to see

Karryn and Cammon still deep in conversation as they all climbed the stairs toward their bedrooms. The casual consort and the lonely serramarra looked poised to become the best of friends.

Perhaps the visit to Fortunalt would not be so bad after all.

SENNETH allowed herself the luxury of sleeping late, though she felt Tayse rise from the bed and leave the room as dawn was barely breaking. A couple of hours later, hunger finally drove her out of bed. She put on a simple dress instead of wearing her preferred trousers—might as well try not to be any more odd than Jasper Paladar already knew she was— and styled her short, unruly hair as best she could. These were the times she missed Kirra the most. She sighed at her somewhat unkempt appearance and headed downstairs.

In the dining room, only Serephette still lingered, and she made no attempt to carry on a conversation. Senneth made a few general observations and then gave up, willing enough to eat her meal swiftly and in silence.

"Do you know where I might find Cammon?" she asked as she rose to leave.

"He and Jasper are in the library with Bryce," Serephette said.

"Who's that?"

"A mystic boy who has provided many fine services to the House," Serephette said in a haughty voice, as if Senneth couldn't possibly understand how to value magic. "The king has very kindly agreed to spend a few minutes coaching him."

"Sounds just like Cammon," Senneth said. "Is Karryn with them?"

A look of distaste crossed the marlady's face. "No. She is down at the training yards, where she goes nearly every morning."

That made Senneth's eyes widen. "Really? She's learning to hold a sword?"

"Disgusting behavior for a serramarra," Serephette pronounced.

"Actually, I think it's wise," Senneth said. "I like your daughter more and more."

Serephette looked doubtful at that, as if approbation from someone as disreputable as Senneth could hardly be a good thing, but Senneth merely smiled, dropped the tiniest curtsey, and left the room.

It was a simple enough matter to exit the house and find the training yards, located on the back lawn near a long, low building that was probably the barracks. Senneth noted with approval that the yard appeared to be well-maintained and that most of the soldiers were using practice blades. Six of the Riders were inside the fence, trading blows with local guards and seeming to enjoy themselves hugely. Senneth assumed the other three were roaming the grounds in the ceaseless effort to keep Cammon safe.

She was surprised to see that Tayse had paired off with Karryn and was walking her through one of the complicated dueling moves that Senneth herself had had trouble mastering. The serramarra was dressed for business, in trousers, a padded vest, and heavy gloves. She listened closely to Tayse's instructions and experimentally swung her blade. Senneth could tell that Karryn didn't quite have the hang of it—but she could also tell that Karryn had had a little practice with a sword.

Just then, Justin spotted her and excused himself from his competition with a solidly built man who looked to be about Tayse's age and rough with experience. He came to lean beside her against the fence that enclosed the yard.

"Look who's finally awake," he greeted her.

"I'm a serramarra. I'm used to a life of idle luxury," she replied.

He nodded in Karryn's direction. "Not that one," he said. "She's been here almost an hour and has been working hard the whole time."

"I can scarcely contain my amazement," Senneth said. "Is she any good?"

"No," he said. "But that's not the point. The point is that she's trying. You can tell all her guards are proud of her for even buckling on a vest and getting her hands dirty."

"How about her guards?" she asked. "They look pretty competent."

A slight frown crossed Justin's face and he shook back his blond-brown hair. "Better than competent," he said. "A couple of them are excellent, and the rest will be soon. Apparently they were all recruited in the past two months when the serra's uncle decided she needed more protection. They've jelled faster than you'd expect from a group of strangers."

She wasn't sure why he seemed troubled. "That's good, isn't it?"

"Well, it's good for Karryn," Justin said slowly, "but it makes you start asking questions."

"What questions? What's wrong?"

He pointed toward the older guard he'd been fighting when Senneth first walked up. "See that man? His name's Orson. See that move he's practicing—using his right hand to slash and his left hand to follow through with a knife? That's a Rider trick. He hasn't got it quite right yet, but it's obvious he's been practicing for a while. Learned it from somebody who knew how to do it."

Now Senneth understood why he was disturbed. "Who taught him? Did he say?"

He didn't answer. "And that woman there—Moss. Watch her. See how she dances back out of the way of a blow? It's a way to counter strength with agility. I've seen Janni and Wen pull off that maneuver flawlessly, and a couple other Riders. But no one outside of Ghosenhall."

"Well—four Riders left Ghosenhall after the war," she said, though she knew he needed no reminding. Not a single absent brother or sister had ever been forgotten by any of the Riders who had chosen to remain in Amalie's service. "Maybe one of them ended up in Fortunalt and took a job for serra Karryn."

He shook his head. "Layne's in Kianlever and Chottle's in Merrenstow, and Selt has rented a house in Ghosenhall," he said. "We know where everyone is, except . . ." His voice trailed off.

Except Wen, Senneth thought. Her loss had been hard

on all the Riders; Justin, for one, had never accepted her absence. She knew for a fact that he had journeyed twice to Tilt, hoping to surprise her at her family's home, and he had quarreled once with Janni when he accused her of knowing Wen's whereabouts and refusing to divulge them. He had even badgered Cammon several times, convinced that Cammon— who could track a friend across the kingdom from hundreds of miles away—must surely know where Wen had run. But Cammon had never given Justin much satisfaction. "Wen is where she wants to be" was all he would say.

Senneth studied Justin's stubborn face. He was the most sarcastic and prickly of her particular band of friends; he was the one who could be counted on to point out your slightest mistake. But Justin, she had learned long ago, was the one who could not bear the idea of misplacing a friend, who could not stand solitude or loneliness. He had lost so many people so early in his life—and he had trusted so few others—that he absolutely refused to part with those to whom he gave his allegiance. It was no surprise he had become a Rider, famed for his devotion to his king. It was more of a surprise that such a position existed in the world, as if tailored especially for Justin's soul.

"So who taught these Fortunalt guards how to fight like Riders?" she asked again. "Did they say?"

"Apparently their captain—the one who held the auditions and hand selected her team—she's the one who's been training them."

Senneth glanced around the training yard again. There were two women on the field, in addition to Janni, but neither of them was Wen. "Where is she?"

His mouth twisted. "She's been called away for a few days. Orson says he's not sure when she'll return." Clearly, Justin didn't believe this.

"Did they describe her? Name her?"

"Willa is what they call her. Orson was vague about her appearance, but Moss talked a little more freely. Small, compact, brown-haired." He met Senneth's eyes. "It could be her. It has to be her."

She glanced over at her husband, now walking Karryn

through a fairly straightforward strength move. "What does Tayse say?"

Justin's face was full of dissent. "He says if it is Wen, she obviously chose not to be here when we arrived and we should respect her decision to stay away from us."

"And what do the other Riders say?"

A small grin came to his mouth. "They think we should go looking for her."

Senneth let out a long breath. "Well. This is an unexpected development. I suppose, no matter what, we should be pleased that Karryn is gathering a strong guard around her. Her mother mentioned that she'd been attacked on the road not long ago."

"Worse than that," Justin said, and proceeded to relate a shocking tale about an attempted kidnapping.

"I wonder if Cammon knew about this when he decided to set out for the southern Houses?" Senneth said.

Justin shrugged. "Who can ever guess what Cammon knows? But he realized there were outlaws on the southern roads. He might have known about Karryn."

Neither of them said the obvious. *And he definitely knows if Wen is here, calling herself Willa.* It seemed unlikely, however, that he would break his accustomed silence on this topic to tell them what they wanted to know. "Well," Senneth said. "Go back to your workout. I'll see what I can find out from Jasper Paladar."

Justin shook off his dark mood and gave her a lazy smile. "What about you? Don't you want to practice this morning, too?"

She glanced down at her dress. "I don't think I'm properly attired."

"Probably do the serramarra good to see how well a woman can fight."

"If this Willa really is Wen, Karryn has already seen a woman fight much better than I'll ever be able to."

"A titled lady then," Justin said. "You must be the best swordswoman among the Twelve Houses. Serra Karryn could profit from your example."

"I don't think I'm along on this trip to show off my prowess as a fighter," Senneth said, picking up her skirts and turning back toward the house. "I'm here to lend some respectability to Cammon."

That made Justin laugh outright. "Then they got the wrong woman for an impossible job," he said.

"I agree on both counts," she said. "But I must go and do my best."

Chapter
32

WEN WAS BORED AND RESTLESS WITHIN FOUR hours of checking in to the quiet little inn on a backstreet in Forten City. She had thought she might take the opportunity to relax a little, but she found almost immediately that she couldn't settle. She'd eaten in the small taproom on the first level of the inn, then retired to her room while it was scarcely a couple hours past dark. Then she just perched on the edge of her bed, too tense to even attempt to lie down and sleep.

If she were at Fortune right now, she would be finishing up dinner at the barracks or heading to the house to consult with Jasper Paladar. If she were at Fortune, she would be looking forward to a night spent in the lord's bed, laughing and making love.

No, if she were at Fortune right now, she would be face-to-face with nine Riders, enduring their questions or their sympathy or their silent scorn.

For so many reasons, she wanted to be at Fortune.

It was pointless to undress and lie on the bed merely to

stare up at the ceiling. So she pulled her boots back on, armed herself with a couple of her more discreet weapons, and headed back out into the night.

It was middle spring now, and the day had been exceptionally warm. Evening had dropped the temperature, but pleasantly so, and the streets were crowded with people made cheerful by the weather. More men than women, more youthful than aged, but sharing a desire to express their high spirits by prowling through the friendly night.

Wen had chosen an inn away from the more commercial districts of the city, but just a few turns down the busy streets brought her to an intersection that was lined on all four corners with taverns doing a brisk business. The first one she tried was too rowdy even for her restless soul, and filled to bursting with what looked like a whole crew of men just off some trading vessel and spoiling for a fight. The second one was a little quieter, though Wen couldn't find an open table. She stood at the bar and ordered a drink, then rested her spine against the counter and sipped from her glass while she watched the other patrons.

Most of them were men intent upon getting drunk; a few were women who had obviously been paid for their companionship. No one looked to be more than thirty years old, although one or two appeared to have at least a little noble blood. Wen found herself watching a card game among six young men, one of whom she was fairly certain was cheating. The rest looked like bankers' sons or merchants' heirs, well-heeled and stupidly confident in their skill. She smiled a little to see them make progressively larger wagers and then exclaim in indignation when they lost.

Sure enough, about an hour in, one of the rich boys cried, "You've marked the cards! No one gets lucky that often!" and pretty soon people were jumping to their feet and knocking over chairs and exchanging wild blows. A few of the other patrons happily joined the fray, while the barman pounded on the counter and called for order. Wen felt absolutely no inclination to enter the fight, even though the respectable young men were obviously no better at fighting than they were at card playing and it was clear they were going to lose the brawl and all their money. No—they were hardly helpless; she was not needed here. She paid for her drink and stepped back into the night.

Cooler out now, but still a couple hours from midnight. She was still too wound up to attempt to sleep. She strolled farther down one of the main streets, looking for a quieter place to try next, and found one tucked beside a millinery shop that was closed for the night. It was a single story high, clean, and well-maintained, and a warm yellow light streamed out from under the heavy oak door. Wen pushed it open and went in.

Ah—far more respectable. The tables were well-polished and widely spaced; the floor had obviously been swept that very morning. As was usual, there were more men than women sitting at the tables, but the women looked to be merchants' wives or shop owners themselves, enjoying a relaxing evening after a hard day of work. Wen was probably a notch below the usual clientele, but it was the kind of place where anyone would be welcome as long as he or she did not start trouble.

She found an unoccupied booth in the back and sat so that she could watch the door and most of the room. The barmaid was an older woman who was probably the owner, or the owner's wife, Wen decided.

"Having food or just drinking?" the woman asked.

"I've eaten, but if you have pie, I'd take a slice of that," Wen replied. "And to drink—"

She looked up as a figure approached the table, all of her senses on high alert. But this was someone she recognized, though she hadn't expected to run into him here. He slid into the booth on the bench across from her.

"And to drink, she'll have a bottle of Rappengrass wine," said Ryne Coravann. "My treat."

The woman nodded, which Wen took to mean she was familiar with this particular patron and knew he was good for the expensive order. "Anything else?"

"I think that will do for now," Ryne said, and the barmaid departed.

Wen was left face-to-face with the impudent young Coravann serramar, who smiled at her as if he had just won a decisive victory in a long-running contest.

"Captain Willa," he said. "What a surprise to see you here."

"Less of a surprise to see *you* here," she said, "though I confess I would have expected you in a place a little less decent."

He laughed at that. He was slouching back in the seat, one arm resting casually on the table. She thought he might have already gone through a couple bottles of Rappengrass wine before she arrived.

"I had a meeting with one of my father's contacts, and this was the place he suggested," Ryne replied. "I was just on the point of leaving for livelier venues when I saw you walk in. What brings you to Forten City?"

"Business of my own," she said.

"I suppose you haven't been fired from your position," he said.

"Not yet. Perhaps you haven't spoken out against me strongly enough."

"I'm waiting for a major infraction. Although, from what I hear, you've really earned your keep in this past week, so perhaps I'll refrain from trying to get you released just yet."

The barmaid arrived with an open bottle, two glasses, and Wen's pie. As soon as she had arranged the items on the table and departed, Wen replied. "What story did you hear? And who told it?"

"Lindy Coverroe was full of Karryn's brush with death on the road back from the Flyten house," Ryne said, pouring full glasses for both of them. "If even half of what she said was true, Karryn was truly in danger."

Wen sipped the wine, which was drier than she liked and oddly spiced. But it went down smoothly and made a warm sensation in her stomach. "Karryn was truly in danger," she said. "If we'd had one less man with us, or one more of our guards had gotten hurt, the outcome could have been entirely different."

Ryne tossed off his first glass without even seeming to notice it and poured himself another. "Who attacked her?" he asked bluntly.

"I don't know," she said. "Where were *you* a week ago?"

It was deliberately provocative, and his eyes gleamed with

humor. "I spent nearly a week aboard one of my father's trading ships that came into harbor here, honoring the captain
with my magnificent presence," he said. "Haven't you missed
me? I've been absent from Fortune for days."

She'd been too preoccupied to notice he wasn't around, but
that annoyed her, so she said, "It was the kind of attack that
could have been hired out, you know. I wouldn't have expected
you to actually be at the scene, taking part."

He drank his second glass a little more slowly, while she
ate most of her pie. When he spoke again, his glass was almost
empty and his voice was grave. "Hired ruffians? Specifically
sent to assault Karryn, you think?"

"That's my guess," she said. "Assault the serramarra—and
kill her. Lindy didn't pass on that information?"

"I don't think she realized it." Now his eyes looked shadowed, almost concerned. It was a look that seemed strange on
that laughing face. "Who would want to kill Karryn?"

"Since I don't actually consider you a suspect," she
drawled, which earned her a faint smile, "you might provide
some insight. Who would want to kill any Twelfth House
noble? And why?"

"Her heir, of course, except I don't know who inherits after
Karryn," he said. "Other than that—someone who feels he's
suffered under her. Been rendered a harsh judgment when he
came to her with some dispute."

"I don't think Karryn's handled any disputes," Wen said.

"Jasper then."

Wen lifted her eyebrows. "You think someone might have
been trying to kill Jasper Paladar, not Karryn?" The thought
made her feel sick to her stomach. For some reason that possibility hadn't occurred to her before. "Has he been a harsh
overseer?"

She expected a flippant answer, but Ryne surprised her by
being serious. "Actually, from everything I've heard, Jasper
is highly respected among the serlords and the Thirteenth
House nobles. Even Zellin Banlish speaks well of him, and he
hates everyone."

"So Jasper is unlikely to be the target. Karryn is, but why?
Could somebody hate her simply because she is her father's

daughter? Could he want to revenge himself on Rayson through Karryn?"

Ryne shrugged. "Maybe, but it makes no sense. The best thing that ever happened to Fortunalt was to lose Rayson in the war. Even if Karryn is a terrible marlady, she would have to be better than he was. Everyone must realize that."

"Then who would want to kill her?" Wen demanded.

He shrugged again. "It has to be someone who covets Fortune."

Wen threw her hands wide in a gesture of frustration. "Jasper has had the heir investigated. It's some backwater lord who scarcely sets foot off his own lands. The man doesn't appear to have ever even *seen* his inheritance."

Ryne gave her a sleepy smile. "You don't think like a woman who wants a title," he said in a chiding voice. "You are too focused on the immediate. My sister and her friends can recite bloodlines that go back ten generations—and possibilities that unfold ten generations into the future."

Wen frowned, trying to unravel that. "You think—it could be someone who would inherit *after* this obscure lord? *His* heir?"

"That's the kind of scheming I would expect from someone who was truly determined to win a House," he said.

"But then—this man and his family are also in danger, are they not?"

"Possibly," Ryne agreed. "Probably."

"Then Jasper must warn them—although, if they are, in fact, the ones who are trying to kill Karryn, the warning will be a bit ironic—"

Ryne drained his second glass and grinned at her. "So, you see that life in the Twelve Houses never fails to be fascinating."

Wen rubbed her forehead. "Give me a straightforward enemy any day," she said. "I was never much of one for scheming and plotting."

"It's much less effort if you have no expectation of inheriting, and not much interest in it, either," he said in a consoling voice.

Wen finished off her wine—she was beginning to feel she

needed it—and poured a second glass. The bottle was almost empty, but she was not going to be the one to signal for a second one. She remembered the conversation she had overheard between Ryne and Karryn about two weeks ago. "You're a marlord's son," she said slowly, "but the property doesn't go to you, does it?"

"No," he said indifferently. "My sister inherits."

"What happens to serramar who don't become marlords?"

He flashed her that dangerous smile. "Their parents usually bestow some fine property on them, and they marry and have children, and those children marry and produce offspring, and in a couple of generations you have another layer of Thirteenth House lords who feel aggrieved because their bloodlines aren't quite good enough."

"But before all these disgruntled grandchildren are born," Wen said patiently. "What happens to *you*? What do *you* want out of your life?"

He had told Karryn he wanted to travel to the Lirrens, Wen remembered, but he didn't offer such a glib response now. Instead his face looked a little lost, a little uncertain; for the first time she saw the vulnerable young man, not the wastrel young lord. "I haven't given myself much time to think about that," he said. "I don't think I like the options ahead of me."

"Can't you marry?" she said. "Aren't there other serramarra like Karryn, who will be marladies in time?"

"Mayva Nocklyn is too old for me and Lyrie Rappengrass too young," he said, so swiftly that Wen could tell he'd thought over this particular idea long before she ever brought it up. "If I wanted to marry for a title, Karryn is really the only choice."

Wen didn't answer that, just regarded him with a long and level look.

He tried to wait her out but failed, finally breaking into a little laugh and shaking his head. "All right, I admit it, one of the reasons my father sent me to Forten City was to see if I thought Karryn and I might suit. She has not been seen much within the Twelve Houses, you know, so no one really had a sense of what she was like."

"And what did you decide?" Wen said in an ominous voice. Silently, she was thinking, *If I have to protect Karryn from*

Ryne Coravann's advances, I will never be able to leave Fortunalt.

He was staring down at his empty wineglass, picking at an imperfection in the stem with his right thumbnail. "I like Karryn," he said in a subdued voice. "Too much to want to saddle her with *me*. I would be the worst kind of husband." He shrugged. "Inattentive and lazy and drunk all the time. She would be infatuated with me at first, but she'd grow to hate me. Who wouldn't? But a more strong-willed woman wouldn't *need* me so much as Karryn might. I wouldn't be such a disappointment to that kind of woman."

"I think you misjudge just how strong-willed Karryn can be," Wen said dryly.

"I would rather be the friend she always likes than the husband she comes to despise," he said.

"You realize there is another possibility," Wen said.

He looked up at her, his expression mocking. "I could reform? How likely do you think that is?"

Wen was suddenly furious. "Look at you. A man who's been given *everything*. Looks, money, charm, bloodline. And you throw it away. You *debase* it. And then you feel sorry for yourself because you have so much and you can't be trusted to use it in a way that's generous." She came to her feet, bumping into the table so hard that she set the dishes to rattling. "You better *not* come courting Karryn, that's all I can say. She deserves someone who can love *himself*—never mind about loving her."

He was staring at her, openmouthed in astonishment, but she didn't wait to hear a response. She just spun away and stalked through the bar, out into the cool air of midnight.

She was halfway back to her inn before some of her righteous rage left her, and her clenched hands began to relax. Oh, that had been wise, that had been courteous—to rail at a Twelfth House lord in such a fashion, when she had absolutely no right to berate him. This time he *would* complain about her to Jasper Paladar, and justly so. She deserved a reprimand for the reprimand she had just delivered.

It wasn't until she was in her own room, washing up for the night, that she was struck by the irony of her last words to Ryne Coravann. How rich that she would criticize someone else for indulging in self-loathing! How funny that she would rant about someone else throwing away every gift, every advantage! She sat on the edge of the bed and buried her face in her hands, fighting hard not to laugh, fighting harder not to cry.

WEN did not accidentally run into Ryne Coravann again. That might have been because she refused to leave her room for the next two nights, and it might have been because he was so busy attending all of the events held by the local nobles to celebrate Cammon's presence. All of Forten City was abuzz with news of the royal consort's arrival. There was even a parade one day down the main boulevard, and people lined up the night before so they would have good spots from which to watch the procession.

Wen told herself she wouldn't go, she already knew what Cammon looked like. But, of course, she couldn't stay away. She joined a handful of other enterprising souls on the flat rooftop of a fabric shop situated along the parade route. All around them at this level, she saw dozens of other people congregating in second-story windows and climbing trees and lampposts to get a better look at the procession.

She felt a moment's panic. Anyone on a roof or an upper-level building could be carrying a weapon, could aim an arrow or a spear or even a rock at Cammon's head and kill him on the spot. This public appearance was too risky; what had Tayse been thinking? She looked around wildly. There, for instance—across the boulevard. Three fairly large men were clustered at the very edge of a tavern rooftop, gazing down with hungry anticipation. Were they just eager to get a glimpse of royalty, or were they nursing secret plans of violence?

One of the men called out to a woman in the street below, and she lifted the hem of her skirt almost to her knee and offered them a saucy smile. The men laughed and applauded.

Wen felt a rush of relief and ridiculousness. She imagined villains everywhere; she thought every stranger was a potential source of harm.

Well, of course, she had learned that philosophy from Tayse himself, and surely it had occurred to the big Rider that this procession down a public thoroughfare could be fraught with danger. Surely he had taken precautions—and surely Cammon himself would be silently scanning the crowd, seeking to identify anyone with a grudge. It was not up to Wen to look for trouble.

It was not up to Wen to keep *this* royal personage alive.

Another hour passed before the procession came into view. Wen and two young men sharing the roof with her had passed the time playing a card game for low stakes. She was a few coppers to the good when the sound of cheering brought them all to their feet. She jostled her way to the front so she could get a better view.

Look at that—Cammon, on foot, inching his way down the wide street, pausing to touch the fingertips of every hand outstretched to him. Tayse was a single pace ahead of Cammon and Justin strode behind him so closely he could touch Cammon's spine. Seven other Riders ranged around him, always changing formation, making it difficult for anyone to guess where they might be next. Wen squinted until she could identify them. There was Janni, with her happy smile and bright attention. Hammond, serious and deadly. Eagon, Rett, Larson. And two she did not know—new Riders, apparently, to replace those who had died in the war.

Although there would be no way to ever truly replace those fallen comrades.

A carriage followed behind, though obviously Cammon had no intention of riding in it. The driver was no one Wen knew, but beside him rode a familiar figure, indeed—Bryce, his red hair bright in the sunlight, his lively face pulled into an expression that apparently was meant to seem solemn. He moved constantly on the seat, twisting around as if trying to get a glimpse of every individual face in the throng. Had Cammon been tutoring him on how to read the emotions of a crowd? Did Bryce imagine he was accompanying the royal consort as part of his security detail? Wen almost laughed.

Sitting on the other side of Bryce was a woman with short white-blond hair and a thoughtful expression. Wen recognized her as Senneth, the mystic with fire in her hands. Tayse's wife. Wen couldn't tell if anyone rode inside the carriage, so she could only wonder if Justin's wife also had accompanied the party.

Justin's wife. How easily the phrase had come to her mind. How little it had bothered her. Justin's wife. When had the pain of that attachment finally drained away? When she spent her first night of lighthearted lovemaking in Jasper Paladar's arms? Had a new infatuation that easily erased the old one?

And how long would it take her to recover from this new passion? Would any successive lover be able to replicate for her the delight she had found in Jasper Paladar's affection?

She shook her head. Worries for a different day. For now, like everyone else in Forten City, she merely watched the royal consort ride by, guarded by his fanatically devoted soldiers; and like everyone else, she waved and applauded, cheered by the sight of his smiling, boyish face.

If it seemed to her that, as he passed the fabric shop, Cammon turned his head and gazed directly up at her, well, that was nothing special. Everyone in the whole city was convinced Cammon had met their eyes. "The king looked straight at me as he passed!" people were heard to murmur, clearly impatient of the lesser title *consort.* Or, "He touched my hand!" Or, "King Cammon smiled at me as he rode by!"

The whole city was alive with a current of excitement that night; no one would be sleeping early. It was no surprise that Wen felt edgy, alive, sparkling with energy. All of Forten City felt just the same.

BY the next afternoon, Wen was thoroughly bored again. Her muscles were starting to feel cramped from disuse. She thought she might have to pick a fight in a bar just to get the chance for a little extreme exercise. Barefoot in her rented room, she practiced difficult moves and did basic routines that wouldn't echo too loudly to the floor below her, but this forced inactivity was likely to drive her mad.

Davey arrived around three in the afternoon with the daily report. She met him, as planned, in a little tavern one street over from her inn, and they shared a drink. "Isn't Cammon *ever* going to leave Forten City?" she demanded. "He's been here four days already."

"He seems to like it here," Davey said. "And serra Karryn hopes he'll stay forever."

She questioned him closely about what was transpiring back in the barracks. He spoke admiringly and at length of the prowess of the Riders, particularly Tayse, who apparently had impressed all of them with his size, swiftness, and skill. "Took on *three* of us at once, Orson and Eggles and me, and never once looked to be in danger," Davey said.

"Well, he's a Queen's Rider," Wen said as if that explained everything.

"And there's another one—Justin—kind of a burly fellow, looks like he might be a little slow, but he's not," Davey went on. "Someone told a story about how he fought off five men and killed them all—trained soldiers, I mean, not just outlaws or bandits. But that couldn't be true, could it? Even for a Rider?"

Oh, it was true, Wen knew. It was just one of the adventures Justin had had as he pursued his dangerous courtship of Ellynor. But that particular episode had almost cost him his life.

"Maybe the story has been embellished a little," she said. "You know how soldiers like to talk."

"He wasn't the one telling the tale," Davey said.

She resisted the impulse to ask after the rest of the Riders. *And Hammond? He was badly injured in the war. Is he recovered now? Janni? Has she hooked up with a new lover who knows how to please her?* Davey wouldn't be able to give her the details she wanted even if she posed the questions. "I hope you take the opportunity to learn from them while you have the chance," she said.

"When are you coming back?" he asked.

His voice was innocent, but she scowled at him. Her guards must have started to notice that she planned to be absent as long as the royal consort was in residence. "When my business is completed," she said.

"Anything we can do to help you finish that business any quicker?"

"No. You have plenty to occupy you at Fortune. So go on back now. But make sure Orson sends someone with a report tomorrow."

He shrugged, rose from the chair, and tossed a few coins to the table before stepping out of the tavern. Wen closed her eyes and rubbed the lids with her fingertips. The whole charade was beginning to be too much for her. Since she had left Ghosenhall, she had never spent this much time with any group of people; she hadn't had to worry about getting to know them so well that they would start to wonder about her identity. It was harder than she had thought it would be to maintain her distance.

A prickle of danger made her eyes fly open. She straightened in her chair, her hand going automatically to the knife at her hip. Someone was watching her, someone was about to leap out and assault her—she had felt this sensation too many times to ignore it now—

She cast one quick look around the room. There. At the door. A bulky figure, coiled and motionless, all his attention on her.

Justin.

Chapter
33

WEN LEAPT TO HER FEET, BUT THEN SHE FROZE. There was no place to flee and she was not about to fight. For a moment they stared at each other across the width of the small tavern, and then Justin's broad face broke into a blinding smile. His lips moved to shape her name, and then he threw himself across the floor to engulf her in a hard embrace. He was so powerful; it was like being crushed by some elemental force, inescapable and life-changing. He lifted her completely off her feet and tightened his hold for an instant before returning her to the floor and letting her go.

"I knew it was you! I knew it!" he crowed, apparently so happy to see her that he was, for the moment, going to ignore all the reasons she had run. "When that woman Moss spun away from me with that little move you and Janni always used—I knew it couldn't be anybody else."

Why hadn't she foreseen that? All the careful training she had instilled in the Fortunalt guard was practically an advertisement to anyone who knew to decode it that a Rider was in residence. But her heart was too full for her to think too clearly. "Justin," she said, her voice shaky. "You stupid man.

Couldn't you figure out that you weren't supposed to come looking for me?"

He gave a scornful snort, one of his favorite conversational elements, and pulled out a chair at her table. Perforce, she sat next to him, perched on the edge of her seat. The young blond barmaid, who had surely noticed Justin the minute he walked in, was at their table in seconds, asking what they'd like her to bring. "Pitcher of ale," Justin said. "Best in the house."

Then he turned his attention back to her, intense in a way that only Justin could be. "Of course we all knew you were trying to avoid us," he said. "Tayse told me not to go looking. But I wasn't going to let you be this close and not try to find you. You've been gone too long, Wen. It's time to come home."

She shivered with longing at the word. *Home*. "Justin—I can't. I don't belong there anymore."

"Yes, you do," he said roughly. "There's a place for you among the Riders, and everyone misses you. I've been to Tilt twice, looking for you, and Janni has gone, and so has Rett—"

Sweet words, inexpressibly sweet, but Wen wanted to put her hands over her ears and block them out. "No, no, no," she said, talking over him, just trying to shut him up. "I can't come back. I'm not a Rider anymore."

Those words stopped him like a blade to the heart. He stared at her, his face stricken, and for a moment she thought she had persuaded him. Then he shook back his sandy hair and obviously decided to try a different tack. "All of us were torn apart by the events of the war," he began.

She interrupted him. "Justin. *The king is dead because of me*. I failed Baryn, and I failed the Riders. I will spend the rest of my life trying to atone, but I cannot undo it, don't you understand? I cannot erase it. It has stained my soul."

He nodded slowly, making no attempt to brush off or minimize her guilt, for which she was profoundly grateful. "I would have felt the same way, if I had been the one beside Baryn when he fell," he said seriously. "I might not have been able to live with the knowledge that he died and I did not."

"Yes," she breathed. "Exactly."

"But you *have* lived with it," he went on. "Two years. And you must have realized by now that your life is still valuable. Maybe there's always this stain on your heart—maybe you never feel whole again—but you feel *alive*. You work around that stain, you put it behind you, and you look forward again. You live."

She stared at him. Never much subtlety to Justin—even his philosophy was blunt as a hammer blow. "I don't think I can," she whispered.

"Wen," he said, "you already have."

At just that moment, the pretty waitress returned, bringing a pitcher and two glasses, simpering at Justin as she poured. Justin, of course, was oblivious to her charms. The only woman in the whole kingdom that Justin had ever noticed was the Lirren girl he had married.

No, that wasn't right. Justin had formed close bonds with Janni and Wen—with Senneth and the mystic Kirra—he was attached to the young queen. Wen had always despaired of catching Justin's attention, but, in fact, she had always had it. It just had not been a lover's attention. It had been a friend's.

And, apparently, it was not the sort of attention that she would be able to turn aside easily now.

Justin nodded his thanks to the blond girl, who departed as slowly as she could. "I've thought about it, over and over," he said, taking a long pull at the drink. "Oh, this is good stuff. Try it. I don't think your death would have changed anything. The assassin who killed Baryn came through *Tir*. The best Rider any of us will ever see. Once Tir was down, Baryn was vulnerable on that side. A blow to the chest, and Baryn was dead. Even if you had died, too, you wouldn't have died defending him. You just would have died." He took another big swallow. "It's better that you survived."

She used both hands to lift her own glass to her mouth, scarcely tasting the bitter brew. "Is that how you would have convinced yourself if you'd been standing on the other side of Baryn?" she asked at last.

He grinned. "Maybe. If I'd have been able to think again after it had happened."

She tried the words out in her mind before she said them, but they didn't hold any residue of pain. "If you'd been mad with grief, your wife could have helped you, couldn't she? She's a healer."

"Maybe," he agreed. "Though she's better with bones and bleeding. Cammon might have helped me through, though. He's got a strange way of dealing with despair." He hitched his chair closer. "Hey! Come back to Fortune and petition Cammon to fix your heartache. I know he'd be delighted to learn you're here."

This almost made her laugh. "Justin, I can't do that! Ask Cammon to make me feel better that I let his wife's father die?"

He grinned. "Well, he'd do it. You know Cammon."

She shook her head again, but she was smiling. She felt as if an iron vise had started to loosen from around her heart, or perhaps her lungs, making it easy to breathe for the first time in years. She wasn't sure how far the clamp would unwind, though; she still inhaled with a certain caution. "So tell me," she said. "All the gossip. What's happening? How is everyone? What are the new Riders like?"

"Well, Tayse is just the same, of course, except even more serious now that Tir is gone. Janni is— No, wait, you don't know! I've got a daughter."

Impossible. "You're a *father*? Justin, no, I can't picture it. Tell me about her!"

He nodded vigorously. "Little over a year old. Ceribel. Looks more like Ellynor than she does like me, but you'd know she was mine if you spent five minutes with her. The most willful child ever born."

"Can she hold a sword yet?"

He grinned. "You know she can. She'll be as good as you are before she's fifteen. Better than me by the time she's twenty."

"I can't believe this. This is wonderful. Tell me more, tell me everything."

They sat there for the next two hours, talking. Once Justin had rattled off the major events in the lives of their mutual friends, he demanded to know the details of her own recent story. He listened closely, interjected comments when he was impressed or disapproving, and finally brought the conversation around to the present day.

"Interesting job you have here," he said. "I would have said I'd never give aid to any relative of Rayson Fortunalt, but I can't help but like the serramarra. I wouldn't want Ceribel to be judged by anything *I* did, but, Bright Mother burn me, it's hard to forget that Karryn's father is one of the reasons Baryn is dead."

"She can't forget it, either," Wen said. "It makes it easier to forgive her."

"So what's your plan?" he said. "How long are you going to stay in Forten City? When can you come back to Ghosenhall?"

She smiled at him. Every time he said it, it was a little less painful. But it never seemed more possible. "Justin. I can't leave her yet. Surely you've heard that she was attacked on the road about ten days ago—"

He nodded. "Heard it from every single person who was with you that day, including serra Karryn herself. Sounds like you were partly lucky, and partly good."

"Exactly. And I need us to get better than good, in case our luck runs out next time."

"You're sure someone will try again?"

"Someone's always waiting to try," she said quietly. "You know that."

He nodded. "But you've assembled a strong group here, and that one fellow—Orson—he's pretty tough. He can slip into your place the minute you're gone."

"I'm not ready to leave yet," she said.

He watched her a long time, his hands motionless around his glass. "Even if you're never going to be a Rider again," he said at last. "Even if you decide to stay in Forten City the rest of your life. You have to stop hiding from us. Come back to us, even if it's just for a visit. Everybody misses you. Everybody worries about you. We need to know how you are. We need you to remember that you're one of us."

She felt shivery again, washed with a familiar panic. "Justin—I'm not sure I can do that. Ghosenhall—" She shook her head.

He leaned forward, intense again. "But you'll come back to Fortune, won't you? Tonight? With me? You'll let Tayse and everybody see you?"

That was almost as frightening—and yet an insistent yearning was pulling her toward Fortune with a force that was almost irresistible. Only part of that was a desire to see Jasper again. Part of it— Oh, Justin was right. Part of it was a longing to surround herself again with Riders, comrades, the friends who helped her shape the very structure of her bones.

"What if they're angry with me?" she whispered. "What if they can't forgive me?"

He put his big hand over hers in a comforting, brotherly clasp. "You're the only one who can't figure out how to forgive," he said. "Everyone else just wants you home."

IN the end, he persuaded her, but only because he vowed not to leave unless she returned with him, and Justin, she knew, was capable of carrying out that threat. So she packed her clothes, paid her bill, and followed him through the crowded streets of Forten City. Now the screws of the vise had tightened again on her heart; now her breathing was shallow and labored. What would Rett say? What would Tayse say? How long would it take them to recognize her when she first stepped through the gate? Would they hold off, would they approach only warily and with some restraint, or would they rush to greet her, endanger her ribs with their fervent embraces?

Perhaps if she slipped inside the barracks first, before anyone noticed her. Perhaps if she had a moment to gentle her wild pulse, a chance to explain to her own soldiers exactly what was about to transpire. Yes, that would be best—she would take control of the situation; she would drop her bags on her bunk and stride confidently toward the training yard, smiling at her old friends—

She would do no such thing. Cammon awaited her just inside the hedge, ringed by Riders, his arms outstretched and his eyes alight. "Wen!" he exclaimed, grabbing her in a most satisfactory, thoroughly *un*regal hug. She could feel the others jostling closer, heard every timbre of voice calling out her name. "I told everybody you were on your way!"

TWO hours of laughing and weeping and talking. Of warm affection and mock recriminations. *Don't you ever run off from us again! Promise me!* Two hours of trying to cram years' worth of history into a few short sentences. *And then Kelti joined—you'll like Kelti; he never gives up.* Wen felt as if she had sat at the most sumptuous feast, gorging herself without restraint. She came to her feet, finding herself dizzy and overfull, satiated down to the last hungry corner of her soul.

"When are you going to come visit Ghosenhall?" Larson asked.

Not, she noticed, *When are you coming back to us?* She had made it clear, during these two hours, that she was not rejoining the Riders anytime soon. She was pretty sure some of them did not believe her—and, after tonight, she could almost persuade herself that a return to the Riders was something she might someday contemplate—but for now they were willing to accept that she was not yet ready to take up her old life.

"I don't know," she said. "There's still a lot to do here."

"If you don't come back, we'll start coming here," Janni said. "'Look, Wen, we've come to visit!' Serra Karryn will start charging us room and board."

"She'll make you earn your keep by working out with her guards," Wen replied. "She'll even have you teaching *her* some Rider tricks. She'll be glad to see you."

Tayse bestowed upon her his rare warm smile. "As long as you are glad to see us, Wen," he said. "We will be here."

He wasn't the sort of man you gave a casual hug to, so she merely rested her hand on his arm as she headed out the door. This had been the most joyful of glad reunions, but now that she was back at Fortune, she had responsibilities to assume. Her own soldiers to reassure.

Another man to face.

THE Fortunalt guard was loitering outside the barracks, which had simply been taken over by the Riders for this clamorous interlude. Not all of the guards, she was glad to see; by her quick count, six were missing. She assumed four were patrolling the grounds, as they should be just after dusk, and two were in the house, where a few nobles had gathered for an intimate dinner. But Orson and Eggles were there, and Moss and Davey—the ones she thought of as her closest friends among this group—and many of the others. All of them were waiting to hear her explanation. All of them wanted to know what she planned to do next.

They clustered around her, silent and a little stunned. She scanned the circle of their faces, made eye contact with each one. She was surprised to find that the emotions stirred up by the reunion with the Riders were still dangerously close to the surface. Or maybe this particular group of people had carved their own places in her heart, and what she was feeling was the strength of her affection for them.

"I guess some of you aren't too surprised," she said. "And maybe a few of you figured it out before Riders rode through the gate. Most of us have a secret or two, and that was mine."

"Now I don't feel so bad about never being able to beat you," Davey said, and a light laugh ran around the group.

"If it makes you feel better, I don't think I've ever beaten Tayse," she responded with a smile.

"What do we call you now?" Moss said. "They said your name is Wen."

"You can still call me Willa, if you like. Or Wen. I'm used to both names."

Eggles was the one who asked the question she could tell they were all thinking. "When are you going back to Ghosenhall?"

"I'm not," she said. "I'll never be a Rider again."

Davey began, "But Justin said—"

Wen interrupted him. "I guess they've left a place for me. But I don't feel like that's the place I belong anymore. Maybe I'll change my mind. But it's been two years, and I haven't changed it yet."

"So you're staying?" Orson asked.

She met his eyes. He could have a number of reasons for posing that question, one of them being that he wanted the position she would vacate when she rode out. But ambition wasn't what she read in his face or heard in his voice. He looked at her now the way Justin had looked at her in the tavern—like a friend who was worried about the reasons she might make a bad choice.

"Staying for a while," she said softly. "I don't know how long."

* * *

SHE waited until dinner was over, waited until Demaray Coverroe's carriage followed Edwin Seiles's coach out past the hedge, until Jasper had had time to discuss anything important with Cammon or Serephette or Karryn. Waited until lights had appeared in the bedroom windows of the upper stories and a few had been extinguished. Waited until at least some of the inhabitants of the house were asleep.

Then she approached the front door on silent feet, nodded at Malton, who stood guard there, and glided soundlessly through the shadowed hallways and stairwells. To find herself just outside Jasper Paladar's door, with her heart pounding and her cheeks hot. A faint light seeped out across the threshold—he was probably reading by candlelight, unless he had fallen asleep with a book open in his hands—

She knocked softly, heard an immediate stirring inside, and the door was quickly opened. Not asleep then. Still wearing the formal clothes he must have donned for dinner. He looked severe and handsome, aristocratic and scholarly. He was so far outside of her own world that at times she was amazed they spoke a common language.

Before he spoke, she almost turned to go.

Then his face lit with a smile of such welcome that she felt treacherous tears rising again. He pulled her inside quickly and shut the door, but he did not instantly take her in his arms. He merely stood there, his hands upon her shoulders, his gaze intent upon her face, studying her as if her skin was printed with a rare and beloved text.

He was not surprised to see her, she realized. So perhaps Cammon had told him of her return—or more likely Karryn, who would have heard it from one of the guards.

"So did you learn what you wanted to learn?" he asked.

"They would take me back," she said.

He placed one of his hands, just so, between her breasts. "And is the stone that has lodged here for two years finally melted away?"

Not *And will you go back to them?* Not *And are you planning to leave me?* He asked first after her own heart. Later, perhaps, he might get around to looking out for his own. "It is smaller," she acknowledged. "I don't know that it will ever go away."

"That's the way of regret," he said. "It tends to be permanent, even when it is manageable."

"I'm so shaky," she said. "I'm trying to think what this emotion is. Maybe it's happiness—I'm not sure I remember what that feels like."

Now he did draw her toward him, very gently, and when she was cradled in his arms, he kissed her sweetly on the mouth. "Strange," he said. "I am trembling as well. I suppose I must have caught this dread disease called happiness. Is it contagious? Could it be you brought it with you when you stepped into my room?"

Which made her laugh, and kiss him back much harder. "Perhaps I did," she said. "Quick, do you know a cure for it?"

Smiling, he began to tug her toward the bed. "One or two, but they're quite radical. Are you brave enough to take drastic measures?"

She tumbled onto the coverlet and he stretched himself beside her. "I am," she said, "but only if you try the antidote, too."

"Well, then," he said, his fingers in the lacing on her vest. "Let us look for remedies."

Chapter
34

SENNETH WAS SURE SHE WAS AS GLAD AS THE next person that the Rider Wen had been discovered, but that didn't mean she wanted to spend the rest of her life lingering at Fortune, listening to the Riders tell Wen yet another story that she might have missed during her sojourn away.

"Isn't it time to go home?" she asked Tayse plaintively after they had been in Fortunalt nearly a week.

Tayse grinned. "I believe there is some event tomorrow at the house of that woman who has been here so much—small and elegant, rather exhaustingly vivacious—"

"Demaray Coverroe," Senneth said instantly. "I don't like her, either."

"Cammon is considering whether he ought to attend."

"He most certainly should not," Senneth said. "Because then Coren Bauler and every other Thirteenth House pretender will vie for Cammon's presence at *his* house, and we will be put to incredible shifts to keep him safe in all those venues, and we won't be out of here for a decade at least."

"Have Cammon and Jasper Paladar settled all the issues they had to discuss?"

"On the first or second day we were here, I would imagine," Senneth said. "Cammon mentioned his idea about assembling a force of guards from all the southern Houses, augmented with royal soldiers, and Jasper seemed agreeable to it. Of course, it probably helped that he knew Nate and Ariane had already approved such a plan," she added cynically. "He might have resisted a little otherwise, not wanting Fortunalt to appear weak."

"Did he consult the serramarra's opinion?"

"Cammon or Jasper?" Senneth said. "Because she and Cammon have been practically inseparable since he arrived, and Cammon's wanted her at every conference."

"And Jasper didn't mind?"

"It pleased him, I think," Senneth said reflectively. "He doesn't strike me as an ambitious man. Competent, yes, and unflinchingly honest. I wouldn't be surprised to learn he is counting the days until he can turn the House over to Karryn. So every time she makes a decision on her own, he feels he is closer to his goal."

"Has Cammon achieved *his* goal, do you think?" Tayse asked.

She looked over at him, surprised. It was night, and she was already curled up in bed. He had just returned from an informal circuit of the grounds and was slowly pulling off his jacket, his sash, his boots. "What goal?" she said.

"Whatever reason he had for making this trip. Was it really to tour the southern lands and try to determine how safe they would be for Amalie to visit? Was it to gain some consensus from the Twelve House overseers about putting together a mixed force to patrol the borders? Or was it to find Wen?"

She sat up straighter in bed. "Surely not even Cammon would believe such a long and expensive journey could be justified by the idea of finding one lost soul?"

"I actually think it's the only sort of prize Cammon really thinks is worthwhile."

"But—but—all this time—and all these people! Nine Riders and seventy guards! The dinners, the bills at the inns! All to locate a missing woman?"

Tayse sat on the edge of the bed. "He'd pour all those resources and more into finding you if *you* tried to disappear."

She stared at him. "How did he discover where she was?"

Tayse shook his head. "I think he always knew. From the day she left. I think he's kept track of her this whole time."

"But why look for her now?"

"He must have decided she was ready to be found," he said, blowing out the last candle and sliding under the covers next to her. "It seems he was right."

Senneth nestled against him in the dark. "I thought you said she doesn't want to come back to Ghosenhall."

"She doesn't want to be a Rider again," Tayse said. "But she's ready to remember that she was a Rider once. That might be all the healing she'll be able to do. But Cammon knew that it was enough."

TO Senneth's great delight, the next morning she learned that Cammon had engaged in one of his spectral conversations with Amalie, and the queen had made it clear that she wanted him to begin making his way home. So they would not be staying for Demaray Coverroe's party that evening—in fact, once they had made their good-byes to their host and hostesses, they would be on their way.

The farewells, of course, took forever, and naturally every single Rider had to whisper a private message to Wen, which delayed them still more. So it was close to noon before they actually set out. Through some indefinable magic, all the residents of Forten City had learned that the royal consort was leaving, so every crone, every mother, every pickpocket, every vendor, had joined together to create an impassable throng of humanity along the boulevards. Senneth despaired of getting beyond the city limits before sunset, so she was relieved when they managed to break free of town before the afternoon was too far advanced.

Of course, the main northwest road passed through fairly well-populated territory, and for the remainder of the day they found enthusiastic subjects gathered at every crossroads that intersected their route. By the time they gave it up and asked for rooms at a modest inn in a small town whose entire population had turned out to greet Cammon, Senneth estimated they had made so little progress that a couple hours' hard riding would see them back at Fortune.

"At this rate, Ellynor will be back in Ghosenhall before I am, and she was supposed to stay in the Lirrens for two months after I left," Justin observed.

"Ceribel will be a woman grown, married with children of her own, before you ever see her again," Senneth said gloomily.

He just grinned. "Well, I suppose when Cammon and Amalie make this trip together it'll be worse," he said. "I'll just have to bring Ellynor and Ceribel with me next time."

Senneth sighed. No doubt he was right; and no doubt she would be on that trip as well.

She didn't bother to rise early, certain that Cammon would be tarrying in the taproom to kiss babies and shake the hands of smiling laborers. But she was surprised, when she wended her way downstairs with her baggage in her hand, to find Cammon conferring with Justin, his boyish face concerned.

"Justin—Senneth—I think the two of you should go back to Fortune," he said. "Catch up with us later when you can. I feel safe traveling on with only eight Riders."

"What's wrong?" Senneth demanded.

It was Justin who answered. "She needs us."

For a moment, Senneth thought he meant Karryn, and Cammon instantly began saying something about the serramarra. But a second later Senneth realized that Justin was buckling on his sword and checking his weapons for another reason.

Wen required his assistance.

Chapter
35

AFTER WHAT HAD SURELY BEEN THE NONSTOP gaiety surrounding Cammon's visit, Wen would have thought all the nobles in Fortunalt would have wanted to slink back to their own private estates and spend the next few weeks in undisturbed solitude. Apparently not. The very day that Cammon set off for Ghosenhall, Demaray Coverroe had scheduled yet another social event, this one designed to celebrate Lindy's birthday. It would be a smaller and more intimate dinner than some of the elaborate affairs that had been orchestrated to impress the royal consort, so Wen gathered. Karryn, as Lindy's closest friend, would be spending the night.

Which meant Wen would be spending the night at the Coverroe house as well.

So much for her plans of spending another delightful evening in Jasper Paladar's bed, as she had every night since she returned from Forten City.

Wen chose Moss, Eggles, and Malton to join her at the Coverroe house. She thought it would be useful to have another

woman in the guard detail in case it was necessary to burst
into a room of sleeping girls. Although she supposed if that
much danger threatened, not even shrieking young women
would care if armed soldiers saw them in their nightclothes.

The Coverroe guards were by now quite familiar with the
Fortune contingent and unsurprised to learn that Karryn's
people would be staying overnight. "We'll clear out a couple
of bunks for you," the captain said. "I suppose you'll sleep in
shifts."

Wen and Eggles were circling the gaudy house, checking
everything over, as the other guests began to arrive. Wen was
standing back in the shadows when a solitary horseman trotted in on an edgy mount and carelessly tossed his reins to one
of the Coverroe grooms.

Ryne Coravann, of course. He was worse than Cammon,
Wen thought irritably. Wasn't he ever going to go home?

He didn't notice her and strode right into the house. Wen
imagined she heard feminine cries of welcome as he poked his
handsome face into whatever salon was serving as tonight's
gathering place.

Once the handful of guests had arrived, the night became
very peaceful. Pacing around the property in the warm dark,
Wen caught very little hint of revelry from inside. Now and
then she heard a light laugh drift out from an open window,
or a few snatches of excited conversation, but for the most
part, the birthday celebration appeared to be a tame and lighthearted affair.

Her own exertions over the past few days had left Wen
more tired than she liked to admit, so she opted to sleep first
and take a later watch. Eggles and Moss took the early patrol.
The bunks in the small barracks were narrower and much less
comfortable than the beds provided to the Fortunalt guards.
Wen thought that Demaray Coverroe was just the type of
woman to spend all her money on extravagant gold doors and
none on practical items of real value. Or maybe she lavished
funds on herself and her daughter, and let those who served
her make do with scraps.

But Wen had bivouacked in worse conditions, and she
easily fell asleep to the sounds of Demaray's guards snoring.
Of course, she slept with her knife still in place on her ankle

sheath and another short blade under her pillow. But there was no need for either. She woke a couple of hours after midnight feeling moderately rested. A few ablutions, a hand through her hair, a tug at her vest to shift it back in place, and she was ready to take her watch.

Malton joined her at the door and they headed out onto the grounds, a little trickier to navigate in the dead of night. But Wen knew the layout well enough to place her feet with a fair degree of certainty. Malton tripped once, and cursed under his breath, but other than that they encountered no obstacles.

Eggles and Moss were awaiting them at the front gate. "We just walked the perimeter," Moss greeted them in a low voice. "No trouble."

Wen nodded. "Get some rest."

Malton made a rude noise. "If you can. Hardest mattress I've ever laid on."

The veteran Eggles gave Wen a brief smile. She was sure he, too, had slept on worse. "When do you want us up again?" he asked.

"The servants will probably rise in three or four hours, but I can't imagine Karryn will be up much before noon," Wen said. "Sleep five or six hours, then come find us."

Moss and Eggles departed. Wen and Malton agreed on a patrol pattern and split up to rove separately for the next couple of hours, meeting at predetermined intervals to compare notes. Malton was yawning every time she saw him, which Wen didn't like, but he was able to rattle off his impressions of noises from the street and sounds from the house, so she was fairly sure he was paying close attention.

As for herself, she rather enjoyed the nighttime patrol. She liked the incomplete silence, the eerie way that sound carried, the ominous, portentous sense that anything could happen without a second's warning. She had trained herself to listen harder at night, relying less on sight and more on hearing; she had also taught herself to sift the breeze for stray scents. She had once detected the presence of an intruder by the smell of onions on his breath.

Dawn whitened the eastern sky, and there were immediately signs of life in the Coverroe residence. Sounds drifted out first—the rattle of pots, the murmur of conversation—and

then came the scents of baking bread and frying meat. The
sun hadn't even completely broken the horizon line when Wen
saw a gaggle of servant girls emerge from the kitchen and
head for the gate, caps on their heads and baskets over their
arms. Off to market for the day's supply of produce, Wen supposed. She counted seven girls, who were joined at the gate by
a single footman, sent out to run errands of his own. Two of
the girls instantly fell in step on either side of the young man,
casting him flirtatious glances. Wen grinned. The oldest story
in the world, retold among the Coverroe staff.

Another hour and the activity became even more brisk. More
footmen stepped out of the front door and began sweeping the
porch and the walk. Gardeners appeared, bending over lush
flower beds. Four servant girls returned from market, weighed
down with purchases. An upstairs window opened and someone shook out a rug. Half of the Coverroe guards emerged from
the barracks and began their first sleepy circuit of the yard.

By about nine in the morning, Moss and Eggles had made
their appearance, wheedled food from the cook, and brought
their spoils to Wen and Malton. "Any sign of the serra?" Eggles asked, but didn't look too surprised at Wen's shake of the
head.

"Do you want us to patrol or work out?" Moss said.

"Might as well work out," Wen said. "Their training yard
is small, but it's adequate for a day."

An hour later, winded and covered in light sweat, Eggles
and Moss checked back with Wen. Malton had returned to the
kitchen door to beg for more bread. He was a big man and it
took a lot to abate his hunger.

"I don't suppose Karryn's made an appearance," Eggles
said.

Wen sighed. "Maybe she plans to move in with Lindy."

Moss was trying not to yawn. "If that's so, I'll have to quit.
I don't like the Coverroe house. I don't like the barracks, I
don't like the lax attitude of the guards, I don't think the food
is very good, and—well, I don't like it."

"Same here," Eggles agreed.

Wen was distracted by the sight of the front door opening
again. Not a footman this time—but not Karryn, either. It was

Demaray Coverroe, followed closely by Lindy, and both of them looked upset. Lindy, in fact, looked terrified.

"Something's wrong," Wen said shortly, and strode across the lawn. Eggles followed her, and Moss ran to get Malton.

Demaray Coverroe spotted them when they were twenty yards away. She clutched a shawl more tightly around her shoulders and actually ran across the yard in their direction. Wen felt her stomach harden and all her muscles burn with readiness.

"Captain—she's gone," Demaray panted, almost tripping over the hem of her gown in her haste to get close enough to speak.

Wen had expected something else—*Karryn has fallen ill, Karryn has slipped and injured herself,* even *Karryn has been attacked by a mad servant in the middle of the night*—so at first the words made no sense. "Gone? Where did she go?"

Demaray shook her head so vigorously her fair curls bounced. She looked like she had been up a couple of hours and had dressed with her usual care, but Lindy, who stumbled up beside her mother at that moment, appeared to have just now risen from her bed. She was wearing a long, heavily embroidered robe over a gauzy nightshirt, and her hair was wildly disordered from sleep.

"I don't know!" Demaray exclaimed. "I don't know where she would have gone or why she would have crept from the house!"

Wen instantly turned a hard gaze on Lindy. "Tell me," she said in a fierce voice. "What have you and Karryn been plotting?"

Lindy had obviously been crying for some time, for her pale skin was blotched and her nose was red. "Nothing! I told my mother! I have no idea why she would have run away in the middle of the night!"

Wen fastened on that phrase. "That's when she left? You're sure of it?"

Lindy stared at her. "No, I—I just said—it was after two before we got to bed."

"Were you sleeping in the same room?"

"No, she was down the hall. We talked in my room after

the party, and then she went out the door and I thought she went to her own room to sleep, but she's not there—something happened to her—" She dissolved into tears again.

Wen turned back to Demaray, who was at least calm enough to talk rationally. "Was her bed slept in?"

Demaray nodded. "Yes. So she spent at least part of the night there."

By this time Moss and Malton had come jogging up, and Wen heard Eggles give them a quick account of the current situation. Moss gasped and Malton swore.

Wen said in a cold voice, "Was there any sign of blood in her room?"

Now Demaray and Lindy were both staring at her. "What?" Demaray breathed. "What are you suggesting?"

"Did someone take her from the house by force?"

Demaray fired up. "How dare you, Captain! I'll have you know that I trust my servants—and my soldiers— implicitly! *No one* in this house would have hurt Karryn, no one, do you understand me? And I'm sure you and your compatriots were loose on the grounds all night. Surely *you* would have noticed if someone had stolen in to abduct the serramarra?"

Wen would have liked to think so, but she had failed dreadfully at a key task before. Who knew what she might have overlooked in last night's casual patrol? And the other guards—still untested, really, still not nearly as reliable, as skilled, as true Riders—

Oh, gods and goddesses, if Karryn had been kidnapped while Wen lay sleeping—

"I'll need to see her room," she said in a brusque voice.

They all followed Demaray back to the house, a hurrying, weeping, grim, desperate band. Karryn's room was on the second story, its door standing wide open as Lindy must have left it when she tripped in and found it empty.

"Look around," Wen ordered her guards. "See if anything seems unusual. Signs of a struggle. Furniture overturned. Blood. See if her clothes are still here."

But a quick search turned up nothing alarming. Nothing disturbed more than it might have been by a young girl's careless occupancy. The bedcovers rumpled, the pillow still bearing the indentation of her head. A glass set on the nightstand, half full of water. The fancy gown Karryn had worn to the party was still hanging in the armoire, but her other clothes were gone, and so was her little valise. As if she had bundled them up and brought them with her when she stole from the house, late that night or very early this morning . . .

Why? Where would she have gone? What possible reason could she have had to run?

"I don't see anything obvious," Eggles said, shaking out the bedcovers one last time, then lifting the pillow as if to check for secret notes beneath the case.

"What's that?" Demaray said sharply, and all of them stared at the small dark bauble lying on the white sheets under the pillow.

Faster than the rest of them, Wen snatched it up. A flat oblong disk of some smooth blue stone, inlaid with a star-shaped pattern of white. It meant nothing to her, but as she turned it over in her hands, Lindy gasped.

"What?" Wen demanded. "What is it?"

"The seal of Coravann," Demaray said flatly.

Wen froze, her hand involuntarily clenching on the token. *Ryne Coravann was here last night.* The last time Wen had seen Ryne, she had all but dared him to try any mischief with Karryn—stupid words, for she had been sure he would complain of her to Jasper, but he had done much worse. He had set out to prove to Wen that he could do with Karryn whatever he wanted. . . .

Demaray whirled on her daughter. "Lindarose Coverroe!" she said in a wrathful voice. "Have Karryn and Ryne been planning to elope?"

"No!" Lindy sobbed. "At least—I didn't think so! They were always flirting—and he would say, 'Oh, won't you run away with me.' And she would pretend to think about it—but she—but he—I mean, they were only joking—"

"Did they joke about it last night?" Wen asked urgently. She didn't know how much longer she would be able to resist the urge to grab Lindy Coverroe and shake her till her head fell off. "Think, my lady! Did you hear them scheming? Even if you thought they were only pretending?"

Lindy shook her head. "No—not really—I mean, they were sitting together, and they were laughing, but—"

Demaray spoke up, her voice troubled. "I didn't think anything of it at the time," she said. "But last night Ryne and Karryn were sitting together, as Lindy says, and having what appeared to be a very intense conversation. As I approached them, they fell silent, and I thought they looked—guilty, almost. I just assumed they had been saying unkind things about me and they hoped I hadn't overheard."

"How would she have gotten out of the house?" Eggles said practically. "We were on patrol all night. I'm willing to swear that no one went out the gate. Are there back ways off of the property?"

"There's a gate in the north wall, but it's kept locked," Demaray said. "She could have climbed it, I suppose—but it's quite high and she would have needed help—" She gave her daughter another narrow look.

"I didn't help her!" Lindy wailed. "I didn't know anything about it!"

"Let's go check that gate," Eggles said.

"She didn't sneak out at night," Wen said, her voice flat and dreary. They all turned to stare at her. "She left this morning. With the maids. A whole group of them departed together just about dawn."

Seven. Wen had counted the numbers, but she hadn't studied the faces. She'd noticed the two maids flirting with the footman, but all the others? A blur of caps and baskets. She hadn't been looking for Karryn in their number, and thus she had completely failed to recognize her. She had failed to protect Karryn from Ryne Coravann's blandishments, and she had failed to protect Karryn from herself.

She had failed.

Again.

"That's good then, isn't it?" Moss said. "If she left at dawn—she's only been gone about four hours. We can catch up with her."

Wen shook off her bleak thoughts. She was feeling numb with disbelief and self-loathing, but a slow fire of pure rage was igniting in her belly and starting to spread upward.

Rage—white-hot and unadulterated—at Ryne Coravann, for plotting this disastrous seduction, probably for a lark, probably just to see how far he could entice Karryn into dangerous pursuits, or maybe to taunt Wen to repay her for her scalding words. But an even more complicated anger at Karryn herself—who *knew* how much this trick would appall and worry Wen, who *knew* how many resources had been expended to keep her safe. How could the serramarra who had insisted that a wounded Garth ride in her carriage so blithely leave behind her devoted guardians? Wen had thought better of Karryn, she truly had. So the bitterness of Karryn's betrayal added a toxic edge to Wen's smothering sense of failure.

But fury was beginning, for a short time at least, to burn away anything but a desire to kill Ryne Coravann with her bare hands.

"We most certainly can catch up with her," Wen said, her voice calm but holding a note that made all of them look at her in wonder. "Lady Demaray, do you know where ser Ryne has been staying?"

"Yes," Demaray said. "The Stilton House. It's a few blocks over from the harbor."

Wen nodded. It was a tall and gracious building, clearly catering to a wealthy clientele; she had never been inside it, but it was a landmark in Forten City. "Then we shall go there immediately and see if we can learn how recently he has left the city—and whether or not he had a companion with him."

She wheeled for the door. "Captain!" Demaray called, and Wen reluctantly turned back. "How will we find out if you locate her?"

"I'm sure Lord Jasper or the marlady will send you word."

"Can we go with you?" Lindy begged.

Wen just gave her a cold look. "No."

Lindy started crying even more violently. "But I have to know if Karryn is all right!"

"We'll go to Fortune," Demaray said. She seemed to have forgiven her daughter for any part Lindy might have played in this fiasco, for she put her arms around Lindy in a comforting way. "We'll go wait with Jasper until the captain comes back with news. Now go. Get dressed."

If Demaray had more instructions for Lindy, Wen didn't wait to hear them. She bounded down the steps, the other three close at her heels, and ran for the stables to throw a saddle on her horse.

She wondered what the penalty would be for murdering a serramar. She was pretty certain she was about to find out.

Chapter
36

WEN AND THE OTHER GUARDS CLATTERED
through the busy streets of Forten City, riding so reck-
lessly that they scattered frightened pedestrians and
angry drivers before them. The Stilton House had its own
stable, so an ostler was standing outside waiting for customers
when they pounded up. Wen leapt from the gelding's saddle,
tossed the groom her reins, and said, "Hold him. I'll be back
out in a few minutes."

The other three were right behind her as she stalked
through the front door and straight to the desk where a well-
dressed and discreet-looking man sat looking over accounts.
He started in astonishment when Wen slammed her open hand
in the middle of his papers.

"Ryne Coravann," she snarled. "When did he check out of
your establishment?"

The man swiftly stood up, assessing her with a professional's measuring eye. All four of them were wearing their fancy
Fortunalt uniforms, pearls sewn into their sashes, and this was
a man who could not afford to offend the local serramarra.

"Indeed, he has not left us yet," he said in a smooth voice. "Would you like me to summon him from his room?"

Wen felt her heart stutter and then bloom to twice its size. They were still here? Upstairs cuddling in the serramar's room, maybe, laughing at her, but still safe? She didn't let any of her hope or relief show on her face. "No," she said in the same menacing voice. "Take me up to him now."

The clerk cast a doubtful look at her tense companions. "But—"

"Now," she repeated.

He made an instant decision, nodded, and grabbed a master key from behind the desk. "This way, please. Sadie!" he called as they passed a hallway. "Come cover the front door!"

Wen gave him credit for moving briskly, leading them up to the third story and two doors down the hall, but when he lifted his hand to knock, she caught his wrist in a hard hold. "Just open the door," she said.

"But—"

She didn't bother to argue, just yanked the key ring from his grasp, twisted the key in the lock, and kicked the door open. Her dagger was already in her hand.

The room was small enough to take in with a single glance, and there was only one body curled up under the thick blue counterpane. Ryne Coravann lifted his dark head from the pillow, staring at the commotion across the room. "What in the red and silver hell—"

Wen was beside him in two strides, grabbing his shoulder and shaking him roughly. He was nude to the waist and clumsy with sleep. He sat up, trying to fend her off, but she kept her grip. "Where is she? Where's Karryn?" she demanded.

"What—? Willa, what are you—why the hell are you in my room? Let go of me!"

He wrenched back, finally breaking her hold, and stared up at her with bloodshot eyes. It was clear that he had gotten to sleep much later than two in the morning, and he'd had a great deal to drink before he sought his bed.

"Karryn's missing," Wen said. "And people seem to think *you* might know where she is."

His face went slack, but it wasn't guilt or furtiveness she

saw in his expression. "Karryn's missing? What do you mean? Didn't she stay with Lindy last night?"

Now Wen's heart stuffed itself back into the smallest possible ball of fear, hard and painful and burning in the middle of her chest. Oh, gods and goddesses, he did not have her, he did not know where she was. Karryn was gone, Karryn was missing, Karryn was lost and alone and somewhere in danger. "She did," Wen said shortly. "And this morning Lindy found Karryn's room empty."

Ryne scrambled out of bed. Not just nude to the waist, it seemed. He began pulling on a pair of fancy trousers that he had apparently discarded by the bed last night. "And you thought I had her? That she had run to me? Thanks for the compliment, Captain."

Wen pulled the lapis disk out of her pocket and flicked it at him. "This was found under her pillow. And apparently the two of you were whispering together a great deal last night."

He'd reflexively caught the token but tossed it instantly to the rumpled bed. "Lindy has one just like it. So does Katlin Seiles—I hand them out like roses. And I surely spent as much time whispering to *Lindy* last night as I did to Karryn."

"The difference is, Lindy Coverroe is safe in her mother's house and Karryn is nowhere to be found," Wen said. She had to work hard to keep her voice from quavering. "I apologize for casting you as the villain—and for waking you up in such a rude fashion. I must go to Fortune and tell her family and then try to decide what to do next."

He looked up through a fall of unkempt black hair as he was pulling on his boots. "Wait five minutes! I'm coming with you."

She turned away from him. "There's nothing you can do to help us."

He grabbed her arm with one hand and snatched up his shirt with the other. "Go order my horse for me," he directed the innkeeper, who had stood immobile at the door this whole time. Listening to the entire conversation, of course, able to repeat this most-shocking but delicious gossip to every store owner and tavernkeeper in the city.

The innkeeper bowed and scurried from the room. Wen

jerked her arm free but didn't take another step toward the door. Ryne was fastening his shirt so rapidly that the buttons weren't aligning with the holes. Eggles, Malton, and Moss crowded closer to Wen.

"If not with the serramar, then where would she have run and why?" Eggles asked in an urgent voice.

Wen shook her head. Her stomach was a roiling mass of acid; she felt like every separate bone and muscle trailed a line of fire. This was terror; this was helplessness. This was the stark certainty that Karryn was in danger and Wen didn't know how to find her. "Did she sneak from the house, planning to surprise Ryne, and run afoul of common criminals in the streets?" she said.

"I'm telling you, Karryn would have had no reason to seek me out," Ryne spoke from over her shoulder. He was shrugging into an overcoat, much too fancy for daytime wear but obviously the nearest thing to hand. "We made no plans. She wasn't running to *me*."

"Do you believe him?" Moss asked Wen, as if Ryne wasn't standing right there. "Do you trust him?"

Wen turned her head to study him. He was buckling on a serviceable-looking sword, and he paused long enough to meet her eyes. His own expression was defiant. But he looked just as worried as she felt.

"Yes," Wen said curtly. "Are you ready? Then let's go."

DEMARAY and Lindy were already at Fortune when Wen's party arrived. "Gather up the others," Wen directed Eggles. "Tell them what's happened."

"What are we going to do next?" he asked.

As if she had the faintest idea! "We'll look for her," she said grimly. "Once we've told her mother and her guardian what we know."

Eggles and Moss and Malton peeled off toward the barracks, taking charge of all the horses. Wen and Ryne bounded up the steps and into the house. In the large parlor just inside the door they found Jasper, Serephette, and the Coverroes gathered in an agitated conference.

"Wen!" Jasper exclaimed the minute he spotted her. "Did

you find—" His eyes went to the disheveled Ryne Coravann and a look of comprehension crossed his face. "Not with the serramar after all, I see."

"He says not, and I believe him," Wen said.

Serephette, who had been standing beside Jasper, now sank to a sofa as if the bones in her legs could not support her. "But then—sweet Silver Lady, where could she possibly *be*?"

Demaray pushed Lindy over to offer Serephette comfort, and then came to stand beside Ryne and Wen and Jasper. She gave the serramar one quick, frowning look. "Captain, are you sure he—"

"Yes," Wen said shortly. "We must consider other options."

"Demaray says you believe Karryn left her house quite early this morning," Jasper said.

Wen nodded but her mind was elsewhere. "I am trying to remember. When I first encountered Karryn—when she was kidnapped by Tover Banlish—she said she didn't think anyone would be looking for her because when he abducted her, she wasn't where she was supposed to be. I don't believe I ever heard how that story began. Where did she disappear from that time?"

Too late Wen realized that, although Demaray knew of Karryn's abduction, she had never been told the name of the man who had played the villain. Demaray looked shocked, but Jasper answered immediately.

"Edwin and Katlin's house," Jasper said. "When she didn't arrive, *they* thought she had decided to stay home. *I* thought she was with them. It was hours before we knew she was missing."

"Had she gone to meet Banlish?" Ryne asked.

Jasper looked at him. "No. She had arranged to go sailing with Coren Bauler, something I had told her she couldn't do unless her mother or I accompanied her. He had been taking all the girls out in his boat, one or two at a time, and Karryn wanted her turn."

Wen's eyebrows twitched together. "Then—did Coren Bauler assist Tover Banlish in the abduction?"

Jasper frowned and Demaray uttered a little cry. "Oh, Jasper, could he have done such a thing? I confess, I'm never entirely certain that I trust Coren, but—"

"He wasn't at your house last night," Wen said.

Demaray shook her head. "No, the party was for Lindy's birthday and I decided we should limit it to her particular friends. And Coren is so much older—it didn't seem right to invite him."

Wen addressed Jasper. "Would Karryn have snuck off to meet *him*?"

"She doesn't like Coren Bauler," Ryne said positively.

"She must have liked him at one time if she wanted to go sailing with him when no one else was around," Wen said.

Demaray turned toward the sofa, where Lindy was holding Serephette's hand and looking just as miserable as the marlady. "Lindy! Did Karryn have an affection for Coren Bauler? Tell me the truth now."

Lindy looked surprised. "Coren? Not anymore. Katlin told us he has an illegitimate daughter that he refuses to support, and since then Karryn can't stand him."

"How did Katlin learn about that?" Demaray exclaimed. "And how *could* she repeat such gossip to young girls?"

"That's not the issue here," Wen said. "Would there have been anything Coren Bauler could have told her that would have induced her to meet him in secret?"

"I can't think of anything," Ryne said in a silky voice, "but I'd be happy to ask Coren in person."

"Yes, I think that we—" Jasper began, but there was a knock on the door before he could finish his sentence.

It was the butler, and he held a grubby young boy firmly by the wrist. "My lord, this urchin has just arrived with a message for you," the butler said. "He claims it was given to him by a man who offered him three coppers to deliver it."

Jasper accepted the proffered note, ripped it open, and scanned it. Wen saw his face blanch. "Karryn is being held for ransom," he whispered.

Demaray threw her hands over her mouth to muffle a shriek. Wen tore the letter from Jasper's hold. In a rounded girlish hand, someone had written:

Uncle Jasper,

I know you're worried, but I've been told I'll be returned unharmed if you will bring two thousand gold pieces to

*a man in Forten City at midnight tonight. He will be
at the White Bull Tavern near the harbor. His name is
Nomis. No one has hurt me. Tell Willa I'm sorry.*

Karryn

Wen handed the note back to Jasper. "Is that Karryn's writing?"

He nodded. Jasper, Wen, Ryne, and Demaray had all drawn closer together, as if to keep Serephette from hearing this new development. "She is alive then, but it is far worse than we feared," Jasper said.

Alive for now, Wen thought. "Is Coren Bauler the type to implicate himself in a crime this serious?" she asked.

"I know he's deeply in debt," Demaray said, sounding troubled. "But I wouldn't have thought—"

"A man who would assist in abduction wouldn't balk at kidnapping for ransom," Ryne said scornfully.

"I agree with Ryne," Wen said. "We need to go ask Coren Bauler some questions."

Jasper dropped to a crouch beside the grimy little messenger, who was looking around the fancy room as if trying to size up what might be small enough to steal. "Who gave this to you, young man?" he asked. Wen could hear the strain in his voice as he tried not to sound too threatening. "Can you describe him?"

The boy shrugged. "He was just a man. He had brown hair and a brown coat."

"Noble?" Ryne asked.

The child shook his head. "No. Not wearing fancy clothes and didn't talk like a fancy man."

Jasper stood, waving him away. The butler pulled the young messenger out of the room and shut the door. "Not Coren," Jasper said. "Though possibly one of his servants."

"What will you do?" Demaray demanded. "You can't possibly pay that kind of money, can you?"

Jasper looked at her. "I think I have to. Karryn's life is certainly worth two thousand pieces of gold."

He spoke too loudly. "What?" Serephette demanded from the sofa. "Jasper, what did you say? Who was that horrible boy? Did he bring news about Karryn?" The marlady rose shakily to her feet, Lindy beside her. Wen saw that Serephette's grip on Lindy's arm was so hard Lindy's skin was pulled and white.

Jasper swung around to face her. "Yes," he said calmly. "We have just received a note saying that Karryn will be returned to us if we deliver some gold. I believe we should do so, don't you?"

Serephette didn't answer, she just moaned and sank back onto the couch.

"Mama!" Lindy shrieked. "She's fainted!"

Demaray spun toward the sofa and Jasper sprinted to the door, calling for the housekeeper. There followed a few moments of confusion as servants rushed in and the Coverroe women fluttered around the prostrate marlady. Jasper ushered Ryne and Wen into the hallway to continue the conversation.

"We shouldn't waste any more time," Jasper said. "I'll ride to our bankers in the city. I don't keep that kind of money on hand. Wen, I know you're thinking you want to lay a trap at the tavern to catch this scoundrel, but I'm not sure—"

"That's exactly what I'm going to do," Wen said instantly. "If nothing else, we need to follow this Nomis to see where he takes the money, so we'll know where Karryn's being held."

"So do you think Karryn was taken by the same person who tried to kill her when you were on the road the other day?" Ryne asked. He was frowning, and Wen assumed that he had a monstrous hangover, but he also looked like he was trying to figure out a particularly knotty problem.

"Maybe," she said.

Jasper shook his head. "But it doesn't make sense," he said. "When we were under attack, it seemed clear those men wanted to kill Karryn. Whoever took her now only wants money. Maybe it's two different people."

"If I had to guess," Wen said slowly, "whoever has her now isn't going to let her live."

Ryne and Jasper both stared at her, their faces studies in disbelief and horror. "No matter who took her, no matter how careful he's been, Karryn will no doubt have seen or overheard *something* that would enable us to identify him," Wen continued. "If he lets her go, we'll track him down. I don't think he plans to let her go." She gestured at the note still in Jasper's hands. "She was alive when she wrote that. She'll probably be alive until the money's delivered, in case he needs her to write again. But after that? I have grave doubts."

"Then—then—you think it's the same person—" Jasper couldn't seem to speak a complete sentence.

"I think he's always wanted her dead," Wen said quietly. "But now he finds himself in financial straits, and he's decided to try to make a profit before he cuts her throat."

"But who would want to kill Karryn?" Jasper whispered.

"The most obvious person," Ryne said. "Whoever stands to inherit this House."

Jasper shook his head. "Deloden Maller hasn't been in Forten City since his marriage! I suppose he could have plotted all this from two hundred miles away, but since he's never shown a minute's interest in this House—"

Wen's brain had stopped registering words with the first sentence. "What did you call him?" she asked. *Deloden, Deloden . . . I have heard that name before. Where? Who spoke it?*

Jasper glanced at her. "Deloden Maller. I told you about him before. He would inherit if Karryn died. Why? What do you know of him?"

She remembered all at once. "I overheard Lindy Coverroe talking about him a few weeks ago. Her mother was insisting they go visit Deloden and his sons. I didn't know who that was, but I thought the name was unusual. Lindy didn't want to go."

"By the Pale Lady's silver eye," Ryne said. His face was blazing with excitement and wrath. "That's it then."

Jasper and Wen both stared at him. "That's what?" Jasper said.

Ryne pointed at Wen. "I told you. Look two or three heirs ahead. Who would inherit after Karryn—and who would inherit after the next man?"

"I still don't understand," she said.

"I would bet you anything you cared to stake—two thousand gold coins, perhaps?—that Demaray took Lindy to the Maller home to try to arrange a marriage between her daughter and Deloden's oldest son," Ryne said. "*She* knew who the next heir was. And *she* knew if Karryn died, and her daughter was married to a Maller, her daughter would be marlady within a generation."

"Demaray . . ." Jasper whispered and fell still.

Wen's mind was racing. "Ryne—it makes sense. Because the Coverroes are strapped for cash, too. Have you *seen* those gold doors on the front of their house? They might be worth two thousand coins all on their own. And Lindy was telling Karryn that they might have to sell the city house because it's so expensive. So the idea of a little ransom money to tide them over would no doubt seem attractive."

"She's ambitious, Demaray is," Ryne said. "She used to throw out all kinds of lures to me—on Lindy's behalf—until my father formally announced that my sister would take over Coravann Keep. Since then, she's been perfectly civil to me, but it's clear she doesn't want me forming an attachment to her daughter."

Wen turned to Jasper. "And you told me that Demaray wanted to be serlady, but the lords didn't vote her a title."

Jasper nodded dumbly.

"She pretended she didn't care when she didn't win a title, but I never believed she was as indifferent as she seemed," Ryne said. "I'm sure she spent all that money on the town house because she thought she would one day be named serlady. And when the Manor went elsewhere—she was already so deep in debt she didn't know what to do. How to cover her losses? Marry Lindy off to the man who would step into Fortune if only Karryn was conveniently dead."

"That's so *cold*," Jasper said, his voice just a thread. "She has eaten at Karryn's house—and acted as Karryn's chaperone—and been a friend to the entire family—"

"And coveted every single one of Karryn's advantages, both for herself and for her daughter," Ryne said. "She's desperate, Jasper. Don't underestimate her."

Jasper shook his head. "No, I—I—but what do we do now? Do we confront her?"

"No," Wen said. For the first time since they had discovered Ryne sleeping alone in his inn room, she was starting to feel the stirrings of hope. "I think I know where Karryn's being held. You keep Demaray occupied while I go find Karryn."

"Where?" Jasper and Ryne said together.

"Covey Park. Demaray's old house north of the city. It's isolated and almost abandoned—it would have been easy to get Karryn there with no one seeing her."

"How did she know Karryn was going to creep out of the house this morning?" Ryne asked.

For a moment, Wen's teeth clenched. "She didn't," she managed to say calmly. "Karryn was still in the house when Demaray came running to tell me she was gone. I too easily believed her tale of Karryn sneaking out to meet with you—I didn't search the house as I should have. The minute the other guards and I rode away, she took Karryn out of hiding, threw her in a coach, and sent her off to Covey Park." She glanced at Ryne. "I owe you another apology. Because I believed in your mischief, I let myself be blinded to true evil."

In reply, he gave her the dazzling smile that *would* have made Karryn run off with him if he'd tried to convince her. Even with his red eyes, uncombed hair, and rumpled clothing, Ryne Coravann was an irresistible man. "My father would have believed the same lie about me," he said. "I can't blame you in the least."

For a moment, Wen smiled back, and then she instantly grew serious. "Jasper, you must keep Demaray here. Don't let her know our suspicions. Tell her you're getting the money together. Let her see you're upset and distracted. Ask for her help with Serephette. But don't let her go home. I don't think she'll want to leave, anyway—she'll want to be here to gauge how well her scheme is going. It's why she and Lindy came over here this morning to begin with."

"And you and I will go after Karryn?" Ryne demanded.

"*I* will go after Karryn, the Fortunalt guards with me," she answered. She paused. "Or—well—I will have to leave some of them behind in case Demaray has hired an additional force to breach the walls here. I can't leave you entirely undefended." Gods and goddesses! If only she had another five or ten soldiers under her command! If only Cammon hadn't left yesterday! A half dozen Riders, even one or two, would do so much to swing the odds in her favor—

"I'm coming with you," Ryne said.

"I don't need to be responsible for the life of another serramar," she said bluntly.

"You won't be. I'll take care of myself."

"Don't argue," Jasper said. "Just go as quickly as you can. And come back as quickly as you can. And—and—bring Karryn with you."

"If she is still alive when we find her, I will bring her back safely," Wen promised. She came close enough to lay both her hands on his arms and stretch up to kiss him on the mouth. He responded with all the fervor of fear and uncertainty and hope. "I imagine we'll be back around nightfall."

"Guard yourself while you're guarding everyone else," Jasper said somberly, and slipped back into the parlor. Wen heard Demaray's voice before he shut the door.

"Jasper! Has there been any more news?"

She looked at Ryne, who was smiling wickedly. "And who was just warning *me* against pursuing ill-advised romances?" he said.

"Shut up," she replied in a pleasant voice and strode for the door. "Come with me if you must, but I warn you, this will be a nasty business and a pretty-boy serramar like yourself may be shocked at what you see."

He laughed and followed her. "I can't believe that you still cherish any illusions about me," he said. "I think you'll find me an asset in this little adventure."

"I might," she acknowledged, pushing open the heavy front door and starting down the steps. "I am desperately short of swords."

A clamor at the front gate caught her attention—two horses galloping up at full speed—and she started in that direction at a run, in case someone was carrying news about Karryn.

No—but these new arrivals were almost as welcome. Justin and Senneth came pounding up the front walkway, pulling their snorting horses to a hard stop right in front of Wen.

"Cammon said you needed us," Justin called, sliding from the saddle. "What's the trouble here?"

Chapter
37

THEY LEFT SENNETH BEHIND WITH A HANDFUL of guards to make sure there was no massacre at Fortune, and then they set out at a rapid pace for the old Coverroe house north of the city. Wen had paused to pick up a few essential additions—including Bryce, the young mystic boy, and a change of clothes from his sister, Ginny.

"You have a plan," Justin said, watching her stuff Ginny's dress into her saddlebag.

"I'm still thinking it through."

Wen couldn't get out of the city fast enough to suit her, but there was one stop they needed to make first. Leaving the bulk of her retinue behind, she carried Bryce before her on the gelding to make a slow pass in front of the Coverroe town house. The gold doors were blinding in the noon sunlight.

"Can you tell me if serra Karryn is inside there?" Wen asked him. She didn't want to make the mistake of careening all the way up to Covey Park when Karryn was still in the city.

Bryce tilted his head as if listening to a conversation two rooms away. "She's not there," he said.

"Are you positive?"

"Yes."

"Good. We'll keep riding."

Wen remembered that it had taken a little more than an hour by coach to cover the ground between Forten City and Covey Park, but riders on horseback made better time. Still, it was close to two in the afternoon when they finally arrived on the poorly maintained stretch of road where the turnoff to the old Coverroe house was located. This much deeper into spring, the trees in the surrounding woods were even more overgrown, thick with new greenery and sprouting twigs.

"There's a house back here?" Justin asked. "Pretty well hidden."

Ryne was looking around critically. "I've been here before, but it was a lot more civilized then."

"Everybody slip into the woods and spread out a little," Wen directed. "I don't want anyone to see you from the road or from the house. Bryce and I will make our way up to the house so he can tell me if Karryn's inside. We'll come back and report—and then we'll make our move."

"I'm coming with you," Justin said.

"So am I," Ryne added.

She nodded at Justin, because there was really no dissuading him when he spoke in that tone, and shook her head at Ryne. "You stay here. One way or the other we'll be right back."

On foot, she and Justin worked their way through the undergrowth of the woods. Justin had hoisted Bryce onto his back, and the little redhead clung tightly and looked around with bright interest, but didn't say a word. Both Wen and Justin used their left hands to push back branches in their way. They had daggers in their right hands in case they needed to engage in sudden fighting.

It took them fifteen minutes to get close enough to see the three-story gray house through the final scrim of trees. The mat of ivy covering the lower levels seemed to have grown even denser with the onslaught of spring, but the place still looked as dreary and unwelcoming as Wen remembered.

Not deserted, though. Two soldiers stood at stiff attention before the front door, and two more were winding past the flower garden, now gloriously in bloom.

"Probably at least two more patrolling the grounds, and two inside," Justin whispered. "Minimum of eight. Could be four more patrolling and four inside. Twelve."

Wen nodded, for she had been doing exactly the same calculations. Not counting Bryce, her own party numbered fourteen, but two of them were Riders.

No. One was a Rider. One *used* to be a Rider. But even former Riders were twice as good as ordinary men.

She looked up at Bryce, who was still riding on Justin's back, studying the house with his fine little features all squinched up. Her stomach tightened. She had gambled so much on the answer to this question! "Can you tell if serra Karryn is inside?" she whispered.

He nodded. "She's there."

Wen felt so much relief that she had to lean her hand against a tree for support. Justin turned his head to ask, "Is she alive?"

Bryce looked surprised. "Of course she's alive!" As an afterthought, he added, "She's mad."

Wen felt the ghost of a smile come to her lips. "That's good. Can you tell if she's—" *Been abused*. No, she didn't want to put any images in Bryce's head. "If she's in any pain?"

He frowned again. "I don't know. She's scared, too, but mostly she's mad."

"Well, wouldn't you be?" Justin said.

"Can you tell how many other people are in the house?" Wen asked.

Bryce concentrated for a minute, but then he shook his head. "They're moving around too much and I don't know them. But more than the ones we just saw walking by."

"Figured that," Justin said. He hitched Bryce up a little higher on his back. "But you've told us what we really wanted to know. Good work."

"Let's circle the house," Wen said. "See what it looks like from the back."

They traced a slow perimeter around the clearing, noting potential entrances and exits. Wen remembered the narrow windows on the upper floors, but she hadn't had a chance to get a good look at the rear section of the house. The vegetable garden had been allowed to run just as wild as the flower garden in front. The door to the kitchen was narrow and recessed, accessed by a crumbling pile of stones that served as steps. Two guards stood watch there, a little more relaxed than their fellows at the front.

"Bad place to try to enter," Justin observed. "And there's no way to get in on the top two stories. Ivy offers a good hand-hold, but not even Bryce could get through those windows."

"I know," Wen said, turning back toward the outer rim of the woods. "But I have an idea."

HER plan was simple enough. She was going to walk right into the house.

She had already changed into Ginny's dress, stripping down right in front of the others, though she did turn her back for a modicum of modesty. "I'll tell them I'm the maid Demaray has sent to keep Karryn comfortable," Wen said.

"They might not believe that," Eggles pointed out.

Wen shrugged. "They're hired blades. They don't know Demaray and what she's likely to do. Besides, who else but Demaray knows Karryn is here? They might think it's odd, but they won't think I'm a threat."

"They'll search you," Justin said.

She nodded. "I know." She'd taken off every bit of weaponry, even her ankle sheath, and handed it all to Moss. "Pretty sure I could take out a couple of these soldiers even without a sword, but I won't have to."

"Do explain," Ryne said.

She nodded at Moss. "She's a mystic. She can move small objects through the air. Once I'm inside, I'll signal from a window—and Moss can send me my knife and my sword."

Orson actually laughed in admiration at that. "Knew there was a reason to keep these damned mystics around." Moss punched him lightly on the arm.

Ryne was grinning as well. "Oh, Rayson Fortunalt would love to know that magic had saved his daughter's life."

"Well," Justin said, "magic and skill with a sword."

"Once I'm armed," Wen said, "I'll create a distraction. Maybe have Karryn scream. I would assume some of the interior guards will enter her room. I'll take care of them. The rest of you then storm the building."

Justin was frowning. "It would be good to have at least one more of us inside before you start your own battle. If it takes us too long to breach the door and there's four men inside—"

She looked at him. "I can hold them off."

"I might be of a little assistance here," Ryne said.

They all turned his way. The Fortunalt guards had obviously been surprised that the serramar had been allowed to ride with them on the rescue mission, but they hadn't asked Wen any questions aloud.

"I don't think this lot will care much about your fine clothes and your noble blood, ser," Orson said.

"That's not the advantage I can bring you," Ryne said. "I can get inside the house without being seen."

Wen let out her breath in a little hiss. "I forgot! Your Lirren blood."

Justin looked deeply interested. "That's right. You're related to Ellynor. You have Lirren magic?"

"Just a little," Ryne said. "But enough to make sure no one observes me slipping inside."

Wen was skeptical. "I watched you that day with Karryn. You never disappeared entirely."

He smiled at her. "It's hard to explain. But I have spent my whole life being able to slink in and out of rooms without being noticed. I can get inside."

"Does us no good if you can't wield a sword," Justin said practically.

"I can," he said.

Wen confronted him. "The truth," she said in a stern voice. "Can you fight well enough to defend yourself against professional killers? Because you'll be dead inside of five minutes if you can't. And much as I prefer Karryn to you, I don't really want to trade your life for hers."

He stared back at her. "Well, I can't fight like a Rider," he said at last.

Orson pushed forward. "Wouldn't have to," he said. "First floor windows—you can hardly see them through the ivy. Creep inside, get to one of those rooms, open the shutters.

We'll wait till the patrol goes by, then some of us will enter that way. It'll even the interior odds somewhat."

Ryne brightened. "I can do that."

Justin glanced around. "Then I think we're ready."

WEN wasn't sure she'd ever appreciated how hard it was to ride a horse while wearing a dress. She tugged her skirts down as far as they would go—not that Ginny's dress was a perfect fit for her anyway—and tried to assume a maidenly expression as she jogged up to the front of Covey Park.

The hired guards at the front gate instantly snapped to attention. One of them called out for reinforcements, and four more soldiers came running. Within seconds, all six of them were clustered around Wen's white gelding, swords drawn, expressions menacing.

This would be a good time for Ryne to try to sneak in through the front door, Wen thought, but she avoided looking in that direction. Instead, she let apprehension mingle with irritation on her face. "Is this Covey Park?" she asked.

"And why would you have any interest in Covey Park?" asked the tallest of the guards, a tall, lean man with a stubbled black beard and a scarred, ferocious face. Probably the captain of this little group, Wen guessed.

She visibly gathered her courage and glared back at him. "Because Lady Demaray Coverroe paid me to come here and take care of the serramarra, that's why," she said.

The lead guard frowned, but he was clearly taken aback. "She didn't say she was sending any lady's maid."

Flashing more leg than she would have liked, Wen slid out of the saddle. She could see them all relax just a little when she was standing among them. She was so short, so unlikely to be a threat. "I don't suppose she told you every single thing she thought she was going to do," she said tartly. "Now can someone take me to her?"

The men stood uneasily for a moment, still not convinced. A few sent covert glances toward their leader, who looked uncertain. "Make sure she's not carrying any weapons," he said at last. One of the younger men, muscular and grinning, stepped forward and began running his hands over Wen's body, through the loose folds of Ginny's gown. It was no accident that he stroked her breast and brought his fingers up suggestively as he investigated the length of her thigh.

"She's clean," he announced. On the words, Wen spun around and gave him an openhanded slap like any self-respecting tavern girl.

"Lady Demaray didn't pay me to take liberties off the likes of *you*," she snapped.

"Hey!" he exclaimed, nursing his cheek, but the other men were grinning. Even the leader seemed to think he'd deserved it.

"*Now* can I go inside and see to the serramarra?" she asked.

The head guard jerked a thumb toward the door. "Take her in."

One of the other soldiers led her inside. She made a great show of looking around with lively interest at the shadowed hallways and narrow stairs. Was it her imagination that the door to the library was just now shutting quietly behind an invisible intruder? "Not nearly as nice as the house in the city," she pronounced.

"I wouldn't know about that," her escort said, then he cupped his hands as if to call someone. "Jolee! You've got company!"

The small, slatternly housekeeper that Wen remembered from her last visit came bustling out of the back region of the house. *Bright Mother burn me,* Wen thought. She looked so different than she had last time she'd been here that she thought it was unlikely Jolee would recognize her. But if she did . . .

Wen would have to take out the soldier first. A hard kick to the groin, gain possession of his sword, slice him enough to keep him out of the battle, then whirl around to face whoever else might be coming through the front door or down the steps . . .

"Well, who's *this*?" Jolee asked, crossing her arms on her chest and looking truly annoyed. "Another mouth to feed? Who is she—one of your doxies?"

"Not mine," the soldier said with a grin. "Lady Demaray hired her to look out for the serramarra."

Wen thought that might evoke another storm of protest, but

Jolee nodded. "Well, good! I can't be running up there every five minutes, bringing her food and emptying the chamber pot. I don't know what Lady Demaray was about, giving me one day's notice that I'd be having all of you descending on me! And everyone expecting to be fed!"

She didn't seem too worried that one of the people in the house was under guard and possibly in danger of her life, Wen thought. Her opinion of the woman, already low, dropped to the cellar.

"Well, nobody told me I was expected to help in the kitchen," Wen said sharply. "I'm just here to see to the serramarra."

Jolee waved a hand toward the cramped stairwell against the wall. "Then see to her! She's upstairs! Someone else will have to take you up because I'm too busy." And she spun around and flounced back to the kitchen.

The soldier was laughing as he led the way up, probably admiring Jolee's feisty spirit. Wen hoped Jolee put up some resistance when the Fortunalt guards moved in, so one of them would have an excuse to knock her down. She herself would like to smash the housekeeper's face.

Upstairs there were only two guards, slouching on the floor before the door to Lindy's old room and playing on a battered old cruxanno board. They hadn't gotten very far into it, Wen noticed, which led her to believe her guess had been right. Karryn hadn't been taken from the town house until after Wen had left it this morning, so she hadn't been at Covey Park very long.

"Maid for the serra," the soldier gave as his concise explanation of Wen's presence. "Supposed to let her in."

One of the upstairs guards came slowly to his feet, giving Wen a comprehensive examination accompanied by a knowing smile. The other guard was too absorbed in plotting his cruxanno strategy to do more than spare Wen a cursory look. He was obviously too stupid to recognize a threat when he saw one, but the standing guard, although he misread Wen, had at least taken the trouble to assess her. He would be the more dangerous one. He would be the one to disarm first.

"Another lovely lady come to help us pass the time," said the guard who'd looked her over. "What's your name?"

"My name is none of your business," Wen said rudely, tossing her head. "Just let me in so I can see to my job."

He produced a key and dangled it before her. "You know once you go in there, I got to lock the door behind you," he said in a teasing voice. "You'll have to be nice to me if you want me to let you leave."

"I'll remember that," Wen said. "Can I go in now? Please? Is that nice enough for you?"

"Nice enough to get in, not nice enough to get out," he said with a grin, and unlocked the door.

He stepped in a pace ahead of Wen, blocking her view somewhat, but she glanced swiftly around the room. It was just as she remembered from that last visit—full of white furniture and blue accents and as much light as the small windows allowed. She heard Karryn before she could see her, sounding as if she sat up quickly from a supine posture on the bed.

"Who's there? What do you want?" Karryn demanded. Her voice was icy, though Wen could detect a tremor that Karryn was clearly trying to conceal.

"Lady Demaray sent you a maid so you don't have to be afraid that me and the others'll help you bathe," the soldier said with a laugh. "Ain't that thoughtful of her, now?"

"I don't want any of Lady Demaray's thoughtfulness, thank you very much," Karryn said. "You can send her away."

"Well, she's here and I think she's staying," the soldier said, moving aside and gesturing Wen forward.

Wen instantly dropped into a deep curtsey, her head down. The sweet gods knew this was the most dangerous moment of all. If Karyn gasped with astonishment when she recognized Wen's face—if she called Wen by name—the guards would instantly realize something was wrong. It would be a matter of seconds before they would all be in a bloody fight that none of them might survive.

Chapter
38

WEN HELD HER CURTSEY LONG ENOUGH TO TAKE a deep breath and figure out just where she would strike the guard if he made a sudden move toward her. Speaking in a subdued voice, she said, "I promise to serve you well, serra," and lifted her head to gaze at Karryn.

Karryn's face was a mask of coldness. "You could serve me best by going directly back to Fortune and telling my uncle where I am."

For a split second, Wen thought Karryn actually had not recognized her. But Karryn's gaze was unwavering on Wen's face and her eyes showed a flare of excitement.

The guard didn't notice. "I don't think anyone's going back to Fortune anytime soon," he said. "You two behave real good, now, and maybe there will be a little supper later." Laughing, he shut and locked the door.

Wen put her finger to her lips to enjoin Karryn's silence, but Karryn couldn't maintain her stony expression a second longer. She mouthed, *"Willa!"* and flew across the room to throw her arms around Wen. Wen could feel the girl's body shaking with tears and terror. She made shushing sounds and stroked the tangled hair as Karryn clung to her.

A moment only, then Karryn pulled away. "How did you find me?" she breathed. "How did you know?"

"It took us a while to piece it together," Wen admitted in an undervoice. "Demaray told us you'd disappeared from your room, and at first we thought you'd run away—"

"Demaray!" Karryn exclaimed, even her whisper filled with loathing. "Willa, she kidnapped me! But she told you I had run away? Why would I *do* that?"

"We found a little token under your pillow," Wen said, watching Karryn's face. "Coravann colors."

"You thought I had run off with *Ryne*?" Karryn was aghast.

"Well," said Wen, trying not to smile, "I was deeply disappointed. I had been so sure you were more sensible now."

"Oh, Jasper and my mother must have been so upset! Willa, I would never run away like that! Not *now*! Not when I understand—" She shook her head.

"But Demaray made a very good case," Wen said. "She showed us your room, where we found no sign of a struggle. What happened? Were you sleeping when soldiers came for you?"

"I was sleeping, but *Demaray* is the one who came in," Karryn said in a bitter voice. "She said a messenger had come from Fortune needing to see me right away. So, of course, I hurried downstairs, but there was no messenger. Only a couple of soldiers. I didn't have time to scream," she added. "I knew you must be just outside, and if I could only make enough noise—but they put a cloth over my mouth and tied my hands, and then they carried me somewhere. Then a few hours later they put me in a coach and brought me here. They brought my clothes along, too, or I'd still be in my nightshirt. I've been going crazy, sitting here, wondering what would happen next. I knew you must be worried about me—but I thought you would have no idea where I was—"

"It took us longer to figure it out than it should have," Wen said. "For which I'm sorry. I should never have gone chasing after Ryne without searching the house first. But she seemed so sure—"

"But why would Demaray do this to me?" Karryn said. "I don't understand."

"We're only guessing," Wen said. "She's been angling to have Lindy married off to Deloden Maller's son—"

"Lindy hates him!"

"But he inherits Fortune after you," Wen said. "And once you're dead—"

Karryn's sudden change in expression made Wen snap her mouth shut mid-sentence. She'd never seen such controlled rage on Karryn's girlish face. "She would murder me for a title," she said in a flat and furious voice. "After all this time of pretending to be my friend."

Wen nodded. "We believe she sent the men to kill you on the road from the Flyten house. She knew you were going there, after all—it would have been easy for her to set the trap."

"Why am I not dead now? Since she has had several hours to kill me."

"Money," Wen said. "We got a ransom note before I left. She seems to have beggared herself in the pursuit of high status. Once your uncle pays the demand, though, I expect your life span to be very short." She smiled. "Or, well, it would have been, except *we're* here."

Some of the rage faded from Karryn's face. "Who accompanied you?"

The question pleased Wen, and she reeled off the names. "Then Justin came riding up with Senneth, because Cammon had sensed you were in trouble," Wen finished up. "So we have a Rider on our side, which will be very handy. Oh, and Ryne insisted on coming, too."

That surprised Karryn more than anything Wen had said so far. Surprised her and pleased her. "Ryne? Is here? To rescue me?"

"Using some of his Lirren magic to help, as a matter of fact," Wen said. "I don't know yet if he'll be an asset or a hindrance, but there was no keeping him in Forten City, so here he is."

Karryn took a deep breath. "What do we do next? Were you able to smuggle a sword in with you?"

Wen laughed silently. "I was not. But I know how to get one."

She quickly outlined the plan. Karryn immediately went to her little valise and pulled out a length of cherry-red ribbon. "You can hang that out of the window," she said. "That will be easy to see."

Together they moved to the bank of tall, slitted windows set into the wall. Bryce hadn't been able to tell which room was Karryn's, so Wen had made sure that the Fortunalt guards were watching all of the upper-story windows. She waited until the next pair of Demaray's guards sauntered past, then she dangled the ribbon outside, letting it flutter in the light breeze. Not too long—she didn't know how quickly the next patrol would round the corner.

Now they would have to wait until someone fetched Moss, and the next set of guards strolled by.

It was about ten minutes before she heard footsteps and low voices below, and two more hired soldiers stepped into view. One made a remark and the other laughed. But their eyes were busy checking out the woods surrounding them, and their hands never strayed far from their hilts. Wen stood motionless at the window and watched them pass.

The instant they were out of sight, she trained her eyes on the patch of undergrowth visible from her vantage point. Slowly, jerkily, sifting itself out of the thicket of interwoven branches, a long, slim shape lifted above the woods and wobbled through unsupported air straight toward the narrow window. There was a minor clatter as the metal bumped against the stone of the wall, and it was quickly clear that it would take a masterful hand to guide the sword through the constricted opening. Wen shot her hand out, closed it on the hilt, and pulled the weapon inside. She felt a slight frisson of magic wash over her wrist and dissipate.

Karryn gave a muffled crow of triumph and clapped her hands together soundlessly. Wen grinned. "One of the best days of my life was when I invited that woman to sign on," she said.

Karryn was peering out the window. "Here comes something else. Smaller. Oh, I think it's your knife."

Sure enough, the slim little dagger came dancing up to the window next, and Wen grabbed it as soon as it was close enough. She looked at Karryn. "It never occurred to me," she said. "But *you* might as well be armed, too. You might surprise them a little."

Karryn glowed with a surge of bloodlust. "Oh, *yes*! See if Moss can send *me* a sword, too."

So Wen flicked the red ribbon out the window again once the way was clear, hoping that Moss would guess why she wanted the extra weapon. They had to wait while another patrol went by, but, gods and goddesses, here it came, a delicate, deadly short sword that Wen recognized as Moss's favorite secondary weapon. Karryn took it from Wen's hands with every evidence of delight.

"Now what?" the serramarra demanded.

"Now we give them a few moments to get into position to attack," Wen said. "I told them to move when they heard you shriek. I suppose you can produce a nice terrified scream, can't you?"

Karryn nodded eagerly. "I've been wanting to scream since Demaray woke me up this morning," she said. "You just wait and see how loud I can be."

It was all Wen could do not to burst into laughter. She was suddenly flooded with the purest euphoria—part of it was battle adrenaline, she knew, and part of it was overwhelming relief at finding Karryn alive and whole.

And part of it was the strangest, most inappropriate belief that life was good, that she was where she was supposed to be, surrounded by people she trusted absolutely, about to fight for an entirely worthwhile cause. Layered beneath it all was the conviction that *she* was the champion, she was the key, the unexpected stroke of good luck.

"Stand a little way back from the door—hold your arm so no one will see your weapon," Wen whispered, setting herself in position. "Ready? Raise your voice."

Karryn loosed the most dramatic screech Wen had ever heard, high-pitched, hysterical, and very loud. Wen widened her eyes in astonishment, trying not to laugh, and heard the guards outside scramble to their feet and start pounding on the door.

"Serra! What's wrong?" one of them called, but Karryn only screamed again, the sound even more agonized. Wen heard the scrape of the key in the lock.

The door burst open and both men came barreling through. They had their swords ready, but neither was really expecting an attack. Wen swept her blade in a roundhouse swing that caught the lead soldier hard in the chest. Not enough to kill him, but surely enough to stop him for a while. He grunted, gasped, and went down, clutching his torso.

Unfortunately, he was the stupid one. His smarter companion instantly grasped the situation and leapt for Wen, his sword already flashing. Wen parried easily, pretty sure she could win any one-on-one battle, but keeping a wary eye on the wounded man and an ear cocked for commotion down the hall.

"Karryn!" she called. "Close the door! Lock it if you can!"

Her opponent growled and lunged for her, a blow that was harder to deflect. He had a lot of power, and it was fueled by rage. She skipped backward, hampered more than she'd expected by the limitations of the dress, and he came after her, raining blows. She fended him off, waiting for an opening, watching for a weakness.

From downstairs came a sudden uproar—voices shouting, furniture smashing, swords engaging—so at least some of the Fortunalt guards were in the house. Could be good, could be bad, depending on the balance of the numbers. Karryn, Wen was able to see, had snaked the key from the hurt guard and locked the bedroom door from the inside. Good girl.

But, oh no, the wounded guard was pushing himself to his feet. His shirt was covered with blood, but he still had his sword in his fist—he might not have been as disabled as Wen had hoped. She must finish off this one before the second one recovered.

Accordingly, she went on the attack, slicing through the soldier's guard, nicking his shoulder, his arm, his stomach. He was quick, though; he pulled back each time before she could do real damage. Better than she'd thought he would be. She still had the edge, but a man like this could get lucky, could land a crippling blow—and if she tripped one more time in these damned skirts—

Her opponent raised his sword for a hard overhanded blow just as the second soldier lurched over to stand beside him. No time for finesse. Wen spun aside as the blade descended, felt it glance along her left shoulder and tear through the muscles of her left arm, and then she spun back. He hadn't recovered from the effort of the swing. She drove straight forward, burying the point of her sword in his heart. He cried out, coughed, gasped, and fell.

Wen whirled to face the second danger and found the wounded guard groaning facedown on the floor. Karryn was standing over him, the bloodied blade in her hand and a fierce expression on her face. Her dress was splattered with red.

"Serra!" Wen exclaimed. "I'm impressed!"

Karryn gazed at her, her face alight with excitement and horror. "He was coming after you! I wanted to stop him."

"And stop him you did."

Karryn stared down at the soldier, writhing on the floor. "Is he—will he die?"

"He might," Wen said. "*I'm* not staying to nurse him."

Karryn nodded, but before she could say anything, there was a furious pounding at the door. "Wen! Serra!" came Justin's voice. "Are you in there? The house is ours."

"We're here! We're safe!" Wen called back. "Give us a moment—we've locked ourselves in."

Karryn flew to the door and quickly turned the key. An instant later Justin and Orson were muscling through. Ryne was right behind them. Justin gave the room one comprehensive look—just in case enemies were still lurking, just in case Wen had been forced to lie—but Ryne leapt straight over the bodies to fling his arms around Karryn. Karryn, Wen noted with interest, melted into his embrace, her ferocity vanishing in a sudden splash of tears.

Justin relaxed, though he still didn't sheathe his sword. "What happened?" Wen asked.

"As planned," Orson said. "The serramar slipped into the house while you were introducing yourself. Opened the windows to the library and four of us managed to get inside. The rest were in place to take on the soldiers on patrol. Then it was just a matter of waiting for the right moment. Serra Karryn," he said, turning to address her, "you could take up a position on the stage. I've never heard such a convincing scream. We actually thought you were being murdered."

Karryn lifted her head from its comfortable spot against

Ryne's shoulder and gave him a misty, if somewhat blood-specked, smile. "I wanted to be sure you heard me," she said. "Were any of our people hurt?"

"No losses," Justin said. "Eggles and Moss were wounded, but not seriously."

Now Orson turned to give Justin an appraising look. "I thought Willa was good, but *you*," he said in a wondering voice. "I never want to be on the wrong end of your sword."

Justin was trying not to grin too broadly. "And yet, there are Riders who can defeat me," he said.

"What's the situation in the house?" Wen asked. "How many of our opponents dead and wounded?"

"Four dead, four wounded, and these two," Justin said, indicating the soldiers on the floor. The flirtatious one dead, the stupid one alive. Wen supposed there was never any predicting fate. "There's a woman, too—I can't determine her place here, but Malton has tied her hands just in case she wants to cause trouble."

"She seems like the troublesome sort," Wen said.

Orson had come close enough to inspect Wen's wound. "That looks nasty," he said. "Hold still and I'll bind it. I'll have to rip the sleeve, though."

"Thanks," Wen said. "I want to change into my own clothes for the return trip, and I doubt Ginny will want to wear *this* dress again. I'll buy her another."

In a few minutes, Wen's shoulder was wrapped, she had had a chance to don her own clothing, and they had all collected downstairs. Moss and Eggles bore similar evidence of battlefield nursing, but that didn't stop them from joining the other guards as they clustered around Karryn, asking her questions and vying for her attention. Wen watched, smiling a little, until Orson addressed her.

"I guess the question now is, what do you want to do with the men who weren't killed?" he asked.

"We'll need to bring them back to Forten City for Lord Jasper's disposition," Wen said. "If nothing else, they can testify against Demaray."

Justin looked sober. "An attempt against the life of a serramarra is a matter for the crown to handle," he said.

"Fine," Wen said. "I'm sure Jasper will be glad to turn her

over to Amalie. But we need to get the survivors someplace where they can be questioned."

Karryn looked over from her circle of admirers. "There's a coach," she volunteered. "It's what they brought *me* here in."

"That's poetic," Ryne said.

Wen glanced around. "Let's split our forces. Leave some behind to oversee hauling the wounded men back to town. I don't want to wait, though—I want to get Karryn home as quickly as possible so that her mother and her uncle know she's safe."

"I'll stay behind with four or five of our men," Orson said. "You take Cal and Malton and Moss and Eggles. And the ser and serra, of course."

"Good enough," Justin said and turned for the door. "Let's get going."

THE ride back was a little more leisurely than the ride out and infinitely more enjoyable. They all jostled back and forth, telling and retelling their parts in the exciting drama and their emotions at various points in the day. All of them expressed the hope that Demaray Coverroe would be incarcerated for the rest of her life. Wen noticed that Ryne—whose fine, crumpled clothing was now covered with streaks of blood and smears of dirt—never once moved from Karryn's side. For her part, Karryn frequently looked over at him with a shy, wondering smile and then looked away.

Well. Wen was not as opposed as she might once have been to the idea of Ryne Coravann courting Karryn Fortunalt. Not that her blessing mattered to Ryne in the slightest, but she fancied it might carry some weight with Karryn.

They were almost inside the boundaries of Forten City when Justin brought his rangy horse alongside her gelding. "Good work," he said. "I hope you're pleased with yourself."

She gave him a wide smile. "I am. In fact. Though it might have been a different story if you hadn't been along."

He shook his head. "I made it more certain. Your group would have managed without me, though you might have lost a man or two. But they all fought hard. I'd trust them behind me any day."

She glowed. It was a compliment to her as well as her troops. "I'm so proud of them," she said softly. "I'm so proud of Karryn. I never thought I'd find people—other people—" *People who were not Riders.* She didn't have to say it out loud. "People I could feel this way about."

"Then you've found your place, I'd say," Justin replied.

She stared at him, feeling as if she'd been struck motionless, though the gelding continued on in his steady way. It had never occurred to her, even as she extended her stay by one month, and then another, that Fortune might become a permanent home for her. Even as she tumbled into bed with Jasper Paladar, she was calculating how quickly she would have to sunder herself from his embrace. She had never allowed herself to think she might stay. She had never thought she might want to.

Justin's smile was small and full of comprehension. "It's all about belonging," he said. "Sometimes you're surprised to find out who you belong *to.*"

She didn't know how to answer that, so she didn't. They had had to slow, anyway, to negotiate the cluttered streets of Forten City. Now and then someone recognized Karryn, and shouted out a greeting or a word of surprise, but Karryn only waved; they didn't slow or stop.

"Gods," Wen muttered at one point as they had to navigate around a roadblock of smashed carts and spilled produce, "if I ever get this girl safely home I am never letting her outside the gates again."

Finally, they were out of the worst of the traffic—finally they were on the quieter residential street leading to Fortune. A few of the guards raised a ragged cheer as they clattered around the final corner.

To find the hedge engulfed in flames.

Chapter
39

MALTON LOOSED A SHOUT AND SPURRED HIS horse forward, but Justin threw his hand up to halt him. "Wait," he said sharply. "It might be sorcerous fire."

Wen looked at him sideways. "I thought Senneth's power was gone."

"She's been recovering it bit by bit."

Wen motioned Cal to ride closer, for he carried Bryce before him in the saddle. "Can you tell?" she asked the boy. "Is it real or is it magic?"

None of them could get too near the rushing, roaring wall of flame. The heat was oppressive, and flickering tongues of fire darted through the air as if tasting the wind. But Bryce leaned out of the saddle, his hand lifted as if he might stroke a streak of hot scarlet.

"Magical," he said in a wondering voice. "I never saw anything like that."

Wen glanced at Justin again. "Still doesn't mean we can ride right through it."

"No, but it means Senneth is controlling the compound."

He raised his voice to a bellow. *"Senneth! Clear the gate! We're back with the serramarra!"*

Almost instantly, the fire cooled, leaving a sparkling trail of embers coiled within the dense branches. The ground around the gate was littered with cinders, but only a few tendrils of smoke impeded their progress now. Wen waved her party forward, to find a whole host of people awaiting them just inside the fence.

"Serra!" Davey shouted, and then Karryn's horse was enveloped by Ginny and six guards. Laughing, Karryn slid to the ground and hugged them, one right after the other, and then picked up her skirts and raced for the front door. Serephette and Jasper were already there, arms outstretched, pushing each other aside for the chance to embrace her first.

Senneth was standing with the Fortunalt guards, wearing trousers and travel gear and looking inordinately pleased with herself. "I see you managed to carry out the daring rescue," she greeted Justin, as he swung out of the saddle. Wen followed suit, and the three of them drew a little apart from the others.

"All Wen's doing," Justin said. "I just provided another sword." He gestured at the hedge, where coals were still smoldering. Wen had the sense Senneth was enjoying the flames so much she didn't want to see them go out entirely. She was amazed to see that the hedge itself was green as ever, seemingly unharmed by its bout with fire. "What's all this?" Justin asked. "Were you attacked?"

"It was a preventative measure," Senneth answered. "At some point the fair Demaray seemed to realize that we suspected her, and she slipped from the house and went scurrying for the gate. I was too far away to catch her and I was afraid the guards wouldn't be willing to use violence. So, not even thinking about it, I just flung my hand out—" She replicated the gesture for their benefit. "And the hedge caught fire. I was almost as surprised as Demaray—although I recovered more quickly."

"Where is she now?" Wen asked.

"Jasper has placed her in one of the upstairs bedrooms. Amie is on guard at the door, and Garth on the ground below her window, in case she should decide to try to escape that way. *I* didn't suggest those positions, by the way," Senneth added. "They seemed convinced that *Wen* would have wanted them to deploy in such a fashion."

Wen grinned. "Absolutely right."

Justin waved a hand at the hedge again. "So then why keep the fire going?"

"I didn't know if she might have reinforcements coming. It seemed like an easy way to keep Fortune secure."

Justin was laughing at her. "You just liked it. It made you feel good."

"Well," Senneth acknowledged, "maybe a little."

"How did Serephette hold up while we were gone?" Wen asked.

"At first I thought she would have some kind of fit—she was so nervous, so afraid, bursting into tears and refusing to be comforted. But when she realized Demaray had taken Karryn, she flew into a cold rage. She drew herself up into this—this *regal* pose and stalked out of the room and went to the library to compose letters to Amalie. And to some of the other lords and ladies, I think. Vilifying Demaray. It gave her an outlet for her rage and terror and kept her occupied while you were gone." Senneth shook her head. "She's a strange woman."

Wen sighed. "She is. I rather like her, but I couldn't tell you why."

Justin snorted. "Because you like battered people that you have to protect."

She punched him on the arm, then turned back to Senneth. "What about Lindy?"

Senneth looked grave. "An excellent question. Was she privy to her mother's scheme? Unless she's a better actress than *I* ever was at seventeen, no. When she first realized what was happening—"

"You mean, when the shrubbery caught on fire as her mother ran for her life?" Justin asked politely.

"Yes—she looked utterly stunned. She sank to a chair and kept saying, 'No. That can't be right. No.' She didn't try to make excuses. She didn't try to defend her mother or claim her own innocence. She just sat there. And then she started to cry. Serephette was out of the room by this time, but Jasper brought her some tea. I didn't hear what he said to her. It's a tangle, though. How can we prove her guilt or innocence one way or the other? And, Bright Mother burn me, even if she had no part in it at all—her life is essentially ruined."

"We could send her to Ghosenhall and have Cammon read her," Justin suggested.

"If he ever gets to Ghosenhall himself," Senneth said gloomily. Wen didn't understand why that was funny, but Justin laughed.

"We can ask Bryce," Wen said quietly. "I don't know if he's as good as Cammon at telling truths from lies, but he's pretty accurate at reading people's intentions." With all her heart, she hoped Bryce would be able to tell them that Lindy was absolutely innocent. And not entirely for Karryn's sake. Wen had never particularly liked Lindy, but she didn't want to think that someone so young could be so wicked, so ambitious, so full of cunning and deceit. She wanted to think such depravity could only accrue after a long and disappointed life.

Justin glanced around. "So what's left to do here?"

"We must make arrangements to send Demaray and her hired soldiers to Ghosenhall for Amalie's disposition," Wen said. "But unless the two of you want to act as their guards for that trip—"

"No," Senneth said at once.

"Then I don't think you have any more responsibilities here. You might say good-bye to Karryn, of course."

Justin reached over to ruffle her hair, but Wen jerked back and glared at him. "And make our good-byes to *you*," he said. "Again."

Senneth was watching her with a faint smile. "Are you sure it's good-bye?" she asked. "Are you sure there's not a place for you in Ghosenhall?"

Wen looked around at the smoldering hedge, at the cluster of guards still talking together with great animation, at the tall, serene façade of the house that, in the past few decades, had hid so much tumult within. She felt a strange tightness in her chest, part happiness, part affection, part amazement that something so dear had almost slipped from her grasp.

"I'm sure," she said quietly. "My place is here."

* * *

IT was close to midnight before the house was settled and Wen could seek Jasper in his room.

Senneth and Justin had left after saying their farewells and promising to carry the entire story to Cammon. Wen and the guards had crowded into Jasper's study to give him their combined report of the day's disasters and triumphs and to hear his fervent thanks. Karryn had been put to bed, despite her protests that she was not tired. Ryne Coravann had been sent off to his inn to bathe and change his clothes, but he had come right back an hour later, saying he wanted to board at Fortune for the remainder of his stay. Everyone had seemed to think this was a good idea.

Lindy Coverroe had locked herself into the room assigned to her and refused to come out. Bryce had loitered in the hallway for about ten minutes before looking up at Wen and Serephette. His small face was as serious as it could be.

"She feels the way I did when I got lost in Forten City once," he said. "She doesn't know where to go and who to trust. She's so sad and she's so—Willa, I don't know the words. She's sick, like she's going to throw up, but it seems worse than that. Like the worst headache you ever had and you don't think it will ever go away."

Wen glanced over at Serephette, whose proud face and majestic bearing showed no signs of softness. "Marlady, I would read those emotions as true. I don't believe she had a hand in her mother's plans."

Serephette drew herself up even taller. "Of course she didn't. She was a victim of Demaray's scheming, as we all were. *I* shall have to care for this child from now on. *I* shall be her mother, and Karryn her sister. We will make sure no more harm comes to her from this day forward." And she swept down the hall with her hand on Bryce's shoulder.

Wen followed them slowly, realizing this meant that she, too, had inherited one more soul to look after.

The number of her dependents seemed to be growing by the hour.

When she presented herself at Jasper's door, she hesitated a moment before she knocked. It had been just a day since she had been here last, but so much had changed—not only in the world around them, but in her own heart. How much of that transformation would show on her face, how much of that would he welcome? She could make no broad assumptions.

But neither could she turn and steal back down the hall without first offering up that altered soul for his inspection.

He flung open the door to admit her, his arms already outstretched. She walked straight into his embrace, burrowing her face against his chest, feeling his arms wrap around her so closely she had trouble breathing. For a moment she was content just to stand there, inhaling his scent, rubbing her cheek against the silk of his shirt. But then with a sigh she lifted her head to signal the time for conversation.

He dropped a kiss on her mouth and smiled down at her. "A day of much terror and celebration," he said. "I am glad I did not know at dawn what midnight would bring."

"It is the sort of day I have trained for all my life," she said. "And the sort of day I hoped would never come. Thank all the sullen gods that it has turned out like it did."

He freed one hand to push at the short tendrils of hair that had gathered around her face. "And here I was convinced you would be berating yourself for your part in how the drama unfolded," he said.

"There was some of that this morning," she acknowledged. "And I see places along the way where I made mistakes. But on the whole I am pleased with what I was able to accomplish, and what resources I was able to assemble, and how the troops I trained performed. I am—I am happy with myself today."

He kissed her again. "Well, now," he said, "let us discuss the consequences of such an unexpected emotion."

He did not lead her to the bed, but to a dainty divan covered in blue velvet and gold thread, and they sat there, curled against each other.

"It has been such a confusing day," she said, almost whispering the words, nose to nose with him and lacing her right hand with his left one. "Disaster! Betrayal! Reinforcements! Rescue! I think it will be weeks before we sort it all out—and there are still so many people whose fates are uncertain. Demaray must go to Ghosenhall, of course, but what happens to her estate? What happens to Lindy? Serephette seems poised to adopt her, but is that the best course? And then there is Ryne Coravann, whom I have liked but never before trusted. Jasper, he was so steadfast today, so devoted to Karryn. I believe there is a true attachment between them, and I don't believe you and Serephette should object if he asks her to marry him."

He tilted her head up just enough to kiss her, then leaned his forehead against hers again. "All true, all important, and I would happily welcome Ryne Coravann into this House," he said. "But at the moment, I don't care about any of that. It is *you*, Willawendiss, you whom I would inquire after. You saved the serramarra—with your wits and your skill and your faithfulness, you snatched her from death and vanquished her abusers. Your faith in yourself is restored. I rejoice with you even though there is a sadness at my core. How soon will your mended heart be chafing to return to Ghosenhall?"

She lifted her head to look him directly in the eyes. The gods knew she had never been much of a flirt, preferring to speak plainly about what she wanted, but this was too important to lay out without a little caution. "How soon would you like to see me leave for Ghosenhall?" she asked in turn.

He toyed with her fingers. "I am committed to Karryn for another five years, as you know," he said. "And I had always assumed that after she turned twenty-one, or after she married, I would return to my own estates. But I have been thinking. They have fine libraries in the royal city, and renowned scholars. I could sell my property and buy a small place in the city. I would be happy there, I think. Happier still if, from time to time, you would consent to visit me in my lodgings."

Wen sat up, for this was not a picture she had ever envisioned. "What are you saying?" she demanded. "That you would follow me to Ghosenhall in five years' time?"

He recaptured her hand, for she had pulled it away, and spoke in a soothing voice. "I know we have never looked so deeply into the future," he said. "I know we have talked in a most tentative fashion, of a night here, a month there, a passion that might wear itself out in the quickest time possible. But I cannot imagine that I will ever grow weary of you—I cannot imagine that a day will ever come when I will not want to know what you are thinking and what you have been doing. I have been trying to devise a solution for how to merge our very different lives, and I think the move to Ghosenhall would do it."

She was so dizzy she thought perhaps she had sustained a blow to the head during the fight this afternoon and she just hadn't realized it till this minute. "You think I will stay here five years and then ask for my place with the Riders again—"

"No," he said quickly. "I realize you will want to join your fellows as soon as you can. But perhaps we might compromise a little, you and I? You would agree to stay here a year— maybe two—and I would spend much of the following three years splitting my time between Ghosenhall and Forten City. It would be difficult, I know, and require a great deal of effort on both of our parts, but I am willing to make any number of sacrifices if it means keeping you in my life a little longer—"

She put a hand to his mouth to stop him. "How much longer?" she said. "Jasper, what are you thinking?"

He pulled his head back and she let her fingers fall. "As long as you are willing to have me," he said simply. "I know I am older than you, and I know I am nothing like those men you admire so much—Riders, and soldiers of every type—but Wen, I do not believe any one of them could love you as I do."

She was shaking her head. "I'm the one who should be pleading to stay in your life a little longer," she said. "You are a nobleman of Fortunalt and I am a nameless soldier!"

"Not true, Willawendiss," he said with a little smile. "You have a very fine name indeed."

She frowned at him. "You know what I mean. Noblemen like you should spend their days with women who are equally noble—and accomplished—and scholarly."

"I married a woman who was all those things, and I loved her very much," Jasper said. "But now I love you very much, different as you are, and I want to spend my time with you."

"Don't you think your daughter would be dismayed to learn of our relationship?"

"Ah, my daughter is very liberal-minded. It comes from so much reading. She will be utterly delighted by you."

Wen was shaking her head again. "Even if that's true, which I doubt, the other nobles of your rank would be horrified to see you consorting with a guard."

"I hardly think I would be looked at with any more horror than Demaray will be for *her* bad behavior," he said. "Anyway, the people of Fortunalt expect a few mismatches in their

House. Remember I told you that Karryn's grandmother ran off with her steward? A Thirteenth House lord and a captain of the guard would not be considered nearly as scandalous as that." He leaned in to kiss her quickly on the mouth. "So what do you think, my dearest Wen? Can I convince you to stay another year, perhaps even two? I will take it month by month if that is what you require, but I do not think I will be able to bear it if you tell me you are preparing to journey to Ghosenhall the minute you can saddle your horse."

She threw her arms around his neck and muffled her laughter against his shoulder. "I have been wondering how to tell you that I do not plan to return to Ghosenhall ever," she mumbled into his shirt. "I have been thinking, 'He believed it was all very well to bed me when he knew I would be moving on soon, but when he learns that I want to make Fortune my home, he will be anxious and uncertain.' I thought that—"

But now he pulled back, urgently, holding her by the shoulders so he could get a good look at her face. "Truly? You have decided to stay here? Why? Why have you forsaken the Riders, who have shown so clearly that they would welcome you back?"

She made a small gesture, all she could manage with his grip so tight on her shoulders. "It's not so much that I would turn my back on the Riders as I cannot turn my back on Fortune," she said. "It has come to be a part of me—all of it—Karryn, and you, and my guards, even Serephette, and now Lindy. You all belong to me. If I tried to leave, I would be lost again. Perhaps I have not been searching for absolution all this time. Perhaps I have just been searching for a home."

He was watching her closely, on his face a mix of hope and uncertainty. "I am part of what gives you a sense of home, I hope. But how much of a part? I would be willing to follow you somewhere else—would you be willing to follow me?"

She returned his regard steadily. "I would," she said, "but I don't want to be made to leave and I don't think you want to go. You might not realize it yet, but you are bound to this place as much as I am. Even if you followed me to Ghosenhall, half of your heart would be here. We have become entangled in this place, both of us. Neither of us would survive the uprooting very well."

A small smile curved his mouth. "Like the hedge around Fortune. Glossy and gorgeous and resilient in the place where it has grown up, but doomed to wither and die if someone tries to transplant it to some more advantageous spot."

She laughed and leaned forward to kiss him. "Just like that."

He drew her forward to settle against his shoulder and spoke with his mouth against her hair. His deep voice fell instantly into the rhythms of verse:

> *I have been used to the beggar's friendless portion.*
> *I have been used to the gods' unstinting wrath.*
> *What wild chance, what fair or fickle fortune*
> *Flung you like redemption in my path?*

"I have no idea what you mean by that," she said. "I just know that I love you and I cannot believe I was lucky enough to find you."

"Yes," he said, "that's exactly what the poem said."

So her days would be delineated now by ballads as well as battles, sonnets as well as swords. There were so many prosaic matters still to settle—from how they might live together to who they might tell—but Wen supposed those were minor details that would work themselves out in time. For now it was enough just to feel this supreme contentment, this ease, this relaxed and sprawling sense of wonder. For now it was enough to see her life taking on this very simple, very solid form—one man's unwavering silhouette to give shape to the formless future, one man's voice to make sense of the rushed and unrhymed days.

THE ULTIMATE IN FANTASY!

From magical tales of distant worlds to stories of those with abilities beyond the ordinary, Ace and Roc have everything you need to stretch your imagination to its limits.

Marion Zimmer Bradley/Diana L. Paxson

Guy Gavriel Kay

Dennis L. McKiernan

Patricia A. McKillip

Robin McKinley

Sharon Shinn

Katherine Kurtz

Barb and J. C. Hendee

Elizabeth Bear

T. A. Barron

Brian Jacques

Robert Asprin

penguin.com